THE FIRST
Mrs. Rothschild

THE FIRST
Mrs. Rothschild

SARA AHARONI
Translated by Yardenne Greenspan

Text copyright © 2019 by Sara Aharoni
English translation copyright © 2019 by Sara Aharoni
Published by arrangement with The Institute for the Translation of Hebrew Literature. All rights reserved.

Previously published as *Ahavatah Shel Gveret Rotshild* by Yedioth Ahronoth in Israel in 2015. Translated from Hebrew by Yardenne Greenspan. First published in English by AmazonCrossing in 2019.

Published by AmazonCrossing, Seattle

www.apub.com

Amazon, the Amazon logo, and AmazonCrossing are trademarks of Amazon.com, Inc., or its affiliates.

ISBN-13: 9781542007276
ISBN-10: 1542007275

Cover design by Shasti O'Leary Soudant

Cover photography by Richard Jenkins Photography

Printed in the United States of America

Spirit within strengthens heaven and earth.

—*Thales of Miletus*

NOTEBOOK 1

Frankfurt am Main, Tuesday, May 8th, 1770

It all began at the window of our home.

I love windows. In the afternoon I linger at the window for a long time. I look over the sights of Judengasse, the Jewish quarter, and cannot get enough. Not of the women carrying yokes with buckets of water, nor of the little *Kinder* scrambling among the carts of goods, the sellers and shoppers, nor of the teenage boys returning from the yeshiva.

And then, one day, as my eyes floated over the figures moving beneath my window, my gaze fixed on him. Tall, a pointy hat atop his head, a briefcase in his hand, hurrying home.

Was that Meir Amschel Rothschild? We all know each other on our street, our one, single street. I had seen him several times in the past. How is it that I'd never given any thought to him or his stature, which seemed to have increased overnight? And why did my eyes chase over his hasty figure until he disappeared around the corner toward his house? And what was the meaning of that breathlessness rising in my chest and the light pinching, that tickling, in my belly?

The next day, from my regular post, my eyes sought his hurrying image. I leaned on the windowsill, glanced impatiently at the constant traffic down the busy street, and prepared myself for his appearance.

My eyes fluttered over the shoulders steadying yokes and the faces of the *Kinder* calling to each other, "Time out!" as they made way for mothers, impatiently following the women's slow, heavy footfalls. Once the disruption had passed, the children restarted their games from the very point where they had stopped.

There, behind a heavily moving cart laden with used housewares, the pointy hat suddenly overtook the coachman, the buckets, and the *Kinder*. As my heart sang, greeting the hat and the man beneath it, both were already disappearing around the bend leading toward the Bockenheimer Gate and Meir Amschel's house.

From that point on, the regular sights of my beloved Judengasse were of nothing more than secondary significance. My entire attention was given to capturing the single vision for which I was standing there.

I treasured the secret in my heart. No one was privy to the storm raging inside of me.

The days floated by, laden with expectation. Days of searching and hope, ending with a void, and then renewed hope for the following day. I stood at our window and waited.

I am very connected to our window. The entire family has grown accustomed to this obsession of mine, and even my decorous and demure mother has ceased chastising me, instead smiling forgivingly at my back whenever I lean down, my hands gripping the windowsill. I don't need to turn to face her in order to see her smile. She pauses for a moment, and then continues on, the smile accompanying her, the rag that's always in her hand, mopping up dust particles before they even land on the furniture. That's what my mother is like—smiling and cleaning. Cleaning and forgiving.

If I didn't have household chores, I would have fixed my body flush against the window all day long, watching the street. This is my connection to the world. Our window faces the street, overlooking lively bits of it, allowing me to follow the traffic of life in our universe.

A universe that is a narrow, dark, and dirty alley named Judengasse. Too narrow for carriages, it is devoid of flowers or trees, but is host to a daily influx of people who fill it with life, which is something to appreciate.

I love our street, where people live in crowded little houses connected like links in a chain. Our house is one of them. Outside our house is a small sign with a picture of an owl on it, and so I like to call myself an owlet. I like to look at the eyes of the owl, which, like human eyes, are fixed in the front of its head, and at the unusually flexible neck that allows the owl to turn its head almost all the way around.

With owl eyes, I follow the bustling life on the street. Almost every other home offers wares for sale on the ground floor, over the stone cellar: all sorts of objects, sewing goods, clothing, footwear, meat and chicken and fish, bread, and, on Shabbat, buns, challah, and cholent. There is a butcher, a cobbler, a tailor, a man who sells talismans for healing, luck, and success in all sorts of shapes: to be worn around the neck, to be worn on the thumb like a ring, or to be hung on the wall of the house.

Whenever a new object goes on sale on the street, I always know who buys it first and for how much. It's easy to tell, because whenever a person acquires a new possession, their walk becomes the languid strut of a proud tortoise. And if that isn't enough, they stop passersby, unbidden, presenting their purchase with self-satisfaction, describing the process at length: what the initial price was, how the negotiation progressed, how many thalers they ended up shaking on, and how worthwhile the acquisition was. Only then do they release their audience, whose entire function in the conversation is to nod lightly, and the longer the conversation lingers, the more vigorous the nodding becomes. And I, watching this, can do nothing more than smile indulgently and lovingly at these people, who are an inseparable part of my life.

In the morning, our street awakens with a bustle of commerce and Torah study. I awake to the work of the day, which includes helping my mother with household chores and my father with his office work, but I linger for just a few moments near the open window, glancing at the students as they walk to take shelter under the protection of the

Torah. I watch as they split up, each age group going to their yeshiva. The youngest boys, accompanied by their fathers or older brothers who carry the prayer book or Bible, go to the religious elementary school at the synagogue. Adolescent boys flock in groups to their yeshiva, and the older boys, the young men, walk toward theirs. Teachers and rabbis pace importantly toward the same destinations, with holy verses, Mishnah, and Talmud books under their arms. Teachers carry pointers used to emphasize each word and each letter. The young and old are all brought closer to the holy language and the Creator, who protectively spreads His wings over us here on Judengasse. Mothers lean out of windows to shake sheets and beat comforters, and older sisters pace back and forth, rocking crying babies, attempting to soothe them.

In the afternoon, once I finish my chores for the day, I enjoy long moments of observation. The groups of *Kinder* join the street traffic in the after-school hours, running around between the people and the carts filled with wares, sometimes falling, even injuring themselves, but then standing and beginning to run again, as if nothing at all had happened. When a row breaks out between them, I always know who dealt the first blow, and they often look up to my window, asking me to judge who is guilty and who is innocent.

I watch all this from the window. What a shame that our house only has one.

As a little girl, my mother used to tell me that, many years ago, before I was born, before Mother and Grandmother, may her memory be a blessing, were even born, the house was filled with windows. It had at least four of them. We could look out from the ghetto over the life of Frankfurt and see the world moving before our eyes. But the people making the decisions in Frankfurt determined that residents of Judengasse were obligated to seal the windows overlooking the street with wood and plaster. Jews must not watch the people of Frankfurt.

They may only have windows showing the people of Judengasse and the open sewer running along the street, spreading its pungent stink. Thus were born blind rooms, devoid of windows.

I remember asking, "Mama, why mustn't we look at them?" and Mother stuttered, like she did whenever she was asked a difficult question, and finally explained that it was because the people of Frankfurt were afraid of the evil eye. I didn't understand. Were they truly that fearful? And what was the evil eye, anyway? Without answering, Mother moved on to other, entirely unrelated matters, but I still had questions, such as, why can't the children on Judengasse play with the children on other streets? And was it true what they said, that the children on other streets had a park? Why were my only friends the girls in the ghetto?

But instead of asking, I extinguished the burning questions inside of me, because I didn't want Mother stuttering again, changing the subject, speaking quickly, almost as quickly as I read Psalms, a skill I'd acquired when competing with my friend Matti.

Even today, as I stride toward the age of seventeen, similar questions often pop up, but I wave them off, changing the subject. Just like Mother.

Ever since, as soon as I finish my chores, I stand at the window.

One morning, I was on my way home after a visit to Matti. I was holding a knitting needle and a ball of yarn, the promising start of a scarf I had begun work on at her home. Suddenly, I lost my footing. I had bumped into one of the obstacles scattered along our street, and the yarn fell to the filthy ground. As I bent down to pick it up, I saw a hand offering the yarn, and another one brushing it off. I looked up and saw that the cordial hands were connected to the tall man I liked to watch from my window. He bent down, and my eyes were captured by his bright-blue ones. I felt lightning strike. His face was so close. My body, still bent over, froze, and the kind man was forced to continue to bend down as well, the ball of yarn still in midair, offered to me.

"There she goes." The twinkle in his eye smiled at me.

Thank you, I wanted to say, but the words evaporated on the way out, and all I could do was clear my throat, take the yarn from his patient hand, nod gratefully, and resume a standing position.

"Hello, Gutaleh." Lightning struck again, and his hand was now holding on to the hat that was removed from his head.

"Hel . . . lo," my response faltered.

"It's nice to see her strolling on the street, just as it is nice to see her looking out the window," he said, speaking to me in the third person.

His voice was offering so many pleasant words, but I only wanted to escape from this vision blocking my path—evade the high forehead flashing me with wrinkles of affection, the black beard adorning his handsome face, the strong cheekbones, the burning eyes, the smiling lips projecting disarming kindness—go home, and quieten the storm raging inside of me.

I was paralyzed. The handsome Meir Amschel, filling my field of vision and making my insides tremble with a new, marvelous vibration, confessing that he'd noticed me standing at the window. I was both flattered and ashamed, a flustering combination. Could it be that my secret was uncovered, that I was caught watching him all these days? I couldn't recall our eyes ever meeting. I would have surely remembered being fixed with that bright blue.

I stood before him for a while longer, straight-backed, but breathless and speechless. After a long moment, I bowed slightly. Clutching the ball of yarn to my chest, I fled for my life.

That day, at dusk, my regular window time, I combed my hair and arranged it carefully, then stood, seeking his tall image among the passersby on our street. The new vibration inside of me accompanied my searching eyes.

And there he was.

He paused, glanced at my window, and bowed toward me, as if returning the favor of that silly bow I had made before fleeing from him. He held on to his hat, the flash of his eyes piercing straight into mine. His smile reflected on my face, raising a twin smile on my own lips. My eyes evaded his and clung to his carefully shorn hair before he returned the hat to his head.

He stood before my window, paying no mind to the unceasing traffic of people, his lips constantly moving, speaking to me voicelessly. As I stood there, trying to decipher the secrets of his words, I feasted my eyes on his lovely looks. His black beard was neatly trimmed, and he seemed to be taking pleasure in the world of the Lord Almighty. I smiled a tiny smile, trying to restrain the fire burning inside of me, and offered a brief wave goodbye.

From that day on, whenever he was on our street, Meir Amschel Rothschild would stand at my window, filling my heart with joy.

A few weeks later he asked my parents for my hand. They said no. I continue to wait.

I've got no one to talk to about it. Not my petty, chatty friends, and certainly not my stubborn father, standing like a fortified wall between me and the intruder, or Mama, who, on this matter, unfortunately, shares Papa's opinion.

Finally, I remembered my good friend, the only one to whom I could tell everything. I awakened my notebook from its long slumber, extracting it from its hidden spot, and placed it on the bit of floor trapped between the beds, to renew our acquaintance. It's been years since I've last written in it. I feel as if I've betrayed my best friend.

Now I return to it, with my pen and ink, pushing the candlestick away and unloading the events of my life onto the pages, all sorts of odd fluttering and trickling things that are better left unspoken.

This afternoon was identical to the ones that preceded it. I put a barrette on one side of my hair and tucked in the other side, and, out of force of a newfound habit, I placed my two bare feet on the wooden floor of our home and leaned a pair of sleeved elbows on the windowsill. Mama likes my made-up words, and says that my inventions are a refreshing addition to our Judendeutsch. Like many other people on our street, we use Hebrew words at home, mixing them in with Judendeutsch.

I rested my face in my hands and switched my eyes to observation mode. This time of dusk, when the day is fading toward oblivion, and the night insinuates its approaching attack of black, invites me to play a guessing game from my perch at the window: Will he come today?

The sun crawls down to disappear behind the wall. People hurry home, rushing to beat the dark. People are not silent on our street. When they arrive home they say a blessing for having held on during the day that had just ended, thanking the good Lord for the precious bread He has given to them, praying to survive the following day as well. But not everyone finds it impossible to get out of the cycle of poverty. A few of them are blessed with a handsome income, and they donate generously to charity. Our family is somewhere in the middle. We are not penniless, but we are far from wealthy. I hear Mama thanking God for the salary Father brings home, and I know that she needn't worry about tomorrow, because Father's coin box is never empty, full enough in fact to even donate a bit to charity.

True, not every person receives an equal amount, but everyone—rich, poor, and those in the middle—live together in love and peace, each person satisfied with their lot and trusting the Lord not to abandon them in a time of need.

The three gates of the ghetto will be locked soon, and after that no one can come or go. Soon, the skies will fill with stars, Mother will light the candles, and we will have dinner and hurry to bed before the last candle burns off.

I count the wooden beams that constitute the roof of the Goldaners' home. I think their house is next in line to collapse, God help us. Two more beams fell off today. They keep detaching and falling from the old houses, like hairs falling from a head, until a few fathers gather together to collect the beams and reattach them, or replace them with new ones. Sometimes they don't fix them in time and the entire house falls apart. Then everyone arrives to watch, say, "Oy vey, oy vey," and rebuild.

As our street empties of people and the ruckus of children, the new garbage appears, clinging to the old garbage, which has become a regular fixture. Dogs and cats burrow through it, especially the piles near the butcher shops and bakeries.

But when Meir Amschel Rothschild arrives, the view outside the only window of our house changes, and his image takes the place of the usual sights. The street becomes more cheerful, the smells and ugliness evaporate, and it becomes the most beautiful street in the world. True, I know no other streets but Judengasse, but I know how I feel, and that is what counts.

Let me rephrase that. I also know the busy Jewish market outside the ghetto, and the short way to the market. From time to time I leave the ghetto to join my mother on a shopping excursion. Until the Christian women of Frankfurt finish their shopping, we Jewish women are forbidden from visiting the market. Mama makes sure not to break this rule, just as she makes sure to obey the long list of decrees enforced upon us, residents of Judengasse, such as the prohibition on silk clothing or jewelry except on holy Shabbat, when we are permitted to adorn ourselves. I've noticed that my mother—whose fine physical appearance is equally important to her as the care she takes with her home and children—makes sure to use this permission to its fullest, and only removes her Shabbat jewelry at the end of the weekend, before she goes to bed. Thanks to her close attention, we've never had to pay a fine for breaking any decree, which has saved us plenty of money.

I've had a chance, then, to become somewhat acquainted with life outside of Judengasse. Sometimes I get the urge to take a closer look at the public parks of Frankfurt, even stroll through them myself, to experience the sensation of feet walking down clean sidewalks and paths, of eyes taking in the beauty of trees, flowers, and lawns. I once shared this desire with Mama, but she looked at me, terrified, and mumbled her way to a decisive order: "Get that crazy thought out of your head and never repeat it again."

My lips are sealed, but the thought lives on. Mother does not understand that people cannot control their thoughts. Even the Roman Empire, which the German people hold so dear, which rules us with an iron fist, ladening us with these humiliating decrees, as if we were a cursed race, cannot control our thoughts. They call us *Schutzjuden*— protected Jews—and charge us an annual tax, which my father must pay, for alleged protection of our bodies and property. It is the tax for the privilege of walking through the city gates with our corporeal luggage in tow. But still, not even the empire can control our thoughts. On the other hand, we do have control of our speech, and can choose whether or not to speak. Therefore I never bring up the matter anymore. I share my secret, my wild desires, neither with my mother nor with any other person.

Mama has called me to come to dinner. The sun has died, and evening has taken over.

He didn't come today, either. I just took a last peek at the street preparing for night. Then I turned from the barren window and headed toward the table. I'll stand there again tomorrow.

New hope lives within me each day.

I had only meant to write about Meir Amschel Rothschild, and here my thoughts have wandered to other days and subjects.

Mother lit the candles in the chandelier before dinner. When she retired for the night, I rose silently from my bed, took the candlestick with the extinguished candle from the nook in the wall, and borrowed a light from the chandelier, which was about to burn out. Now I shall place the pen back on the dresser and make sure to close my favorite inkwell, the one made of porcelain and decorated with spread-winged angels. I shall carefully hide the notebook under my mattress, and blow out the last of the candle, whose wax has coated the candlestick with a colorless film. Morning and night, we children are warned against fire. The houses on Judengasse are made of wood. We've had enough disasters here as it is.

Sunday, June 10th, 1770

My return to the notebook was a sign. I'm sure of it. The resuming of writing is my good-luck charm. How else can I explain the shift that has occurred today?

I'm still out of breath. I cannot settle down. I take a quick break and continue writing. The events of the last few days crawl into my mind and do not leave. I feel that what has happened to me today marks the beginning of a new era in my life. It sounds silly, writing such pompous words, "a new era in my life." You'd think I was Maria Theresa. I'm only Gutle (nicknamed Gutaleh by all), daughter of Wolf Shlomo Schnapper, a Jewish moneylender from Judengasse, the broker of a small princedom named Sacksen-Mainingen. But who cares? This notebook is mine alone, and I can write in it whatever I fancy.

I'm so glad Father gave it to me.

I recall the events of two years ago, when I was fifteen years old and helping my father, as usual, arrange his messy work desk and wipe off the dust that had collected over the past week. My father is accomplished in the speed with which he is capable of putting disorder in anything he touches, and it is my job to restore order over and over again. This task of arranging his desk had been handed down to me ages ago by the tired hands of my mother, Bella, who had announced it was time she relieve herself of this single, exhausting task among her many, and give it over to me, knowing my obsessive affinity for order and cleanliness.

Well, I sorted the papers strewn over the table as if after a blizzard, and there, right next to the tattered old expense ledger, filled with words and numbers in my father's horribly illegible writing, I discovered a new, thick, glorious ledger, like a well of fresh water next to a pungent sewer. I took hold of it, flipped through its clean pages, breathed it in, and held it to my chest.

Father, who had just finished counting his daily income of coins and placed them in the heavy wooden box, suddenly asked, his smile warm, "Would you like that notebook?" I nodded and clutched it to my chest. That night I whispered to it, making sure not to wake up my younger siblings, sleeping in our room crowded with beds and soft breathing, "I choose you as my best friend. I'll tell you everything." I placed it carefully under the mattress, and from that day on have occasionally pulled it out late at night, sitting down on the floor, the way I am right now, and unfolding my day onto its pages. Since I am in charge of making the beds in our room, I have no fear of my secret being revealed.

Four weeks ago I decided to begin writing again, after a long hiatus. I opened the notebook, but before I dipped my pen in ink, I felt the voyeuristic urge to skim through what I had written long ago. From the distance of time I can attest to having been quite the childish girl. Everything made me giggle for no good reason at all, just like my friends. Now I certainly *feel* mature. I am no longer tempted to continue laughing with my friend Matti about the crumbs in the beard of Limping

Ephraim, who lives in the crumbling house, or about Mr. Stern's wig, placed crookedly atop his head, or the powder that stains his shoulders. He continues this habit, even though it worries his mother sick, seeing as how he is breaking the decree forbidding Jews from powdering their wigs. I certainly no longer feel the need to mock the rips and patches on the shirts of the children in our neighborhood.

I do my best to use clean, literary language in my notebook, because written language is more important than spoken language. The written word must be treated with respect. True, it is not the holy Bible or the tales of our sages—both of which I love so much I have memorized whole passages—and yet, each kind of writing has its own dignity. Since I like to curl up inside my memories without sharing the existence of my secret notebook with a living soul, no one can mock the flowery language I choose to use in the history of my life. I'm using that phrase again.

What's wrong with me? The answer must lie in my *Aufregung*, and I have a very special reason for my excitement.

Now let me start from the very beginning, and tell everything in the correct order.

I stood at the open window like I do every day, my eyes seeking nervously, wishing to capture the image of Meir Amschel Rothschild emerging from the dusk. Ever since my father's second refusal of the match, he has not turned up on our street. Eight long weeks have gone by since the day he appeared again in our home, standing tall, and requesting to speak to Father. He giggled with (enchanting!) apology for assuming the role of both matchmaker and match, said that his late mother and father would have certainly been happy with his choice, and announced that he loved Gutaleh (me!) and promised that she

(I!) would want for nothing in his home. But Father ran his eyes over Meir's faded coat, hesitated for a moment, and to my great sorrow turned him down again, and Meir Amschel Rothschild left our home, never to return.

I almost went to the neighbors, to see if they knew anything. Perhaps he'd decided to return to the yeshiva? Or maybe he'd been called back to work at Oppenheimer's bank, far away in Hanover? And if one of these were true, when was he planning to return? But I was concerned that my interest would disclose my emotions, and so I locked and bolted shut the doors of my mouth.

Instead, I wandered the street, seeking my beloved.

One day, my feet carried me north toward the Bockenheimer Gate. His house was near the gate, at the back end of the street. My shoes sank in the muddy road, where the paving stops and the ground grows sticky the closer one gets to the Hinterpfann—the rear frying pan—what we call the houses that were built in the backyards of other buildings when there was no more room on the street. I stood by his mossy apartment and yard overflowing with garbage, filled with alert expectation. At the front of rear house number 188, proudly ignoring the sight of the filth on the ground, was a new, round, colorful sign with glowing gold letters:

M. A. ROTHSCHILD
AUTHORIZED VENDOR OF THE COURT OF THE VENERABLE LANDGRAVE WILHELM OF HANAU-HESSE

The symbols of the Hanau and Hesse princedoms were painted on both sides of the sign.

A warm wave washed over my abdomen. Meir Rothschild, one of us, was authorized as the court vendor of the crown prince, Wilhelm.

Just like my father, but Meir Amschel Rothschild was a young man, twenty-six years old at most, and already a court vendor. Hanau was small, but Kassel was the capital of the larger princedom, Hesse.

Well then, Meir Amschel had not returned to the yeshiva.

I walked closer to the ground-floor lobby, which housed the dark rooms belonging to him and his brothers, Moshe and Kalman. Used objects and a few wooden boxes were scattered on shelves and along the walls. Moshe, Meir's younger brother, and Kalman, the youngest, disabled brother, were both leaned over their goods, serving customers. Moshe noticed me and raised his eyebrows with a question. I cleared my throat and pointed to an embroidered handkerchief that peeked from a wooden box. He yanked it out and muttered, "Two florins." I picked up the handkerchief with the small hole with one hand, and with the other fished two florins from the pocket of my dress, buried them in his outstretched hand, and hurried home, breathless, another fruitless tour under my belt. I took up my customary post at the window.

Perhaps he'd found a match outside of the Judengasse? Perhaps in Hanover? People must appreciate his abilities there. I felt lost. How ridiculous of me to expect him to appear as usual at my window and look at me, removing his hat and bowing toward me as if nothing had ever happened.

I imagined now that he'd installed that sign with the nobility symbols on the front of his home, he wouldn't be back to ask for my hand again. Oh, God, what would I do if his heart now belonged to another, while mine was captivated by his charm?

Tears rose in my eyes, blurring the approaching image. I stared at the fan moving from side to side, and felt waves of self-pity. I was so miserable. What had I done to deserve this? What sin was I being punished for? I yearned for him. All I wanted was to see him, to follow his silent words. And he wants my presence too. Or wanted. I was tortured by the thought of him no longer yearning for me.

I ran the pads of my fingers over my eyes, wiping away the dampness. I glanced distractedly at the fan, and was shocked to find that it was not a fan at all, but rather Meir Rothschild's hat, waving in his hand. My eyes were fixed on his hat with surprise, and now that he'd noticed that I had awoken from my reveries, he bowed at me, his lips opening into a smile, his short black beard also taking part in the movement. I looked down awkwardly at my fingernails, which I now noticed had a layer of spices underneath them. Inside I was jumping for joy, but my face was restrained to the point of bursting. After a few moments I found the courage to move my eyes from my fingernails and slowly raise my head to face him.

But the street was empty.

He had vanished. A true mystery. Had he really been there, or was it a vision of my raging imagination? I could swear it happened. I leaned my torso out the window in an attempt to follow his shrinking figure, but could see him nowhere. I stifled a shout. What a fool I was. How did I let this chance pass me by? Days upon days I stood at this window, waiting for the twinkle of his eyes, his friendly smile, and now that he was finally there, I had avoided his face and stared instead at my fingernails. Why had I clung to my damn nails so long that I lost my beloved?

I paced the small room, tormented by the thought that I'd missed my last chance. I must pray.

From the corner of my eye I saw my brothers and sisters following my route around the room. I'd been blessed with five *Geschwister*: three sisters—fifteen-year-old Bella, who was probably out with her friends, eleven-year-old Braineleh, and four-year-old Vendeleh; and two brothers—Meir Wolf, who had recently had his bar mitzvah, and six-year-old Amschel Wolf. I turned away from them, and they quickly returned to their usual endeavors, always able to make a ruckus: playing catch, fighting over sticks wrapped in fabric—each sister claiming exclusive ownership of the "doll"—Amschel Wolf riding Meir Wolf like a horse while waving his hands and bellowing with laughter. I drowned in my misery, allowing my feet to lead me from one wall to the next in our small room.

As I noticed Vendeleh carefully following my footsteps, I began to hear new sounds in the house, different from the normal noise. I immediately put an end to my pointless pacing. "Hush," I told the children. Curious, they stopped their rumbling, obediently falling silent. Even little Vendeleh played along. I put a finger to my lips and they nodded in agreement. I approached the door quietly and opened it a crack. I listened, never removing the warning finger from my lips.

I wasn't dreaming. He was here. It was him. He hadn't given up on me. He hadn't chosen another. Father, do not turn him down. Please, kind Father, please.

Vendeleh sensed my alertness, clung to me, and searched for my hand. I took her little, searching hand, and closed my eyes in prayer. When I opened them, I saw that Vendeleh, Meir, and Braineleh had also closed theirs. Only rambunctious little Amschel peeked around him.

"Gutaleh!" I heard Father calling me.

I jumped, covering my mouth with my hand to hold in a squeal. My siblings opened their eyes all at once, their mouths gaping, and turned their questioning eyes on me. Even they knew something meaningful was about to happen.

I turned to them, put my finger to my lips again, smoothed my dress, and ran a hand through my hair. I closed the door quietly behind me, and walked to the next room on tiptoe, my hands in fists.

Mama and Papa were seated in their chairs. Before them stood Meir Rothschild—tall, his narrow shoulders leaning toward them, his right hand holding his hat, and his left hand placed with (captivating!) looseness on his waist. He turned toward me, his eyes meeting mine, his mouth curling in a restrained, victorious smile. I couldn't resist his firm features. He shot me an amused look with his blue eyes, and smoothed his beard, and I wanted to get to the nearest wall and lean against it so I could stop the trembling of my knees.

Wednesday, June 13th, 1770

We strolled down our alley for hours. The stench of filth had vanished, or perhaps merely chosen to avoid my nose. Even the sticky slime on the sides of the road was invisible to me. The constant dimness of the walled Judengasse made room for a glowing light, the light of his eyes, which illuminated my heart. Just Meir Rothschild and I, hovering above ground, passing by people, seeing their lips spreading in a smile toward us as they cleared a path, looking up at us. His hands were crossed behind his back, and mine swung alongside my body with the pace of our footsteps. Since noon our feet had trodden the alley from south to north and from north to south, back and forth, and even twilight did not signal the end of our wandering.

I'd pictured these moments for days and nights, returning to them again and again, hoping and praying for them to come true. Today they have become a reality, pleasing every fiber of my being, and I feel insatiable. The combination of the feeling in my heart and the physical sensation of my body is new and wondrous to me. Is this what they call love?

His light laughter swept me away, infecting me. "The more they multiply and grow," he repeated for the twelfth time, looking toward the horizon.

It's been three days since my father gave the stubborn lad his permission to take my hand in marriage. He mentioned his appreciation both for Meir's persistence in choosing his wife, and his exceptional debut in the business world. He could have listed these two qualities in reverse order—after all, the material world is the source of our sustenance. Father kept repeating that "one cannot take lightly the noble title given to this boy by the royal court. This sheds a new light on the candidate." Even the Hinterpfann's landlord eventually granted Meir and his brothers' request to sell them a quarter of the house. Father was therefore convinced to give him my hand, the hand of his eldest daughter.

Hallelujah! I'm engaged! We celebrated our betrothal last night in a small gathering at my parents' house, and today we walked together, liberating the flickering of fire between us. As early as this gathering, when my father wasn't looking, Meir tickled my ears with that same passage: "The more they multiply and grow." A few hours ago, his eyes aflame, he interpreted it for me.

"The more your father tortured me and rejected me, the more determined I became. In fact, with each rejection I increased the quota of our anticipated happiness. When I first visited your father, I was determined to marry you. After he turned me down the first time, I decided I would marry you and have five children. After he turned me down a second time, I decided to marry you and have ten children: five boys and five girls, in pairs, boy-girl, boy-girl. And if he'd turned me down again, I would have doubled the number of children once more. That is why I said, 'The more they multiply and grow.'"

How impressive. Where did he gather such courage? Or should I call it arrogance? Where was that passage from? But I mustn't ask. I must restrain myself. It is enough that he has chosen me of all the girls of Judengasse. I watched him silently, and from within the storm roiling inside me, tried to digest the new facts of our blessed future.

He must have read my mind, for he began to explain. "This passage has been on my mind for quite some time. Look, Gutaleh, look around you." He took the forefinger of my right hand softly, shifted it right and left along the Judengasse, and said, "Do you see this street?"

I saw nothing, so enchanted was I by the touch of his hand.

"The street," he tried again.

I nodded, not fully fathoming his intention.

He let go of my finger and used his hands to demonstrate. "The more they were oppressed, the more they multiplied and grew," he called out, raising his hands left and right. "Everything your eyes see is torture. When the first eleven Jewish families were brought here, three hundred years ago, by the order of Frederick III, the torture was small. Merely a separation of the Jews—'Enemies of the Cross and Christ,' as they were called—and the gentiles. I assume that those hundred and two Jews did not rejoice, having been deprived of the right to live among others. But their troubles were not so bleak. Within their isolation they were graced with a large space where they enjoyed freedom of movement, and were able to live according to the Torah with no interference. But the geography has remained the same since 1442, while we have multiplied. An area meant to contain three hundred Jews now holds three thousand, crowded inside two hundred houses. Every space is filled with walls, rooms, houses upon houses. It's become very uncomfortable, as you can plainly see."

Meir focused his eyes on me, then looked away to the horizon. I followed every movement and every glance. I did not want to miss a thing. I felt as if he were spreading a path for me into his world, and oh, how I longed to be a part of it. So many questions were racing to the tip of my tongue, but I had to hold back, as was expected of a decent, well-educated young woman. I joined his gaze at the horizon, attempting to understand him. He seemed pleased with the curiosity he'd awakened in me.

"You know, Gutaleh, my father, may his memory be a blessing, deliberately removed me from the ghetto and sent me to continue my education at the rabbinical school in Fürth, near Nuremberg. That is where I gained much knowledge of the Torah and the Talmud, as well as fluency in three languages—German and Hebrew as speaking languages, and Aramaic in order to interpret scripture. He expected me to become a rabbi. When my parents died, my uncle sent me to Hanover. These two different paths opened my eyes to things I could not have seen from here. In Hanover, I spent six years specializing in commerce in the Jewish bank owned by Jacob Wolf Oppenheimer. I felt filthy rich, not necessarily with funds, but with knowledge. And so I decided to return home to my younger siblings, to the place where I grew up, and run my business in Frankfurt. But upon my return home, proudly carrying my intellectual luggage, I came across a band of hoodlums who demanded that I pay my Jewish dues. *'Jude, mach Mores!'* they shouted. What I truly owed them, I thought, were two slaps in the face, each. But they expected a different kind of respect, and I had no choice but to step aside, take off my hat, and bow."

He stopped short. His eyes caught mine. "I had to make this gesture, bowing and removing my hat, for scoundrels. Do you see the level of torture? And that wasn't the end of it. After letting them have their fun, I reached the ghetto gates, the iron chains and those hateful heavy wooden doors, and had to wait like a beggar for the guards to let me into my own neighborhood. You should know that none of this happens in Hanover. This inconceivable treatment—closing ghetto gates to us merely because we are Jewish—is an exclusive trait of Frankfurt.

"But this wasn't the end of it, either. When I finally approached my house, my neighbor called, 'Hello, Rothschild,' reminding me that for many years Jews had been deprived of the right to a last name. People now call me by the color of the sign outside my ancestors' home: *rotes Schild*, red sign. I am disenfranchised in many ways. As I was about to step into my home, I saw my brothers, Moshe and Kalman, surrounded by the crates of useless rubbish they are forced to sell for a living. Gentiles enjoy the right to sell anything and do any kind of work. But we Jews are forbidden by the guilds from working all kinds of jobs or selling anything of value. Our only option is to sell used household goods and rags or work as money changers."

I recalled the torn handkerchief his brother Moshe had salvaged for me.

Meir looked around with a sigh. "We're tossed into the filth, ordered to stay here, and are then criticized for smelling like the devil. Do you see how absurd this all is?"

He wasn't expecting an answer, which was all good and well, seeing as how I was speechless. What could I say? We lived on the same street, but my vision was limited, while he could see for miles. I was captivated by his wisdom. I'd never considered life in the ghetto in these terms before. It was clear that his departure had allowed him a different perspective.

The light went on in his eyes once more. "That is why I've reached an unequivocal conclusion." A sweet smile adorned his face, and his hand rubbed his black beard. "Come, sit here, and I'll tell you my secret." He quickly gathered a few logs that were strewn about, smoothed them with his large hands, brought them close together, and offered me a seat. I sat down quickly, so as not to disturb his train of thought, and fixed my eyes on him. He sat beside me, his shoulder accidentally rubbing against mine before he drew away with a casual apology and continued with determination: "The more they were oppressed, the more they multiplied and grew. We shall multiply our family, as well as our wealth. Our power will be in our money. A poor man is as good as dead, but money carries dignity, and I plan on earning us plenty of dignity.

"It is a powerful thing. We shall use it to break through the walls of the ghetto and set ourselves free. It will be our revenge, the Jewish revenge, avenging all previous generations."

I widened my eyes at him. Before I knew it, I burst out laughing. I couldn't stop myself. "Break through the walls? Leave the ghetto? You're out of your mind, Meir Amschel Rothschild." I shook my head.

"I know it sounds crazy, but I'll make sure it becomes a reality. Even God didn't create the world in one day. It takes many days to make big changes. But we are destined for respect and destined for life outside the ghetto. We *will* leave the ghetto. *Everyone* will leave the ghetto." His decisiveness was awe inspiring. He circled the neighborhood in the air with a quick finger and added, "Then we'll see who's crazy."

I said nothing, but my head, as if possessed, continued to shake from side to side like a pendulum, refusing to partake in the fantasy.

Meir glanced at me before looking out at the horizon again. Suddenly his speech became slow and quiet, as if emerging from the depths of his belly. "Gutaleh, you saw how your father changed his attitude toward me once I came across a bit of money. That is also why the gentiles will come to respect me. Then we'll see if they dare say *'Jude, mach Mores'* to me. You'll see. One day we'll leave the ghetto. It will happen. If not in our time, then in the time of our children."

I felt the air between us filling with sweetness. I was living a fairy tale.

"I know what I need more than anything is freedom. I need freedom to take initiative, to find an opportunity for competition. If I plan my steps right, a combination of hard work, industriousness, and the skills I've acquired will take me far. I have no doubt about it. If financial success is what determines our place within society, then we must make sure we find that place in spite of our Jewish origins."

He took my hand and helped me up. I stood before him, ready to follow his lead. He took light hold of my waist and lifted me up, spinning me around. He and I laughed until my head rose high into the air and I could see the windows. I asked him to stop, and when he let go I whispered breathlessly into his ear, "People are watching."

He glanced up and spotted heads peeking out of windows. They saw us seeing them and retreated back inside, shutting the windows behind them. An amused smile appeared on his face, while I buried my eyes in the ground. Even though I knew it was inappropriate for a man to hold his fiancée's hand, let alone her waist, how could I have refused his touch?

"Gutaleh," he whispered back, his breath tickling my ear, "when we leave the ghetto, we'll be able to stroll together wherever we like without anyone watching. Now let me take you home before your father collapses with worry and regrets ever agreeing to give me your hand in marriage."

◆ ◆ ◆

I lay still across my bed, my eyes closed and my heart awake, beating quickly. The rustle of my siblings' breathing drowned out by the racket in my head. My mind was so crowded. Soon, I would marry my beloved. I could still feel his hands fluttering over my hips, his breath on my ear. The warm, pure physical proximity making my insides churn. I couldn't catch my racing breath. An inflaming sensation of anticipation surrounded me, dropping me into the burning heart of love and desire. I became acquainted with the femininity flowing through me. I yearned for his piercing eyes, coveted the touch of his hand, the flutter of his lips. Longed for his voice.

He isn't like the other young men in the neighborhood. Something about him is different, superior. I try to comprehend what makes him so special. It must be a combination of things. A quality mixture that had imbued a single person, Meir Amschel Rothschild. First, his striking looks: his strong, tall body, his sparkling eyes, his bright face. Next, his familiarity with the great big world, and the way he ties what he'd learned in Torah and business to his firm opinions. And the dreams he weaves, the confidence he projects, the determination, the enthusiasm, the energy. And then, along with these—the tenderness and warmth, the deep-blue eyes, the tickling whispers—all these enchant me. We only recently said goodbye, and already I cannot wait to see him again.

I can feel how, in our evolving relationship, he removes his shields, revealing what's hidden beneath, and the thought is so flattering. I try to understand him. His world. His life. His thoughts.

I think the principle he'd adopted, "The more they were oppressed, the more they multiplied and grew," was inspired by losing his parents at a young age. This adversity did not merely fail to defeat him. Rather, it strengthened him, preparing him for a life of independence.

A thought materialized: I am diving into my new life with the sober knowledge that a life lived with him will not be ordinary. Meir Amschel Rothschild is a riddle that will be solved one step at a time, and I am ready for an extraordinarily adventurous future. I turn my gaze inward and see how narrow my world is compared to his, as narrow as our alley, the Judengasse. And I am certain that, thanks to him, I'll be learning plenty about life outside the ghetto walls.

When I was a child, Mama used to tell me fairy tales, and I liked to imagine they all took place outside the walls. When Father told me stories from the Torah, they occurred to people who had gone across the walls, to great, faraway places. Now I am impatient to start my new life.

Ten children, he told me. I put a hand on my heart and the other on my flat stomach. We would have ten children. That's what he said, with confidence, with determination, without a blink, as if all he had to do was speak, and it would come true. And I believe that is indeed the case. I am the only partner to his plans. I am an inseparable part of the future he's planning for us. There's no doubt that Meir Amschel Rothschild will be a great man. And I will be the wife of a great man. His wondrous strength and power will radiate into our children.

Papa, thank you for giving your permission before it was too late.

I let out a yawn. For the past few hours I had not let go of the memory of his hands on my hips, of thoughts of him. Dawn was threatening to rise and there was much to do. I gave myself over to the webs of sleep and curled within them. A moment before the final surrender, Meir's caressing smile appeared again, and the touch of his hands was burned into my dream.

Wednesday, June 20th, 1770

The next morning, I let go of the depths of sleep at the touch of a small hand on my cheek and the busy sounds of a waking house. I opened my eyes a crack, as if drawing a curtain. My little sister's face blurred before me. I rubbed my sleep-bound eyes and lingered in an indulgent yawn. I stretched my arms, covered my head with a blanket, and immediately shook it off. I turned to face Vendeleh and noted that her face was glued to mine and clouded with worry. I held her close and kissed her lightly on both cheeks. "Good morning, Vendeleh, you beat me today." I tried to sound casual, intentionally ignoring her concern.

"Everybody's already awake, Gutaleh. Are you sick?" she asked in her soft voice, observing me worriedly.

"No, of course not, I'm completely healthy." Her question chased away the remains of sleep. I sat up in bed at once.

"Then why didn't you get up?"

"Because I didn't fall asleep until late."

"Is it because of Meir?"

"Yes, Vendeleh," I said quietly, "it's because of Meir. Don't tell anybody."

Vendeleh said nothing. I looked at her again. Her face was missing its magical smile.

"What's wrong, Vendeleh? Why are you sad?"

"I hate Meir Rothschild."

I gasped. "Why, sweetheart?" I asked in a matter-of-fact tone, stifling my emotion.

"Because Mama said after you marry him you'll move into his house. I don't want you to leave us. Why can't he move in here?"

"Don't worry, sweetheart," I said, calmer. "We've got nowhere to run off to. We'll stay right here, on Judengasse. I'll come visit you, and you can come see us whenever you want. What did you think, that I'd give you up?" I wrapped my arms around her skinny shoulders. "Meir is going to love you. He's a good person and he loves children."

"Are you sure he loves children?"

"I'm certain." I looked away to hide the tears in my eyes and the lump in my throat.

"Then I love him too," Vendeleh decided, and was off to chase the rambunctious Amschel, who had pulled on her hair as he did every morning, trying to get a rise out of her.

After a quick breakfast, Mama took my hand and led me to the master bedroom. We stopped at the locked chest, and she handed me the key. I unlocked the chest, and Mother took items out one by one: linens and blankets and towels, a tea set, a tablecloth and matching napkins, nightgowns and lace clothing. I put my hands together with satisfaction. "It's so pretty, Mama! When did you prepare all this?"

"I've been putting it together since you were born, my child. I just kept adding to it." Now she pulled out two old books, ran her hand over them, and offered them to me with awe. I recognized them. Ever since I was a child, Mother read them almost every night, sometimes reading passages out loud to us children. I took them from her, infected by her attitude of sacredness. Two books of morals, *Brent Spiegel*, by Rabbi Moshe Altschul, and *A Good Heart*, by Rabbi Yitzhak Ben Eliyakum.

"Read them every day."

"But they are yours, Mama. They fill your evenings."

"I've read them enough, child. I remember every line and letter by heart. From now on, they are yours."

"Thank you, Mama. I'll remember and do that, just like you."

Mother leaned down to pull a bundle wrapped in cloth from the bottom of the chest. "There are twenty-four hundred florins here. A little help for the beginning of your road together. I wish you a happy life with Meir. He'll be a good husband." She closed her eyes and spoke a silent prayer. Then she watched me with concentration, running a hand down my face. I rested my head on her shoulder and broke into tears.

"Cry, my daughter, these are good tears. They wash out your eyes and the mean heart of anyone who is jealous of you. You're embarking on a new path, and God will be at your side." She stroked my head.

Between sobs, words escaped me uncontrollably. "Mama, I love him. I love Meir Rothschild."

"Of course you do, my child. And he loves you. Look at how he fought for you. That's it, enough crying for today, you've got work to do." She patted my back, trying to soothe both of us, pulled out the napkins, and placed them in my hand. I held them carefully.

"Embroider," said Mama, picking the sewing box off the wooden dresser.

I put my arms around her neck and kissed her cheek. Embroidering is my favorite chore. Every comforter in our home, stuffed with goose feathers by Mama, was embroidered with flowers—my proud handiwork.

"Sit here," she suggested. "Otherwise the children won't let you work."

I put the napkins down on Mama's little table, threaded the needle, and picked up one napkin. I held on to its edge, and embroidered the initials M. A. R.

I thought about what Meir had told me, about his last name. My parents had known his father, Amschel Moshe Rothschild, and his mother, Schönche, may their memories be a blessing, the way everyone here knows everyone else. But that wasn't enough for them. They went to the effort of studying his family history and exchanging details and impressions, ignoring my burning ears as I eavesdropped hungrily on their conversations. At the cemetery was a plaque engraved with the name of the very first Rothschild, Isaak Elchanan Rothschild, who died in 1585. A quick calculation: that was 185 years ago. The red sign decorated the gate of Isaak Elchanan's home, which was located at the southern edge of Judengasse, not far from our home. When Naftaly Hertz, Isaak Elchanan's grandson, found himself in financial distress, and was forced to move to a Hinterpfann at the northern edge, he took the red house sign with him, and ever since, the family had been living there, having adopted "red sign" as their family name.

Amschel Moshe, my Meir Amschel's father, died when I was only four years old, and therefore I cannot remember him. But Mama and Papa knew him well, and whenever they speak of him their voices are filled with appreciation for his efforts, his charity, and his hospitality. But I could also hear the hint of reservation on my father's part, due to Amschel Moshe's financial standing, which was lower than my father's. I myself had no reservations. On the contrary, the fact that Amschel Moshe had worked as a silk trader in spite of the prohibition placed on Jews to trade in luxury items, the fact that he had been a money changer, and, before his death, started his banking business, aroused a kind of admiration in me toward Meir Amschel's deceased father. There, I thought, like father like son, brave, fearless.

I looked at the embroidered napkin. The letters on it—M. A. R.— led me to recall the new sign he'd affixed outside his home. I closed my eyes and envisioned the royal court of Landgrave Wilhelm, elector of Hanau. Meir Rothschild of the dark Judengasse, his father's successor, would step, in due time, out of darkness and into the light. He would achieve greatness. He's already on his way. I know it, just as I know there is blood running through my veins.

Saturday night, June 23rd, 1770

I stood at the window again today. Ten days have gone by since I went on a walk down the alley with Meir. According to rumor, we seem to have blown fresh air into our little neighborhood, making a significant contribution to the gossip on the street, where people cling to each other, feeding on any fragment of change that occurs in any of the individuals composing our world.

Our names are rolling off people's tongues, and Meir Rothschild is enjoying praise for his persistence, which paid off. They say he's proved once again that nothing can stand against his will. In commerce as in his personal life—his actions are calculated to the last detail. My father's name—Wolf Shlomo Schnapper—is also spoken by all with a hint of appreciation, and he enjoys a pat on the back for giving Meir his approval. There is a general agreement that what tipped the scales was Meir's financial rise, which impressed my father, himself a successful trader.

People can say what they will. I care only about one thing: I am going to marry my beloved. To me, Meir Rothschild is the whole world.

Each day at dusk, after the household chores are complete, I stand by the window, hoping he will come and we might go on a walk, so

that I may hear the sound of his enthusiastic voice. Questions crowd my
mouth, but I know how preoccupied he is with his business and understand he may have trouble getting away. And nevertheless I remain
standing in my regular spot, accepting the ticking hours with love, and
clinging to the thought that each new day carries new hope.

I completed the embroidery to my excited satisfaction, and placed
the folded napkins in the chest. Vendeleh never leaves my side, as if
wishing to drink up my company before we part. She had climbed on
the chair she'd dragged over to my spot by the window, and was sitting
on her knees, swinging her feet behind her, her eyes following and hopeful, just like mine. Suddenly she let out a squeal: "There he is! There he
is, Gutaleh! He's coming, he's coming!" She pointed toward the handsome young man walking toward us, smiling widely.

I rubbed her back, trying to settle her down, and especially trying
to calm my own heart, which had begun to beat like a drum, competing with the volume of her voice. Meir came closer to the window,
waving his hat at us, and Vendeleh waved back. He signaled to me
to come downstairs, and I replied with a demure smile and a nod,
needing no words.

I stepped into my shoes and was about to head out, but Vendeleh
was grasping the ends of my dress. "I want to come too, please. Take
me with you."

I looked at her, concerned. I had not predicted this development.
Of course Meir had to meet me out on the street, since there was no
chance of privacy in our small home filled with children. If he saw fit to
put off his important business in order to see me, this could not be the
right moment to involve Vendeleh in the precious time he'd set aside for
us. How would he react if he saw this little one tagging along?

Her pleading eyes didn't leave me. I couldn't bear to turn down my
lovely, sensitive sister. I bent down and took her hand. "I'm letting you
come with us just this once, and only for part of the meeting. Then we'll
drop you back off here, all right?"

"All right. Thank you, Gutaleh, you're so kind," the little one said, cheerful.

"And you promise never to ask again?"

She hesitated for a moment and I gave her a piercing look, until she finally blurted, "I promise never to ask again."

"I'll go out first, and you put your shoes on and stand at the window. I'll signal to you when it's time to come outside."

She ran toward her shoes and I hurried outside, kissing the mezuzah hastily on my way out, without giving my racing heart a chance to slow down. I told Meir about my sister's wish to join us. I was afraid of his response, but he eliminated my doubts in a flash. Rather than answer, he turned to the window and signaled to Vendeleh to come. I relaxed.

When she arrived, he picked her up, raised her into the air, higher and higher, and she laughed with joy and fear. When he put her down, he said cheerfully, "Want to race?" He pointed at the finish line, right by the house that had collapsed today, a group of people already working to restore it. Vendeleh nodded and told me to give the cue. They ran, Vendeleh working her little legs as hard as she could, while Meir held on to his hat, trying to maintain a reasonable distance in her favor.

I walked over. They were waiting at the finish line, holding hands. Meir welcomed me with a defeated face, announcing in the most convincing voice that he wasn't used to losing races, but today he'd lost to a young, pretty girl named Vendeleh, and it was only right that she win a prize. He led us down the path to his Hinterpfann home. A group of children dawdled behind us, gaining numbers along the way. From a pile of junk he fished out a rag doll. Vendeleh's eyes lit up. He smoothed the doll's dress, led Vendeleh to the sign, and announced to the gathering audience that had been watching his treatment of the glowing child, "I, Meir Amschel Rothschild, authorized vendor of the Court of Venerable Landgrave Wilhelm, elector of Hanau and crown prince of Hesse-Kassel, hereby present this prize to Miss Vendeleh for her victory in the race."

He handed her the doll, removed his hat, and bowed to her. The audience cheered, and Vendeleh lowered her head bashfully. She looked at the doll and then at me. I nodded encouragingly, and she reached her tiny hands out, brought the doll to her chest, offered Meir the bud of a shy smile, and returned her eyes to the muddy path. I followed the two of them with my eyes, willing to drop everything at that moment and marry this wonderful man who loved children so much.

We made our way back along the curving street. Vendeleh skipped ahead of us, the bundle of hair at the nape of her neck skipping along with her, the doll in her arms. She said goodbye to us by the house, and prancing joyfully, disappeared at the entrance. I said a silent thanks for the way my knight had ensured our privacy from this point on.

Finally, we were alone. I held on to my blue-and-black-striped scarf, pulled on both its ends, and fixed him with taunting eyes.

"What is it?" he asked.

"If I had a hat, I'd take it off right now, Meir Amschel Rothschild."

In a flash, he took his hat off and placed it on my head. Now he turned his open, inviting hand to me.

I laughed, removed the hat from my head, and took a deep bow, reaching almost to the filthy floor. "Wisdom and sensitivity don't always go together, but with you I suppose anything is possible." The words spilled out of my mouth without consulting with my mind and without considering that, as a newly engaged woman, a little more restraint might have been expected of me.

He brought his mouth close to my ear. "If we were alone right now, without these people's eyes staring from the windows, encircling us, I'd call you 'my beloved' and dance with you right this minute."

A hot wave washed over me. This incidental declaration of love was spoken with full intentionality. What should I do with it? How should I treat this sweet confession? I crushed the ends of the scarf with my fingers, my eyes turning upward toward the narrow sky, searching for a refuge in which to bury the beating of my soul, and instead meeting the heads peering through the windows. The ridiculous sight undid the knots in my tense body. I covered my mouth to stifle the laughter that threatened to pop out. Meir Rothschild's presence managed to awaken waves of laughter that I, an adult now, had thought were no longer possible. I guess even adults have stores of laughter just looking for release. I returned his hat, put my hand on his inviting arm, and was glad to be led down the road by him. I considered all the gossiping tongues I was pleasing, and was surprised to find I didn't mind. On the contrary, it only made me feel warmer.

"I'm not that special," he said in all seriousness, one hand returning the hat to his head, the other serving as a resting spot for mine, one leg sent forward to kick out any obstacles from my path. "Anyone who has brothers and sisters, and especially those who've lost their parents and remained alone with those brothers and sisters, cannot help but feel connected to children and relate to them."

"How are your siblings?" I was reminded to ask, aligning myself with his gravitas while simultaneously following our path as he led me around a pile of garbage blocking our way.

"Well, let's see. My sisters, Bilkha and Gutelkha, are very happy in the families they've started. Every year I am informed that my value as an uncle has risen with the arrival of another niece or nephew. I think that's the most cheerful part of my report. My brother Kalman is not at his finest. His handicap is making things difficult for him and it breaks my heart, though he himself has accepted his limitations, never complains, and does his best as a money changer. I even added coins, medals, pearls, gems, and antiques for him to sell. Unfortunately, I don't think he can hold on much longer. Only a miracle can save him. Sometimes life is cruel to the wrong people."

I only see Kalman on our street occasionally, but other than a passing sense of pity at the sight of his weak body, I've had no other feelings toward him. Now, reflected in his brother's eyes, Kalman's face takes on a new, surprising facet. I feel a desire to know him better, familiarize myself with his strong personality, anchored inside a fragile body.

"And as for my brother Moshe," Meir Rothschild continued, "from him, a grown man only one year younger than I am, I expected better."

"What's wrong with Moshe? I see him working industriously, selling used goods." *Such as the handkerchief,* I wanted to add, but held back.

"That's just the thing. He's investing all his energy in a profession with an income that is barely sufficient for basic survival. He's just gotten married, just a few weeks after turning twenty-five, and now must provide for a family."

"I suppose he has no other choice. You yourself said that we Jews are limited in our commerce possibilities."

"True. But we must remove these limitations. We cannot go on this way. The ghetto is closing in on us. If we don't break out, we'll suffocate. Look, Gutaleh—we step out of our small homes to get some fresh air, and what kind of air do we have to look forward to? Unbearably stifling."

"That's the air we've got, and we make do with it. I don't see what's so bad about it."

Meir's face wore that distant look again. I think I'm growing used to it. It's always followed by a lesson about his life or life in general. He said nothing for a few minutes, and I could sense it coming. What would he teach me this time?

He spoke slowly. "Gutaleh, this is Judengasse air. Other places have different air. Air that does not contain the smells of mildew and sewage. Air that invites you to expand your lungs and breathe in properly."

"Tell me about those places."

"Poor child, I must find a way to get you out of here so that you can see with your own eyes what takes place beyond the walls and beyond Frankfurt. It is unimaginable that only men have the right to go out of town for business, while women and children remain buried in here."

I trembled. "I don't feel buried. I'm alive and well. Here I am, walking freely at your side."

He shook his head. "When a person is cooped up between four walls, they cannot imagine what goes on outside of them. We Jews are adaptive creatures. We find our way in any situation. You want to know what it's like? While we're crowded in this tiny ghetto, just fifty cubits away is an expansive world with spacious, stable homes, not tiny houses, piled up and crumbling like ours. In the outside world, the streets are wide and sunlit, more than just one narrow, dark alley. The people there dress up and walk leisurely down the street any time they please. They aren't locked up as if in a cage. Their tender feet pace paved sidewalks, while we Jews, lucky to enjoy their world every day until sundown, not including Sundays and holidays, wallow in muddy paths we must share with carts. Our feet are as rough as the carts' wheels. And on top of all that, they can work in any field they wish, without boundaries. Do you understand? They have light, air, freedom. That's why their faces are saturated with the color of life. They aren't pale, like the faces of Jews in the ghetto. You cannot imagine how pale your face is in comparison with those of the elegant women descending from carriages with fur coats on their shoulders and gloves on their delicate hands, walking leisurely down paved sidewalks."

I was lost in reverie about this great big world he'd spread before me. The more I thought about it, the more I decided I didn't like that world. The large homes and the wide streets and the elegant women—I didn't like any of those. They looked condescendingly over my Judengasse, reframing it between four walls. I put my hand on my face. I never thought about my paleness. The thought that I looked lackluster to him compared to Frankfurt women bothered me. "And those women . . . the elegant women . . . with color in their cheeks, they must be beautiful," I whispered from between my four Judengasse walls, and immediately regretted it. I hoped he hadn't heard.

But Meir has ears like a cat. I must remember that from now on.

"Beautiful?" His laughter rolled. "Gutaleh, my Gutaleh, all that color on those elegant women's faces—both the color of life and the artificial color of their makeup—can do nothing to bring them even close to the beauty of Judengasse women. Our women are the prettiest."

That cheered me up. I know physical beauty is not my most prominent quality, but I liked knowing that those gentile women Meir sees are no prettier than me. And I, even if I am pale, my body is strong, and I would never allow the paleness of my face to decide the fate of my body. "What kind of job would you like to see your brother performing?" I resumed the conversation with a sense of relief.

"I'd be happy if Moshe joined my business and helped me develop it. I opened a *Wechselstube* in our used-goods store. We sell antique coins. Like I said, Kalman is helping me run it."

"Who buys that kind of thing? I think people need useful items. What would they do with antique coins?" Once again, my mouth got away from me. Though I keep reminding myself to be subtle, not shoving my big nose into his business, which is none of my business, so to speak, what ends up happening is that my lethal curiosity, combined with the unrestrained thoughts in my head, does not allow me to take a passive stand and merely listen.

Fortunately, Meir didn't mind what I had said. In fact, he took it seriously. More seriously than I did. "From the point of view of someone who lives here, you're right. Of course I can't sell antique coins to the people of Judengasse. Six years ago, when I first went to the Frankfurt markets and fairs, I sold fabric, wine, leather. As a side venture, I changed money. That's not bad at all for a start. I accumulated some money. But I also learned that serious money is not to be found in normal commerce, but in luxury commerce, which includes antique coins. And what is serious money? The kind great people with deep pockets pay. The kind of people who live in grand homes, castles, and palaces. Those kinds of people are interested in antique coins." He pulled a folded page from his pocket and carefully unfolded it. "Here's the catalog I made."

I took the page from him with reverence. I saw straight lines written in his careful, elegant handwriting, surrounded by decorations. "You did all this?"

He nodded. "And you know who's held this very catalog in his hands?"

I shrugged.

"The landgrave Wilhelm himself."

"Meir, I hope you aren't teasing me. How did you meet him? How did you manage to be let into his palace?" And wordlessly I added, *You're so young, so much younger than my father. And, well, let us not forget—you're Jewish.*

"Well, of course I did not knock on his chamber door and say, 'Hello, I'm Meir Amschel Rothschild from Judengasse and I'd like to visit my friend Wilhelm.'"

This time I didn't even try to stifle my laughter. He's funny too, my smart, sensitive man. A riveting and amusing conversationalist.

But now he wasn't laughing. His face was severe. He sounded like a grown man, versed in the ways of the world, explaining things to a young, inexperienced child. Nevertheless, I knew he wasn't condescending, like the privileged people of Frankfurt. He was only trying to bring his head closer to mine to acquaint me with the way his brain worked. "It's a long story, which involves a prolonged, well-planned preparation," he said. "Each step led to the next. It's like a tower, one floor constructed over the next, and none can be skipped, or the entire structure falls apart."

"We've got time, and I'm curious to hear all about it," I said quickly, my eyes fixing on the wrinkles that formed on his forehead. When he speaks seriously, his forehead switches to wrinkle mode, and I enter listening mode.

"I'll tell you, and when you get tired of listening, please do not hesitate to stop me. I warn you, when I talk I tend to forget myself."

"Fine, I'll remember that," I promised. God, he is so gentle and considerate.

He nodded with satisfaction. "I owe a debt of gratitude to Hanover. That's where my path began. That's where sobriety and comprehension budded. I worked as an apprentice in the Oppenheimer family's Jewish bank in Hanover. The first years were rather disgraceful. Apprentices are treated like servants. But it didn't bother me. I saw before me the possibilities that spending time at a commercial bank serving nobles would bring. I performed all the useless tasks they gave me with devotion, patiently waiting for my time to come. I gradually found my place in more and more significant activities, which justified my patience and answered my expectations. My time spent there was great business training. I reached the conclusion that only those who dare, succeed. I told myself, if the Jewish banker Oppenheimer did it, I, Meir Rothschild, can do it too. From that point on, I began to design a system of rules that I use as milestones for success. One of them is creating contacts."

"Contacts?"

"Yes. Contacts are like threads. Woven properly, they can lead you to the correct destination. But first, you must detect the appropriate contacts. And to detect them, you must develop your sense of smell."

"Your sense of smell?"

"The sense of smell can constantly evolve. Sniffing helps me stay up to date and use the information for my own needs. Sometimes I smell trouble, other times treasure. I'll give you an example. In Hanover I worked as an errand boy in service of General von Estorff, one of the most prominent collectors of ancient and rare coins. I took devoted and professional care of his affairs. Sniffing around, I discovered that General von Estorff had been employed by the court of Landgrave Wilhelm in Hanau, where he served as an advisor. So what did I do? I continued to nurture my relationship with the general even after leaving Hanover. I came to see von Estorff on a friendly visit, and as expected, he was glad to see me and even made the effort to introduce me to his friends. That way, I got the chance to introduce them to my own friends: antique coins from Russia, Palestine, Bavaria; medals and antiques passed from one generation to the next. I praised my special goods. I was not used to speaking in their style. I remained faithful to the style of the ghetto, but I proved to them and to myself that this would cause no problems. Since *I* didn't see my language and style as a problem, they were led to reach the same conclusion, that they must accept me as I am. They listened to me, perused the catalog, listened and looked again, and . . . bought." Meir clapped and cried, "My first achievement!"

I listened to his story, analyzing it much faster than I was used to, and drawing conclusions. My wise Meir did not let language limitations get in his way, and had no qualms about speaking like a simple man. As it turned out, that was another winning formula. With his murky German, mottled with Judendeutsch, and with his heavy Judengasse accent, he captivates everyone—both the noble and the lowly, and everyone in between. Where did he get that kind of confidence?

His story did wear on, as he'd warned me it would. A quick look around revealed that the day had folded up and disappeared, and that evening was slowly emerging, as if making sure first that the coast was clear. I felt each detail of his story becoming a part of me. I knew no one else had enjoyed such a confession from him. This was reserved for me alone. I wanted to hear more and more.

He went on, and I made sure not to break his train of thought. "Success breeds success, I kept repeating to myself. Therefore I must not rest on my laurels, but move on."

As Meir spoke, I tried not to give in to the sensations his lips and voice aroused in me. I focused my thoughts on his words—everything he said was food for thought.

"So I sat down to carefully produce more and more catalogs. I sent over two hundred of them to princes and dukes, some close, others farther and farther away," he said. "And I expanded my circle of acquaintances. But my desired objective was the landgrave Wilhelm of Hanau, because he could open new doors for me. I pulled some strings with General von Estorff and arrived with him at the landgrave's chambers at the finest timing, while the landgrave was in the middle of his beloved chess game. I took a look at the sixty-four black-and-white squares and the few pawns remaining on the board, and hinted to the landgrave a move that led him to announce, 'Checkmate.' He squealed like a little boy. While he was pleased with his victory, I hurried to present to him the finest array of rare coins and decorations. I could not have asked for a clearer path than the one that opened before me and led to my signing my first deal with the most influential landgrave. From that point to applying for a position as a court banker, the road was smooth, with no true obstacles, though a few delays. But who am I to become discouraged by postponement? I had achieved the main thing, arriving at the coveted moment and placing the sign outside my home."

"Sounds like a fairy tale."

"A fairy tale? Indeed. And just as in fairy tales, it began a long, long time ago." He fell silent all of a sudden, looking up with a childish smile on his face. He must have been thinking about the fairy tale, I thought. Suddenly, he returned his eyes to me and said purposefully, "I think I've burdened you with more than enough details for one day. I'll tell you the fairy tale the next time we meet."

I nodded. Indeed, it was late, and I had to get home.

He walked me to the door, bowed deeply, and blew me a kiss. I smiled bashfully, my eyes filled with gratitude.

Wednesday, June 27th, 1770

I believe my feet have never encountered our street the way they do
these days with Meir Rothschild. I have definitely never walked it with
such focus and concentration as I do now, taking in so many shards of
information, which grant me the feeling of having been reborn.

Before our next meeting, I pinched my cheeks lightly to give them
the shade of life. The manner with which he welcomed me, examining
my face with surprise, lifted my spirits, giving me permission to make
it a habit.

After a long walk, catching up on the events of the last few days,
with me marveling at how activity-filled his were, he suddenly said,
"Well, darling, I owe you the fairy tale I promised several days ago."

I closed my eyes. I used to love Mama's fairy tales, and have been
recounting them to my brothers and sisters for years. I listened to Meir's
voice, wandering through the world of fantasy. "I was ten years old. It
was a short while before Father sent me to the yeshiva in Fürth. I was
strolling, as usual, with some friends by the northern gate, near our
home. We followed passersby, carriages and horses, hoping that someone might be in need of an errand boy or a porter. Most of the time we
returned home with a few coins, the fee for our work. Suddenly, my

eyes caught an elegant carriage harnessed to three horses. I watched it, prepared to continue to do so as it drove past, but to my great surprise it came to a halt right beside us, and one of the horses almost knocked me over. I evaded the horse's mighty hoof at the very last moment. As I was catching my breath from this near accident, I heard my friends crying out enthusiastically, 'The landgrave! The landgrave!' I looked up and saw a boy our age wearing a velvet cape laced with silver fringe sitting alongside an old, dignified-looking man.

"The old man apologized to me, looking at us as if we were animals in cages, waiting to be sold for slaughter. Then he spoke warmly and amicably: 'You are correct, children,' he said.

"'At my side is the heir to the Hesse throne. I am his tutor. You must never have seen this remote princedom and its capital of Kassel. Since we were visiting Frankfurt, we were curious to take a look at the Jewish ghetto.' He looked at us again, and I looked at him and at the landgrave, sitting silently, looking quizzically at our ragged clothing. The old man carried on: 'Seeing as your holiday of Passover is drawing near, the landgrave would be glad to grant you some coins as a gift.' Not a minute later, a shower of coins fell upon us from the landgrave's hands. The boy stood on the edge of the carriage, amused by the sight, while I was appalled to see my friends kneeling down to collect the charity.

"I demanded that they hand over everything. Then I approached the old man and gave him the coins. 'We do not need handouts,' I said. The old man gaped at me and my friends, but then took the coins from me and asked that I join them on a tour of the place and reveal the secrets of the street to them.

"I took advantage of my first opportunity to serve as a guide. I explained that since our street was too narrow for their carriage, they had to leave it outside the gate. I led them by foot down the street and through the alleys, among houses and shops, pointing out the synagogue, the bathhouse, the yeshiva, the guesthouse, and the mission, explaining the purpose of each establishment, as if I were an experienced guide. I puffed out my small chest, explaining with an air of importance that outsiders came especially to see our great rabbis—some young men coming to study at our yeshiva, others arriving to ask our rabbis questions of Jewish law they were unable to have answered elsewhere.

"The two of them thanked me for the fascinating tour and the detailed explanations, expressing how impressed they were by our schooling, our prayers, our cleanliness and purity, and the efforts we put into our sustenance. They were especially impressed by the custom of *gemilut chasadim*—acts of kindness. When they were about to board their carriage, I reached out my hand.

"'I think you've forgotten something,' I said.

"'And what is that?' the teacher asked. 'You turned down the coins we offered earlier.'

"'We do not accept handouts, but I will gladly receive payment for my guided tour.'

"The landgrave reached into his pocket, fished out a handful of coins, and placed them in my outstretched hands. 'Goodbye, Meir Amschel Rothschild,' he said, speaking my full name, which he had wanted to know during the tour. 'I, Wilhelm, landgrave of the Hesse princedom, promise to never forget this special day and your wonderful guidance. If you ever require my assistance, please come see me at the palace. My door will be open to you and I would gladly oblige.'"

"What a story!" I cried. "And what a marvelous ending. A fairy-tale ending."

"No, Gutaleh, this isn't the end."

I watched him, arching my brows.

"I thanked the landgrave for his generosity," Amschel continued with satisfaction, "and answered, 'And I, Meir Amschel Rothschild, would be glad to provide you with my services when the time is right.' The young landgrave nodded, climbed up to his elevated seat, and drew away in his carriage with the ringing of cymbals, and I turned toward home with heavy pockets and mutual promises recorded in my brain."

I'm getting to know this man who never ceases to surprise me. A man of principles who would never accept a despicable handout tossed at his feet, but would nevertheless demand what he has earned. A man of vision and courage. And he was only ten years old at the time! I took a long look at the big man at my side. I required no words.

He returned my look, aware of the profound impression his story had left on me.

"Well then, you both kept your mutual promises to each other," I finally said. "Did he recognize you when you came to see him at the palace? Did you remind him of the past?"

"No, Gutaleh, he didn't, nor did I remind him. I'm saving that card for the right moment."

"And why is that?"

"Because right now I have other tricks up my sleeve."

I looked around. Twilight had turned our street gray. I looked up. Above us stretched a narrow canopy of sky, dotted with stars. It is indecorous for a young girl to stroll with a young man in the dark.

He saw what I had seen, and quickly said, "I have yet to bring you up to date on my goals, which I had begun to describe to you the last time we met. I must tell you that the next step was my most coveted target."

"It's late. I suppose we'll need a few more strolls for me to get caught up on all your goals," I said, though secretly I prayed for him to keep going. I was willing to spend the night out on the street with him, though I knew the scolding I would have to look forward to from Mama, and—much worse—Papa.

"Oh, you're caught up. This coveted goal I speak of is called Gutaleh."

"I was on your list of goals?"

"Let us be accurate, my dear. You are at the top of the list. You even appeared in my application for the title of court banker, sent to Wilhelm. I wrote, 'His Highness the Landgrave, I put my faith and hopes in his highness, who would be most gracious and benevolent to accept my request and grant me this honorary title, which holds the power to promote my commercial career and assist me in the fulfillment of my personal plans. These two paths, converged, would send me to the highest peaks of happiness in the city of Frankfurt.' By 'personal plans' I was of course referring to you, my beautiful lady."

I, little Gutle, was included in a letter to Landgrave Wilhelm. I must record this stunning detail in my memory.

And what made him so convinced that Papa would eventually agree to his pleas? Before I could find my bearings and say a single word, he surprised me again:

"And I must ask you, my beloved Gutaleh, if you'll marry me according to the faith of Moshe and Israel."

I felt my face catch fire. I said a silent thanks for the darkness of the street, concealing the color of blood that must have been burning through my cheeks. "Yes, but . . . what's the rush?" I asked foolishly.

What have I done? What was I saying? This is what I had yearned for: to marry the man who had conquered my heart.

As was his custom, Meir replied with gravity, listing a series of answers for the imbecilic question I had blurted. "Gutaleh, how long can we continue to stroll up and down the same street, the only roofs above the curious faces of neighbors? Do we not deserve a proper roof over our heads? I am opening up, telling you my secrets. Isn't it only right that this exposure be kept private, just between us? We plan on having ten children, and we must allow time and space for this plan to come to fruition, mustn't we? And, most importantly, I want you by my side because I love you. Don't I deserve this? Don't *we* deserve this?"

I wanted to answer yes to all of his questions. A hesitant smile stretched across my face, then disappeared. I was paralyzed. A deep fear seeped into my golden dream, my dream who was standing by my side, proposing the offer of my life.

"Are you sure?" I finally asked.

"Sure about what?"

"About your proposal. Are you sure I deserve you? You are all-knowing and all-powerful, while I'm just a . . . little fool."

He took both my hands in his. "Look into my eyes, Gutaleh."

I did as he said. I was babbling, which meant I was in love. In the darkness of the evening, his eyes lit up like fireflies.

"Never make this mistake again. Do not call yourself a fool. You are not a fool. In fact, you're the brightest, wisest girl on Judengasse. First, I love you, Gutaleh, and that in itself should be enough. But, as I am wont to do, I also sniffed around and quickly found your three most wonderful qualities: warmth, wisdom, and industriousness. I want you, and I yearn to build my home and family with you, from the foundations to the roof beams. It's no coincidence that I'm thinking of ten children. You can make it possible. You'll be the foundation stone, my support and strength. You're the one I need. You're my best deal. I can't wait for the wedding. *How beautiful you are, my darling. Oh, how beautiful! Your eyes behind your veil are doves.*"

How handsome you are, my beloved! Oh, how charming! I answered in my heart.

Sunday, September 2nd, 1770

I'm married! Thank the Lord! I'm a wife! My name is Gutle Rothschild, or, more accurately, Frau Gutle Rothschild, wife of Meir Amschel Rothschild, court banker of his highness the landgrave Wilhelm, elector of Hanau and the crown prince of Hesse-Kassel, resident of Judengasse.

It happened four days ago, a date that will remain in my mind forever: August 29th, 1770, six days after my seventeenth birthday.

After calculating the days of my cycle to determine when I am a *niddah*—a woman impure for sexual relations due to monthly bleeding—and after making sure we did not deviate from the annual quota of twelve marriages, as determined by the law of the Holy Roman Empire for residents of Judengasse, and based on the fact that Meir is already of the minimum marrying age allowed by the same law, having already turned twenty-five, plus an extra year for the books, we set a date.

During the *Spinnholz* reception on the Saturday night before the wedding, my mouth had a life of its own, stretching into a constant smile, though I knew I had to show restraint and behave with modesty and moderation. I could see panic on my mother's face, her eyes demanding that I rein in my smile, but even they could not make me conform. The smile simply would not leave my face. Meir Amschel smiled too. One smile invites another. His kind eyes beamed with satisfaction.

The night before the wedding, Mother took me to the *mikveh*, the purifying baths, after I conducted the necessary checks and counted seven clean days. When I walked out of the baths, Mama took both my hands and whispered, "Gutaleh, you were born once when you emerged from my womb, and now you are reborn—pure, clean, and untarnished—into marriage."

There was a great to-do on the day of the wedding. For the first time in my life, I felt beautiful. I covered my corset with a tight bodice, over which I wore a smooth, white dress with delicate lace on top, its ends skirting my glimmering shoes. The corset made my waist look narrow, and I floated through the room, trying to convince myself that this body, enjoying compliments, was mine. The room became stifling as the women surrounded me, never ceasing their praise and advice. Their chatter, mixed with the bustle of the household, made the noise inside of me even louder. *It's happening,* I thought. *Today I will become Frau Rothschild.*

I sat up in my chair before the mirror, pinched my cheeks, patted the powder puff over my face and neck, and thought of the color covering the faces of the women of Frankfurt. Not only did the thought not bother me, in fact it lit up my face with a special, feminine glow that reflected from the mirror and made my heart swell. I had beaten them all. Meir, a wondrous combination, a kind, special, successful, smart, honest, handsome, and beloved man (and this is only a partial list of his sublime qualities), had chosen me as his wife. I scattered some powder on my carefully coiffed hair, put lipstick on my lips, and gently painted my cheeks.

Mama urged me to hurry up and finish applying my makeup. She gave me a quick kiss on the back of my neck and latched a pearl choker around it. For a brief moment, our eyes met in the mirror, and I detected the twinkle of a tear in hers. My kind mother was as excited as

I was for my big day. I swallowed a smile at the sight of the many necklaces around her neck and the gemstone bracelets around her wrists. She was making the most of this legal opportunity to show off her jewelry, all of it at once. My beloved brothers and sisters stood in their places, obedient, the boys suffocated by their tiny ties, the girls proud in their glamorous dresses. Only sweet Vendeleh twirled around in her fancy dress, stumbling, falling, getting up, and twirling some more.

I left the house, arm in arm with my mother on one side and with Bilkha, Meir's sister, on the other, each of them carrying a burning candle in her free hand. I was led down the path to the big synagogue, looking all around me at Judengasse, wearing its holiday best.

A large crowd filled the sides of the road, blocking the filth and broken beams with their bodies, ensuring a clear path on the way to the synagogue. Congratulations and best wishes were spoken from all directions, and I answered with a nod and a glowing smile. My heart had love for everyone: for the crowd sharing in my joy, for my mother and father, thanks to whom I was about to marry my beloved, for my siblings, and an even greater love for my dear Meir, my one and only. I was curious to see his face and his elegant outfit.

A cellist and two fiddlers, who had traveled from the nearby city of Offenbach, began to play loudly. I paced like a princess along the cheering crowd. All I was missing was a scepter. The parade followed us, accompanying the musicians in song, dance, and clapping. The closer I came to the windows of the synagogue, the larger the crowd behind me became.

I visit the holy synagogue on holidays and days of commemoration. Whenever I visit, I circle my eyes all around, taking in the grandeur and sanctity. Upon the opening of the Torah, I focus my gaze on the elegant Torah crown with the pomegranate on top.

Now the outskirts of the court were dotted with burning candles. Atop a wooden plank stage, my eyes caught sight of the handsome groom standing beneath the chuppah stretched across four poles, held by four yeshiva boys. Who was this regal young man waiting for? Could he possibly be waiting for me? Was I dreaming? Would I soon wake up, the spell broken?

I did my best to stop the tears from ruining my makeup. He stood tall. To his left were his brothers, Moshe and Kalman, and my father. My groom's suit was elegant, covered with a snow-white *Kittl* flowing down below his knees, his black beard well trimmed, and a yarmulke on his head. A wide smile was on his face, and his shimmering eyes caressed mine.

I stood still. I thought I could hear my own heart pounding. Mama and Bilkha stepped onto the stage, and Meir descended to meet me. His proximity had me intoxicated. I fought off the powerful urge to rest my head on his shoulder. With a tender gesture he pulled the veil over my face. I felt safe under the mesh, hiding the fire burning inside of me.

We walked together toward the chuppah. My memory of the ceremony is muddled, as though I had been drunk. Bilkha and Gutelkha took my hands and circled my groom with me seven times. We sipped our wine. The rabbi and community elders said the seven blessings, and Meir sanctified me with a valuable wedding ring that weighed a whole ounce. The ketubah was read, Meir stepped on the glass in memory of the ruination of the temple, the musicians played cheerfully, circles were formed, one for men and another for women, and I, swept up with joy, gave myself over to the dictates of my body and moved within the women's circle with no desire to stop. Once the ceremony was over, Meir took a tiny bite of the *schalit*—a wedding-day pie—then came over and put a small, warm piece in my mouth. I felt the flavor of the *schalit* and realized how much better it tasted thanks to the sensation of Meir's fingers on my tongue. I kept repeating to myself that this was the happiest day of my life, and that no one in the entire world was happier than I. Then I corrected myself: no one in all of Judengasse, at least.

For a moment, Meir's eyes rested on the impoverished people of our street, celebrating our marriage. I looked at them too, how they delighted over the hearty meal and the sweets, drinking the wine, and fingering the gift coin placed beside their plates. I thought of this fine custom we kept for the benefit of the less fortunate, and how now I had become a partner to this custom as well.

◆　◆　◆

Later, in our bed in Meir's home, our home, I lay awake beside my man, whose rhythmic breathing was testimony of his serenity. He was tender with me, making all my fears of the first night fall away. Lovemaking had opened a secret door to a strong storm of excitement, bringing with it a pure, completely unbridled lust. I became acquainted with a secret world. A shared tremble, ours alone, the final tightening of our bond. I am lucky, I told myself, attempting to summarize the evening, give in to exhaustion, and join my love in sleep.

A tiny tickle in my stomach interrupted my tranquility. I wondered about it. What could possibly bother me on the happiest day of my life? The more I thought about it, the more I was surprised to find that a single sentence spoken by my beloved was echoing through my mind. At the doorstep, Meir took my hand and whispered in my ear: "Tonight I made the deal of my life." Am I not the love of his life, but rather the deal of his life? Even after our lovemaking, when my ears waited to hear the declaration of love I needed, he did put his arms around me, but the only sound he made was a sigh of relief, and I was convinced that even now he saw me as nothing more than merchandise, profitable goods that held certain advantages that turned it into the deal of his life.

There, I'd cracked the riddle. Now that I had identified the root of the problem, the pain sharpened, and the path to sleep had been derailed, transforming into full wakefulness. The thought took control of my wedding night and left no way for me to resist.

I had no doubt about the sincerity of his love, but I needed the warmth of his words on my first night away from my childhood home.

This warmth was more necessary to me than the impressive, happy ceremony prepared for us.

Warm tears drenched the pillow under my head and continued to flow for a while longer, until finally I pulled the blanket up to my chin and sank into the darkness of slumber.

In my dream, I was sitting in the yard. Before me, arms crossed, sat ten little children, all the same age, five boys and five girls. Meir was holding a stick and teaching them the daily sermon. I tried to catch his words, but the only one I could make out was "deal." I came closer, and he raised the stick to signal to me not to interrupt, calling out, "Deal! Deal! Deal!" The word burst out of his monstrous mouth, echoing all around. I wanted to shield my face, but my hands refused to obey me, dangling at my sides. I wanted to shout, but my voice betrayed me and refused to emerge. I awoke with a start. The sound of my panting filled the room. It was morning.

Meir took me in his arms and held me to his chest.

"I had . . . a dream . . ." I blurted out the shards of words onto his shoulder.

"False dreams shall speak out," he quoted.

I remained in his arms. His soft voice blurred the image of the dream. Finally I pulled away slowly, sitting on the edge of the bed. I offered him a meek smile. His kind eyes, tinged now with a hint of worry, called out to me. How could I have imagined him as a monster? He kissed my cheeks and my mouth, and I gave myself over to him, wishing to cleanse myself of this awful dream.

"I'm sorry for waking up this late."

"I'm not sorry one bit, my lovely wife. You've given me some time to make necessary arrangements. Look at this letter, addressed to her highness, Frau Gutle Rothschild." He pointed to the dresser, atop which was an envelope.

"Is that for me?" I marveled.

"Do you see another Frau Gutle Rothschild here?" he answered with a question of his own, looking around him, as if to make sure no other Frau Gutle Rothschild was hiding somewhere.

I smiled at his taunting, sniffed, and took the envelope. I opened it carefully and pulled out the letter. I immediately recognized the handwriting and the watermarks.

> *To the honorable Frau Gutle Rothschild,*
> *You have granted me a special honor by accepting my invitation to share the rest of my life with me. It is well known that living with me is no easy task, seeing as your man is not one of those who live a life of serenity. There is a fire burning inside of me, and bringing it out into the world with efficiency and purpose will only be possible with full cooperation from a personality such as yours. Therefore, your modest acceptance of me as your husband is infinitely blessed. I promise you that I am prepared to spend all of my energy and strength in order to justify your readiness. It would be an honor and a pleasure to do everything within my means to keep you satisfied all days and nights.*
>
> *My darling, more precious than gems and pearls, you have it in your power to help me build the foundations of our home. I shall place the supports and infrastructures of our shared future in your hands. I gain confidence knowing that in doing so, we are fulfilling our superior duty of raising our ten children, showering them with love and warmth, and providing them with the most suitable education. If we also succeed in sharing our wealth with our Jewish brothers and sisters, we shall bring even more peace and tranquility to our consciences.*

*If my busy schedule will not allow me to declare daily
just how much I love you, I hereby declare in advance my
great love for you on this day and every day that follows.
Please remember this whenever your soul desires words of
love and affection when I am not at your side.*

    Yours forever,

    Meir Rothschild

    Happiest man alive

I finished reading and stared at the letter for another long moment. Then I read it again. I took the words in small gulps, tasting them, one by one. I placed the letter on the dresser and covered my face with my hands.

My crying emerged in small, broken, choking sobs, growing from one moment to the next. Meir pulled me close. I buried my face in his neck, my tears dampening his shirt.

"My emotional wife, my love," he said, his breath tickling my ear.

"I . . . don't deserve you," I managed to say without letting go of him, ignoring the spreading spot of wetness.

He took hold of my shoulders and steadied my moist face before his. "Gutle Rothschild, never say anything like that. I only hope I can be worthy of you. I, with all my shortcomings, could not have dreamed of a better wife. The blessed Lord gave you to me, and I shall be thankful to Him for the rest of my life."

"Meir, you have no idea what kind of thoughts ran through my mind last night."

"I know, my dear. I know."

"I beg for your forgiveness. I had unkind and inappropriate thoughts about you."

"I never stop sniffing around, even in my sleep. I could sense your unrest and had an entire night to wipe away your tears, carefully, without waking you up, and then get deep inside your head and try and fish out what it was that was bothering you. I assumed it was my coarse remark as we walked inside last night that upset you." He paused for a moment before continuing: "If you listen carefully, you can hear the sound of my scruples. It's deafening."

I smiled, speechless.

"In order to correct my errors," he said, "I put pen to paper, and by the light of the candle, wrote from the bottom of my heart. All night long you writhed, torment apparent on your face. I was mad at myself for causing you this, and on our first night of marriage, no less. When you awoke with a start, I was angry with myself for having caused you such distress. Please forgive me, my dear wife. I promise to be more considerate in the future. You are altogether beautiful, my darling. All the riches in the world cannot compare to my love for you."

"You are . . . so special. You never cease to surprise me. You . . . you're superhuman, Meir."

"Superhuman. I like that. Now, would you care to join me for breakfast, Frau Gutle Rothschild?"

Thursday, January 10th, 1771

I continue to write in my notebook, which I had made sure to bring to my new home.

I am with child! The morning sickness subsided and has finally disappeared altogether. My growing belly is concealed by cotton dresses that flow down to my ankles. I made them from Meir's selection of fabric. I am proud to be carrying the first offspring of our new family. I feel that pregnancy becomes me, affording me a grace that I had never had before. For the first time in my life, I enjoy a sense of beauty, and I hope that it stays with me for a long time to come. An amusing thought occurs to me: perhaps I had been too hard on myself all this time, and I am not as ugly as I had always thought myself to be. I've always had these white teeth. And the smooth skin is not a result of pregnancy. My fair forehead and beaming face are also part of the package. I have made a joyous discovery: I am pretty!

Now thin blue lines stretch under my skin, and I wonder if they'll disappear after I give birth. I would be willing to keep these lines if only I can also keep the beauty.

Nevertheless, people staring at my belly make me uncomfortable, almost as if I were naked before their gazes. This is why I go to all this effort to conceal its size. It's interesting to find that the longer, less abashed looks come from women. Still, I do not like it.

I have wrapped my head with a coif, in accordance with Jewish law. My stature as wife is multiplied by the fact that I am the wife of Meir Rothschild. I have tied the ends of the coif together around my neck. I like to pull some of my hair forward, so it shows in front, to reduce the exposed part of my high forehead.

Vendeleh will be here soon to keep me company. My little sister makes sure to fill the space Meir leaves when he is gone from morning till night, often two, three, even four days in a row.

It is a woman's way to sit in her home and a man's way to go out to market and learn wisdom from the people.

Early in the morning he opens his eyes to the new day.

"Why don't you sleep for a while longer?" I ask him.

"Look, Gutle," he says, removing his nightcap. "When I sleep, luck is awake to keep me safe. But if I sleep too long, my luck will go to sleep as well."

I decided to take care of my own luck and to keep him awake for both of us. All of Meir's suggestions and pleas that I not wake for him and continue to enjoy my bed, gathering strength for the rest of the day, were no good. While he prays, wearing his tefillin, I smooth the sheet that still contains his body heat. Then I pick up the coin he left for me by the pillow, cupping it in my hand, and placing it in a simple wooden chest under my bed. That is Meir's way of saying good morning. Since there are no flowers where we live, he makes one coin blossom for me each morning. "The coin you receive every day," he said, "is first and foremost a testimony to my love, but it is also a reminder to you and to myself that we are on the right path to bring us honor."

When Meir goes out to the shaharit prayer at the synagogue, I go into the kitchen, pour a bit of well water from a bucket into a small bowl, boil some tea, prepare breakfast, and pack up food and drink for the day: bread, water, cheese wedges, and a few pieces of the *kugelhopf*

I had baked the previous night, before going to bed. Meir always says, "Every Judengasse woman knows how to make *kugelhopf*, but yours rises higher and tastes more delicious than anyone else's."

Meir pays special attention to fulfilling mitzvahs, the daily Jewish laws, and I must help him carry out these moral deeds by preparing a kosher lunch. On days when he lingers outside of the house he avoids eating cooked foods and makes do with bread and vegetables, which do not provide sufficient nutrition for a hardworking man.

After we say goodbye, I go to the window to drink in a few more moments of sweetness from his tall figure crossing our threshold and his glimmering eyes lingering in front of the sign. When he walks away I cover my face to preserve the kisses he'd showered on my cheeks, nose, lips, and chin. My hands run down to my belly, trapping the warmth of his soft hands. This is how I conclude the moments of morning serenity that recharge me for the new day, blending the routine of housework, sewing in preparation for the birth, and dealing with the different people who live in the house, into each other.

First I strip the bed and hang the sheets and comforters from the window to air out. To this day I ask myself if there is any point in this action, since on the one hand, the sheets must be cleaned from the smells of sleep, and on the other hand, at the window they absorb the stench of the street. The interim solution I have settled on is hanging them out the window for a short while, convincing myself that this brief period would be sufficient to drive out the smells of sweat and breath, but short enough to avoid absorption of street smells. I adopted Mama's habit of perfuming comforters and pillows, but more than any perfume, I love the smell of sheets fresh out of the laundry. Hanging them in the open field every six weeks clears out unpleasant scents. How nice it is to be able to do the washing and spread the wash on the grass outside of the ghetto.

I have not written in the notebook Papa had given me in four months. My hands are full. Besides, I don't want any of the house's tenants finding my notebook. To this day, I have shared the secret of my writing with no one, not even Meir.

We share our lives in this small home with Moshe, his wife, and their baby, and with poor Kalman, who has remained single due to his disability. Luckily, Meir took care in advance to pay a hefty sum to distant relatives of his who used to live with him, and in exchange they agreed to move out. They went to crowd the home of other relatives, whose wealth they shared. And still, these are tight quarters. I love Kalman very much; he is like a brother to me. Perhaps because of his disability. I am touched by his efforts to perform everyday tasks without asking for help, and it takes an effort to stand on the sidelines, witnessing his difficulty without embarrassing him by offering assistance.

But when it comes to the other tenants, God have mercy on me.

Disorder rules every corner of this house. Unlike my parents' home, where the chaos is caused exclusively by my father, here several partners have come together for what appears to be a competition over the amount and originality of the mess they create in the house. And I, frantic, follow the tracks they leave behind, pushing my way between pieces of furniture, and picking up items of clothing that have fallen from their bodies and were forgotten on the kitchen floor. I place the dirty dishes in the sink to be washed, and mop the floor without being able to fathom why people must spill water from the barrel that is always there. When will they learn to perform the simple task of wiping off mud from their shoes before removing them at the door? The crowdedness becomes unbearable because of how they live.

Quiet is another coveted necessity that is never sufficiently in stock.

Who knows how much longer we will have to share the same space? There are no apartments for sale or lease on Judengasse, in spite of the scandalous prices charged for the shapeless, tasteless apartments that open up every few years, only to be snatched up by the quickest bidders.

I feel the burden of the communal life at home, shoving its way into my personal life. Everyone is involved in everything. Yenta, Moshe's wife, who has a right to this home by virtue of her marriage to Moshe, searches my eyes each morning for signs of a fight with Meir. My quiet sobbing on the first morning of our marriage had piqued her interest, creating a false impression that had yet to be erased. In spite of the bump poking out of my loose dress, clear evidence of our love, and in spite of the tenderness Meir shows me in public, she never ceases her attempts to detect convicting signs. Let her do as she pleases. I will not give in to the temptation of a fight. *Do not answer a fool according to his folly, or you yourself will be just like him.*

What more is there to say? Meir is unaware of his sister-in-law's suspicions. He does not spend much time at home with the extended family. Moreover, he is ignorant when it comes to relationships between women, as men are wont to be. Only a woman can understand her friend, or her foe, for better or worse. I do not bother Meir with this kind of nonsense. He is concerned with important, crucial matters, and I mustn't fill our time together with unimportant gossip.

I feel proud to be a confidant to my husband's business endeavors. Our home is filled with many pairs of ears, some of which prick up as he speaks, especially those belonging to Moshe and Kalman. But when he speaks, he is addressing me alone.

But while our small space is crowded with secondary characters, I do my best to maintain eye and ear contact with my Meir. Sometimes these efforts are trampled under the weight of overinvolvement by our large, busy family, and Meir sends me up to our tiny bedroom, which, when luck shines on us, is free of uninvited guests.

In our room, we draw the heavy brown curtain that surrounds our bed, and when we are alone, hidden from prying eyes, he pulls out a sweet from his pocket and drops it in my mouth. In these days of pregnancy I am addicted to candy. As I roll the sweet flavor over my tongue, holding back sighs of pleasure, he puts his mouth to my nose as a preface to a whispered dialogue, and I feel the tickle of his breath and push him slightly to allow my eyes to tour the contours of his lips—which move with childish fervor as he outlines his convoluted road map—and linger in the sparkle of his blue eyes. I close my eyes at the touch of his hands searching for my body, and already feel myself rushing toward him, wishing for the magic to never end.

I wonder at this thirst of my pregnant body. Would this not be a time for restraint? Meir seems entirely unconcerned with this question, sharing this thirst with me, curling up with me and joining together with me for mutual satiation.

I know he loves me, even though I wish he'd say it more often. But in our conversations he is businesslike, and I carry out my duty to remain focused and not interrupt his train of thought. I therefore listen, but my own train of thought is derailed, and in my mind I burn for his mouth, which never stops talking, and his body, calling me to him, and yearn for the night, for my legs intertwining with his in our narrow bed, until I catch myself and return to my deceptive concentration. Some of what he says enters my mind and blends in with my own thoughts, while other parts escape and flutter about. But those words will never be heard by other ears—and this is most important.

I like thinking about my part and role in his world. Though he is independent and original in thought and deed, he is fed by the warm, homey atmosphere that has formed between us. He holds the reins, and I accompany him on his wondrous way. I do not need to advise him on matters of negotiation. My heart's intention is enough to bring the best out of him. This is why he told me, "Gutaleh, I need nothing but a seeing eye and a listening ear, and most people do not like to sacrifice either." And I, I am willing to give him my eyes, my ears, and my heart.

I fixed my eyes on him, asking why he blessed me with such honor. He answered promptly, "A man must always take care to honor his wife, as there is never any blessing in a man's house but for his wife alone."

Today, once again, Meir went to visit Hanau, the palace of Landgrave Wilhelm, stocked with rare coins for Carl Friedrich Buderus, the landgrave's head financial broker. The thought of the landgrave's behavior makes me uncomfortable. I still recall the shock I felt upon first hearing his life story. And I continue to learn new facts about life outside the ghetto walls and outside greater Frankfurt. I am especially entertained by stories of the mannerisms of nobles, their wives adorning themselves with diamonds and pearls, with glittering tiaras and elegant dresses with fur collars.

But the landgrave's unholy lifestyle is a very unusual thing that has caused me immense embarrassment. I do not understand how such a high and mighty man, officially married and whose wife has borne their children, can take lovers and fill the world with his offspring. Some of these children are from forbidden relations with his mistress, Frau Rieter von Lindenthal, who has easily given herself over to this married man due to his wealth and stature.

Meir has found a path to Buderus's heart, and the two men's relationship is growing closer. Considering his position as the frolicking landgrave's head financial broker, I am not thrilled by this budding connection between Meir and Buderus. But since I never stick my nose in Meir's business, I have sentenced myself to silence on this matter.

But Meir needs no words to know that I am concerned.

"Understand, my Gutaleh," he began in his familiar style, answering the question I had yet to pose. "I am not held responsible for other people's life choices. I am responsible for myself and my morality alone. The landgrave's hedonistic lifestyle is as interesting to me as the dust you wipe off the shelves. I choose my friends according to my heart's—or my pocket's—desires. My true friends are the ones chosen by my heart, and they are honest people. The others are intended to lend a hand in my career path. And if their arms are long enough, I may choose to take hold of them and help myself gain speed. *A man must always know who he is sitting with, who he is standing before, who he is visiting, who he is speaking with, and with whom he signs his deeds."*

I looked at him, trying to process his words. I thought of the Jewish morals compared to gentile depravity.

He read my mind once again. "Don't forget that even King Solomon, one of ours, was no saint. On the contrary, Solomon's harem was ten times bigger than the landgrave's. Beware of boasting about our pious Jews."

I burst out laughing. "I needn't say a thing. You see right through me." Will I ever get used to living with such an extraordinary individual?

"No, Gutaleh, do not crown me with a title that belongs wholly to the one and only up in heaven. He has only granted me a few crumbs, like my powerful nose."

I did not argue. I do not wish to waste any words. When I say nothing, he speaks, and when he speaks, I learn.

"I'll tell you another thing. Every person has a weakness. All I have to do is sniff it out, find the weakness, and use it in my favor. The landgrave, Buderus, and other people with deep pockets living in the royal palace are enamored of antique coins, and that is the weakness I'm interested in." He brought his face closer to mine. "Now, learn another rule," he said, tickling my ear and turning his head left and right as if to make sure no ears were pressing against the thick fabric that separated our room from the others. "Keep secrets. The less you say, the harder it is for your enemy to uncover your ruse. Secrets are the most important weapon."

"Why are you talking about enemies and secrets?" I wondered, mimicking his whisper. "We're only speaking of business, not the battlefield."

"My dear, the world of business is a nonstop war, and its rules are no different than the rules of combat. First, you must constantly be conquering targets, just like in a war. Second, there are competitors in business, and they are your worst enemies. They are prepared to cause you to fail in any way possible to make sure you do not stand in their way. Third, the road to success is littered with victims. To survive, one must identify the strong in advance and join their side. Do you understand? This is war."

As he spoke, I recognized the fervor heating within him. I thought it my duty to make sure it never died out.

"Each transaction must be carefully examined," he continued. "One must dig deep to recognize hidden land mines. A fox walked on the riverbank and saw schools of fish swimming frantically. He asked, 'What are you running away from?' They said, 'From the nets people use to catch us.' He said, 'Would you like to come up to dry land and live together with me as our ancestors once did?' They said, 'You, who are known as the cleverest of animals, are nothing but a fool! If we are careful where we live, then we must be three times as careful where we die.'"

Meir could tell I enjoyed the fable. I love fables and fairy tales. He offered another.

"First, looks can be deceiving. One must examine every aspect of a deal. A bear stood at the market, adorned with gems and pearls. People said, 'He who is brave enough to pounce on the bear may take its treasure.' A smart man said, 'You are focusing on what is on the bear, while I look at the teeth in its mouth.'"

"You are very bold, Meir Amschel Rothschild," I said. "Are there any limits to your boldness?"

Meir smiled his beautiful smile.

Today he will go to Hanau again, to see Buderus. He will give him the coins and take hold of his long, helpful arm. He told me that Buderus is the landgrave's favorite, wisest broker. The dairy profit plan, which was Buderus's brainchild, had captivated the heart of the landgrave, whose lust for money exceeds even his lust for women. The brilliance of the idea is in its simplicity.

Buderus proposed to change the practice of deducting fractions of pennies from bills, and—wonder of wonders—the landgrave's dairy profits rose incalculably. The landgrave was thrilled by this brilliant idea that allowed him to cheerfully fill his pockets with piles of coins, and determined to give the talented broker full responsibility for the accounting of his great wealth.

Buderus's affection for Meir is not surprising. Who can understand it better than I? And when affection is coupled with an addiction to unique coins, even I—not a great expert on commerce—can reach the simple and obvious conclusion: the budding friendship between Meir and Buderus may prove to be in our favor.

I heard Vendeleh and quickly closed the notebook. I have not told even her about it. Her voice sounds so much prettier than the other voices of the house. Even the baby in my belly was glad to hear her, and kicked joyfully.

Wednesday, October 2nd, 1771

I am a mother! Hallelujah! Is there any greater joy? Meir is beside himself. He has already canceled several business meetings and will not let
go of the little treasure, bundled in soft blankets he chose carefully from
his wares. The sweet baby girl I have birthed with the help of Olek, the
gentle and considerate midwife, has planted new emotions inside of
me. They are reminiscent of feelings that have thus far been reserved
only for Vendeleh, but they are joined by a new nuance of sentiment
that I cannot explain.

I cannot get enough of her. Every twitch or yawn, every peal of
laughter, stretch of the arm, cry, or peaceful sleep awakens my maternal
instincts. If a year ago I was impressed by how much I've matured, it
was nothing compared to how grown-up I feel now. I am willing to
sacrifice anything for this tiny creature.

Meir is also trying to adapt to his paternal love. Every little gesture
she makes has him crying with excitement. From the outside we must
look like two children delighted by a new toy, but when it comes to
the care of this new figure that has entered our lives, we are mature and
serious.

The birth took place on August 20th, three days before my eighteenth birthday and nine days before our first anniversary. The month of August is one of celebration in my home. The sweet sound of her crying made me sigh with joy and wiped away my fears. I nursed her, and with each nursing I felt defeated by exhaustion, drained of all power. I closed my eyes and relaxed my body, falling into a deep, peaceful sleep. When I awoke, the happy father was standing in front of me, holding the swaddled baby in his clumsy arms. I was worried he might drop her, and with a sudden urge reached out to take her, and quickly smiled at him in an attempt to soften the impression of my concerns.

"Good morning, darling," he said. "Here is the first harbinger of the House of Rothschild." And he placed the baby with effortful care in my outstretched arms. "And now she is safe and sound," he added with a wink.

I divide my hours between sleep and wakefulness according to the schedule set by our daughter, Schönche, may she live a long and happy life. We named her for Meir's mother, may her memory be a blessing. Does my little sweetheart know what she has brought into the chambers of our home and of our hearts? Does she know she is the bud marking the commencement of bloom in our family? Our neighbors visit and quote to me, *A firstborn daughter—a good sign of boys to come.*

Monday, May 4th, 1772

I have two favorite seasons: spring and fall. I read about flowers and trees blooming in spring and cannot decide whether to laugh or cry, because there are no flowers or trees on Judengasse. For us, blooming is exclusively human—every baby is a blossoming flower. A week ago I went shopping in Frankfurt and gazed longingly at the tops of green trees towering over the park that had been created in place of the old dikes. I knew that beyond them, the men and women of Frankfurt were strolling leisurely. I must have lingered there for too long, because suddenly I heard a voice behind me call, "Juden!" and I rushed away from the forbidden spot without turning back.

I must keep this incident secret, lest Mama find out. More important, I must adhere to rules and behave more responsibly, now that I am a mother.

I like spring because my Meir, who blooms and grows all year long, is his best self this time of year, when the fair takes place in Frankfurt, and the two of us—sweet Schönche and I—enjoy him even more than usual. All year long, except during the spring and fall fairs, Meir goes away on business outside of Frankfurt: in nearby Darmstadt, Mainz, and Wiesbaden, and in the capitals of more remote princedoms, requiring many days spent traveling in a carriage. We mustn't expect such noble clients to even dream of sinking their expensive shoes in the filth of our yards and entering our wretched apartment in search of *Schätze*—treasure—amid the mélange of used goods. There is no choice for Meir but to travel far and wide in his carriage to visit the elegant homes of the wealthy.

Traveling by carriage is far from comfortable. The rocky roads, the buttocks slamming against the wooden seat. But Meir never complains. Instead, he is grateful for his title as "court vendor," which allows him to travel, and always goes out with a twinkle in his eye, a twinkle that grows even brighter upon his return home.

But during fair season he is not forced to venture far from home. Every evening he returns home from the great Frankfurt fair with an exciting pile of ducats, florins, and many other coins that have passed from the hands of one merchant to the next, to be finally gathered in his. He places the happy collection in the money-changing office he has created in our home and turns to our small room to shower us with a special kind of love, full of smiles and laughter. He has taken to tickling Schönche, causing her to flee from him, but soon enough she returns, staring at him, waiting eagerly for the next round, which is not long in arriving. He grabs her hands and feet, spins her around and throws her up in the air, and she squeals with fear and excitement, seeming to demand, "Again!"

There is no doubt that financial success at the fairs improves his mood. At auctions attended by the biggest collectors from Germany and around it, he offers a respectable selection of coins and medals. It is a mystery to me why serious people make the effort to travel to Frankfurt, only to separate themselves from fine sums of money in exchange for pointless luxuries.

It seems that Meir, an undoubtedly serious and responsible man himself, is also captivated by these frivolities. Every once in a while he has trouble parting with the charms of a rare item that he claims is worth a fortune, and decides to keep it. It seems collecting is becoming a significant aspect of his personality.

He takes daily inventory of his coins in the free space remaining on the floor of our room: Greek and Roman coins of silver and gold, rare coins from Germany, France, and Sweden, all lined up. Behind them, battalions of medals and prints. He looks at them and calls them by name, then looks off toward the horizon, that indefatigable gaze. That is when he treats me to tidbits of history and art, and I listen and focus on what's most important: his fiery voice, his moving lips producing gems, his rising and falling brows, his body that sways as he speaks, as if in dance or prayer. At the same time, I never cease to marvel at the stores of information with which he constantly fills his hardworking brain. Finally, he collects his soldiers, returns them to their box, sorry to see them go, the following day or week, to foreign fields, making way for the next shift.

I myself find no interest or purpose in these coins, other than that they produce the money we use for sustenance and for the purpose of buying and selling new collections. Nevertheless, I do not dismiss things I do not understand, for perhaps there is a point to these items that I simply cannot see. It is just as Rabbi Yossi taught us in the story of the blind man with the torch. Rabbi Yossi said:

"I used to dislike the saying, 'I grope at noon as a blind man gropes his way in the dark.' For I thought, what difference does it make to the blind man whether it is dark or light? Until one time I walked in the dark of night and saw a blind man walking along with a torch in his hand. I asked him, 'My son, what need do you have for this torch?' He answered, 'As long as I have a torch, people can see me and save me from danger.'"

Some of the money is saved in a separate box, lined with velvet. One day, we will have our own home, shared with no one. True, we are not equal citizens with the noble Frankfurters, and, as "protected Jews," we do not have the right to our own land, but we can buy a house. I yearn for the day when I can stop being so wary.

My marriage would be more whole without the bothersome worry that the sounds of our lovemaking may cross the curtain and reach others' ears. Woe is me. The thought alone is shameful enough to spoil pleasure and turn the pure act into sin.

I yearn for the day when I have the power to decide the way of life in my home, without any of my housemates whispering names behind my back, names that I would rather not put in writing, as they make me feel so forlorn. I have no desire to show weakness to the extended family I have been forced to live with. I therefore restrain myself, projecting a calm, carefree attitude, and treating the entire household decorously, even those who do not deserve it. When the growing irritation threatens to drown me, I retire to the window, look outside, and allow my anger to subside.

I love the window of our home, though it is a far cry from the one at my parents'. Since our home is rear facing and the window does not overlook the street, all I can see is the dirty entry path, surrounded by a mess of houses. Nevertheless, looking out the window pulls me away from the events of the house and sends my mind in a positive direction.

And now, for some good news. I am pregnant again. The baby inside of me is growing and kicking. I tell Schönche all about her baby brother growing inside of me, and we both caress him, causing him to answer us with stronger kicks. They are unlike Schönche's kicks: stronger, violent even. Schönche seems just as impatient as I am to meet him, but I always explain, "We must wait several more months. The longer we wait, nurturing him, the more he will grow and come to us *gesund und munter*, safe and sound."

Is that true? I hope so. The number of infants who die in Judengasse has me reeling. I do not share my concerns with Meir. I want him to be happy every single day. It is enough that he works so hard and travels so long in the bouncing carriage. I mustn't burden him with pointless worries and doubts.

I know he expects a boy this time. He rubs my belly, listening to the groans coming from my womb, sharing stories of the deals he made on his latest voyage, as if speaking to a business partner.

Dear God, please do not disappoint him. Give my Meir a healthy son.

Wednesday, June 10th, 1772

Today I had a visit from Matti, my most beloved and favorite friend, although with the urgency of real-life events and the hard work of the day-to-day, I have little time to think of her.

I jumped at the sight of her and we embraced lengthily. I allowed the awakening longing to take pleasant hold of me. Then I excused myself to go brew some tea, which we sipped slowly while eating Matti's butter cookies. "These are for you and for the hungry baby inside of you," she had announced after our embrace, letting go of my plump body, which cradled her thin frame, and pulling the tin of cookies from the cloth bag at her feet.

Between sips, we each painted pictures of our current lives. I learned more about her fiancé, Isaac, who lives near the Hinterpfann, and whom I often see walking to work at the amulet shop, a heavy sack on his back, or returning home with the empty sack folded under his arm. The two of them, Matti and Isaac, have been seen recently, walking along Judengasse together, the windows of the street opening for chatty observation that brings a smile of recollection to my face.

"He is hardworking, but is quite stingy," Matti whispered to me.

"Well, what about it?" I said, trying to reassure her. "Does he love you?"

"He does. His face turns red when I arrive, and his normal stutter worsens in the first few minutes of our encounter."

"This is a good sign, Matti. He is in love with you. You are lucky," I explained, experienced as I am, and feeling as if years separated us, though we were born in the same year and the same month of August. "And what about you? Are you fond of him?" I asked.

She blushed. "Would you like to know just how fond?" Her eyes shone and her mouth tightened in a secretive smile. She leaned down to her purse, pulled out a diary, and placed it on the table. "You're the first I'm showing this to," she whispered. "I read Elkaliti and Hendilekhen's diaries and decided to keep one too."

I swallowed. The names of our friends, Elkaliti and Hendilekhen, rolled naturally off Matti's tongue, but to me they sounded like a barely coherent reminder of an old tale.

All atwitter, Matti did not notice my discomfort. She ran her hands over the thin diary printed with large, colorful flowers, and I envisioned the more mature cover of my own notebook, elegant in black over white.

"See what I wrote, Gutaleh," she said and began reading. *"Have I found my heart's beloved? Sometimes the answer is yes. Other times, I cannot find an answer . . ."*

I listened to her descriptions, her dilemmas, her coquetry. I tried to follow her hasty alternations between doubts and decisiveness, and felt myself drowning in the confusion, until finally the sound of Schönche's crying as she awoke from her nap saved me from complete oblivion.

We said goodbye, promising to meet again soon, and as Matti left with the purse containing her diary, I thought of the cheerful lightness of her youth as opposed to my own serious, mature life. I was satisfied by the refreshing encounter, and as I caressed my daughter, curled up in my lap, and thought things over, I realized that my friends were writing in order to present their creations to others, while I wrote for myself alone, my only confidant the notebook, which has become an inseparable part of the space under my mattress. Every night as I lie in bed I feel it beneath me and say a silent hello to it from the other side.

Sunday, November 1st, 1772

Tonight I reach for my notebook with shaky hands. What can I say? What I had feared most has occurred.

My trepidations have come true, full force. My maternal feelings have taken a harsh beating. My son, to whom I have grown attached with bonds of love strengthened by each kick, has emerged from my womb, but has not seen the light of day.

I insisted on looking at him, but Olek the midwife covered him up and placed him far from my view. "Gutaleh," she said softly, clearing her throat from tears, "close your eyes, rest. God will take care of you. You will have many more children."

But I wanted to see him. "Let me see my son," I pleaded with draining strength.

She took my open hand and tried to soothe me with tart apple wine, but I pushed the cup away and continued to beg, almost voice-lessly. "He's my son," I cried faintly. "I have a right to see my son. My son. Let me see him, just for a moment." I knew very well he was a boy, my boy, the unlucky one.

She undid the blanket. He was lying in the same position as he had in my body, his eyes closed. *He is sleeping,* I told myself. *Perhaps he will awake in a short while? Perhaps he will awake and I will laugh madly and say, "We were wrong, my son, you are alive, you just wanted to rest a while longer."*

"You are alive," I cried out, laughing, wailing, trapped in a thicket of pain and anxiety.

Olek rushed to wrap him up again and I panicked. "No, not his head! He has to breathe. Let him breathe! Don't close it."

Then I collapsed. I remember nothing else.

I woke up the next day. Everyone was standing around me, watching me. Meir, Mama, Father, Vendeleh. All the people I love. They all smiled at me, and I looked into their eyes and saw the cloudiness within. When I burst into tears they all joined me, weeping as one. *Poor dears,* I thought. They tried so hard to be strong for me, and I just spoiled all of their work. Even Meir could not control his traitorous, aching, warm, loving tears, pouring shamelessly from his eyes, disturbing the equanimity he had tried to demonstrate. *He lost a son too,* I thought. I must be strong for him. I must wipe away his tears.

He leaned down toward me, kissed my cheeks, and wiped my tears, and I clung to his kind face, rubbed my cheek against his stubbly cheek, and mixed my tears with his.

"The Lord did not allow him to suffer in this world. He took him into His lap without torment," he whispered, then stepped back to make room for my other loved ones.

Vendeleh wailed for a long time, throwing her arms in the air and begging to curl up in bed with me. Mama was shocked by the thought and pushed her away from me, and Father took advantage of the ruckus to come closer and whisper, "Gutaleh, you are the same as other women, even your mother. They have all lost offspring, but they never lost hope, and they had their babies. You are stronger than all of them. I'm certain you'll overcome this."

Mama came near. "The wound is fresh, my child. But it will heal with the birth of your next child. You were the cure for my wound. Remember that."

Mama never told me she'd lost her first child. I had healed her wound. I am not her firstborn, then. I had an older brother. He died. I was surprised to learn about it.

My dead child was never of any age. With no age, there's no sitting shiva.

I held on tightly to my little Schönche in the days that followed. I pressed her to my grieving chest and went on with day-to-day life without showing any weakness. I sent Meir off on his business trips, presenting him with my strong façade. No one knew what was going on inside of me. There was no comfort in the upsetting fact that death had also been the lot of other unfortunate babies. I lost my baby. I had a score to settle with God. I wanted to know how many pages He flipped through in order to determine who to torture next. How many merciless knocks on the doors of innocent people's lives does He allot the Angel of Doom? Are we all just pawns to Him?

On my own, I allow myself to cry without interruption, but when Meir returns, my eyes are dry.

In spite of my efforts to get over the tragedy that has hit us, I am unable to stop the image of my lost son from rising in my imagination, with his serene face and his closed eyes, an image that digs and pricks at the depths of my bleeding heart. This image is mine alone. Wherever I turn, there it is. Olek had been right when she tried to stop me from seeing his face. She was using her experience to help me, but my persistence was stronger, and now I am punished for it.

Wednesday, October 20th, 1773

The ways of the Lord never cease to baffle me.

I have a healthy son. Meir and I are infinitely happy. My son, Amschel Meir, may he live a long and happy life, has healed the wound of his brother who did not survive birth.

My screams during childbirth had released my fears and nightmares. From the moment my son emerged into the air of the world, I focused all my organs on the sound of his crying. "Why won't he cry?" I asked. "Is he all right? Tell me he's all right. Don't wrap his head . . ."

Olek was busy caring for the newborn, and only said, "He's fine, we won't be wrapping anyone this time."

After what seemed like an eternity, my son finally cried, and I cried along with him. Mama, who never left my side throughout the entire process, took the reins and my hands and said, "Gutaleh, listen."

I fell obediently silent.

"You have an angel baby. He is your cure. Look at him. He's draining your nightmares away. The evil is gone, evaporated, and from now on you'll be happy. Look at him and see that I'm right. See what a lovely baby you've delivered into this world."

She was so right. I look at my son, may he live forever, my little Amschel Meir, and something happens on the path from my stomach to my throat. It's called happiness. A little scar after the wound scabs over does not dull the measure of happiness.

Bless the Lord, now Amschel Meir is circumcised. We celebrated the bris in glorious joy, and four days later I began to cook again.

My heart swelled to receive this new love, crying and sometimes even smiling at me. Will my heart be able to contain ten such loves? I think it would be able to contain even more.

Oh, how the merciful God makes sure to fill the void left after something is taken away.

Tuesday, July 30th, 1776

In spite of the difficulties hindering our paths, and in spite of the tests the great and mighty Lord puts us through from time to time, to teach us that not everything in life comes easily, our family continues to expand, and now another healthy child has joined us, a brother to Schönche and Amschel Meir. Our little boy is named Shlomo Meir, after my father, and will soon turn two years old.

Our wealth is also growing satisfyingly, and I feel the flapping of dignity's wings.

"Money brings dignity," Meir told me over six years ago. Indeed, Meir's dignity, both among the people of Judengasse and among his important clients in Frankfurt and elsewhere, is growing in direct proportion to the number of gold coins he earns, in spite of the fact that nobody knows the exact number.

Meir walks around Judengasse like a noble, though he continues to wear his tattered, yet wondrously clean, coat, as well as his old pants. He often encounters the current fashion at royal palaces—elegant, high-collared jackets and robes laced with golden fringe, all made by the most famous tailors in France and Spain, but he would never agree to try them on. Their only custom that he adopts is wearing a white wig, though he does not powder it as they do, because Jews are forbidden to do so.

But we do not have the kind of wealth that other rich families on our impoverished street have, those that have prospered since long ago. I find it hard to believe we could ever reach the financial status of families like Speyer, Reis, Elissen, or even Schuster, Hass, or Goldschmidt. But I am proud of my Meir, who with his own two hands, two feet, and singular brain, has made such a significant change in our financial situation. And judging by his enthusiasm, it's easy to trust that his plan to bring honor to our family will come to fruition. I myself am prepared to see it as having come true already. But looking at Meir, I can tell that this handful will not satisfy a lion such as him.

We continue in our old ways, never spending our hard-earned wealth on useless goods. I do not shop more than before, but only in accordance to the needs that have been growing along with our family. I do not wear fancy clothes, in spite of the fact that we have plenty of fabric, as it is a big part of our business. Most days, I put on a loose cotton dress, befitting the proportions of my body, which is often pregnant. I save thriftily, never underestimating the value of a coin, even though there are more around now than I can count.

In spite of the modesty with which we live our lives, people on our small street know everything, and the parade of beggars knocking on our door has become a regular sight. Meir never turns them away. Whoever enters our house hungry leaves it satiated, but he whispers to each of them not to spread the word of what they were given. He claims "Anonymous giving is a true mitzvah," and quotes the Talmud: "Rabbi Yanai saw a man giving a coin to a poor man in public. He said: 'It would have been better not to give at all than to give him in this manner and shame him.'"

I must point out that this desire of his aligns with his desire to keep our financial standing secret. "Secrecy is the key to success," he always says. Considering his collection of sayings, it would be more accurate to say that secrecy is *one of the keys* to success.

I should also point out that there is one *geshtin*, one beggar, who has captivated me more than the others, perhaps because she is always wrapped in rags. We have scheduled times for her to visit, and she always leaves our house with some food, a coin, and a bit of fabric, her attentive ears filled with passages from our holy Torah to strengthen her crumbling dreams.

As a rule, I do not write in my notebook in the daytime. The traffic of life flowing through the house does not allow the appropriate conditions for surreptitious writing.

Once, I was tempted to write in daylight, and as I should have expected, I was interrupted. Shlomo, my youngest, bumped into one of the sacks strewn in the corner of the room and stumbled. After making a face, he made a quick calculation and surmised that crying would be a more efficient way to pull his mother away from her business and make available a pair of hands to give him a pain-relieving hug, so he broke into a sharp wail. The ruckus of crying made me jump, and I knocked into the inkwell. With the swiftness of an acrobat I held on to the edge of the inkwell and steadied it, preventing the ink from spilling. I cradled little Shlomo in my arms, got a bandage, and dressed his knee as if he were bleeding. The crying subsided. My son loves bandages. They are perfect for attracting attention. For him, I was willing to be a makeshift medicine woman.

Well then, our home has grown very crowded. The foyer is at capacity, too narrow to contain the wares that fill it to the brim. The floor has boxes stacked up along the walls, large boxes on the bottom and smaller ones on top. The nooks have been filled with sacks packed so tightly that there is no room for air between them. Sometimes, poorly placed sacks fall to the ground, and occasionally they hit one of the children, making them stumble.

Meir and I toy with the idea of moving to a larger house, both due to his concern for the storage of goods, and because of my difficulties during lovemaking. At night when he awakens toward me and I respond to the lighting fire, desiring to go along with the flame twinkling between us, we make sure to stay completely silent. This kind of vigilance sends warning signs to my body that do not align with the twinkling and often diminish its intensity or even turn it off altogether. One night, when our yearning for lovemaking awoke, his hands embarked on a riveting voyage over my body. I closed my eyes, surrendering to the pleasure, and in my compromised position momentarily forgot my usual vigilance and let out a fervent moan, which made its way past our separating curtain and straight into the ears of Yenta. Like a person whose land was invaded, Yenta pounced out of bed and hissed from the other side: "I demand some decorum. I will not have debauchery in my house."

The fire died immediately, and I, breathless, wished for my own death. I turned my back to Meir and buried my face in the blanket, wallowing in my mortification. The next day, I avoided Yenta's eyes, reduced my presence around the room, and generally carried myself as one who has lost something on the floor. Since then, whenever he comes close to me, my body hardens on its own accord, and Meir slowly helps me loosen up, and then grow aroused in a more restrained fashion.

The hope for a house lives on in our hearts, but reality slaps us in the face. The number of people wishing to rent or buy a home is much higher than the number of available apartments. When one becomes available, many flock to purchase it before its price rises. In fact, it has been several years since we have heard of a house cleared of its tenants being offered up for sale or lease. Young couples are forced to continue living in their parents' house until a miracle occurs and a place is found for them.

In light of the situation, Meir has taken initiative and contacted the Holy Roman Empire headquarters in Frankfurt with a request to alleviate the distress of the residents of our neighborhood and make expansions. He explained to the empire clerks that in no other city in Germany are Jews treated in this manner. Not only are we limited to twelve weddings a year, but no residence is arranged for those twelve couples, not to mention the exaggerated prices of the small homes that only become available every few years.

Though he was turned down, and also criticized for the "unstoppable arrogance of the Jewish nation," he has decided not to give up, and if I know my man, there's no doubt he will continue to fight in the name of distressed couples.

Meir went to look at the home of Johann Wolfgang von Goethe on Großer Hirschgraben Street in Frankfurt. "We are an arrogant nation?" he muttered to me upon his return. "What did I ask for? Neither a palace nor a garden. All I asked was for small homes for young families. And that is what they call arrogance? They have eyes, yet they cannot see."

This wasn't the first time Meir lingered near the Goethe house. Johann Wolfgang von Goethe is a writer, a poet, and a scholar. The family palace, with its twenty glamorous rooms and expansive yard, was bought for the same price asked in exchange for a modest Judengasse apartment of three dark rooms, with no yard and no windows. And yet, even this kind of apartment is not available on our street.

I myself am not jealous of the Goethe family, its monstrous castle, its ostentatious lifestyle, or its superior status. I do not even envy the family's private bathroom. Even if the Messiah rode into Judengasse on his donkey to announce that from now on we were allowed to leave the ghetto and that I was invited to live in Goethe's palace, I would thank the Messiah politely for his attention to us Judengasse residents, but clarify in no uncertain terms that I, Frau Gutle Rothschild, will never live in a palace.

So far, I have given birth to five children. Two have been taken from this world, and three have survived: Schönche, Amschel Meir, and Shlomo Meir. I have already allotted some painful words to the matter of the first son I had lost. My second, born only three months ago, emerged into the world, worked hard to sob meekly, and thus ended his time on earth. I washed my pain with tears, smoothed a wrinkle, stood up straight, and walked out into my life like any other person. I am experienced, and I know that the cure for my pain would be the birth of the next child. I await his arrival patiently.

In spite of the hardships of this place, and in spite of the crises that God uses to test me, I look life in the eye and see that it has granted me fine measures of happiness. I am happy with my husband and with my children.

The many tasks I must perform at home never end. Whenever I have a few moments' rest I sew clothes from leftover fabric. Still, I make sure to leave some time for my children's education. Schönche has attentive ears and is very interested in stories. Amschel is a worrier, and can often be found lost in thought, his small forehead covered with wrinkles that attest to a temperament that is anything but calm. It seems that from the moment he emerged from my womb, Amschel has been concerned with the world to which he'd come. He even rejected the pleasure of breastfeeding, pursing his lips and shutting his eyes tightly, and my breasts ran dry after a few months. I must teach him how to smile, and it would be best for him to spend more time with his friends. On the other hand, little Shlomo smiles effortlessly at the whole world, and is a neighborhood favorite. On Shabbat eve, after they return from the baths, the children don clean clothing and join their father on his way to the synagogue. A line of men in their Shabbat clothing, carrying tallit pouches under their arms, surrounded by a jolly cloak of children, make their way to prayer. On Saturday the streets are cleaner than they are on weekdays.

When they return home, Meir places his hands on my head, blesses me, and recites "A Woman of Valor" while the children arrange themselves in a row by age, from eldest to youngest, and each of them in turn places their head under their father's hands to receive his blessing. Then Meir washes his hands and walks silently to the cloth-covered dining table and its two burning candles in silver candlesticks. Meir maintains his silence as he pours the wine, picks up the silver goblet filled to the brim, and blesses it: "The sixth day, thus the heavens and the earth were completed in all their vast array . . ."

I look at the light in Meir's face and run my eyes over the illuminated faces of my children. *The light of a person's face on Shabbat is nothing like it is the rest of the week.*

Meir takes a long sip and passes the goblet to Moshe and Kalman, then to the women and children. Once the goblet is drained, he begins his Shabbat songs, and we all join in. After that, he rips bits from both challahs and says hamotzi. The plates are filled with cholent—my handiwork. I do not order our meal from the famous cholent maker of Judengasse, the way many of my neighbors do. Instead, I make sure my family has homemade food of my creation, food that satisfies every mouth around the table, with leftovers for the following day.

At the end of the Shabbat, the guests Meir invites during the maariv prayer at synagogue all convene for the havdalah blessing. Wonder of wonders—there is always room for everyone.

The children stay close to their father all through Shabbat. He tells them and his little nieces and nephews the stories of the Torah and drags rolls of fabric from the foyer. They cloak their small bodies in the fabric and play the roles of Eve, Adam, and the serpent, and Meir climbs onto a chair and rumbles in the voice of God over and over until they are all exhausted. Then he turns serious, asking all sorts of questions, such as, "Do you know why the Torah is compared to a fig?" And they come close enough to touch his hand, his arm, and his thigh, hanging their wide, quizzical eyes on him. He smiles and answers, "All other fruits have waste: dates have pits, grapes have seeds, pomegranates have skins, but figs can be eaten whole. The same goes for the word of the Torah—it is without waste."

Meir, such a sensitive soul, never forgets my affinity for magic words of love. "You are beautiful, my wife," he whispers in my ear. He never spares any words of seduction that will lead us to a full fulfillment of Shabbat pleasure whenever we get a moment alone, away from the eyes of our multiplying housemates. Then he softens the hardness of my body and assures me that no one can hear us and loves me with a fervor equal to the fervor with which he conducts his business. I make sure to keep my mouth shut, and when we are finished I listen for a while longer to assure my conscience that no one else has heard us.

On weekdays when Meir does not go on his business trips he uses every hour of daylight for work, even working by candlelight until the wee hours of the night. Surrounded by the entire household, all following his skilled gestures, he leans over the table, picks up an inkwell, a feather, and a piece of paper, and prepares catalogs to be mailed to nearby and distant princedoms all over Germany. The catalogs offer coins for individual sale and in entire collections, ancient gems, ancient figurines, rare statues, and pictures in diamond-studded frames. The gems would surely inspire Mama to cry out with excitement, which would delight Meir. I'll ask him to give her a few.

I am not too familiar with the German language, and even Meir still makes errors. But this does not undermine his confidence, which is forever high. He even goes so far as to attach personal letters to the catalogs from time to time, written horrendously, according to him. "They won't notice the spelling mistakes," he explains, "because words are spelled differently in each princedom, by arbitrary decision for which I can find no rhyme or reason. And the errors will be forgotten once they feast their eyes on my goods."

As someone who greatly respects the written word, I squirm whenever he smiles at a sentence that he knows full well is riddled with mistakes. But at the same time I am lost in a feeling of admiration for his courage to carry on.

As compensation for his lack of writing skill, Meir takes special care with the appearance of the catalogs. He binds them in gorgeous leather covers printed with captivating golden letters. Sometimes he asks for low prices, even loss prices. The first time he did this, he noticed my raised eyebrows and explained with a wink, "Today I'll lose some money on one, two, or three products; but tomorrow I'll get back my losses from ten new customers whose trust I have earned, and they will be prepared to pay heftily."

When he offered to mail items to customers and promised them they would be able to mail back any in which they were not interested—at his expense—I didn't even raise one brow. I know his tricks of war are calculated to the last detail.

Meir's cunning maneuvers never break the rules of integrity and morality. His honesty and generosity, along with his patience and pleasant voice, grant him entry to the big world of business. Many of his customers return to him and recommend him to their friends with deep pockets. His integrity gives me confidence, and his success gives me the strength to continue and maintain our home with its ever diminishing space.

Wednesday, November 20th, 1776

Throughout the years, I've made sure not to intervene in Meir's business transactions. I find that life runs smoothly as long as I don't stick my nose in his affairs.

But this time I broke my own rule, and we had an awful fight. For the first time in our relationship, the walls of our home shook, and so did the walls of my heart. This all happened after I found out about the landgrave Wilhelm's tricks—the lowliest kind—and saw Meir as an accomplice.

Lately, Meir has become more involved in the banking business, handling the discounting of bills of exchange. In order not to break the flow of his work with his customers, when he goes on the road he transfers this responsibility to the trusted hands of his brother Kalman. Thus, his customers enjoy uninterrupted service and are not inconvenienced by his absence. Meir explained the complex business of money changing until I was able to understand it as well.

"Take, for example," he said, "a man who has a bill of debt from a royal family or a house of commerce that will be due for payment in the future. What if he requires cash immediately? He approaches a banker, hands over the bill, and receives the amount of cash stated on it, minus commission. When the date of payment comes around, the banker sends the bill to the palace or house of commerce and receives its full value in exchange."

The bankers who deal with the discounting of bills are well established and have wealthy customers. Competing with them, which seemed like a lost cause, stirred Meir to action. His eyes lit up at the new target, which he decided to conquer by any means necessary. With that in mind, he put to work the array of artillery at his disposal, from utilizing his connections with Buderus to lowering the commission incomparably. And so he succeeded in breaking into the exclusive business and reaching the bill owners, inspiring the fury of more experienced bankers.

One of the biggest owners of bills was no other than Wilhelm, the mighty landgrave. Wilhelm agreed to work with Meir as long as he could receive his gold for a not-too-hefty sum. But the landgrave continued to employ his old money changers, only placing small bills in Meir's hand. But Meir did not give up, whispering to me behind the curtain, "Once the first obstacle is removed, the rest will fall into place. All I need is patience."

Patience, which is naturally bitter, bore its sweet fruit, and Meir was asked by the landgrave to cash a bill of exchange for an amount I never imagined existed in commerce between two individuals. We could not control our cries of joy, which could not be contained by the curtain and the wooden walls of our room. Gossiping lips and listening ears inside and outside the house went into action.

Just as we broke our habit of keeping secrets, a new and significant piece of news came back to me. One of the neighbors, a small-time money changer, came to my doorstep and began to yammer: "The landgrave's bill of exchange was given to him by the government of his majesty the king of England, King George the Third. And in exchange for what?" he asked, and then immediately answered his own question.

I could not bear the answer the money changer spewed at me. I felt my jaw tightening. Before my eyes rose the image of the landgrave taking part in this atrocity: sending a *riek*—a squad of mercenaries—to be used as cannon fodder in his cousin King George the Third's war against the rebellious American colonists.

From this horrific image, a thought invaded my consciousness: the awful thought that Meir, through his bills of exchange, has been participating in this inhumanity.

I slammed the door in the face of the chattering changer and remained standing, paralyzed, in front of the closed door. I don't know how long I stood there before finally feeling hands taking hold of my shoulders. I paid them no mind. My feet were planted, my eyes fixed on the door.

Meir took my hand and pulled me toward our bedroom. From the corner of my frozen eyes I caught sight of Yenta's victorious eyes following us there. She must have seen this as confirmation of her suspicions about the relationship between Meir and me.

Meir sat me down on our bed and demanded that everyone else leave. He drew the curtain, leaving just the two of us there: the man contributing to the recruitment of mercenaries, and me. My eyes came back to life, and fixed on him with resentment.

"Tell me what happened, Gutaleh."

"You . . . you are . . . recruiting mercenaries," I said, my face twisting. "Cannon fodder," I finally managed.

I saw his lips moving, but my ears could not take in the words. I have no idea how long he went on. I was lost in my own thoughts, exhausting myself. At some point I must have fallen asleep.

I opened my eyes. The black cover of night blinded me, but I could feel Meir lying awake beside me. Then, suddenly, he began to talk to me, without touching me. Now my ears were free to listen.

"Gutle," he said, calling me by my real name, not my nickname, for the first time. "You saddened me greatly today." He fell silent for a moment, as if pausing for air, before continuing. "In one fell swoop you made me the executor of the king's orders. I thank you for raising me in rank and appointing me the legal minister of the king of England. But no thank you, I am not interested in the position. When will you learn that I am not responsible for or involved in the way nobles and rulers live? Who am I, Meir Amschel Rothschild, a stinking Jew from Judengasse in Frankfurt, worth less than a mosquito, who at least has the ability to bite and then flee, to say anything to the landgrave Wilhelm or to the king of England about their actions? Who am I to tell them 'You are behaving poorly'? Whether or not I handle the bills the landgrave receives from King George would make no difference at all. The king would accept the mercenaries either way. A bill broker is meaningless when it comes to the principle question of taking the lives of innocent people. The decision has been made and passed through the self-important channels of the government. Wilhelm, just like his father, has turned the horrid sale of soldiers into a profitable business. My heart goes out to all those miserable peasants who are recruited under duress, and to those who evade enlistment and are later caught and punished with twelve whippings. They suffer even more than we Jews do.

"I won't hide the dire truth from you. For each enlisted soldier, fifty-one thalers are paid, and more money is paid for every wounded soldier, and three times as much for casualties. But who am I to change this? I am an innocent party to a business transaction revolving around exchanging bills for cash. That is my entire role. I have no hand in the transferring of people, in their injuries or deaths. The money I receive is not tainted. Money is money, no matter how many hands it changes. It does not tell anyone where it came from and where it is headed. It is handed from one person to the next. I am innocent. You have turned me into something I am not. And I will continue to be what I am my entire life. All around me, people behave atrociously, but I continue in my blameless path."

As he spoke, my eyes remained open, attempting to adjust to the dark. Slowly, they began to uncover dim details. I recognized his arms folded on his chest without shifting, his frozen body. I ran my eyes over his face. No muscle twitched other than his lips, from which words emerged. Naked words, without adornment or artifice. He and the truth of his life. His smooth, whole, unbreakable integrity.

Threads of fear began to wrap around my throat. I was losing my Meir. Those bitter words, "You upset me greatly today," settled in my mind, pricking my gut. I imagined the sorrow filling his eyes. Would he forgive me for this great insult? Would he forgive me for turning him into something he was not? I did not doubt his innocence and purity. But how could I turn back time and undo the events of the day? Why did I not go about my business, letting him go about his, as I always did? This could have all been prevented if I had just controlled myself.

A sour wave of regret washed over me. Where could I go from here?

I curled up on the edge of the bed, keeping my regrets to myself. I had to thaw the frost that had formed between us. But how? I had no idea what to do, and my reservations had yet to fall away completely. Meir spoke well, an argument convincingly delivered, but I still did not feel at ease about this deal, even though it was not my decision to make. Though Meir's hands were clean, he would eventually be receiving the money. Just knowing where it came from muddied my spirits. And I knew where it was going: it was going to me. I had no wish for this money. How could I tell Meir that? I do not know how to please him, nor how to insist on this matter. Woe is me if I say something, and woe is me if I don't. Good Lord, why does life continue to pile up challenges?

My brain was filled with noise. A bitter distress squeezed my chest, climbing up my throat, filling me with stifled passages. I crushed the ends of the blanket in my hand. My lips moved voicelessly: *Have mercy on me, Lord, for I am faint. Heal me, Lord, for my bones are in agony. My soul is in deep anguish. I am worn out from my groaning. All night long I flood my bed with weeping, and drench my couch with tears.*

All of a sudden, I felt a large, soft hand running over my face, wiping away the tears, bit by bit. I closed my eyes, indulging in the sensation. *Please don't stop,* I asked silently. And he didn't. He continued to caress my face, my head, and my neck silently. I realized that in all those moments or hours of the great sorrow I had caused him, he never frowned at me, nor raised his voice. I opened my eyes and looked at him. His face was close to mine.

He spoke softly. "Gutaleh, do not torment yourself over this. Your kindness, the human emotion burning inside of you, is what led you to this outburst. You were upset, but also right from the point of view of a person who has always lived an honest, fair life. It does not sit well with your conscience. Still, all I ask is for you to never doubt my integrity. It is strong and will never leave me for as long as I live. If you have even the slightest doubt about that, it would cause me to lose my mind. I have no desire to defend my actions again. And when it comes to the money, you will not have to see it. Before it even reaches me, it will already be passed to new hands."

Never doubt my integrity. I held on to that. I knew that I would forever keep this promise.

The chaos inside of me slowly died down. I did not speak. He spoke for me, allowing a new peace to grow inside me. Once again, he understood me without my having to explain myself. That is my man, who sees what is hidden, who recognizes sense and morality, and understands words of wisdom. I must adjust to this incredible, heartening truth. How I love the wondrous combination of his tender soul and his powerful presence.

"Let all evildoers die, the king of England and the landgrave, a death of evildoers that is befitting of them and of the world," I said, breaking my silence.

Meir smiled and answered with a quote of his own. *"A man must not pray for evildoers to leave this world. For had the Lord God not sent away Terah, who was an idol worshipper, we would not have had Abraham."*

How much truth there was in those words. "May your mind rest at ease knowing you have put my mind at ease," I mumbled, pushing against him.

Wordlessly, our hands searched, our fingers interlaced, and our bodies came together to please one another with divine delight.

One day, Meir left for a journey that had been planned to last several days, but surprised me by returning the very same day. After dinner, he turned to me gravely. "I returned to you early," he whispered, "and I ask that you make yourself available. We have a long conversation ahead of us."

My heart almost jumped out of my chest. What was it this time? The word "conversation" sounded rough and distant. I searched his face for clues, but other than the profound gravity of his eyes, I could find nothing. He could not have returned early to discuss the mercenaries again. What was it, then?

I distractedly prepared the children for bed. Schönche, my love, obeyed with the perfect maturity of a five-year-old, urging her brother, Amschel Meir, to join her, and even tucking him in under his warm, woolen blanket. I put two-year-old Shlomo Meir in his crib near his brother, and asked Schönche to sing him his lullaby. Schönche, bless her soul, hopped lightly out of her bed, came closer to him, and sang with a soft, gentle voice the song "Schlaft, Kinder, Schlaft" while tenderly rubbing his back, just as I do. I said good night to my children and walked to our bedroom, noting that my daughter's kindness had somewhat dulled the storm raging inside of me.

Beyond the drawn curtain, Meir was waiting on the edge of the bed. I paused, watching him.

"Gutaleh, you look as if you're expecting a difficult conversation. That is not the case. Our conversation is meant to clarify for you and myself what we must do with our lives."

I took a deep breath and took a seat next to him, resting my head on his shoulder. He kissed my covered head and then turned my face toward his.

"Listen, Gutaleh. For the past few days, after the incident in the parlor of King George . . . ," he began, and I thought, *What a fine name he's given our unpleasant scuffle: the parlor of King George.* "I've been thinking long and hard, Gutaleh, about the way of life I have chosen, and the way of life you entered into as my partner, without a choice." He took a breath, and I listened carefully. My eyes never left his face. "When I think of my actions, I know for certain that God is at my side. There is no doubt in my mind that the hand of God is guiding and directing my footsteps. It is not the will of God to have us sitting idly, lamenting our helplessness. We must act. We must work hard, persistently, industriously, studiously, with planning and forethought, all the while striving for success. Our success would be the attainment of our goals, an objective blessed by the Lord. The harder we work, the more the Lord will repay us. It was best put in Proverbs: *'Do you see someone skilled in their work? They will serve before kings.'* He who is quick, efficient, and talented must be encouraged until he reports directly to the king."

Then Meir fell silent, and I used this pause for one small question. "Why are you telling me this, Meir?"

"Good question," he said, encouraging me. "Because recently there has been much criticism of me."

"I accepted your explanation, rest assured," I said.

"You are fine, we have no more difference of opinion on that matter. But people talk. Some complain about the fact that I make money, as if there is fault in the desire for financial prosperity."

"Who are these people?"

"All sorts of people who hate seeing Jews setting financial success as a goal. They believe we Jews are ordered to be God fearing, to focus on prayer and love of the Lord."

"But your financial path does not contradict, God forbid, fulfilling the mitzvahs and believing in our holy Torah."

"You are right, but in their eyes attention to the material is a demerit. Recently, the newspapers have been publishing criticism of wealthy Jews."

"And what do you think about that?"

"I remain faithful to my way. I believe that everything we do is for the best. We do not live idly. We work hard. God surely watches us with satisfaction. He loves hard workers of all kind, be it agricultural, commercial, or any other endeavor. The important thing is that we behave according to the standards of the Torah. We are honest. Moreover, without having decided it in advance, we have chosen a modest way of life. Money does not cause us to lose our minds, nor change our manner of life."

"If you live in peace with yourself, why are you concerned about what people say?" I asked. I could not accept the distress in his face.

"Because we Jews have always suffered from how we appear in the eyes of the gentiles. Whether we were starving or rich, they have always found an excuse to hate us. The more money I make, and I plan to continue to make money, the more excuses I must provide to our enemies."

We were both quiet, thoughtful. The thought of someone else's actions affecting the whole of society rattled me, especially when it came to my Meir.

He turned to face me again. "It is ridiculous to think of me negatively affecting an entire people, but with the path I've chosen and the objectives I've marked for myself, I must be aware of the risks. I might sully our people's reputation if alongside the honor I had wanted to bring them I also invite the fury of the gentiles over my success."

"Now I am completely confused. All you want is to become rich in order to bring honor to us, your family, and to us Jews. And now you are worried about tarnishing the Jewish people. This is a blatant contradiction. Which is it, honor or tarnish?"

Meir laughed, as if he'd just heard an amusing ditty. I listened for sounds from the nursery, making sure the children were all asleep. The silence put my mind at ease.

Meir filled his lungs with air and let it out with a quiet whistle. "The way up is riddled with thorns, and thorns, by nature, prick. But they do not have the power to stop my ascension. The attempt to tarnish will continue to follow me in the paths I tread, but at each step, the flag will continue to wave, bearing the word 'honor.'"

"Meaning, eventually honor will win out," I concluded, cheerful as a little girl who had just cracked a complex riddle.

"Yes, but that is not the end of the story, seeing how success follows success, and the honor will grow endlessly. There are only interim steps on the climb. This is our will and this is the will of God. Therefore, I see the way of life I have chosen, the fulfillment of my destiny, as a mission."

"This mission is the purpose of your existence, our existence," I said quietly, trying to process the connection between his choice of a path and God's blessing, and a mission.

"Indeed. Since this is the will of God, He provides us with the necessary tools: the energy required for hard work, the industriousness, the persistence, and . . ."—here he looked at me for a long moment before continuing—"and therefore He has chosen us as a couple, knowing full well that we are the right pair to fulfill this mission."

Thursday, March 28th, 1782

Does repeatedly beating a person end up strengthening them?

It does not sound right to me, though it is spoken with profound gravity and good intentions from the mouth of any man wishing to comfort me, as if they were the words of God.

I prefer my Meir's theory, adding it to his collection of wise sayings: "When a blow hits two people at once, it is divided between them, and each one wants to make things easier for their mate, therefore opening wide the half-closed door and revealing the wondrous world awaiting on the other side."

The wondrous world awaiting has given me two more children: Nathan Meir, four-and-a-half years old, and Isabella, one-and-a-half years old.

Between the births of these two children I was tried once more by the Lord, forced to say an agonized farewell to a newborn who died before even receiving a name. I am not like all the other righteous people, who say that those who rejoice in their suffering deliver redemption to the world. Nevertheless, I washed away my pain, smoothed the wrinkle, stood up tall, and along with Meir, linking my hand with his, said, "The Lord gave and the Lord has taken away. May the name of the

Lord be praised." And now we have brought a sweet little thing into the world, the fifth of our living children.

And now my face and heart are focused on my children, may they live long and healthy lives.

A mother's heart is divided into chambers devoted to each of her children, each chamber a magical world in and of itself. My children are all very different, each of them with his or her own way of melting the heart and garnering praise. Nathan, my fourth child, is nothing like his siblings. From the moment he developed opinions, he seemed to have one single passion in life: to defeat his siblings in every possible matter. His intelligence comes through with gems of sentences, on par with quotes from the venerable writer Johann Wolfgang von Goethe. Along with the collection of Meir's words of wisdom, I have started to gather gems from young Nathan Meir. Here is one: "Papa is here—a time for cheer." True as day and rhymes too. Has anyone ever seen this in a child not yet five years old? The greatness of this saying lies in how it goes straight to his father's heart. With just a few words, he has bought a place of honor in his father's heart, and now, when Meir comes home, Nathan is the first to receive a greeting.

Nathan's charm is not overlooked by one of our regular visitors, Carl Friedrich Buderus of Hanau, the head financial broker of the landgrave Wilhelm. Buderus is the only Christian customer who visits our home, and he does so with growing frequency without recoiling from the appearance of the street or the crowdedness of the house in general and the sales room in particular. Rumor in the neighborhood has it that when Goethe stumbled upon our street and glanced in from the northern end, near our home—the filthiest, smelliest end—the tender soul was so shocked and revolted that he had to plug his nose and flee the area. As soon as he was beyond the ghetto gates, he threw up, relieving his tortured guts.

Buderus, on the other hand, felt right at home, and with the open, natural way he carried himself, created a sense of familial, warm intimacy. He did not grow up with luxury and twenty palace rooms. He too lived in the gutter as a child, and feels no need to flee or empty his delicate stomach. With a pinch of humor, he tells us about his childhood outside of Frankfurt, and we laugh along with him. But in secret I shed two tears, one for him and his family, the other for us and the rest of the Judengasse people.

The handsome, tall man with the robust build and the jovial and elegant appearance makes sure to come see us during the week, respecting Shabbat and holidays, during which Meir avoids discussing commerce. Even when it comes to urgent matters, Buderus waits patiently until the end of the holiday.

When he comes, he removes his jacket and reveals his dress shirt with the silver embroidery and light-colored tie that dangles down to a matching vest. His shoulders are so wide, as if designed to carry the burden of his master's palace. Before he embarks on the matter at hand, purely business, he turns to the children, who gather around him, chattering and chirping from the moment he arrives, examining his face and outfit with curious, cheerful eyes. Instantly he becomes a mischievous young man, hopping like a goat, meowing like a cat, hanging out his tongue like a thirsty dog. He ruffles their hair, arches his brows, rolls his eyes, pretends to punch them, and threatens to chase them. The children squeal with ecstatic terror, trying to entice him to follow them out of the house, but then he pounces, easily gaining on them between the walls of our home, and finally takes hold of them with his large hands, acting as if he were about to devour his prey, and only releases them after they promise not to follow him into their father's study.

Buderus pats nine-year-old Amschel's back in encouragement for his following in his father's footsteps and showing an interest in learning his trade and becoming like him, and advises him to continue down this path. But out of earshot, he whispers to Meir that he expects Nathan to surprise them when he grows up. He lingers with Nathan, flooding him with complicated math problems, and the child, both knowledge thirsty and arrogant, replies with formidable accuracy and confidence.

I tend to agree with Buderus about Nathan. His unique intelligence has not evaded me. Nevertheless, I have no doubt that each of my children will succeed in their own way. I believe that each person has a tailor-made destiny, and must only take care to direct themselves toward it.

After he wipes away white powder that has fallen from his wig to his shirt and smooths his rumpled clothing, Buderus finally enters Meir's study and closes the door behind him. The children lurk on the other side of the door, eavesdropping and taking in every word. Meir knows they do this, but never sends them away. On the contrary, he steps out for a moment and nods at them, to signal to them that their presence is known and welcome. Many times, after the business talk is concluded, he tasks them with different chores, which they accept with obvious gaiety, as if they had just received a handful of candy.

Meir is keen to have the children adapt to his business way of thinking and behaving. He has made it a habit upon their waking in the morning to lead them to the front door, where they feast their eyes on the sign out front. Each morning, except mornings when Meir is away, they obediently follow him outside, some still yawning, others wiping the sleep off their eyes, others still with a burning urge to urinate after the long night.

"Look, Gutaleh," he said one night as we lay in bed, my eyelids fighting off the fluttering of sleep, "our children will be my successors. The business is growing, and I have no interest in bringing in outsiders. My only partners will be my sons. The secrets of the trade must remain in the family, otherwise everything will be lost."

"There is time," I answered, half asleep. "They need to grow up first. Some of them have yet to be born."

"You are right. I say this now because I fear for Kalman. Up until this point I used my brother's help, but this won't last much longer. I must prepare."

I thought about poor Kalman. His disability is worsening, and his health is deteriorating. While I pondered this, growing melancholic, sleep landed on me with full force, dropping me, helpless, into its lap.

Sunday, August 24th, 1783

Kalman is gone, may he rest in peace. God has released him from his misery.

A burdensome silence screams from all directions. Kalman, that good man, beloved by all of us, is gone. Even the children do not frolic as they usually do. Isabella searches for me, clinging to me with her little hand, not gurgling as she normally does.

How can one handle the loss of a loved one? I wondered. Even everyday activities require a special effort. I must find a way to overcome the sense of grief. When one of my babies dies, a new baby arrives to take their place. But who can take the place of poor Kalman?

As usual, Meir had an answer. "You will fill his role in my study," he said, searching my eyes for a reaction.

My heart soured. I stared into his eyes, trying to determine whether or not this insane idea was serious. His eyes were not laughing. This was no joke. Nevertheless, how could I take the place of the deceased Kalman? I cannot find words in Judendeutsch to describe this chilling sensation. No, I cannot take dear Kalman's place.

Besides, how could I find the time to fill this role, when my hands are already full with housework and our plans to have more children? I said nothing.

"Try it and see," he said. "You've helped him recently, learning bookkeeping. Just imagine you're still helping him. He'll be watching you from above, appreciating your help. Out of everyone, he would have chosen you as his replacement. I know you are busy, but you are the one who decides your schedule in the study. You do not need to spend any more time than you can afford to in there."

I took a breath. I must have forgotten to breathe while he was talking. I am no match for Meir's powers of persuasion. His words invade the heart and reach the brain, performing the necessary actions in both. I recalled our conversation just before Kalman died, when Meir determined that his children would become involved in the business. They are still young. It would only be right for me to take their place for the time being. And besides, I have some experience helping my father with bookkeeping, and more recently, Kalman.

I felt my way to the desk and sat down with awe. I looked around. Here I was, embarking on a new path. No longer the homemaker of the Rothschild family, but the bookkeeper of M. A. Rothschild. I work for a living. My financial contribution is minuscule compared to the gold bars, the coins, and the bills that Meir handles, but I have a respectable position—dealing directly with my husband's accounting.

I opened the old ledger and recalled my private notebook. Some notebooks are out in the open and others are hidden. The one on this desk is exposed, documenting the life cycle of the financial business, but only partially. Meir has kept two notebooks for a while now. The second one is secret and kept in a box, and it alone contains the accurate report, which is different from the one appearing in the exposed notebook.

"There's no other choice," he explained when I asked him about this. "As Jews, the government limits us, requiring us to use roundabout means in order to achieve our goals. Don't forget that I plan on bringing plenty of honor to our household, and in our world honor is anchored to money. This will also benefit the rest of our persecuted people."

His explanation made sense, but nevertheless, was it fair to present the government with a partial report of our financial standing? His entire business path has been characterized by integrity, but when it comes to the tax authorities Meir deviates from his habit and feels perfectly at ease with himself and with the opportunity to rebel against the many decrees posed against us Jews, paying the government back, at least in part, for years of mistreatment.

On this matter, I had reservations. But who was I to decide matters that were none of my business?

Meir regrets my reservations and fights my silence with silence. But his silence is rumbling.

And all the while, he continues to address the heads of the Holy Roman Empire with requests to remove the decrees, widen our street, and allow Jews out of the ghetto.

After a few days of bookkeeping I now feel like an experienced employee. My spirits are higher, though I still conduct silent conversations with Kalman every day before placing my round bottom on his chair. When Meir is away on business trips or at fairs I handle debt collecting, payments, and mail. I think I'll be able to get Schönche, my eldest, involved in office work soon. For the time being, twelve-year-old Schönche, industrious and orderly, assists me in household chores and in caring for her younger brothers and sisters. They listen intently to her stories, and she reminds me of myself and the way I cared for my own siblings. My sister Vendeleh is married now, and has a one-year-old son. She lives at my parents' house with her family, waiting, like many others, for an apartment to become available.

◆　◆　◆

Many nights, Meir tosses and turns in bed. He is preoccupied with the embargo the ghetto rabbis have placed on Moshe Mendelssohn's translation of the Pentateuch. The rabbis, led by the head rabbi and the head of the large yeshiva, the venerable Rabbi Pinchas Horowitz, have spoken out against the Jewish thinker, determining that the translation of the Bible into German, though it is spelled in Hebrew letters alongside the Hebrew original, is heretical and brings shame on the words of our sages. It seems that, more than anything, they fear for their own honor. For hundreds of years, the ghetto has offered organized religious education in a *heder* and a yeshiva. They take pride in educational prosperity and turning the ghetto into a center of attraction for those seeking answers in Jewish law. And now, a man named Moshe Mendelssohn has come to transform our biblical Hebrew language into German and change things around.

Forty-seven Jews on Judengasse have already ordered the first volume, but Meir is hesitant. Tempers have been flaring at the synagogue and the shops, and the entire street has turned into a roiling hub of argument.

On the eve of the Hebrew month of Tamuz of last year, Rabbi Pinchas Horowitz gave a sermon at the synagogue, harshly criticizing Mendelssohn and his book. The echoes carry through our street to this day.

At night, before lovemaking, the subject came up again. As usual, he did most of the talking, and I did most of the listening.

"I will not hurt the honor of the rabbis, the venerable Rabbi Horowitz, and the pride of the butcher, the cantor, the beadle, and the undertaker, who are all of unified opinion. They asked me to join the embargo, arguing the importance of maintaining the ghetto's reputation as a center of religious study. Any change, so they say, could cause damage."

"They are probably right. I see no fault with what the children are learning. Why change it?"

"We mustn't stagnate. In study, just like in commerce, things must be constantly renewed. Had I continued selling used goods, I would not have gone far. Think about Moshe Mendelssohn. This brilliant man is trying to bring a fresh gust of progress, illuminate our Torah, and this is a golden opportunity to bring new light into the darkness of the ghetto. And we, in turn, seem to be telling him, 'Excuse me, sir, there is no room in our narrow ghetto for such light. We will carry on with our holy language and our Judendeutsch. We have no need for German.' Do you see how absurd that is? On the one hand, we fight for equal rights, but on the other hand, when Joseph II himself issues an empirical charter of tolerance, stating that 'the Jews are human, just like us,' what do we do? With our own hands, we extinguish the light he has sent to us, as if telling him, 'We'd rather stay in the dark. We have no desire for change.'"

I accepted his explanation. I thought, *How odd, to feel the wind of enlightenment in our bed.* "What do you plan to do?"

"I am torn between the two sides. On the one hand, the desire to maintain what we have and avoid a civil war, and on the other hand, the need to renew, to open our eyes, to evolve, to blend in with our surroundings."

"And if you had to decide?"

"We'll wait and see."

"Waiting is hard."

"Of course. I am a man of action, not waiting. But I must take into account the sensibilities of the people who create the image of this place."

I thought, *Why stick our heads between two large mountains?*

Meir finally found a measure of mercy toward the rabbis, and in spite of his desire, did not purchase Mendelssohn's book.

I must admit that I am curious to read it, though I know I would not understand a single word, for though the letters are Hebrew, the language is German. Moshe Mendelssohn urges us to let go of Judendeutsch and adopt the German tongue. This is a challenge only the younger generation can face.

Monday, December 12th, 1785

Oh, Nathan, Nathan. How much effort is required to restrain a child with a great mind and equally great arrogance? Several contradictory sensations are at war within me, but one wins out: my commitment to reduce the suffering of his siblings by his hands.

I had gone out to the butcher's and returned with a kosher chicken, and before I could even reach the door I could hear shouting and crying. I guessed that Nathan was responsible and quickened my steps.

Before I could begin to pluck feathers, I separated the combatants, and called Nathan to join me in the kitchen. "Read to me from your Talmud while I take care of the chicken."

Nathan grabbed the Pentateuch interpretation and came into the kitchen with me. He faced the Wailing Wall, looking like a ball someone had cast aside and forgotten.

"Say goodbye to that gloomy expression. One mustn't frown while holding the Nachmanides interpretation. Read me something."

He twitched his face around, fighting against the lines of anger, and put on an effortful smile. The result looked quite dismal on his flushed face.

"Open the book. What will you teach me today, son?"

He flipped through the book and read some of Nachmanides's innovations. He focused on his schoolwork, while I shoved my hands into the chicken and extracted its organs, my ears turned to Nathan and attentive to the other rustles and tumults of the house.

A short while later, things settled down, and Nathan asked to be excused. I accepted his request and made myself available to Isabella. We sang Hanukah songs together while I riffled through the pile of clean laundry and picked out the items of clothing that needed patching, threading a needle and sewing to the rhythm of the song. Isabella likes to watch my fingers as I work and wants to try sewing herself. I think she will soon learn the craft of patchwork.

I thank God above for imbuing me with the power and wisdom to handle my children properly. And yet, I cannot deny the relief I felt when I see my mother and father coming in to take some of the burden of responsibility from me. It is a true redemption.

Whenever Grandma and Grandpa are here, the house is filled with loud cheers, and our faces stretch into joyful smiles. My children gathered around their grandmother and were immediately joined by their cousins, Moshe and Yenta's children, who see my parents as substitute grandparents. Their eyes fixed on the bundle in my mother's hands, and their mouths hung open as the string was untied and the delicacies were extracted one by one and served into eager little hands.

I watched them, the group of children, whose scuffles were a matter of routine, both between siblings and between the cousins who shared their lives, and I considered the spell these sweets cast on everyone and how much power they had to make fights temporarily forgotten.

With full mouths, some of them spilling down their chins and dripping onto their shirts, the children then turned to my father, who had settled into a chair, and plopped down on the floor around him, prepared to hear his stories.

I led my mother into the kitchen and gave her two gems Meir had left for her.

"Oh, Gutaleh, these are beautiful, but I cannot accept them," Mama said, holding the gems close to her chest.

I looked at her twinkling eyes and realized how much they resembled Schönche's. This realization brought tears to my eyes, which now shone like hers. If there is anything in this world that makes my mother's eyes shine, it is pearls and precious stones.

"Mama, Meir asked me to give these to you."

"How chivalrous of him. Rather than sell them for a fine price, he gives them to me. How can I ever repay him?"

"Oh, Mama, you have repaid him by giving birth to me. Had I not been born, he would not have come to badger you about marrying me."

Mother caressed the gems and buried them carefully in her purse. From there we moved on, as was our habit, to sharing secrets—about Yenta, Nathan, my bookkeeping work, and my world at large. I listened to her advice and waved off her criticism of my hard work, smelled the scent of her love, absorbed it, and then released her out to the rooms full of life and noise, to play with little Isabella.

As my parents embraced their grandchildren, I turned to the tasks that beckoned, waiting for me at every turn.

Tuesday, October 10th, 1786

It's early in the morning. The dim light of the street makes its way to our house, hesitant to disrupt the rest of the slumbering. They are all still deep in dreams. Meir is on another business trip. When I do not find my good-morning coin upon awakening, I know it's going to be a day of longing. When will he return, today or tomorrow? The longer he lingers, the more he advances his business, but the sooner he gets here, the faster he cures my yearning.

I also miss him as a father to his children. I sense that our children require a more available father figure. When I sit with Vendeleh, my beloved sister, and she speaks of her husband, who spends evenings with her and her children, I bless her for this fortune and share her joy, but also feel a light twinge. I suppose nothing is ever perfect. If Meir is more successful in his work than anyone else, the price is paid by his children, who are robbed of a father. It is a daily loss, other than Shabbat, holidays, and a few other odd days when they are lucky enough to see him before they go to bed at night. I am grateful to our holy faith for uniting our family for celebration and quality time with our children.

So many things happen that I can hardly find the time to sit and write them down.

Well, where should I begin? Of course, with the expansion of our family. Two years ago, a new offspring lit up our world: our daughter Babette, may she live a long and healthy life. Everyone's attention was turned to her, as is our custom upon the arrival of a new baby. With each birth, my belly shrinks for a limited time, making room for my heart, which expands to receive the new child. I am amazed at the flexibility of the heart, able to expand with each birth to create another magical chamber, pushing its way among the older ones. Our Babette delights us with her contagious laughter and her scampering all over the house. As luck has it, the space in our small home and yard allows her to push her speed to the limit.

And that brings me to the most surprising news of all: we've moved!

Yes, we have moved out of the house with the red sign and into the house with the green sign. And though green is the color of our new sign, our family name will forever remain Rothschild.

I am happy. True, I have felt happy many times before, but happiness can appear in many forms, and these waves of joy are my favorite so far—the happiness of a person who lives in their own home.

And here I am in my own home! Mistress of my own domain! Everything in it is mine, and the life that is conducted within it is lived by my guidance. Each person is a king in their own home. Do you see, dear notebook, what this means? It means I'm happy. I do not need any more rooms. I do not need a glorious castle. I have what I wanted, and for that I thank God up above and my Meir for leading me here. *The Lord grant you that ye may find rest, each of you in the house of her husband.* Therefore, a woman cannot be at rest unless in the home of her husband.

How did this happen?

Well, after over a decade of waiting, a year ago, in the middle of the cold Hebrew month of Kislev, a house for sale on Judengasse caught

Meir's eye. For the first time, he deviated from his habit as a merchant, and without any negotiation handed over the asking price: 11,000 gulden, the going price for a palace in the noble city of Frankfurt. He explained this unusual step with convincing simplicity: "I could not afford to give the seller any time to reconsider his actions."

Meir says this is double what Goethe's parents paid for their palace. Nevertheless, he walks around like a man who has just made the deal of his life, constantly measuring the length and width of our house with his steps. He sold our part of the Hinterpfann house to his brother Moshe for 3,300 gulden, and three months ago we moved into our new house and said the sheheheyanu blessing.

I have had quite enough of sharing a home with my sister-in-law. Not only could I not bear her lifestyle, but I had to pretend I was comfortable and happy in her company. It is no wonder therefore that now, after years of keeping everything in, in these very moments, as I hold my favorite pen and write about my new home, I am tickled by light waves of pleasure.

We took our things—the pots and pans, the dishes and barrels, the beds and comforters, and everything in between—and arranged them in our new abode.

I am amused by the image of the moment of purchasing, which had become quite an event on our street. The first to announce it was the synagogue beadle. After that, the town crier went out into the street to sound the news in the ears of residents. I stood in the window of our old home, unable to believe my ears. Meir Amschel Rothschild's name echoed over and over like a shofar, and my skin was covered in goose bumps to match my swelling heart. And if those two weren't enough, here was another surprise: the rabbi of the synagogue himself participated in the signing of the sale agreement, holding a burning candle for a blessing. This is what he does on special occasions, and he saw the buying of our new home as a very special occasion indeed. The congratulations we enjoyed in light of this event were more heartfelt than any wishes we'd received for the birth of all of our children, combined. The reaction of the people of Judengasse added several more titillating layers to the lovely tumult inside of me.

This home is also mine in another way: I have an actual part in its purchase. I pulled out the hidden boxes containing my good-morning coins—they had filled quite nicely with time. I placed them at Meir's feet. "This is my contribution to the acquisition," I announced festively.

He looked at me, his face falling. "Why, Gutaleh? These coins are yours. Save them for a time of need. Do not worry about the money. God has taken care of me and given me the necessary amount."

"I have other savings for a time of need. These coins were for a time of want, and there is no greater want than this."

Meir's eyes lingered on my face, then he nodded understandingly, his face lit up. "This home is yours, Gutaleh. These coins you are paying for your home are of the greatest value. They are coins of love. Our home will be enveloped with love."

He picked up one of the boxes and opened it. "You have me working like a dog, Frau Gutle Rothschild. Have you no mercy? Do you have any idea how long it's going to take me to count all the coins in these six boxes?"

I smiled at him and pulled an empty box from under the bed. I set it beside one of the full boxes and plopped down to the floor. With a gesture, I invited Meir to sit next to me. I picked up a handful of coins and began to count them out loud. Then I placed them in the empty box and said, "Each coin joins the others to create a large sum." Meir rubbed his bottom cheerfully against the floor, picked up a fistful of coins, counted them, and repeated after me, "Each coin joins the others to create a large sum." Thus we continued counting the sum of our love through one box, two, three, shoulder rubbing against shoulder, hand touching hand, all around us the children watching the piles of coins passed from one box to the other.

Well, the house is mine in every way possible. I place the new good-morning coins that appear on my pillow in a velvet-lined box, asking myself what dream they are about to make come true for me, now that the dream of the house has come true.

Our new, beautiful house is in the center of the Judengasse, right across from the bridge leading into Frankfurt. It is on the east side of our street, eight houses away from the central synagogue. Its façade faces the street just where it widens. The house has four windows (!) which allow some light to filter into some of the rooms. This is not the stifling, rear-facing house with the footpath covered in garbage where I lived for the first sixteen years of our marriage.

This is a house worthy of a life, in spite of its small rooms, some of which are dark.

The house is four tiny stories high. Its walls and floors are made of brick, wood, and slate. Outside is a bell that rings whenever a guest enters, and Meir or one of the children go downstairs to welcome them.

The first floor is a foyer with a water pump. That is one of the wonders of the house. No more must I drag my feet, carrying buckets of water from the well to the house. Few Judengasse people enjoy such luxury, and I am still consumed by discomfort about the many luxuries I enjoy.

From the foyer, stone stairs lead up to the second floor. The door to the right is the entrance to our sweet little bedroom. We have managed to squeeze in our bed, covered with clean pillows and comforters of fine linen. The small nooks in its walls are stacked with neatly folded sheets that answer all of our family's needs from one laundry day to the next—six to eight weeks apart. On the smooth wall between the nooks is a Star of David matching the one in the study, to protect us from evil and imbue us with strength to carry the burden of life and succeed in our paths.

The left door leads to an open balcony, also small. That is the cream on top of this delicacy. The forbidden gardens of Frankfurt now filter into my home through a tiny, open square—a miniature garden all my own. I covered the railing with planters of different sizes. I water the young plants slowly, so as not to choke them, God forbid, as if they were suckling babies. Drops dance from the mouth of the watering can, and the plants bloom like well-fed children, trusting their mother never to forget them. They welcome me with modest, colorful blossoms, canopied by the intense green of pine trees.

The balcony is the solution to my dreams of visiting the gardens of Frankfurt, dreams I have had often, and for years. I curl up in my precious little corner, and envision it as a green thicket of trees. I only regret the fact that it overlooks the backyard, which is no sight to behold, being blocked by the wall that surrounds the Judengasse and protects the people of Frankfurt from our lurking eyes. According to some ancient decree, we are forbidden from observing the secret lives of Frankfurters, and thus their homes, their gardens, and their open fields remain hidden from us at all times. But I must thank the Lord for the fact that my blooming balcony receives natural light, unlike the rooms of the house, which remain in partial darkness. Each day the balcony is caressed by a touch of modest, languid sunlight, and for that I must give thanks. This is a stroke of luck in a place where even the mighty, glorious sunbeams have joined forces with the people of Frankfurt, ignoring Judengasse and maintaining the separation.

Our family mostly spends time on the balcony on the weekends, and sometimes on weekday afternoons. This is where Meir plays with the children or reads them holy books with interpretations, and I serve them fruit and watch them with pleasure. On weekdays, I make efficient use of the natural light that smiles at us from the narrow bit of sky above, and I sew, embroider, patch, and knit sweaters and scarves for Meir and the children to use on cold days. The sounds of joy flow from the rooms to the open balcony, their echoes scattering in the open air. We celebrate Sukkot on the balcony, the pine branches serving as our sukkah's cover, and a few stars trapped between the vines peek in on us, blessing us with touches of light for the holiday.

How unfortunate that Meir is so often on the road, the free time he has to devote to our children diminishing gradually. On the other hand, how fortunate that we have Shabbat as our day of rest, to narrow the gap of the week.

A third door on the second floor opens into a back room. This is the study. The contents of this room separate it from the rest of the house, providing it with its office characteristics. On the wall hangs a good-luck charm—a stone carving of a Star of David. When Meir is not away on a business trip, he leans over his desk or sits on the high stool beside it. Most of the time he stands, to balance the long hours of sitting during his travels. When Meir is away, the stool becomes available for my plump or thin bottom, depending on whether or not I am pregnant.

Recently, Schönche has also been taking part in the work. She comes to the office, glowing in the new dress she received from us to celebrate her joining the family business.

Luckily for her, she inherited her father's handsome features, and combined with her feminine contours, she's a good-looking girl. It's no wonder, then, that she's already being courted. But we mustn't rush. She's only fifteen years old. My owl eyes have caught sight of the most persistent suitor, Benedict Moshe de Worms, who visits often under the guise of shopping, while his mind is entirely concentrated on a different affair, embodied in my eldest daughter. He frolics around her without taking his eyes off her face. I am familiar with this kind of fervor, but for everything there is a season.

This study is where the changing business and the sale of used goods and sewing notions takes place. The large wooden closet affixed to the wall contains notebooks and accounting ledgers, along with a perfectly neat stack of papers. A large, heavy iron chest at the corner of the room contains bills and coins and is locked with a formidable bolt.

It was Meir's idea, and was meant to create an illusion. Only those in the know are aware that, to open it, you must remove the lid on the back.

But that isn't all. Meir has taken care of all safety measures in the house. The entire money chest is misleading—a sophisticated trick—because it appears innocent and unsuspicious. Most of the bills—as well as the updated ledgers, documents, and important contracts—are kept in hidden shelves inside the walls of the study, and others among wine barrels, sacks of lentils, spices, and sausages tucked in a secret cellar accessible by a door hidden in a false wall that Meir had designed and built himself.

And that isn't all. An underground tunnel leads from our secret cellar to the cellar of our neighbor, Schiff, who lives on the right side of the building. If we needed to, we would be able to evade the evildoers who see themselves as representatives of the law, escape into our neighbors' home, and continue to flee from there.

Our kind neighbor Schiff, who welcomed us to our new home with salt and bread, lives in the "Ark." Above the door to his home is an engraving of a ship. In fact, our home and Schiff's are two halves of the same building.

I must point out that, in addition to the secret cellar, we have a second cellar, accessible through a hidden door in the floor of the foyer.

Enough about secrets. Let me move on to the third floor. The living room.

This is where we spend the majority of our time together. When guests come it serves as a fine parlor. I am proud of the living room and make sure to keep it clean. Among our regular guests are my parents, who come to Shabbat dinner with my favorite sister, Vendeleh, her husband, Pinchas, who always arrives carrying a bowl of fruit compote, and their two children, Yaakov and Frumit, who mix with our children as if they were siblings. The rabbi visits us at Shabbat's end along with other synagogue goers, who join us for the havdalah ritual.

Another guest who comes from time to time is Buderus, of course, who never stops praising our new home and complimenting Meir both for the move itself, and for the way in which he made sure to fill every space in the house. Dozens of crowded alcoves have been carved into the walls. "Your home is like one big walk-in closet. If I ever need a hiding place, I'll know where to go," he said jokingly, and I chuckled at his mischief. Who knows better than he that only we Jews suffer from a constant fear of threats and blows, be it emotional abuse or robbery at best, pogroms at worst. The great princedom of Hesse-Kassel, where the landgrave and his entourage have moved following the death of his father, must be one of the strongest princedoms in the Holy Roman Empire, if not the strongest. Would a lion hide in a mouse's burrow?

Our living room's greatest advantage is the fact that it features four long, narrow windows overlooking the street. I do not have much free time to enjoy these lovely windows, but there they sit, in all their length, whispering their invitation whenever I walk by. When I sit there with the children, I place my chair close to the window, bounce one of my beloved babies on my knee, and enjoy both worlds: sitting together with my family, and maintaining a relationship with the outside world.

A metal chandelier dangles from the ceiling, its concave base holding a candle that is lit every evening. On Shabbat eve we place six candlesticks on the table in the corner of the room, three on each side, and in them we burn candles to turn the room festive with their brightness. The wooden chairs around the table have high backs.

The sofa and chairs in the center of the room are upholstered with a velvetlike fabric in green, my favorite color, reminding me of the color of vegetation, which is missing from our street. Holy books stand together on the shelf against the wall, and Meir likes to read them to the children. Alongside them are the two morality books I received from my mother, *Brent Spiegel* and *A Good Heart*, which I like to feast my eyes on often. In the corner of the room is a round wooden dresser, upon which rests our marital bouquet, which has known better days and is now a permanent decoration, carrying within it memories of the days of modesty and hope, and reminding us of the starting point in every phase along the way.

On the fourth floor are two small, dark bedrooms, and along the walls are the beds, facing the street. Since these rooms are too narrow to contain any closets, Meir has built closets under the staircase, using the indentations in the walls, under the ceiling, and in the attic. In this manner, each part of our home has a function. Separating the nurseries into a boys' room and a girls' room allows the children to get undressed without averting their eyes. I visit the two bedrooms each night, leaning over each of my lovely children, feeling their breaths on my face, and praying that their sweet serenity, the expressions of children who trust the kindness of the world, will stay with them for the rest of their lives. Then I return to the living room, pick up either *Brent Spiegel* or *A Good Heart*, and cleanse my soul with their enlightened letters.

And now to my kingdom of kingdoms: the kitchen.

The location of my small kitchen near the water pump is the biggest advantage of my kingdom. Water is a perfect match for a kitchen. At the back of the kitchen is the fireplace, where I place the cauldron. A burning lump of coal is stationed permanently in a small metal mesh, maintaining the flame. On the other side of the kitchen is a small cabinet containing cups and plates, and on the front wall hang pots and pans—my loyal work tools.

The kitchen, filled with the smells of cooking, is where I spend a large part of the day. Here I am the exclusive ruler. If Meir is the captain of the business, then the kitchen is where I, Frau Gutle Rothschild, command the ship.

My time in the kitchen does not revolve only around cooking. It is mostly devoted to thinking, planning, and chatting with the children. Among the clinking of pots and pans, as my hands knead, peel, chop, ball, boil, and clean, my mind is constantly at work.

A time for pondering. For clarification. For raising questions. And, most important, a time to pay mind to my children. My beloved children, some still buds in my lap, others, stumbling toddlers exploring the wonders of their existence, others still thoughtful youths with a zest for life. As they mature they require more and more attention. Simply feeding them is insufficient. I must give thought to improving their education and put effort into maintaining their souls. They come home after a long day at school, and their eyes plead with me to ask, to listen, to advise. In matters of schoolwork, yes, but even more in social affairs. Where people meet, there is tension, and where children meet, unresolved tension can lead to blowups, and to fragile souls. My eyes are open to see and my ears are open to hear even what is not said. Their eyes speak, and I do everything I can so that my children can live their days with happy eyes.

More than the rest, I worry about Amschel Meir, my oldest son. He is an introvert, and it is my job to spur him into action and coax his worries out of him. And he has no shortage of worries. Even after he completes his homework, answering each question in turn, and even after his tutor rejoices over his perfect answers, he continues to tinker and revise and wonder if anything is still missing. His imagination tends toward ideas whose essence shrinks down to a small bit of sorrow. And why should a child like him, who has yet to bear the full brunt of life, have to carry such a burden of anguish and frustration? Time spent with his father imbues him with peace and confidence, making me sigh with relief, but also raises a worrisome question: What will he do when he is forced to part with the hand holding his and bear the troubles of life alone?

I hope time, as well as my treatment of his tender soul, will remove his worries and strengthen him sufficiently, in a measure appropriate to the reality that drags us along.

Among the walls of our lively home, filled with laughter, conversation, words of Torah and wisdom and wit, in line with the passage

"May your home be an eternal house of wisdom," fights and scuffles also occur, accompanied by teasing and cursing in a language whose origin is outside of textbooks. It is obviously my position to improvise appropriate channels for peace between the adversaries.

The seed of calamity is Nathan. Though he is the fourth child and the third son, he has his heart set on uninhibited control, and insists on making the decisions, a fact that riles up the other fighting roosters, especially the older ones. Not only does he incite the chaos, but he also emerges victorious from every fight. His power is in his mouth, and to this day not a single child has been found who can withstand his sharp, quick tongue. When he is furious, this tongue spews fiery arrows at his siblings, as if they were ignoramuses, which they are not, of course. Each of my children is smart and intellectual in their own way.

He never compromises, not even when it comes to petty things. For instance, the most recent bit of drama: dishes were piled on the dining table, which is also used for doing homework. These dishes had been cleaned and polished by two pairs of hands: mine and dear Schönche's, my little helper. Nathan looked unhappily at the crowded table and went to do his homework in our bedroom, at the tiny desk in the corner. On my way to grab another rag, I walked by the room and peeked in at Nathan, leaned over the desk, concentrating on his work. As long as he keeps busy, there is peace and calm all around. On my way back, rag in hand, I caught Amschel entering our bedroom as well, and placing his books absentmindedly on the edge of the shelf. Nathan looked away from his notebook and toward the books that had invaded his space, and then toward his brother, finally letting his eyes rest on him.

"What's this?" he muttered, pursing his lips with distaste, his usual expression before a row.

"Oh, these are two new books," Amschel answered matter-of-factly. "I'm putting them here until the table becomes available. Carry on with your schoolwork, little brother."

Nathan scrunched his face and snorted. "How dare you?" he railed. "Just because you were born before me does not give you any special rights, except one: you'll die before me too, and the sooner you leave this world, the better."

I was unhappy, of course, both with the content of his words and with the rage that accompanied them. I knew for certain there was only one way this fight could end, and it would not be a desirable end by any means. Nevertheless, I stayed out of it for the time being. I ran the rag over the furniture, wiping away dust while watching what was happening out of the corner of my eye.

Amschel was about to answer his brother, but then thought better of it, turned his back on him, and began to head out the door.

"Where do you think you're going?" asked Nathan.

Amschel offered no response.

Nathan tossed the books aside, letting them crash loudly to the floor. Amschel turned back, looked angrily at his poor books, and raised his fist at his unruly brother. But Nathan was faster. He evaded the blow and punched his brother in the stomach. Amschel writhed with pain, and I rushed to his aid, scolding Nathan. Amschel pushed me away and swallowed his tears. He gathered his books and went into his bedroom, where he lay in bed. In the privacy of the bedroom he allowed me to look at his belly, and after I ran my hand tenderly over it and made sure he was feeling better, I went back to see Nathan, who was sitting at the desk, staring at his notebook.

"Your behavior is shameful," I said.

Nathan kept his eyes on his notebook.

"You must apologize to your brother," I urged him, still upset, due to both Amschel's physical pain and his humiliation, and because I wished their father could be there, standing between them, instead of me. But he, as usual, was away.

"Amschel is the one who put his books on the shelf and he was about to hit me. I was only defending myself. One of us would have been hit, and I wasn't going to volunteer to be the victim. He made two mistakes." A well-reasoned argument, conveyed precisely.

"And you had no part in it?" I insisted.

"My part was in defending myself."

"And how about some generosity on your part? If you'd only let him put his books down, this could have all been avoided."

"He didn't ask permission, he just put them there, as if he didn't even need to ask."

"Had he asked, would you have agreed?"

"Maybe."

At least he was being honest, I told myself, seeking weak encouragement to settle my nerves. Still, I fixed him with a scolding look. "A little kindness on your part would go a long way, Nathan. Go ask him how he is doing and tell him you did not mean for this to happen," I concluded, leaving the room to ponder why it is always Nathan performing the violence, always prepared with an accusation of someone else, leaving me bitter, unable to refute his arguments.

Oh, how badly I need Meir at home. In times like these, the quickest solution I can think of is to turn the scuffling parties' attention to their father's presence. Then the cries and threats die down instantly, raised arms drop to the sides of bodies, and innocent looks dart all around, trying to evade the threatening eyes in the doorway.

Aware that my children, just like their father, have unending resources of energy, I've found that the most efficient way to put out fires is by channeling that energy toward performing tasks. They are eager to accept them, though sometimes even this can start a battle, and then I find myself in the midst of an exhausting brawl. To prevent such tiring scenarios, each child must be directed toward a task suitable to his or her talents. I quickly learned that the most desirable tasks are those connected to the business. I therefore tend to aim the boys toward accounting, and Meir, who instinctively understands why a gaggle of children has suddenly convened around him in his office, gives them envelopes and packages to mail, each according to their carrying abilities.

I believe that good can come from bad, and that the day is not far off when my sons will use their capabilities for more significant business errands. Meir is already laying the groundwork, and I know that no training is better than that provided by a person who has hard proof of success.

◆ ◆ ◆

My three sons—Amschel, Shlomo, and Nathan—are doing very well at school. Meir and I are pleased with their progress in all subjects: reading, writing, Torah, prayer, the Pentateuch with Rashi interpretation. Amschel has already started studying the Talmud, and will transfer to the primary yeshiva next year. My sons can quote whole passages by heart, recite complex interpretations, and read Hebrew and Aramaic as well as they can read Judendeutsch.

But though they may be smart and studious, they all have wandering eyes, and they all wander toward the same focal point: their father's business. This curiosity intensifies with the years, though I must point out that Meir accepts this weakness of vision with pride and love. While they pore over books, their lips mumbling holy words that often bore them to death, their eyes slant toward unholy affairs, and Meir winks at me: "I am happy with their studiousness, but more so with their wandering."

"Don't you wish one of them to become a Rothschild rabbi, and make your late father's dream come true?"

"Mmm . . . ," he wonders, then replies, "Let's just say that I respect Torah students, and even more so rabbis. But when it comes to my sons, I prefer for them to be holy men of banking, taking after their father."

I myself still hope that one of my sons makes Meir's father's dream come true.

Wednesday, October 11th, 1786

Another night is here, and once again I'm writing away, asking the clock to slow its pace and allow me to deliver the flood of words emerging from my heart through feather and ink, onto the page.

While we are on the subject of celebrating our new home, a new celebration has arrived. For years, ever since receiving the title of court banker, Meir has been fighting to receive a travel permit. His applications were denied again and again without any explanation. Nighttime and Sundays were strictly prohibited, and it seemed they would remain that way forever.

Well, his efforts have finally borne fruit. A justice of the peace in Frankfurt has granted him the coveted permit. The meaning of this is only clear to me now: Meir will be able to conduct his business much more freely, exempt from the series of humiliations and prohibitions he used to experience at the Judengasse gate.

My admiration for this accomplishment multiplies in light of the rumor of Goethe's failure to procure the very same permit. Goethe, who has recently been appointed secret advisor to the Duke of Saxe-Weimar, tried to use this position in order to procure a travel permit for his protégé, the Jewish man Lub Reis, who serves as court banker for the duchy of Saxe-Weimar. But Goethe failed. Lub Reis did not receive a permit.

My heart ached for the man, one of ours, who did not get his wish, but I must admit that at the same time I felt elation, thinking about my Meir succeeding where Goethe had failed. A twenty-room palace is no guarantee for success with the government.

Meir has taken this permit as a divine decree ordering him to never rest. He is expanding the scope of his business and his voyages, and I hope and pray that he can handle it. The shaky carriage rides and the hours spent sitting on hard wooden benches are making his piles worse, and he is in constant pain.

Sometimes, while meeting with one of his deep-pocketed customers, in the height of negotiation, his buttocks urge him to close the deal right away, screaming soundlessly, sending hints as sharp as razors. Meir attempts to conceal his uncontrollable writhing, walking in silly circles, placing a hand on his forehead comically, as if thinking hard, and, once he has felt the dampness of blood in his underwear, to the surprise of his counterpart, suddenly closing the deal, naming the lowest price of negotiation. He slams the ancient coins on the table, grabs the bag of money without counting its contents, bows in parting, and hurries to the door without turning his back to his customer. Once he has left, he embarks in a running dance, to the satisfaction of the customer, who has enjoyed both a successful transaction and an amusing negotiation.

I try to convince him: "Do not sit for too long. Sitting makes piles worse," but it is no use. Luckily, God made Shabbat, the day of rest, which creates breaks in his schedule, limiting his absence from home and forcing him to rest. On Fridays, I prepare a bowl of warm water for him to sit in, after which he massages the blushing part between his aching buttocks with olive oil, hoping to feel some relief for several days.

"Your poor stomach," I say, taking pity on him. "It accumulates and accumulates, and you sit and sit, and nothing comes out."

"Why is it so stubborn?" he asks, prolonging our medical discussion.

"It's your anus that's the stubborn one. It holds on to the filth rather than set it free."

Meir loses himself in thought, and from the thicket of his pain a jolt of laughter is released. "Did you just say *filth*? You aren't talking about that caricature, are you?"

I look at him blankly for a moment, but then the caricature materializes before my eyes, infecting me with Meir's laughter.

A week ago, Meir placed a German newspaper in front of me. I cannot read German. What was I to do with the paper?

"Turn the page," he ordered in the tone of a man in the know.

I did as he said. On the second page I found a caricature of Meir, showing him squatting in order to defecate, but rather than excrement, banknotes emerge from his bottom.

"Do you know what it says?" Meir pointed to the title, answering immediately, emphasizing the word: "Filth."

This is people's way of criticizing and ridiculing a successful Jew. His wealth makes them uncomfortable. According to them, Jews must focus on Torah studies and not show any interest in money, and they're allowed to express their discomfort through any means, especially the press, where they are immune to any response.

And indeed, we have no way of responding.

◆ ◆ ◆

There are two sides to Meir's absences from home.

It would be dishonest for me to ignore the benefit of his departures. They allow me to answer the children's unmet maternal needs and spend all my time with them without feeling guilty for turning my attention to them at their father's expense. The time I have allows me to devote larger chunks to each of them, more for some and less for others, according to their needs.

But this should not be taken to mean I do not miss my Meir. On the contrary, I am rich with longing, accruing it with interest, packing it carefully in the satchel of my heart, along with the love coins—the good-morning coins that I keep in the chest. As they say, "A woman yearns for her husband when he is on the road." As the days wear on, my level of longing rises, and when my heart is overcome I can begin to feel stifled. After the day's work all I want is to curl up in our bed, cling to his body, and absorb moments of peace and comfort from the sound of his voice, his caresses, his body heat, until I fall into a sweet sleep. Though I am strong and able to move mountains, run my life, and answer my children's needs, big or small, before I say goodbye to the day and give in to slumber, I need Meir by my side, as if I were a baby myself.

But since I know he will come, if not tomorrow then the following day, and if not the following day then at the end of the week at the latest, I am able to restrain my emotions and pep up to deal with the challenges of waiting.

Before he even walks in, I am informed of his imminent arrival by the children crying out from the street, "Papa's here! Papa's here!" or the neighbors calling, "Gutaleh, come to the window, see who came to visit." I rush to the window, ripping off my apron, tucking stray hairs under my coif, and pinching my cheeks like a girl about to head out to a meeting with her lover. Meir takes long strides toward our home, answering those who greet him on his way. When he is close to the house, he looks up at the window, removes his hat, bows, and reveals an enchanting smile, awakening within me an urge to cover him with kisses.

Seeing the sunrise in his eyes in spite of his fatigue and suffering on the road, seeing the beauty of his face, becoming enveloped in his embracing arms, waiting in trembling expectation to the night of love-making we have to look forward to—this is the gift I wait breathlessly for when he returns from his trips.

Among those seeking Meir's services was a high-ranking man named Karl Anselm, prince of Thurn and Taxis. Meir's contact with him has contributed to an unusual spurt in the growth of our business. Meir told me that Anselm's Italian family has been managing the errand services of the Holy Roman Empire in Rome for many years now. The son, Karl, who had inherited from his forefathers a franchise to manage the post and errand service, has transferred his center of activity to Frankfurt, as was the custom of those who wished to promote their business, moving away from the outskirts and closer to the heart of the city. As it turned out, Frankfurt provided the necessary conditions for success.

We are fortunate to be living in this central city, Frankfurt, and to have Meir so involved in the city's commerce. Meir tells me about life outside of the ghetto. If it wasn't for him, I could never have imagined just how bustling it is. The constant traffic of people, horse-drawn carriages, sellers and buyers, civilians and soldiers, servants and porters, Christian merchants and Jewish merchants, money changers, coachmen, guests from nearby and visitors from afar, people with deep pockets and people with shallow ones, all rubbing shoulders in the port city on the banks of the Main River.

Meir forges his way among all of them. He speaks fervently of his goods, offering, persuading, signing deals with regular and random customers, and acquiring more and more potential buyers.

The demand for postal and errand services is constantly growing, and Anselm's hands are filled with work and bills of exchange. Meir is asked to discount bills for him regularly, and is entrusted with short-term loans. With his pleasant demeanor and spirit of self-sacrifice with which Meir performs his role, he has managed to win Anselm's heart. Of course, due to the scope of his work, Anselm also employs other bankers, and yet a respectable portion of this bill work is given over to Meir.

But Meir is not the kind of man to make do with this. His far-seeing gaze is in constant motion, coming up with new ideas and translating them from concept into action. This time, his speed of thought and depth of perception have led him to form a new area in Anselm's errand service: a news service, as he calls it. One of Meir's keys to success is the acquisition of knowledge. "Knowledge is power," he says, then adds, "The first to know is the first to act."

A never-ending source of knowledge is hidden in some of the postal envelopes. All one has to do is to sniff the right ones out and be the first to open them, before they reach their destination. After committing all information to memory, one must seal the envelope in a way that raises no suspicion, and make immediate use of the new information.

Meir's restless brain has caught on to Anselm's ways. The man is not above the aforementioned method if it means he can pass on information to the emperor and be paid a pretty sum. "If Anselm is doing it, why shouldn't I?" Meir concluded, and I recalled a similar conclusion he'd come to when he witnessed the success of Oppenheimer, the Jewish banker of Hanover. I dared challenge him. "Is it moral to open other people's letters?" Meir answered my question with a question of his own. "Is it moral and fair that they open ours?" Then he explained: "Gutaleh, such are the rules of war. Until someone higher up dictates clear and fair rules of commerce, people will do whatever it takes to promote themselves by their own standards. All means are permitted on the road to achieving goals, as long as they are not in contradiction with the existing laws. Of course, we must also make sure not to break the decrees posed by our holy Torah."

In order to establish his role, Meir asked Anselm's permission to see the letters. He dug through them, coming up with some information of value that he'd collected from the letters and presented to a surprised Anselm. From there the road to clinching a collaboration between the two was as quick as the flick of a letter opener.

I do not feel comfortable with this choice Meir has made. Is it corrupt? My heart asks me, but I say nothing. I am not an expert on all rules, and if some rules are missing, other people are responsible for making them. At the same time, I wonder about his statement, that he is in constant competition and must do everything in his power to win, as well as his statement that if someone is permitted to open the letters of Jews, why shouldn't we Jews open the letters of our gentile competitors? There is some truth to that. There is no doubt that in his ambitious attitude and his determination to overcome the competition, he is showing spirit. Only the bold can win.

I am certain it is God's will that we succeed.

◆ ◆ ◆

I turned down the children's beds and tucked them in. I sang Babette a lullaby, told Isabella the same story twice until her long lashes came together, then told it a third time for Nathan, who demanded to hear it too, alone. I stood near each of my beloved children, listening to their soft breathing. They are innocent angels in their sleep, peaceful and delicate, submitting to the graces of slumber. Through sleep, they become charged with power, and when they awake they will demonstrate their new energy.

I love my children's energy, but this does not mean I do not wish for a bit of peace and quiet. And they, these beloved children, growing before my eyes, filling my heart to the brim, they need it too.

Now I will sit down to make up for lost time.

A few months after we moved our belongings to the new house, the landgrave Wilhelm left Hanau. His servants and aides packed up his things, and along with his wife and children, his mistresses and bastard children, his servants and horses and chariots, he left Hanau and rode through the valley, through Fulda, until he reached the princedom of Hesse-Kassel, where his father, Frederick II, had ruled and which he left to his son upon his death. I am describing this move because of its meaningful effect on our lives.

Meir is very concerned about the future of his business. The landgrave, who has given him the title of court banker, is now far away from us—out of sight, out of mind, out of pocket, and out of business. Just when there has been significant progress in their relationship, the landgrave abandons his seat in Hanau and travels all the way to Kassel, capital of the great Landgraviate of Hesse. Kassel is not as accessible as Hanau, which is only an hour from Frankfurt by carriage. Getting to Kassel requires many days of travel. It seems like all of Meir's hard work is coming to nothing, and we are at a dead end on one of the most important roads to our success.

I recalled the ten-year-old Meir's encounter with the landgrave, and the young landgrave's promise that he would never forget the special day he spent on Judengasse, promising that his door was always open if Meir ever needed help.

Perhaps this is the time to remind the landgrave of this? But what good would a reminder do? It cannot shorten the geographic distance.

The wrinkles on Meir's forehead have deepened. I've pushed away the children whenever they try to approach him. "Papa is bound by the shackles of his own thoughts, and we must give him some quiet and time until, with God's help, he reaches the appropriate conclusions."

Meir gathered his items every day, with attention, with laborious insistence, with careful examination, sleeping less, putting off everyday tasks, and temporarily putting off business trips. He did not rest until he could present an impressive collection of rare items: coins, medals, pearls, precious stones, and valuable works of art. He placed them one by one in a padded box, which he then carried with special care, as if carrying a newborn. Finally, his treasure hidden in a secret compartment of his carriage, he traveled 150 kilometers north, to Kassel. I said goodbye to my man and his high hopes with moist eyes, then rushed to our room, took hold of the Star of David hanging on the wall, and said a prayer.

The landgrave did not try to conceal the sparkle in his eyes when he saw the contents of the box, and was eager to accept the goods for the extremely discounted price he was offered. It seemed the plan had succeeded, and Meir's loss in this sale was calculated against the next steps he would take. If this treasure reminded the landgrave of Meir's involvement in some of his transactions, it would be enough.

Unfortunately, the venerable man, busy handling the great wealth he had just inherited (rumor has it he had come into over 100,000,000 gulden) and lost in an intoxication only money can cause, turned to his more important business and left Meir standing alone, arms spread, embarrassed, and staring into space.

After some time, someone took hold of his spread arms from behind and put them in their regular place, near his body. Meir got hold of himself and turned around, his concerned face meeting the affectionate one of Buderus.

"Do not lose heart, my friend," Buderus whispered, embracing him. "Some water flows freely to the lake, while other water must pass over rocks and bumps before it can settle. The important thing is not to back down, but to wear down those bumps and pass over them."

Meir nodded in agreement and thanked the man meekly. He shook kind Buderus's hand. The man had recently become one of his most devoted customers, and his growing business required Meir's assistance in the management of investments in bonds and real estate.

Meir's been sniffing around Landgrave Wilhelm's business transactions for a while. Whenever one of the big bankers is found to be taking care of another discounted bill or another loan for the landgrave, Meir feels as if someone has punched him in the stomach. Dealing with competitors is a difficult summit to climb, since these are experienced bankers who have been handling the business of the father, Frederick II, for dozens of years, and have naturally gone on to handle his son's business as well. These old bankers are tough as nails, and their names, spoken by Meir, make me furious: the Bethmann brothers, Preye and Jordis, Rüppell and Harnier. Even the Jewish one, Fiedel David, does not sound pleasant to my ears. I envision them standing in a row, aiming their cannons toward my Meir. I loathe those overfed thieves, taking all the cake for themselves, not leaving even a crumb for anyone else.

Meir's hunger for financial success is insatiable. If someone would only let him, he would prove that his services are more efficient than the services of all those oily bankers put together. He sees for miles, and plans for the future. I believe in him and know that even if a wide crack forms in his path, he will know how to seal it, and eventually arrive at his desired destination.

Tuesday, December 1st, 1789

I have no time to write, but I must document one detail until I have time to write more extensively about others.

Meir came home from one of his business trips. He kissed me hastily and shook my shoulders. "Gutaleh, remember these three words that are worth more than gold: *Liberté, égalité, fraternité.*"

"What's that?" I laughed, trying to interpret his excitement.

"It's French."

"French? Since when do you speak French?"

"I don't. But we are lucky enough to be living in historically important times."

I looked at him blankly.

"Listen, Gutaleh." He was panting as if someone had just told him he had another son. "Human rights have just been defined in France: *Liberté, égalité, fraternité.* Liberty, equality, and fraternity."

"Well?"

"Don't you see?"

"What does that have to do with us Jews?"

"We are people too, are we not?"

"Since when do we count as people? And what do we have to do with the French, with all due respect to this impressive declaration?"

Meir looked at me forgivingly, as if saying, *I won't let you kill my joy.* "That's the thing. From France, these rights will eventually reach the Jews, and then our path will be laid out."

I truly did not mean to spoil his good mood, but I could not accept this baseless giddiness. A few depressing words stood on the tip of my tongue, but I chose silence.

Meir turned away from me and my silence, frowning.

Saturday night, October 9th, 1790

Our God, God of our fathers, may this month be a month of blessings. Blessings of goodness and blessings of joy. Salvation and solace. Livelihood and good fortune. Good life and peace. Forgiveness for sins and transgressions. May this new month be the end to all of our troubles.

God be exalted, the downfalls in our life lead to new heights.

As usual, I shall begin with maternal news: there are now two new Rothschilds running around our house: two-year-old Kalman and six-month-old Julie, may they both live long and happy lives.

I won't say much about the baby girl we lost three years ago, before Kalman was born, nor will I write her name, because the wound is still bleeding, and will continue to bleed. No new baby can heal the loss of a baby who received a name, lived in this world for a short while, and became a part of my heart before suddenly writhing in my arms, her small body burning with fever. Nothing helped, no cold compresses, lukewarm baths, or potions prescribed by the doctor. Her eyes, which tore me apart, pleading for help, grew tired and slowly closed. I breathed heavily along with her, trying to fill her with strength to continue inhaling and exhaling, but she grew distant, continued to wilt, slowly and painfully, until finally she grew limp, taken from this world, leaving her misery quiet and hidden in the back of my heart.

Her death carries the weight of the deaths of all my lost children. An entire chamber of my heart is filled with longing for her, a longing I know will never stop. Longing for her sweet scent, her soft body, her small gestures, her little kicks, her smile, her cries, her gurgling, her suckling, the way I rocked her in my arms, the warmth of her body against mine, her rhythmic breath, every part of her face and body, her eyes closing at the sound of the lullaby, her pleasure as I bathed her with warm water and soap.

Mein liebes Kind. My dear child. Pain takes a thousand forms. Sometimes it pricks, other times it crawls. Sometimes it pinches and other times it weighs heavy. Sometimes it groans and other times it screams. Sometimes it is silent, other times it tries to speak. Now it is crawling up my stomach as I try to decipher its words.

I ache for the things I didn't have the chance to do with her in her brief life. I never had the chance to comb her hair and tie it in a bow. I never had the chance to adorn her small body in Babette's dresses, which she had inherited from Isabella and Schönche, and which were waiting, folded, in one of the alcoves. I had yet to tell her stories, teach her cooking and sewing and reading and writing, and I had yet to guide her through the secrets of life.

They say that when a child enters the world, an angel comes down from heaven to watch over them. Where was her angel?

Meir and I lingered in the cold lap of our tragedy for a while. There is no comfort in knowing that death visits many homes. The pain, which hit us mercilessly, is our private pain. Would crying release our grief? But God has abandoned us.

We spoke little. Words were so fragile.

Together we experienced moments of hope and together we felt their bitter end. When crisis knocked on our door, our emotions were diluted by their constant overlapping. His tears flow from my eyes, mixing with mine.

Why? we asked. We received no answer. God works in mysterious ways.

With time, I was surprised to feel a robust thread emerging from the clench of pain, tightening our already strong bond even more. Meir felt it too, and the way he held me and was held by me was more powerful than words. We applied the salve of love to our wound.

After some time, I leaned on the strength of our union and decided it was time to stop our downward journey into misery. Against the feeling of annihilation, which was taking hold of our hearts, unmooring us, my household insisted on its right to be rebuilt. Decisively, I pulled Meir up from the depths of mourning and sent him on his way. Success can cushion his pain, balance his mood, and pull me up along with him, even if I never toss aside the shroud of grief, I will weep in secret. Sorrow turns out the lights, but I wish for light to shine constantly on my family.

I gather the remains of our grief, shove them deep into a neglected compartment, subjecting my will to the sanctity of my family, and making room for the sounds of life and the sight of light shining on the faces of my loved ones, like the sun that had been hiding behind the clouds and has now appeared upon their scattering.

Strengthened by the knowledge that I hold the colors and the brush and the choice of color, I chose to paint the gray walls in bright shades.

Thus I walk, sometimes my eyes weeping but my heart cheerful, other times my eyes laughing while my heart sobs, trying to lift my spirits and convince my mind that there is no point in feeling sorrow.

What more can I say? This is enough. I had already determined not to go on about this. The ink cries, the page is stained with tears. I push aside the event to the bottom of my memory, though it continues to force its way to the front, and I turn my back on this sharp slope downward, and instead will dedicate my words to the upward path. I must give thanks for what I have.

◆　◆　◆

The chambers of my heart knock about against each other in the tumultuous racket of life. In contrast to my moments of worry, due to the illness of one of the children or the elusive changing mood of another, requiring deciphering and care, there are other moments filled with satisfaction, pride, hope, and gratitude.

My two oldest sons, seventeen-year-old Amschel and sixteen-year-old Shlomo, whose faces are tinged with buds of red hair, have achieved the peak of their ambitions—joining their father's business. They work together all day long, from the early morning until the late evening. Their talent for business, a result of the sights and sounds they have absorbed from the office in our home, is now awakening in all its glory. Meir watches them with his kind eyes and lets out a sigh of relief when he sees their eagerness and their abilities, action backed by witty thought. He is not afraid to task them with jobs that are normally given to more experienced employees. No more small errands. They know the business, and are now participating in the Frankfurt fair for the second time. Over dinner, they report the commercial success they've enjoyed, such as buying an item for a low price and selling it for a higher price, and they search for approval in their father's eyes. The conversations around the dinner table grow ever louder.

The French Revolution and the Storming of the Bastille are making their marks on the Frankfurt fair. Meir is aware of the market trends, and has prepared for them in advance. The luxury items that have covered his stalls have been replaced with consumer commodities, which are now in high demand, and therefore significantly more expensive. These changes have done wonders for the business, and Meir is constantly coming up with ideas on how to use the situation to our benefit.

And lo and behold, he has become the greatest wool, cotton, and flour merchant in the area, enjoying the much-needed help of his older sons.

Meir makes daily use of his travel permit, leaving Judengasse whenever he chooses. He is not even limited by the ghetto gates, now locked in honor of the crowning of Leopold II as Holy Roman emperor, following the death of Joseph II, and he walks out freely. He smiles at the thought that for the first time he, a Jew, is permitted to enter the central cathedral grounds and watch the crowning parade. But since he was ordered to remain hidden behind one of the houses, he decided he was in too much of a rush anyway, and while the royal parade made its way through the city streets before a gathering crowd, the cannons thundering, he turned his back on the vision and continued to his destination.

Obviously, our small home can no longer contain the amount of goods that are growing at dizzying speed. Meir has rented storage facilities outside of the ghetto, and those are growing constantly as well.

To me, the words "storage facilities outside of the ghetto" sound like something out of a fairy tale. We, residents of Judengasse, have goods stored outside of the ghetto? This is unheard of. The wonders Meir works are inconceivable to me, but once he's accomplished them they become obvious. I ask myself what we would do without them.

The upward direction of Meir's business activity compensates for the difficulties in his relationship with the landgrave Wilhelm. Meir goes to Kassel, capital of Hesse, from time to time, but other than extensive descriptions of the elegant capital, the many gardens, and the glamorous Wilhelmshöhe Palace, he has no real news. Buderus goes above and beyond, trying to improve Meir's prestige in Wilhelm's eyes. He keeps repeating Meir's noble qualities to the landgrave: his integrity and modesty, his extraordinary service, and his energy and intelligence, which are incomparable among big bankers.

Meir has great hope for Buderus's influence on the landgrave. Recently, Buderus has been promoted in his majesty's accounting department. This was the result of yet another financial trick suggested by Buderus. Seeing how the number of Wilhelm's illegitimate children was on the rise, Buderus suggested that for each bastard birth, the price of salt be increased by one kreuzer. Wilhelm calculated the projected profits. He never imagined, in his greedy mind, that his children would become part of his blossoming business, making him thousands of thalers. He calculated his projected profits and informed Buderus of his promotion with the same breath.

Buderus quickly took advantage of his master's fine spirits, and when the man opened his eyes, having indulged in his financial hallucinations, Buderus placed Meir's letter in his hands. This is what he had written:

> His venerable majesty, the honorable Landgrave of Hesse and its capital, Kassel,
> I approach the honorable landgrave with the utmost obedience and deference to remind him of the devoted service I had offered him during his time as landgrave of Hanau.
> I must thank his majesty for a second, a third, and a fourth time for his great generosity and the honor he has bestowed upon me with the title of "court banker."
> I have no doubt in my mind that, considering our relationship of mutual appreciation, this title will continue to hold true now that the venerable landgrave rules over Hesse-Kassel.
> Holding on to the connection that has been formed between us, and with great appreciation for his majesty's integrity and kindness, I now dare turn to him and offer my continuing and growing services, based on the fact

known by his majesty and the state revenue service, that all my payments have withstood the test of pristine care.

I am therefore offering my services in the bill business, and promising that I will match the highest of all prices offered thus far for his majesty's bills by any of his bankers.

At his service always,

Meir Amschel Rothschild, court banker

The landgrave beamed with happiness from the flattery, a hint of curiosity reflected in his eyes. Buderus wasted no time, hanging on to that hint of a chance, and complimented the letter's author, while undertaking to provide information about Meir Rothschild's financial assets.

He prepared an initial list titled "Meir Rothschild," and this is its essence, as was passed on to Meir:

An extremely impressive scope of assets—please ignore the fact that in the Jewish community's accounting ledgers a capital of only 2,000 gulden appears and there is no sign of his properties, because the owner keeps his income secret; proven honesty, accuracy in debt payment (which gives him an advantage in receiving credit); consistency in offering the highest return for any service related to bills of exchange; fast, reliable, and devoted service.

Next, Meir was required to provide numbers. It was obvious that his insistence on keeping his income secret made things more difficult for Buderus, and our modest lifestyle did not provide testimony for ownership of great assets. Therefore Meir, as a one-time, unusual measure, agreed to provide his friend with the confidential numbers, after securing a promise that these would never leave Wilhelm's chambers.

The fruits of these latest efforts have not ripened, considering the volumes of credit that are constantly streaming into the hands of the business opponents. But Meir is patient. His first tiny bit of credit, for the amount of 800 pounds, was received with stomach spasms. His sniffing, envious nose did not miss the fact that at the same time, another court banker, Fiedel David, received credit for the amount of 25,000 pounds.

"It's like setting an obstacle for one runner while the others stride ahead, obstacle-free," he complained in the privacy of our room. But in public he displayed perfect equanimity, even thanking his benefactor for the trust he has put in him.

After waiting several months, Meir made a second application to the landgrave for credit in the amount of 10,000 pounds. This time, the landgrave approved an amount of 2,000 pounds. I buried the insult deep in my growing belly, and along with my Meir, put on the serene face of a person who knows their future.

It is not easy to be the wife of a man who does everything in his power to bring honor to his family.

But at the same time, there is no greater honor.

Sunday, July 1st, 1792

We have ten children! Five boys and five girls.

In spite of the difficult tests God has put us through, He took care to complete our coveted minyan. The eldest, Schönche, and after her, Amschel Meir, Shlomo Meir, Nathan Meir, Isabella, Babette, Kalman Meir, Julie, Henrietta, may she live a long and healthy life, who is just over a year old, and baby Yaakov Meir, may he live a long and healthy life, who was born a month and a half ago, on May 15th.

I look at my Schönche. The years have improved her looks. Her face is beautiful, in spite of its paleness, and her lithe body curves in all the right spots. My daughter is in love. She often asks about my love for Meir, and whenever de Worms's name comes up, her face turns red, which adds vitality to its pale complexion. I now believe that this man has forged a path to her heart. She is ready for marriage.

I must sleep. The sky will soon part with the fading light of stars, making way for the rising sun, and I have yet to close my eyes.

Tuesday, October 30th, 1792

The course of my life and my family's life is strewn with mysterious, convoluted question marks. Once the existing questions are answered, new ones appear. The enigmas of my life make it fascinating, complicated, and filled with activity: a vibrant fabric of life, changing constantly, and it is only due to lack of time that I cannot document it all in my notebook, not even most of it. And yet, I manage, from time to time, to steal a moment to fulfill this need to write, which brings me comfort and release.

Two important events have taken place in Frankfurt in the past year. The first was the crowning of Francis II as Holy Roman emperor, after Leopold II, crowned only two years ago, had passed away. The Jews did not attend the crowning ceremony due to an ancient and explicit prohibition. Once again Meir decided to forego the questionable honor he had been given, to show up and watch the parade from one of the windows, choosing instead to put the time into his business.

I mention the crowning because there was much debate on our street about the uncertain future of the Roman Empire, all because of the second event, which took place eight days ago, shaking the foundations of Frankfurt entirely, and the ghetto specifically. Rumors of the

French Revolution and the Storming of the Bastille on July 14th, 1789, have spread and made their way here. We have been following the news of the incarceration of Louis XVI along with his wife, Queen Marie Antoinette—daughter of Francis I, once the Holy Roman emperor, and the strong empress, Maria Theresa.

I have cultivated an interest in Marie Antoinette. Ever since the day she was mentioned in Meir's conversation with the boys around the dining table, I ask about her, and as experts in extracting reliable information about the events in Europe, they are glad to deliver gossip spiced with sensational scandals from the royal French court.

Her picture often appears in the newspaper. I look at one of hers from better days, smiling handsomely, wearing a magnificent dress with a cinched waist and a wide skirt, a hat decorated with feathers and flowers, and expensive jewelry. So graceful and so regal. Standing in front of the painter, she could never have guessed that her life was about to change irrevocably. Considering her situation today, there's no escaping the thought of how tumultuous life is. No one knows what a day might bring. One day you're a queen, the next a victim of the people's frustrated outburst.

I am ambivalent about the queen. On the one hand, I understand that her heart is merciful, concerned for the impoverished of France. I was touched by the description of the tragic event that took place on her wedding day, when the fireworks burst into flames, and hundreds of people were trampled to death while fleeing. Who understands the meaning of fire better than the people of Judengasse? And she, Marie Antoinette, took pity on the families of victims, cared for them, and even donated her monthly allowance to them. They say she advised her husband, the king, to collect taxes from the nobles, but the nobles protested. This behavior is certainly honorable as far as I'm concerned.

On the other hand, her actions and words in the royal court were unacceptable to the French people. Her royal lifestyle, her exhibited wealth, and her wastefulness inspired their fury. They picked on her clothes, her jewels, and her expensive shoes, claiming she had taken those from their hungry mouths. And who understands the sensitivity of the simple people better than those who were born and raised on Judengasse?

They further condemn her permissive behavior, calling her a man chaser and a hedonist. This queen attracts fire.

True, she must live in the palace and live the court life, and everyone knows that this Austrian woman was expected to behave like the French ever since her marriage, but could she not have acted more modestly, shown more discretion with the number of outfits she displayed to the public, if only in order to better consider the emotions of her people, who are starving for bread?

On the matter of the bread, rumor has it that the French people have attributed the saying "Let them eat cake" to the queen. Meir is convinced that this unfortunate statement about the bread and the cake was not spoken by Marie Antoinette, but rather by her sister, Maria Carolina, queen of Naples. "Anyone who makes the slightest effort opening Jean-Jacques Rousseau's book from 1766 can find it quoted there," he said confidently, adding, "Marie was a ten-year-old at the time, four years before marrying Louis. She could not have imagined becoming the queen of France."

I try to fathom the people's rage. As long as people live without having to worry too much about their livelihoods, they do not question the royal family too thoroughly. But the moment their source of income is taken away, they look up, examining what goes on in the ivory tower. When they don't like what they see, they mercilessly judge the traitors they had previously trusted, and every bit of rumor that reaches them becomes a convicting fact. The fact that Louis and Marie did not come through for their people was enough to add more and more bills of indictment, which pass between people like a fire spreading through wooden houses.

But I mostly want to talk about the vision of the French soldiers that have burst through the open gates of our ghetto, and the arguments they have started among us.

For several weeks, we tracked the French soldiers' campaign, commanded by the glamorous General Adam Philippe, Comte de Custine. His name is spoken by Judengasse residents along with a shaking of the head, as if to say, "Beware." After General Beware's soldiers conquered Speyer, Worms, and Mainz, it was Frankfurt's turn. The soldiers, intoxicated with victory and striding toward battle, continued on to Frankfurt, and the city council convened an emergency meeting. It was clear that Frankfurt would be conquered too. The council reached a quick decision, and eight days ago the gates of the city were opened to the invaders in order to prevent total destruction. Above the armory building, located outside of Bockenheimer Gate, the French victors raised the flag of the revolution.

I sat with Meir and our children near the window in the living room, our eyes wide at the sight of new traffic on our street. The same alert faces were seen in all the other windows. Our home was filled with suspense and expectation, making us all fall silent. I placed little Yaakov on my lap with his face toward the window. I hugged my seven-month-old baby, and watched the odd company of soldiers marching down our street, carrying the three key words of the French Revolution: *Liberté, égalité, fraternité*. Liberty, equality, fraternity.

Little Yaakov was riveted by the sight. His body, only recently adjusted to crawling on his stomach, now stretched up, his feet trying to hover over my knees, his small fists punching the air with special excitement. He shifted his eyes between them and me, his face beaming. He blurted out enthusiastic sounds, as if trying to say something.

Until now, I naively believed that conquering soldiers wore the aura of victory. That their appearance projected power and force. That their uniforms were ironed and their shoes perfectly polished. That they wore shiny badges on their shoulders, their threatening weapons raised into the air. But to my surprise, General Beware's exalted army had none of these features. His soldiers looked like a bad joke. Had they not been our enemy, I would have offered them some M. A. Rothschild fabric to improve their pathetic appearance. Their tattered, torn, and filthy clothing would embarrass even the most impoverished of Judengasse residents.

I recalled the landgrave Wilhelm's cannon fodder. His mercenaries were poor souls sent by force into the battlefields in order to fill the landgrave's cashbox. They had no motive for fighting. All they wanted was to get home safe, and the fulfillment of this hope was extremely doubtful. On the other hand, these soldiers marching before us now had come here out of faith in their cause. True, their exterior was peculiar and pitiful, but the light in their eyes attested to the inner strength that pushed them onward. I suppose it was their vision that imbued them with force. The words *liberté, égalité, fraternité* have a special magic, which they were now trying to implement outside of their own country.

And in that case, how should we treat them? As invaders who must be forced out? Or perhaps as our saviors, who would remove us from our ghetto, just as they had granted equal rights to our Jewish brothers in France?

Are they our enemy or our kin?

I addressed this question to Meir, who went out to sniff.

The street is divided. Opinions diverge, burning, shaking, threatening, urging, confusing. Some people support loyalty to Frankfurt, while others wish to take the side of the French invaders.

Meir followed his heart, which followed the majority opinion: we must not support the French.

On one of these mad days, I took hold of thread and needle, preparing to patch up Kalman's pants. These pants, which ended below the knee, began their life on Amschel's body. From there, they underwent a series of ruthless incarnations with Shlomo and Nathan, who in their unrestrained play damaged the fabric, and finally, they ended up on

Kalman's legs. The fabric, which has suffered through frolicking buttocks, has been worn down and patched up again and again. It is safe to assume that this was the final patch, putting an end to the misery of thread, needle, and pants combined.

Meir sat down beside me and began to explain while my hand nervously rubbed the end of the thread that threatened to fall out of it.

"Look, Gutaleh," he began. "We all understand that there is an opportunity here. But if this opportunity doesn't come through, we'll be in great trouble."

I didn't look at him. I kept my eyes insistently on the end of the thread, saying, "The French have given freedom to the Jews of their country. Why should we turn our backs on them?"

"All right, Gutaleh, let's follow your line of thinking for a moment. Let's assume we welcome these soldiers here with flowers, assuming we had any flowers . . . If the French succeed in changing our fate and removing us from here, how wonderful. But if they are defeated and driven out, we would be seen as traitors by the city council, the emperor, and the entire government. They would never forgive us for it, imposing even more decrees and embargoes on us."

I crushed the thread violently.

"Gutaleh, look at me."

My eyes clung to the thread.

"Tell me, what would you have me do?" he demanded.

"Tell the whole truth." The words landed heavily on the patch.

"The whole truth begins with the fact that I would like the French to rule the world and impose their new order upon it, according to their beautiful ideas." He paused to give me time to take in his words.

I looked up at him. *Go on,* my eyes begged him.

"I want us all to leave the ghetto tomorrow and live like everybody else, equals among equals."

I nodded.

"I want to continue to dream these beautiful dreams."

I clung to his eyes.

"But I have to stop floating on air. I have to steady my feet on the ground."

My forehead wrinkled with a question.

"Understand, my darling, we do not live in France. The new world-view that started there might reach us here too. But this kind of thing doesn't happen in a day, or even a year. You cannot compare the Parisian way of thinking with the way of thinking in Frankfurt and its nearby cities. The difference is enormous. Austria and Prussia will not let those kinds of ideas come true right away. We must let them trickle down slowly, until they fill the abyss of this place's worldview."

He searched my eyes to make sure I was listening.

"Since these new ideas will not be easily accepted here," he continued, "and neither will surrender, we must assume that the defeated soldiers would try to return their lost honor sooner rather than later, and then we would find ourselves facing them once more, no French, no liberty, no equality, no fraternity."

"What else?" I asked, my voice broken, when he paused to look into the horizon.

"You know I am not eager to take the side of those who have hurt us and our brothers. On the contrary—I'll never be able to forgive and forget years of cruel humiliation. I despise them and yearn for them to be punished. But reality dictates that I go against my desires. For the time being, I must remain sane, and the practical implication of sanity is to win the hearts of my customers, offering them a kind smile."

I dropped the thread.

Thursday, December 20th, 1792

Meir was right, and so were most of the Judengasse people.

On December 2nd we could hear the battle that was taking place just on the other side of Bockenheimer Gate. We hid inside our homes, embarking on a passionate dance of guesswork, whose main, undeclared purpose was to dull the sensation of fear and helplessness. The guesses did not indulge us for long. A few hours after the first explosion was heard, news spread through the street: the French have been defeated by the Prussian forces.

Meir sighed with relief. The whole of Judengasse sighed with relief. I sighed too, just barely, certainly not with relief. The lead we had, that small thread, had dropped out of our hands. Redemption, which had been so close, was now far away again, and who knows when it would be back, if at all. I was not a partner to the rhythmic calls of the Jewish crowd: "Down with the French! Long live the king of Prussia!" To me it felt like exaggerated ingratiation. They might as well have been calling, "Wonderful! Continue to humiliate and oppress us!"

Cheers echoed through our street, but my heart was filled with the melancholy of defeat.

Do not gloat when your enemy falls; when they stumble, do not let your heart rejoice.

People are saying that General Beware, whose star had faded, licked his wounds and blamed the defeat on us, the Jews of Frankfurt, who had treated his soldiers with hostility.

I feel for the French general. I feel for our defeated people. I feel for the missed opportunity. I am not excited about the glowing light in Meir's eyes. He is on the side of the gloaters. On the other hand, I have no intention of putting that light out.

I ponder what might have been, had we acted differently. There may be truth in Meir's words—perhaps our behavior worked against us. Our victorious rulers would have rushed to punish us heftily for our treason.

I look at the wall surrounding us and try to take comfort. The wall isolates us from the world, but at the same time it embraces us, as if to say, *My dear children, do as you please, carry on with your life, I am here to protect you.*

Tuesday, October 22nd, 1793

I am shocked. Louis XVI was executed. A French mob watched giddily.

And if that wasn't enough, after months in prison, Marie Antoinette was executed as well.

Six days ago, she was decapitated by guillotine. I heard that her chopped head was presented to the cheering crowd.

My divided heart soured. While I can't blame the hungry masses for gloating, I still lit a yahrzeit candle and said a prayer for Marie Antoinette's soul.

How the tables have turned.

Monday, December 7th, 1795

I recall the early days of our engagement, the moments when I realized that life with Meir was bound to be fascinating. Today, twenty-five years after getting married, I can admit I could never have dreamed of a better life.

I am used to beginning my entries by recapping familial events. This time I have special news to report: my eldest daughter, Schönche, is married! It isn't too hard to guess who the groom is—it is Benedict Moshe de Worms, the patient and persistent man who reminds me of Meir in the old days. He stood guard until he found the appropriate time to send over his parents to make a match. And my Schönche, who had been so coy around him, answering his beseeching looks with such delicate, surreptitious signs, had suddenly begun responding to his tortured courting out in the open, her face constantly beaming.

My son-in-law is handsome, generous, industrious, smart, talented, and, most important, he loves my daughter, and treats her like a princess. Meir is pleased, if only because Moshe is the son of a successful court banker. "I shall give my child to a man befitting of her status," he had told me often. "Her father-in-law must be a court banker. The honor of the Rothschild family will remain with it for generations."

Luckily, Moshe de Worms meets the condition set by Meir for marrying into a wealthy Jewish lineage, and the match was made. His father expressed his warm gratitude about marrying into the family of the equally successful Meir Rothschild. I thought about my father, a court banker in a small princedom, who also saw my marriage as a multiplication of his family's honor. I find that court bankers all have something in common: they respect each other and marry into each other's families.

My Schönche, beautiful and delicate, her pretty head now covered with a coif, walks around cheerfully, with sparkling eyes. Each morning she descends from their tiny room in our house to the study and takes special care with her bookkeeping job. The generous dowry her father gave her, 5,000 gulden, is worthy of her and her chosen one. Besides that, they were promised, as is our custom on Judengasse, a place to live for the next two years, until they find a home of their own.

The house is more crowded than ever—we are now thirteen. But this new addition seems to have added another spark of happy light to our family. The young couple deserves an isolated corner for intimacy, and so we had a wall built within the girls' room, allowing a bit of privacy at night, with the hope that the small chamber where the lovebirds sleep would soon give way to a chirping baby bird.

In spite of the admiration Meir has for his young, hardworking son-in-law, he vehemently refuses to bring him into the family business.

"Gutaleh," he said when I hinted at my displeasure. "Remember, the key to success is the ability to keep a secret. When a secret is revealed, it ceases to be a secret. I can only trust my sons to keep it."

Meine lieber Eidam, my dear son-in-law. I look at him and wonder if he, like my sons, has the talent to keep this golden key safe. I believe he does, and tend to believe that Meir thinks so too. But a man like him does not take such risks, and who am I to stand in his way when his abilities are proved every single day.

My owl eyes can sense Moshe's sensitivity. The efforts he and Schönche make to hide their hurt feelings tug at my heartstrings. I pray for them, hoping time heals the ache and helps them adapt, and finding comfort in the fact that Meir himself is finding ways of appeasing his son-in-law. When we convene around the dinner table he goes out of his way to shower Moshe with attention.

My son Nathan and Moshe have formed a special bond. They have a language that excludes us. They carry on conversations that sound as if they are made up of a mélange of foreign languages, and while I struggle to understand what they have just said, they have already moved on to joking about their bright yet odd ideas and patting each other's backs like old friends. I watch those two and wonder how it could be that the age difference does not deter them. Moshe is only four years older than my son Amschel, but they have no interest in a friendship, while Nathan is eight years younger than his brother-in-law, and yet the two behave like twins. It is true that Nathan has always considered himself wiser and more mature than his siblings, who have, in turn, adjusted to this image of his. And yet it is astounding to me that a stranger who has just joined our family also treats him as the eldest. The relationship between them seems to be quickening my son-in-law's integration into our family.

And yet, I have some reservations. Without a doubt, it was my eldest son's responsibility to form a connection with his first brother-in-law and assist him in fitting into our family. But I mustn't fight reality, which has rules of its own, sometimes clear, other times hidden. I must accept the difference between my children and appreciate each for his or her virtues. Amschel remains my anxious, worrying, old-fashioned son. The worry lines on his forehead warn against special risks in business deals, the lowering of profits in a specific transaction, or the chances that tomorrow a business might deteriorate. Nevertheless, he has one invaluable virtue—the responsibility he demonstrates with every step he makes. This quality is priceless in a complex family firm like ours.

Amschel, Shlomo, and Nathan all come together to bear the brunt of the work and business trips. The training and guidance our sons have received over the years are bearing choice fruits, as befitting a quality tree. On the one hand, they assist Meir in expanding his business with the landgrave Wilhelm. On the other hand, they expand the business by supplying the Austrian army. And on the third hand, they continue to trade in linens.

◆ ◆ ◆

One day, Buderus rushed into our study. Veering from his usual style, he ignored the younger children, who saw his face flashing by and ran to him, screeching with delight. He strode toward the study, slammed the door behind him, and sat alone with Meir for a long time. No one was allowed entrance.

When he left, his face grave, the three sons were called urgently into the office, and the murmurs that sounded from in there attested to the preparation of a complicated plan. An eternity later I heard him call, "Gutaleh!"

I opened the door. Four anxious men looked at me like beasts ready to pounce on their prey. I looked at Meir imploringly.

"Gutaleh, we are heading out. Please prepare provisions."

I stayed, planted in place.

"Gutaleh, I'll explain everything later, there's no time right now. We must leave."

"For how long?"

"For as long as we need to," he answered breathlessly, sweeping the papers off the desk and into his briefcase. Schönche, Isabella, and Babette held on to my apron and rushed into the kitchen with me. Together we assembled a pile of sandwiches, vegetables, and bottles of water.

When I was reunited with the secretive group four days later, the mystery was solved. My four heroes sat victorious in the living room and tried to beat each other to the punch in the colorful descriptions about the events that had taken place.

As it turned out, in his peculiar visit, Buderus informed Meir about developments with the landgrave, spurring him into immediate action.

According to Buderus, Wilhelm had tracked the invasion of the French soldiers with mixed emotions. While his business sense pushed him to side with the French, his crown determined that he must join those opposing the French Revolution, including Austria, Prussia, and England. He agreed to join the opposition to the French on the condition that the English grant him an award of 100,000 pounds. His demand was accepted without argument, and the landgrave was now in urgent need of banking services.

From then on, the door was opened wide to Meir, and his business took a giant leap forward.

The Rothschild men's full entry through that door was preceded by the actions of my three clever sons, who stood before the roadblock and removed it with a series of steps that inspired my maternal admiration.

This time, Buderus was the one who did the sniffing. He described to Meir a hopeful scenario of profound disagreements between the landgrave and the most prestigious Frankfurt bankers: the Bethmann brothers (led by Simon Moritz von Bethmann) and Rüppell and Harnier. The negotiation between them and the landgrave had reached a breaking point, and they were at a loss.

"We must do something before harmony is restored between the landgrave and his bankers," Buderus advised Meir and his cabinet.

My three sons appeared before the worried Bethmann brothers, removed their hats, took a bow, and promised them "excellent and certain mediation" with the landgrave.

The unassailable—and, one might add, esteemed—Frankfurt bankers looked quizzically at the bold Judengasse boys, listening with sour faces to their broken German, their expressions more scornful than the one Goliath gave David. They were about to send away these ill-mannered young men who dared address them with such unrestrained enthusiasm and bizarre propositions.

The direct look the three Bethmann brothers gave the three Rothschild brothers before sentencing them paralyzed and silenced the Rothschilds. The Bethmanns looked at the wild appearance of the Jewish natives, peering at the tattered clothes hanging off their bodies, looking as if they had come from a more primitive age, and examined their eager faces. Under the guidance of Simon Moritz von Bethmann they discussed the topic and decided that these "animals" might succeed where they, the great professionals, had failed. They looked at them once more and decided, "Their appearance poses no threat. They will never be our competition."

They offered the eccentric boys a paltry fee and sent them straight into the lion's den: Wilhelm's Wilhelmshöhe Palace.

That was all my wonderful boys needed. Their theatrics, combined with the fact that they were clearly from Judengasse, a place so isolated and shut off from the world—these all did the trick. And there you have it: the fish took the bait and was caught in the net.

Meir, who watched it all unfold from his hiding place, congratulated them on overcoming the first obstacle and led them to the landgrave's palace in Kassel, practicing their next role in the great play of life.

My boys did not disappoint at the palace, either. Standing like soldiers before the landgrave, as if he were their commander, delivering the words of flattery their father had instructed them to say, they softened the cold heart of the landgrave. What helped persuade the landgrave was the fact that Buderus was with him at the time, and quickly encouraged Wilhelm. The words "his majesty," "his highness," and "kneel at your feet" rolled out of the three boys' mouths like a refrain, echoing through the regal room.

The desired result was quickly achieved. With bags of money in their hands, my three wonders parted with a salute, rushing over to the venerable bankers to declare their success.

The most highly respected—and, at this time, shocked—Frankfurt bankers, listened to them repeating their story again and again, checked the contents of the bags they had been given, shook their heads to make sure they were indeed awake and not dreaming, and then got ahold of themselves and let loose a tirade of praise for themselves, their wisdom and resourcefulness in choosing this trio of amazing, excellent, harmless mediators.

The terrific mediators' hands were soon filled with work for the bankers, who glowed with satisfaction, and their path to Kassel was clear, frequent, and essential.

As they were now in charge of mediating with the landgrave, and the landgrave was growing used to their presence, it wasn't long before they began deviating from the direction of their mediation, and rather than represent the highest-ranking Frankfurt bankers, began to represent their father, the Jewish Meir Rothschild.

In those days, Denmark, which was already in debt, badly needed a loan. Wilhelm wished to help his uncle, the king of Denmark, but knew that lending money to a relative could quickly veer into gift territory. He needed, then, to conceal the source of the loan. Since the distinguished Frankfurt bankers were identified with the landgrave, my Rothschilds were tasked with the mission.

The landgrave was pleased with the Judengasse team's work. But there were others who were furious about it. The Bethmanns. At first, the smug brothers wondered at the lack of interest the Danish treasury had shown when they offered to take care of the loans. When they asked further, the royal court informed them that someone had already taken charge of the loans. They pressured the treasury to disclose the entity handling their business.

"It's made up of a few brothers," they said.

"We're brothers. What brothers are you referring to?"

"Brothers working under their father, a good, decent man who smiles at everyone."

The Bethmann brothers had enough of these riddles. They demanded immediate answers.

"What are their names?"

"Rothschild, I believe," the treasurer answered impatiently.

Only then did they fathom the situation. They were furious, but it was too late. There was nothing they could do.

The landgrave, with the tireless encouragement of Buderus, invited Meir to handle the discounting of English bills, to the additional chagrin of the bankers whose power had been undermined.

News often comes in droves. I had yet to calm down from the picturesque descriptions my wonder boys were offering, when life winked at me meaningfully. I was drowning in smiles.

What happened, you ask? Well, along with the happy news from the princedom in Kassel, we caught wind of a useful relationship with higher authorities, those anchored in international relationships. It was a result of Meir's sniff work and his decision to act quickly and surreptitiously before others could find the treasure that seemed to have knocked on his door, saying, "Take me home!"

Once again, I found that when God closed a door, He opened a window. All we had to do was pay attention. And that is Meir's wisdom.

Frankfurt, the city that makes our lives harder and closes the doors to the world on us, suddenly opened a vital, welcoming door for us to walk through. As a central city of the Holy Roman Empire, Frankfurt was sucked into the war between the allies—England, Prussia, and Austria—and France. When Meir heard that the allies were gathering their forces in Fischerfeld, which bordered Judengasse, the wheels in his brain began to turn.

To the question in my eyes, he replied, "The military requires provisions. I must strike while the iron is hot and be the first to make an offer."

"What will you offer? What do they need?"

"They need everything. These are people. As such, they require food and uniforms. They've got horses, and so they need hay."

"And where will you get these provisions?"

"I don't know. I'll make the offer first, and worry about that later."

My heart skipped a beat. My Meir has not disappointed yet, and nevertheless, this was no ordinary client. This wasn't a routine merchandise order. By God, this was an army retaining a commitment for immediate, ongoing supply for its thousands of soldiers. Meir had never dealt with such supply, in these kinds of quantities and this kind of frequency. Where would he get it from? How would he deliver it? "He is mad, my man," I told myself out loud. "I'm sure of it." And his madness worries me. Oh, God, please never make him put his resourcefulness to the test. This time, it is his integrity at stake.

"May God keep you safe as you come and go," I said by way of parting, placing a hand on Meir's head, the way I do with my small children. I felt that this time I must offer assistance. But what kind of assistance can Gutaleh Rothschild offer?

Prayer. I ordered Schönche to gather her sisters—Isabella, Babette, Julie, and even little Henrietta, my darling four-year-old sweetheart. We stood for a long time in a pure circle of women in front of the Star of David hanging on the wall. I opened a book of Psalms, and the girls joined my songs of David.

Meir headed toward the gates of the military base.

With the pride of a born-and-raised Frankfurter and an experienced businessman, he walked with his head held high past soldiers of different ranks, who all stepped aside to make way for the vigorous man who, one must admit, looked odd in his garb and speech. Soon he was standing in front of General von Weimar, who was in charge of supply to the Austrian army.

General von Weimar, whose seat was in Frankfurt, from which he took care of the needs of all soldiers in all units across the empire, received Meir more or less the way we Jews would have welcomed a man announcing the arrival of the Messiah.

To Meir's surprise, which he hid well, the general invited him to sit down and offered him wine. Meir made do with one glass, while the general drank heavily. The wine did its work, opening the heart of the great general to Meir, as if the man had always been his confidant. The general, his heart now open, described the many requests coming from all the German provinces, piling up there at the headquarters, most of them involving demands for items the general was unable to procure. "You see, my friend, this is what happens when an ally such as Prussia decides, out of the blue, to change its stance with regard to the French, signing the Peace of Basel, and leaving Austria alone at war," the intoxicated man concluded.

Meir nodded with empathy, as if to say, *Indeed, hard times, my dear general. But you are not alone. I am here with you.*

A contract was signed on the spot.

The two said goodbye, and Meir turned to leave with a calm, confident step. Only when he left the general's line of vision did he start to run, like a man fleeing from a herd of beasts.

He met and asked and studied and researched and haggled in smooth Rothschild fashion, and as in a demonic dance, twirled and signed purchasing agreements for merchandise, their books riddled with a long series of zeroes, which, together, came to millions of gulden. He signed a contract for wheat supply with one, then rushed to the next to sign an agreement for all sorts of foodstuffs, and a uniform provision contract with a third. Then followed work horses, hay, saddles, tents, and more and more equipment. Everyone who signed knew Meir and admired his great business prowess. Now that they were aware of his connections with the Austrian army, their admiration grew tenfold.

Upon his return home, he went up to our room, and I quickly followed. He plopped down on the bed and settled his breathing.

"Look, Gutaleh," he roared, intoxicated, a burst of laughter escaping him. I waited for him to speak.

But the news was postponed, because at that moment Meir closed his eyes and departed for the night into a world filled with zeroes. I had to wait for the next morning to appease my curiosity and hear the rest of the sentence.

"There are contracts, Gutaleh," he said as soon as he opened his eyes. "Lots of contracts. A main contract with the general and subcontracts with those debited to him. Gutaleh, we've succeeded. Do you understand? I am the main supplier to the Austrian army. We are in the international arena, do you understand? We've done it."

I hugged him. "Yes, you did, Meir, as always. Praise God."

I attributed the success to him, but I knew that it was the work of God. I didn't share the whole story with him—the fact that the girls and I had a part in it too, the part related to the Lord's approval of his genius moves.

He stood up all of a sudden. "Where are the boys?"

"Shlomo is in Kassel, Amschel and Nathan are in the study, awaiting orders."

"Yes, we have plenty of work to do, and this time we cannot do it all on our own. We need strong helpers. Draw a bath and prepare clean clothes."

I hurried to heat water in the kitchen washbasin while he wrapped tefillin.

In spite of his rush, Meir did not skip his usual morning prayer at the synagogue. When he returned, he asked to have his breakfast in the study. Amschel and Nathan, who had joined him for prayer, had already received word of the exciting developments. I served their breakfast, and Kalman and Yaakov also joined the hustle and bustle in the room. Meir spoke fervently, outlining the plan. Suddenly, his eyes fell on the two young children.

"I'm waiting for you to grow up," he told them. "You have work ahead of you as well. You'll learn from your older brothers and grow up to be like them."

Kalman and Yaakov put their hands together. A light went on in their eyes. They glanced at their older brothers, indulging in the sweet taste of the compliment they received from their father.

More contracts were signed in the following days: contracts for the provision of groceries and equipment, and two important partnership contracts, one with Wolf Loeb Schott and the other with Beer Nehm Rindskop, both successful business owners with the added advantage of being Meir's relatives. These partnerships are a great help in his ability to meet his obligations.

In my opinion, there are two friendly armies: there is the Austrian army and there is the Rothschild army. The latter feeds the former through good sense and hard work. The more exhausting the work, the more energy it provides to the exhausted.

The Rothschild army. Who would have thought . . .

And I wonder if there is any way of getting life to sign a contract that never expires.

Because, as far as I'm concerned, I'm willing to go on like this forever.

At the same time, another thought plagues me: Is it seemly to have our profits founded in war? All I can hope for is that, with time, our money will start coming from peace.

Tuesday, October 18th, 1796

I have learned my lesson: I must never tempt the devil. He lurks everywhere, just waiting for human beings to slip up and spur him to action.

And I've learned something else too: it's best to remain modest in every situation, even when I am talking only to myself. When life does well by me, I must not gloat. I must restrain my urges.

Indeed, my entire life I have been modest and thrifty. My clothes are modest, my meals are modest, my house is modest, my behavior is humble. *You have found honey, take as much as you need, lest you overeat and throw up.* I even hoard my good-morning coins. They are something kept private between Meir and I alone, just like our lovemaking, and such they will remain forever.

But now I am lamenting my sin. I broke my rule of modesty and committed the sin of avarice. In a moment of weakness I got carried away, expressing in writing my childish excitement over our progress.

What was I thinking? I tried to control life. I wanted to sign life to a contract that never expires. Who am I to do that? I, little Gutle from the Judengasse prison, dared put myself in God's place. That is not my way. *Do not boast of tomorrow, for you do not know what it will bring.*

We've been plagued by a great tragedy, one that befalls us every two decades on average. Another fire erupted on Judengasse. But this time, the magnitude was enormous. *All of Diaspora is like a burning pyre.*

I am broken. Fallen apart. Guilty. I have sinned and caused others to be punished. Had I not gotten carried away by my greed, we may have been able to continue from where we were before the fire. Everything might have been different. Everyone would have carried on with their lives at home. Meir would have gone to synagogue each day, speaking, as usual, with the yeshiva students and enjoying some Torah. *Man must never tempt the devil.*

The hostilities around us were the source of this evil. We had followed the goings-on in the military arena with worry. A new name has risen from the French military. A young general named Napoleon Bonaparte was instilling terror all around. Legends of him passed between us as fast as the fire licked through the wooden houses standing in its way. Napoleon was leading his forces proudly, and last spring he defeated the Austrian soldiers in Lodi. From there, he and his soldiers continued in our direction, and within a month they were outside the Frankfurt walls. The Austrian forces were put under siege. The city council suggested a surrender, but the Austrian command refused.

Anxiety took over Judengasse. People walked around with their heads hanging, their ears ringing with their own cries against the defeated French from years ago: "Down with the French! Long live the king of Prussia!" But things change so quickly. This time we are meant to stand by Austria's side, rather than Prussia's. Prussia left the battle long ago. The French are now on the offense, not defense. And we, the Jews, where do we go from here?

On July 14th the French began bombarding the city with cannon-balls. Fires erupted here and there but were all put out. Our anxiety rose to new levels. Don't let them get to us. Just leave us alone and depart toward prettier, more enticing places.

But they chose not to answer our prayers.

Experts walked among us, offering interpretations to any willing ear, explaining that Napoleon's only intention was to bomb the Austrian ammunition reserves, and therefore there was no need for worry. We were out of his line of attack. We hoped this was true.

But we failed to take one thing into account: human error. The overzealous soldiers indeed aimed their cannons toward the ammunition reserves, but some of them missed their target, and the cannons hit the neutral part of town—Judengasse.

In the darkness of night, the sky lit up over our street. A horrid racket broke the silence that fell in one of the breaks between bombings. The windowpanes shook. The moaning of cracking wood stopped the hands of the clock of our lives, and all movement froze. A banging came at the door of our house, and we all ran out. Our neighbor had already fled. One quick look was enough for us to realize we'd stumbled upon one of the worst events to ever occur on our street. We looked up. *The fire of the Lord was falling from heaven.* The flames rose at once above us, a terrible canopy of fire spreading from one house to the next. A unified row of homes that used to stand as one for years upon years collapsed with mighty explosions.

The frozen expressions on people's faces thawed at once at the sight of scalding licks of fire, and cries of woe were swallowed in the eruptions. People were running amok, no direction, no purpose, no point. What were we going to do?

Meir called to me, "Take the children and run outside, out of the ghetto!"

The children. The children. Where was everyone? Yaakov was in my arms, his head in my lap. Henrietta and Julie were holding Isabella's hands. Moshe de Worms held Schönche, then raised her in his arms while she protected her belly with one hand and gripped his waist with the other. For a fraction of a second her eyes met mine. The look in her eyes was familiar, frightening—she was in labor. A spasm of terror ran through me, threatening to take over my body. God, where are You? *Do not desert me, for a tragedy is near and there is no help.* Where was Kalman? There were Kalman and Babette, bleary-eyed and holding hands. And the older three, where were they? The three boys and their father were dragging chests and boxes out of the house.

"Run!" I cried. "Run!" everyone repeated. "Run"—a single word, a survivor of the Judengasse vocabulary. All other words had been scorched in the fire.

The flames galloped wildly, rising in a rainbow of colors, orange, red, yellow, their ends painted blue and gray. They seemed to have no intention of receding. Indeed, they were gaining speed and trampling the foundations of our existence with scalding breaths. Onward to the parting of the Red Sea. But there was no water here. Where was the water? Put out the fire. Who was going to put it out? Where were the Frankfurters? Why weren't they coming? *Do not abandon me, my savior God.* Everybody was rushing, running, some carrying children, others whatever they could take hold of, what little property they bought with their hard work. Fleeing for their lives through the wide-open gates. No more energy. Must run. Cannot let go. No looking back. Pillar of salt. Come on, get through that gate. Onward, to the river, to the Main.

We collapsed on the banks of the Main, touching the ground where water met land. Beneath us, we felt the chill of wet sand. We checked our bodies for injury, our children, our families. Panicked shouting: Where is the child? There he is, calm down. He's just fallen asleep, escaped into slumber, and will soon wake up. There, he's crying. Cry, my child, cry for me. What is this, you're crying too? And you? Why is everybody crying? We are saved, we're here. Don't cry. Yes, we are saved, but look behind you. The street is still burning, cloaked in flames. A ceaselessly moving burning horror, consuming our world without paying any mind to the elderly and the newborns. Newborn. Schönche. Where is Schönche?

"Schönche!" I cried hoarsely and rose to search for her.

A wall of women stood on a patch of dirt. From deep in its center came stifled moans. I picked up my pace. All around, women were saying, "Gutle is here, Gutle is here." I pushed through the circle of arms and legs and made my way to the center.

On a blanket lay my daughter Schönche, legs splayed, limp face colorless, writhing with pain. Beside her leaned my sister Vendeleh, running a wet cloth over her forehead, whispering words of encouragement. In front of her kneeled Olek the midwife, repeating her instructions over and over again. All the necessary equipment was laid on a towel at her side.

That miraculous woman. Even in the most horrid moments, she never forgot to carry with her the provisions of life.

I rushed to my daughter, sat beside her, and took her hand.

"Good timing," Olek sighed, her worried face illuminated by a flash of hope.

"Schönche," I whispered, trying to steady my voice. "My Schönche, do as Olek says. Push, my child. Push."

Schönche looked at me, her eyes helpless.

"God is my fortress," I said for both of us. I think she might have squeezed my hand weakly.

Olek nodded at me to continue, and I nodded back. I wanted to return my tired daughter to my womb, to feed her through the umbilical cord and transmit my energy, my blood, to her, so that she might complete her mission. I concentrated my full attention on giving these to her. *Take it, take all my strength,* I thought. I spoke to her softly. "Schönche, you can do it. I'm here. Mama is helping you. It's going to be all right, you'll see. Push the way I told you. Remember? That's a good girl. Just like that. More, more, a little more." Schönche squeezed my hand strongly. "Good, my Schönche, very good, you're doing wonderfully. Just a few more pushes and we'll be done. Strong. Yes, stronger.

Yes, just like that, just like that, just like that. *Please, Lord, save us, please, Lord, let us succeed."*

The baby slipped right into Olek's hands. A thin cry broke the wall of women, who all cheered. I mumbled words toward the heavens: *A life of Yours You have given her.*

"That's it, you see, my hero? You did it," I said quietly, finally letting my voice tremble. I kissed her dripping forehead. "That's your baby, look at him. He's a hero too, just like his mother. A baby bringing life back to our street."

Olek wrapped the baby and put his mouth to his mother's breast. Schönche had trouble holding him, and Vendeleh came closer so she could carry his minuscule weight. His first few sucks made Schönche shiver. She trained her eyes on me, and for the first time that night, a thin smile stretched across her face.

I went to Olek and wrapped my arms around her. "Thank you, our guardian angel, sent to us from heaven," I whispered, finally letting the tears run down my cheeks and the shoulders of our savior, who was crying as well.

Our hot, merciless enemy took twenty-four hours to suffocate and die. It left smoking clouds of stench in its wake that would stay with the street's residents for many days.

With a faltering step, we returned to our ruined street, which had so recently been full of life, now occupied by the sadness of death. Our eyes refused to take the image in. The black crumbs of soot fell slowly, buried between the broken houses and unrecognizable black objects. Beneath the layer of haze over the street, the dimensions of ruin and destruction were revealed. Our eyes burned and our breathing was heavy, and not only because of the heat and smoke.

Half the houses, or, to be exact, 119 houses, were in shambles. Twenty-one houses were badly damaged. The beautiful synagogue had turned to dust. Two thousand of the three thousand residents were left homeless. Weeping people insisted on digging through the remains of their lives, fishing out hidden fragments from the depth of the ashes.

In light of the situation, the Frankfurt Senate released provision decrees to carry us through until we could resume our normal lives. The homeless were allowed to live outside of the ghetto for a limited time, until their homes could be repaired or rebuilt. As for those whose homes were only partially damaged, the decree forbidding them from leaving the street after dark and on Sundays continued to apply.

But we all realized that the senate, being subject now to the French flag waving over the city, was powerless and lacking the energy to enforce such decrees. It was too busy licking its wounds, having no time to take an interest in the state of the Jews, for better or worse. Just as it does nothing to assist our recovery, so does it not check too closely as people come and go.

As for us, our green house was only lightly bruised. The porch, the pine tree, the flowers and plants, were all gone, but the rooms of the home remained intact, and the sooty walls were repainted. A piece of shrapnel remained stuck in the façade, crying out its testimony of the cannon fire.

Miserable people crouched down by the ruins of the synagogue, searching for a place to pray to God to abandon His wrath. For the time being, our home is open to the worshippers. We have cleared out one of the rooms, brought in the Holy Ark and the Torah Scroll, and hold minyan prayers until the synagogue can be rebuilt.

My devoted, concerned neighbors and I take turns caring for the unfortunate souls hardest hit. We take day and night shifts in the shelter that has been spared by the calamity and is now housing the sick and impoverished, children and elderly, who need financial and emotional support.

Meir took advantage of this opportunity—the senate sleeping—and immediately got in touch with Trautwein, the biggest leather merchant on Schnurgasse in the center of town, not far from the ghetto, from whom he rented storage spaces. Our house has been cleared of large quantities of goods, which are now stored in warehouses a half hour's walk outside ghetto walls.

As we lick our wounds, we are faced with the knowledge that the French, celebrating their great victory, have decided to impose fines on every private asset in Frankfurt. The fines come in different amounts, and can be as high as 2 percent. I looked at Meir questioningly, and he gave me a reassuring answer. Luckily, our capital appears in official registers as 60,000 gulden, a handsome sum, but substantially lower than the real amount.

The secret numbers of the wealthy on our street were suddenly revealed to all. People said the declared capital of the great Michael Speyer was reported at 420,000 gulden.

Truth be told, in spite of my bookkeeping position, I do not follow the true sum of our capital. I am consumed by my anger at the French. Rather than fine us, they would have done better to compensate us for the terrible disaster they had brought upon us. *If a fire breaks out and spreads into thornbushes so that it burns shocks of grain or standing grain or the whole field, the one who started the fire must make restitution.* I take comfort in the fact that they are not fining our full assets. Luckily, the real numbers are still deep in our secret burrows, and have been spared by the fire.

My heart is roiling with anger. I am filled with rage toward the privileged Frankfurters. Seeing the flames rising from the ghetto, they should have offered to lend a hand. Not only did they sit idly by, but they chose instead to mock our escape. Goethe's mother, who believes herself to be a very knowledgeable woman, is speaking ill of us because we locked our doors behind us as we fled, making it impossible for anyone to enter the burning houses and put out the fire. I want to tell Catharina Elisabeth Goethe, "Is this your way in life? Teasing less fortunate souls, making them a laughingstock? Are we amusing to you? Do you have no better sources of amusement? And another thing: Would you allow me to set your palace on fire and then stand on the sidelines, watching as you undid the locks of your home and elegantly put out the fire that took hold of your expensive possessions?"

And while I was at it, I would have remarked on her family's habit of belittling Jews. Goethe the son has followed in his mother's footsteps, judging our language unfavorably and announcing publicly that "the sound of Judendeutsch is grating to the ear." Oh, Goethe, Goethe, how tender and precious are your ears. Please forgive me for the rough screeching of our language.

It occurred to me to invite Catharina to my kitchen and please her subtle taste buds with my Jewish stews. A bite of my fine cholent would silence her complaints forever.

The honorable Frau Catharina is lucky to never have me as a guest in her palace. Had she invited me, she would have experienced with her own Frankfurter eyes and ears a decisive response to the nonsense she lets slip like sneezes, nonsense that is nevertheless accepted by her ingratiating, hypocritical friends as word of God.

◆ ◆ ◆

While we, unlike many others, have escaped the fire with only minimal damage (and I must thank the Lord for once again protecting us), I search my heart and find that I am anything but calm. First, we were just a footstep away from death and from losing our home. The terrible sights of the fright, the fleeing, and my Schönche's difficult birth are etched in my memory.

Second, the loss all around us rings in my ears, and I am a full partner to the pain and grief of our friends on the street. It has been three months since the event, and the deathly sorrow that descended has stayed with us to this day.

Third, the more I ponder this event, the more I find I cannot let go of the bothersome sense that I am partially to blame. Guilty of the sin of avarice.

From now on, no more boasting.

Sunday, July 2nd, 1797

There is much to report of my family, some good and some bad.

I am plagued by a new breed of disquiet. My son Amschel married in November of last year. This is odd. You would think I would be pleased by this news, but things are not simple, though some say there is hope.

Let me explain everything from start to finish.

First, the bride. Her name is Eva. Eva Hanau. By all accounts, she is considered to be a "good deal," to use Meir's expression. He is the happy father, happier than everyone else, including the bride and groom. With this marriage we have joined a Jewish lineage that meets the requirements. Eva, like me, is the daughter of a court banker. Like me, she is marrying at seventeen, a wonderful age to start. As a wedding gift, Meir gave Amschel the impressive sum of 30,000 gulden, and accepted him as the first partner in the family firm. Eva was hired as a cashier in our office, and divides the workload with Schönche, filling in for her in the first month after the birth of her child.

Schönche recovered from giving birth during the fire, and now has a son, Binyamin, and a daughter, Rebecca, four months old.

Meir explained his decision to give Eva the job while not offering one to his son-in-law, Moshe de Worms, in no uncertain terms. "Our sons, being our confidants, have the right to join their father's business, and therefore their wives will be gladly accepted as well. Our daughters do not have this right, and therefore their husbands are to be kept separate from the Rothschild family's business dealings. Nevertheless, I am not mistreating my daughters. I will be sure to grant them a respectable allowance that would make their lives comfortable and remove any possibility of their lamenting my choice."

Well, everything seems fine with regard to Eva. She is a young maiden, the daughter of a court banker—two details that are sufficient to satisfy the parents of a groom. According to Meir, she is perfect. In my eyes, she has one major flaw.

I must admit, she is attractive, and some would even go so far as to say she is pretty. I won't argue, though I've seen prettier women. At first she seemed to me like a smiling doll. This was during those first weeks, when she treated Amschel with open affection. But this brief period in their shared lives quickly came to an end, and with it went the affection and the smile, and instead a constant gloominess settled over her doll face.

At any rate, I must say that her beauty cannot compensate for the great flaw. There is no love.

I am concerned by the notion that Amschel married Eva due to his strong urge to please his father. He does not love her and she does not love him, either. A loveless marriage is doomed to fail. Some say that love comes with time, but I believe that if love has yet to arrive after eight months of marriage, it has missed its chance, and will never appear.

Amschel and Eva were invited to stay with us until they find a home of their own. Because she is under our watchful eyes from morning till night, I never miss a detail of Eva's demeanor: neither the boredom on her ashen face, nor her efforts to remain outside her husband's sight, nor the care she takes to stay just out of his arms' reach, nor the longing looks she gives Moshe de Worms, compared to the cold looks she gives her husband.

I am not happy about the fact that both couples, Schönche and Moshe, Amschel and Eva, live so close together under our roof, though I have full faith in my son-in-law's loyalty. Out of the two, he surely prefers his fertile wife to the dry sister-in-law wooing him like a blind woman who has lost her cane.

Luckily, Moshe de Worms is a man of initiative, and since he calculated that in just a few months, the time allotted for them to stay with us would expire, he has devoted many hours to searching for a home, and has recently announced that soon they would move into one of the new houses on our street that had been renovated after the great fire. His determination and industriousness match the rhythm of life in our family. He does wonders in his own business, and sometimes I feel bitter to think that this business is not part of our family firm. He has also been proving himself to be a loving, considerate husband and an exemplary father. But what's done is done. The founding father has set rules, and these rules will always stay with us.

Perhaps it is best that he does not set foot in the same place where his sister-in-law spends her days. I have no desire to see Eva standing too close to Moshe. She seems to have memorized his schedule and makes sure to stand at the doorway and smile at him as he enters and leaves.

Meir is not aware of these things taking place right under his nose. In all matters concerning women, he continues to demonstrate the naivety of an adolescent. My woman's eyes can see in the fraction of a second what his man's eyes fail to notice for hours on end.

Perhaps it is for the best for him and for keeping the peace. I do not share the information with him because it would not be right to bother him with domestic affairs when he is so concerned with exterior matters.

But I must not take this severe matter lightly, and I mustn't let it go, for any slight deviation could turn this deformed bud into a defective tree with no chances of recovery. I am the owl mother who must keep close watch on the chicks in my nest.

I didn't let the thought linger for long. I knew I had to execute my plan without further delay. So, in light of these unwanted developments, I've decided to take matters into my own hands.

It began at dinner, when the dull bore stared at Moshe, oblivious, only the blush rising in her face attesting to some life coursing through her veins. It seemed she'd forgotten what to do with her fork. Rage rose in my throat. My upper lip trembled, and I could no longer taste my food. My eyes wandered over her face, and I could easily recognize the heat inside of her. With great determination, I decided now was the time to ferociously protect my son's marriage and stifle the dangerous flame while it was still small.

I filled my glass with apple wine, downed it in one gulp, and twisted my face due to the sourness of both the wine and the situation. I placed the empty glass back on the table, then quickly shoved the compote bowl with the ladle into Eva's confused hands. I spoke loudly, attempting to awaken her. "Eva'leh, here are the bowls. Put one ladleful into each bowl and give it to the person sitting beside you."

She cleared her throat. "Yes, yes, of course, yes," she answered, as if just waking from a deep sleep.

At the end of the meal, after the dishes were rinsed, the kitchen empty, I went to the wakening bore, still sitting at the dining table, and rasped into her tender ear, "I'll be waiting for you in the kitchen."

She must have hoped I was just asking for help, for she put on an apron when she walked into the kitchen. I glanced at the pot bubbling with bath water. My blood boiled. I stood behind her, straight-backed and determined, undid the apron with a flick of the wrist, shoved it into her hands, and said the words that had been waiting impatiently on the tip of my tongue, right into her face. "When we are sitting around the table, it would be best for each woman to look at her own plate, rather than at another woman's."

She looked at me with hesitation, gauging how serious I was, but I whipped my answer at her without skipping a beat, before I had a chance to lose my temper. "Oh, I am serious. You'd better get that deep into your head."

Now she had no doubts as to the gravity of my intentions, even if she still wasn't sure of their meaning. She took one step back and fixed her eyes on me with a wrinkled brow, while I continued to stare knives into her. I already knew that a quick mind was not one of her strengths, so I allotted my words the necessary time to penetrate.

Suddenly it dawned on her, and with realization came embarrassment. Her pale face, which had lost its coloring before, was now ashen, then burned with patches of shame. Her eyes darted around the walls of the kitchen, like a prisoner seeking an escape route. Seeing that it was hopeless, she lowered her head. The smell of regret mixed with the other odors of the kitchen. She was speechless. She cleared her throat and finally breathed out, "I'm sorry. I don't know what came over me. It won't happen again, I promise."

"Neither at the dinner table, nor anywhere else," I clarified.

"Of course." She looked at me as if wanting to say something more, then thought better of it and looked away. Tears were in her eyes. She lingered in the kitchen for a moment longer before turning to flee to her room.

The flame had been put out. The burn will likely require some time to heal.

Tuesday, October 10th, 1797

Life, by its nature, occasionally offers unpleasant surprises. Along with the peaks that charge us with energy and motivate us to action, obstacles pop up, blocking our path in the marathon of life, disrupting our routine. Just when we think that all our problems have been resolved, life appears before us, hands defiantly on hips, to replace the old obstacles— the ones we've toiled to remove—with new ones.

Like a lowly meddler, the obstacle nests in a dark corner, waiting for its time to shine. It looks around, checking, testing, poking out its head, craning its neck, shaking its shoulders, and proceeding into the field.

The worst kind of meddler is the one born of a life of continuous comfort. It has indulged in it as it pleased, and now under its wing it stirs, pounds, digs, and tramples. *A lion does not growl from a treasure of straw, but from a treasure of meat.*

I feel as if I'm speaking in riddles. I must organize my thoughts.

First, I'd like to make it clear that we needed to recruit outside employees into M. A. Rothschild. That in itself is all well and good, because while Meir and the boys planned, traveled, bought, and sold, other employees could perform the smaller tasks, without which no plan could be executed. Thus, we hired coachmen, porters, and other workers, in numbers of which I cannot possibly keep track.

Our Judengasse community showers Meir with respect, a respect founded both on his financial standing and on his generous donations. Though Meir makes sure to donate anonymously, most of his contributions are found out sooner or later. In spite of his proven ability to keep his mouth, and ours, shut, he cannot control the mouths of strangers, who praise the philanthropist and send more and more beggars to his door.

"I have yet to find a way to give in silence and retain that silence."

"The important thing is—you give, Meir."

"That's true. That is better than the way some people talk about the need to give and leave it at that. To those people I say, 'Do not say you want to give. Go on, give!' Only then do they reach for their pockets."

"That's a wise saying. You should add it to your collection." I seem to have become an obsessive collector of his sayings.

"No, Gutaleh," he corrects me. "That isn't my saying. Goethe coined it, trying to demonstrate the idea that words without actions are meaningless."

I was pleased by his answer. *He who delivers words by the name of their speaker delivers redemption to the world.* I said, "Goethe is all right. But I always thought wise sayings stem from life experience, and only those who started at the bottom have the necessary life experience to compose such statements. But it turns out even those who live in ivory towers can have insights."

Meir laughed and put his arms around me. "I don't know what you have against Goethe. He's a very creative man, and very wise. You love collecting sayings. Here are a few more from Goethe: 'I love those who yearn for the impossible.' 'A correct answer is like an affectionate kiss.' 'Knowing is not enough; we must apply. Willing is not enough; we must do.' 'As soon as you trust yourself, you will know how to live.' 'If you wish to know the mind of a man, listen to his words.'" He looked at me gloatingly, as if having just administered the winning blow.

I considered these quotes. Indeed, they were wise. "I am not claiming he is not smart or creative," I explained. "But I do have a resistance toward condescending people."

Meir, who has not a condescending bone in his body, enjoys lots of affection and respect from the residents of the street. His reputation has made him popular throughout the entire street.

Rabbi Shimon says: There are three crowns man can wear: the crown of Torah, the crown of priesthood, and the crown of royalty, but the crown of a good reputation exceeds them all.

One of the consequences of this attitude on the street is the decision to appoint Meir head of the managing committee of the Judengasse community. The position he received on the day of election at the synagogue, near the open Torah Ark, is an honorable position indeed. As part of his duties, Meir spends his days meeting people whose luck has run out and who are hungry for bread. The committee responds compassionately to their dire state, determining assistance according to need: medical treatments free of charge, financial aid for the homeless, support for needy widows and orphans. My heart warms when I think of the sense of accountability on our street, and all those who donate to charity.

One memorable incident involved a man who captivated our hearts. One day, a Jewish man named Hirsch Liebman came to our home and bowed at the doorway. "My name is Hirsch Liebman," he said. He kissed the mezuzah and entered.

In the privacy of the study, the man begged Meir to take him under his wing. "I'll serve his honor in exchange for a salary," he offered. "Please do not send me away with some change. I am not asking for a handout, but for work. I do not want to survive on charity, but no one will hire me. Please, hire me as your loyal servant, and I will perform any task sir gives me."

The man's distress, along with his determination to work and his insistence to refuse gifts, all touched Meir's heart. He always preferred industrious people. Hirsch Liebman reminded him of his early days as an apprentice at the Oppenheimer Bank in Hanover. He accepted the man as his protégé.

Liebman quickly proved his worth. No request was too large or too small for him. He carried heavy sacks of gold and silver coins to their destinations, and even offered his help in the kitchen, demonstrating surprising skill in dishwashing and clearing trash. As he deftly juggled tasks, he rooted himself in our midst, becoming an inseparable part of the household. From morning till night, we could see him going up and down the stairs, cleaning or carrying something. In the midst of the children's scampering, the traffic of visitors and customers, he created more movement and sound in our crowded home. When a knock came at the door, he hurried down the stairs to receive the guest.

Hirsch Liebman had dinner with us every evening, and at night left for the room he rented after he began working for us. The next morning, he returned to our house. In order to afford his steep rent, he shared his home with five roommates.

If Meir was impressed with the man's energy and determination, I was enchanted by his coy smile, his modesty, and his submissiveness. Our son Kalman clung to him after school, and rather than scuffle with his sisters, enjoyed offering help to our employee. Hirsch bent down over the packages, pulled out one bag at a time, and gave them to Kalman, saying, "Help me, please." The little one hoisted the bag onto his back, a perfect impersonation of the way Hirsch carried the goods. Together, they went up to the study. Once they placed the merchandise on the floor, Hirsch would say, "You saved me!" and it was as if he gave Kalman candy. I was so touched by him that I almost cleared a room for him in my heart, but I was afraid the other rooms would protest, having already achieved seniority.

The things that took place from this point on feel like madness. The details of the events have been made clear to us gradually, with the help of the legal authorities who handled the affair. These revealed a clever, cunning man who had calculated every step in advance.

One day, while Shlomo was busy with some customers, Hirsch went into the study, as usual. The large closet contained bags of money delivered the previous day, each containing 1,000 gulden. Hirsch went to the closet, pulled five bags off the shelf, hoisted them onto his back, and walked out.

He hid the loot in his home, in a wooden box under his bed. For a full year, no one knew the box even existed, nor did we realize the money was gone. Hirsch carried on with his work as usual.

I am nauseated when I think of the compassion and affection we felt for him, and how hard we tried to give him a warm, homey feeling, as if he was part of our family. After dinner, while the girls helped me clear the table and wash and dry the dishes, he would check the dying flames in the woodstove, pick up the coal pan, fill it with logs, and toss them into the burning coals. Then he'd return to the table, pick up some bread and salt, and, with everyone else, listen to Meir say the after-dinner prayer. Meir would then tell stories from the Torah to the younger children before they turned in for the night. Finally, with the older children, he would debate the words of the sages. He once surprised his listeners by dividing the decrees of the Torah into "dos" and "don'ts." Meir was a fan of learned scholars.

About a year after the theft, Hirsch got a new roommate, whom he did not like. He moved his loot, hiding it in his parents' home in Bockenheim, in the princedom of Hesse.

How was the crime revealed, then?

Well, one day Meir hurried to answer a knock at the door. Outside was an unfamiliar gentleman asking for Hirsch Liebman. Hirsch was out on an errand. "He isn't here," Meir said. The man left, and Meir put the event out of his mind and returned to work.

The next day, the man returned with the same question and received the same answer. On the third day, Meir grew tired of answering this gentleman's calls. He demanded that the man explain what he wanted with Hirsch. The man fidgeted uncomfortably, evading the question. His behavior seemed suspicious to Meir, who stared at him, crossing his arms in a demonstration of waiting.

Finally, the man spoke. He introduced himself as a mediator who had performed a transaction for Liebman, for the purchase of bonds in the value of 9,000 gulden.

When he heard the sum, Meir's jaw dropped. His assistant, whose entire salary was two and a half gulden a month, one gulden of which went toward his rent—how could he possibly afford four-figure bonds?

"Sir, why are you so confused?" the man asked.

Rather than reply, Meir demanded more information about the essence of the relationship.

The mediator divulged another detail, according to which Hirsch had instructed him to keep the matter of the bonds secret, and that if the man ever had to explain the connection between the two of them he must say that they sold hay together.

Meir brought the matter to the attention of the court. From that point on, we experienced many days of tension and emotional distress.

To the judge, Meir said he did not blame Hirsch Liebman for having side businesses. This was how all Jews fought to survive. But these dealings would not be enough to gain him such hefty sums. Moreover, he said that a partial examination of his study proved that some gold coins, gold medals, diamond rings, and other valuables were missing, worth a total sum of 30,000 gulden.

The investigators showed up at the home of Hirsch's parents, and were surprised to find a venerable treasure trove, including bonds, gold coins, gold medals, gold candlesticks, gold goblets, and eating utensils of silver and gold. Our property was returned to us, and Hirsch was arrested.

Meir demanded that the investigation continue, even handling it personally. He had a strong desire to reveal everything that had been going on under his nose, and punishing the man who had tricked us. *"Even my close friend, someone I trusted, one who shared my bread, has turned against me."* He muttered the Psalms passage under his breath with a red face, and turned to me with a clenched jaw. "People like him are the reason the gentiles speak ill of us, just like the Jewish beggars, the listless *Betteljuden*, who wander from here to there, stealing from Jews and Christians alike. Even though they are a meaningless minority, they create a twisted image of the Jewish people, strengthening the reasoning behind not granting us normal civil rights."

Amschel, Shlomo, and Nathan's increased activity in the firm allowed their father to devote some of his business hours to the investigation.

It was a meaningless bother, but one that drove him mad. I hoped the trial would be over quickly. I couldn't bear to see Meir suffering. My dear man, who influenced the rulers of princedoms, equipped the Austrian military for battle, imported merchandise from the great England, and exchanged money with the elite of the business industry—this man now wallowed all day, trying to hide his burning sense of failure, all due to some unimportant worm that wasn't worth a second glance. I prayed for this nightmare to be over soon.

One evening as Meir returned home, I informed him, "The worm has retreated."

His eyes lit up. "Was the detective here?"

"Yes. He had a few last questions for you. You'll go see him tomorrow morning."

That night Meir tossed and turned in bed. After a few sleepless hours, I caressed his head until he fell asleep in my arms. Sometimes, even the greatest men need a helping hand.

The investigation was finally complete. All accusations were proved. The lowly thief had constructed mountains of lies in his defense, all of which came tumbling down, until he finally broke and revealed his plan, its execution, and its outcome.

He was sentenced to death. None of his begging helped to mitigate his sentence. People are sentenced to death for even smaller misdemeanors. It seems awful to me to take a human life. It would have been better for him to spend the rest of his life in prison, agonized by his conscience.

Though justice had been served, our home was not yet free of worry. Meir paced around our room, his mind tortured by conflicting thoughts. On the one hand, he behaved like a man whose honor had been trampled. "Who knows," he kept telling me behind closed doors. "Perhaps there are others who have wronged me without my noticing. Perhaps my sniffing skills have deteriorated."

I said, "You've checked your belongings over and over, making sure nothing is missing. And as for your sniffing skills, they have neither faded nor gone away, as your work attests."

"Perhaps, perhaps," he sighed, resting a hand on his fatigued face.

My heart wept. Assets bring worry. This was not what I had hoped for. But still, I turned to Meir to plead, "Do not cry over spilled milk, and certainly not over useless, murky water."

Meir was not convinced. "It is precisely because it is useless and murky that it hurts so much. I would have rather been hit by cannons."

On the other hand, he bitterly regrets the fate of the sinner. "I should have made him confess and repent privately, here, at home, not in a gentile court. I conspired with our enemies against one of my own. I, who always work so lovingly for my people, have let my emotions get the better of me, and took part in deciding the fate of one of them."

"I believe that confession and contrition would not have satisfied you."

"But a death sentence will?" he hurled, and I knew he was right. The tables have turned. The verdict, a thousand times worse than the sin, now causes the petitioner regret. His suffering, caused by his scruples, won't be relieved easily.

I scrub his shirt on the washboard. How easy it is to clean clothes, and how difficult to clean a conscience.

And nevertheless, my mind assures me, new events put an end to older ones. We have a fascinating life full of achievements ahead of us. And most importantly, I put my faith in Meir's strength of spirit. We must be patient. God will turn sour into sweet.

God, hear my prayer.

Friday, March 2nd, 1798

Purim is a joyous, busy holiday.

I have prepared a *mishloach manot*, a food package with delicacies, for our neighbors and for the less fortunate. The list of paupers grows with every passing year. If there is any complaint in my words, it is directed at the Lord, Who is tasked with caring for the welfare and well-being of His creatures. I myself enjoy preparing and giving the packages, and only worry that I might accidentally forget one of the homes expecting it, and commit the sin of causing a family anguish on this festive day.

The decree to prepare *mishloach manot* is a fine one, bringing people closer together. Maimonides improved it even more when he emphasized that offering packages to paupers was the most important part of the ritual.

My children are excited to take the packages from me, eager to deliver them to their respective homes according to my list. I urge them to hurry up and get the job done before sunset, as the decree must be performed in daylight.

Wednesday, April 4th, 1798

Our home is full of blessed Rothschilds, and especially now with the addition of my two grandchildren—Binyamin and Rebecca, the heart-melting children of Schönche and Moshe. And yet the house still feels spacious.

This magical space is the result of the transfer of all sacks, chests, and piles of fabrics and other goods to rented storage outside the ghetto.

A natural relationship forms between my youngest children and their young nephew and niece, who all live together. My children—six-year-old Yaakov, seven-year-old Henrietta, and eight-year-old Julie—have taken Binyamin and Rebecca, the baby they see as a smiling little doll, under their wing.

I will not deny that the proximity between the many residents of our home also offers a constant source of conflict. Among the small children these are minor, passing scuffles, forgotten a moment after peace is restored. They cannot be compared with the conflict that forms between the older children. An outsider witnessing those might think they were representatives of enemy countries in the midst of heated cease-fire negotiations.

Everything starts off well enough, but from there things spiral into Rothschild-style battlefronts. I think I've already mentioned the heart-warming details about my three sons, Amschel, Shlomo, and Nathan, who have become an inseparable part of their father's firm. Shlomo was the second to be accepted as partner. Without his sons, Meir would not be able to rule his kingdom. They act with fervor and wisdom, and, just like their father, never rest. Ideas formulate in their minds at the same frequency with which ingredients I mix in the cauldron become a stew. Their ideas crystallize into actions, which bring results fine enough to stimulate ideas to come.

This is all fine and good. But here lies a seed of conflict.

"Your suggestion is dangerous. It contains too many question marks and too few exclamation points. I object to it entirely." This is how the anxious Amschel speaks during a business consultation.

"You're an imbecile. You understand nothing. Your thinking is terribly slow. I cannot deal with you, you won't understand what I'm saying, anyway." This is how my son Nathan, who is impatient to the point of rudeness, expresses himself. Nathan is purposeful, and does not have much patience for people who can't keep up with his speed of thought. His words are preceded by an exasperated look at the ceiling and a whistling huff. He is so unlike his siblings in temperament and appearance. He is not tall, rather wide, has red hair, and is quick to lose his temper, as redheads are wont to do. He has endless energy and creativity, and he thinks independently. He is smart and ambitious. These last few qualities he inherited from his father. The rest, probably, from his forefathers.

"Enough, you two. We don't have to choose one way. There are all sorts of possibilities. We only have to decide what to do now and what to do later." That is peacemaker Shlomo. What would I do without him?

They are all wonderful in their own way. If only they wouldn't bicker all the time!

Thus continues a long series of arguments, teasing, voice raising, roaring, huffing, and puffing, in which their father often partakes, though I must admit that it is thanks to him that they don't come to blows, which until recently was an essential part of their fighting.

Sometimes this friction finds its expression outside the house, in negotiations with customers. All three of my adult sons take part in negotiations, but the most prominent is, of course, Nathan. He often finds himself at a dead end. He persists, and the other party persists as well. He protects his honor and will not compromise, and the other party does the same. Words of insult gather on his tongue. At this point, before the transaction is shattered irrevocably, Meir pushes his way in, appeasing, softening, smiling, sacrificing his honor, and lowering the price until a handshake seals the agreement.

At the debriefing, which takes place later, in the study, Meir emphasizes to his belligerent sons the need for softening, friendliness, compromise, subtlety, generosity, and calm. They nod distractedly, and Meir knows they have no intention of changing, and that they will continue to handle their disagreements in their own way.

Who knows, perhaps they need a few more years to learn how to calm down and ease up. Or maybe, in this new era that is coming into existence before our eyes, this is the kind of conduct that is necessary. Time will tell.

And nevertheless, I am concerned by Nathan's behavior, which is growing more and more extreme. His impatience often reaches unbearable heights. He feels crowded in our home. He needs space.

He's been spending more and more time in the kitchen.

◆　◆　◆

Nathan took the knife from me and peeled potatoes. He is not skilled in this task. I watched him toss the thick peels into the garbage and ached at the terrible waste. *He should peel off the skins of the importers of English fabric, who charge us higher prices every day. He would be more useful in that mission,* I thought. But I kept my mouth shut, waiting for him to open his heart.

"Mama," he whispered to me. I took the peeled potatoes and cut them into cubes. We both pretended to concentrate on our work. My ears were alert, and my eyes, although fixed on my hands, followed his motions closely from their corners.

He sighed.

My mouth stayed shut. If I breathed a word, something might go wrong. Silence is a sign of wisdom. It's best to keep quiet and listen. I am skilled at listening. I have been thoroughly trained by life with Meir. It is no accident that God gave me two ears and only one mouth. He has designed me to listen more than I speak.

He fidgeted beside me. The longer I remained quiet, the more likely this fidgeting would make way for speech. My kitchen is the best motivator for talking.

"I know Papa loves me. I know he has the business's best interests at heart, and that what is best for the business is best for all of us."

What an impressive preface. My smart son knows what he is talking about. But of course he wasn't getting his hands dirty with the potatoes just to praise his father. My clever son chose a diplomatic way into something that would likely end not as diplomatically. I had the patience to go through all the necessary steps until I reached the finish line. That's another skill of mine. I am Meir's wife, after all.

"But he thinks only he knows what's right."

There we go. I said nothing, only looked at him. My son, smart like his father, can read people's eyes. He needs no words.

"All right, Mama, you're right. Papa has proved himself. He is the founder. He's the one who turned the family business into an empire. I salute him. I know he could not have come this far if he hadn't been right all along."

How lucky that I said nothing. He had taken my place in the conversation. Rather than preach to him about his father, my silence led him to speak my own thoughts clearly. I decided to let him carry on. He was about to make his point.

"But he's got to understand that what was right back then is not right now," he said, raising his voice. "Times are changing, Mama. People do not stay the same. The world keeps evolving, advancing. Needs change, and behavior changes in accordance with them. That is the case in life, and that is the case in business. The chariot must continue to move. If it doesn't, it will lead us nowhere. You must remember how badly I had to fight Father to agree to hire outsiders. It was like talking to a sack of fabric, rather than a great merchant. It drove me mad. What was he thinking? Why didn't he open his eyes to see reality? Today is not yesterday. Today is a step toward tomorrow. Hirsch Liebman was an exception. Not everyone is a thief or a traitor. Some people are honest. Look at Geisenheimer. He goes above and beyond. Papa drives me mad. I've had enough. I can't do it anymore."

A persuasive argument, I thought, *though if I were him I'd make my tone less aggressive.* But taking into account his upset, I made no remarks nor assigned any demerits. He was right, though this idea was nothing new. He had been projecting this attitude in every business disagreement recently. And as for Seligman Geisenheimer, the young and talented bookkeeper, I agree. Meir is in full agreement on this matter as well. Geisenheimer has put order into the study with the help of Schönche and Eva, who are his cashiers. He even recommended that Meir hire a tutor, Dr. Michael Hess, to complete the general education of our Yaakov. The liberal teacher has managed to impart upon our six-year-old an education superior to that enjoyed by his older siblings. I was still waiting for Nathan's bottom line. It would come, that much was certain. His entire body showed his passion.

At this point, we had finished peeling and slicing, and had begun cooking. I put down the spatula, washed and dried my hands, and handed him the towel. I sat down on a chair, and he dragged another chair over to sit across from me. He began to clear his throat. What was he cooking in there?

I looked at his tense face. His eyes were fixed on the ceiling. His head was a spot of gold.

I resisted the urge to take him in my arms, kiss him, and say, "Relax, son. Whatever happens, I'm at your side." I had to stop my tongue if I wanted to be of any use to him. My face was open to receive any kind of message, my head nodding in encouragement.

"Look, Mama, I've got to think, but I can't think here. I'm trapped. I want freedom. See, freedom of thought is like air, and I don't have enough air. I feel stifled."

I kept nodding. Fear poked at my insides. Though I wanted to ask him to scatter the fog and focus his thoughts, I forced myself to put on a peaceful face.

"I don't know how or when or where, but I have to get out."

"What do you mean, out?" I spoke for the first time—a rational, obvious, legitimate question.

He sighed, and I wanted to cry.

"Mama, I truly don't know yet, but I had to speak to you, to share this with you, to prepare you."

"Son, I understand you need freedom. But leaving one place means going to another. What is that other place? What destination do you have in mind?"

"Someplace far away. I'm not sure what kind of place yet. In the meantime I'm here, and we'll talk again soon."

He kissed my cheeks, which are accustomed to being kissed by everyone in my household but Nathan. His smile wasn't able to smooth out the worry wrinkles on his forehead, or the ones on mine.

My son is thinking of leaving home. He's young, only twenty-one years old. He doesn't even have a match yet. Where would he go?

I hope these are passing thoughts, just landing momentarily in his mind, only to disappear as quickly as they had come. But deep down I know: my Nathan is a determined man. Fickleness is his least favorite quality. What's going to become of him?

Sunday, August 5th, 1798

My kitchen conversations with Nathan grew more frequent. The blush spread over his cheeks, competing with his red hair. The initial thoughts he'd voiced to me not only did not disappear, but rather took hold of his tired mind, sharpening and branching out, growing flesh and bones.

The more conflict he had with his father and brothers, the more prepared he became to leave. The conflict that separated him from Meir brought him closer to me. Their paths were diverging, the gap between them increasing.

I am attuned to my son's distress, and I cannot stop his flight.

"I've got it!" my little Archimedes shouted one day, and I followed him into the kitchen. "England," he said, his eyes shining. The words bubbled out of his mouth: "Why should I pay more here when I can buy directly there? I'll get rid of him and take his place, that's what I'll do—"

"One moment, for God's sake, what's the rush? Wise words are spoken slowly. Speak so that I can understand. Why England?"

"Because I'm sick of working with that arrogant English broker. He's a simple textile broker, but he behaves as if he owns all of Europe. You know the goods we import from England are our most important business. You can check Geisenheimer's books. And the prices of goods from England keep rising because of the commission, which goes directly into that wretched Jeffrey's pocket."

"That's his right, that's how he makes a living. And for goodness sake, enough swearing. You wouldn't want our customers cursing us because of our prices."

"That's just it, Mama. Because of him we're forced to raise our prices so we can make a small profit too. I'm sure people are angry with us, and it isn't our fault."

"So what is my genius's idea?"

"I got the idea after a bad fight with Jeffrey. I asked to see his newest fabric samples. I must not have spoken very delicately, and he was offended and refused to show them to me. So I said, 'No matter, I'll go to England and check the samples myself.' Do you realize how brilliant that is? I'll go to England and send Papa the best fabrics from there, without paying exaggerated brokerage fees."

I burst out laughing. I couldn't help myself. He looked at me, trying to decipher my laughter, but I couldn't stop long enough to explain myself.

"All right, Mama, I get it. You think my idea is stupid. And I was naive enough to think you'd help convince Papa."

His disappointed face stopped my laughter short. It could have easily turned into crying. The line between the two is so thin. But I stopped my tears short too. "No, you misunderstood. I just find it funny that your greatest idea was formed in such a typical way for you—out of a fight. The more you fight with your siblings, the more brilliant ideas you have."

He nodded and held me tightly.

I protested. "I can't breathe, Nathan. Let go of your old mother, she needs some air." He let go and looked into my eyes. "So I take it you like the idea, Mama."

"It's impossible for me to like any idea that keeps my son away from me. And what's more, it involves many risks."

He looked at me with disappointment again, and I rushed to complete my thought. "But since you like it, I accept it. I believe you'll find a way to make it work, with all its repercussions."

"Talk to Papa, I can't have another fight with him. Please tell me you will."

I said nothing. I hesitated to grant his request. Finally I said, "You must present a detailed plan to your father. If need be, I promise to intervene on your behalf."

Sunday, August 26th, 1798

Outwardly, the next few days were tranquil. If the study itself could speak, it would have likely said something like, "What happened? Are these different people?"

"I don't know what's going on. Something isn't right."

No, this was not the study speaking, it was Meir, who received no answer.

I kept quiet, and so did Nathan. He was fully invested in preparing his plan. He kept me abreast, and I was proud of him for the depth of his analysis, for the precision he wielded, and for the creative solutions he suggested. In truth, my sense of pride was strengthened because only I knew his secret. It is a cautious pride. I do not brag, I am only proud. And there is a difference. There is no cockiness in me. A mother's pride is always allowed.

Nathan, preoccupied with planning, found no time for his regular combativeness, and his demeanor in the study was more peaceful than we'd ever seen it.

But this was not the only reason for the new mood in our home and office. I looked at Nathan's face and saw it twinkling. I attributed the twinkle to two sources: the milestone he has to look forward to, and moving away from home.

My hunch was confirmed in the kitchen.

"You know I'll miss you, Mama," he confessed, flushed and embarrassed.

I've always known he had a hint of human sensitivity. For the first time, my maternal instinct was validated. "We'll miss you too, Nathan, so much," I said, stroking his cheek.

"I know, but it's easier for you. You're all together here. The longing will be shared by all of you. I'll be there by myself, carrying the full brunt of longing, sharing it with no one. Do you understand? I'll be all alone."

"You can change your mind, Nathan, it's not too late."

"Oy vey, forget about it, *mama-lieb*. I'm going through with this. Don't even think of trying to stop me."

Now I knew he was sure of his decision. There was no point in trying to change his mind.

"All right, son, I won't badger you. I'm only interested in this longing you mention."

"I'll miss you most of all, Mama, your quiet. You offer good advice in small doses, but never make me feel like you're intervening."

"I think you've picked the wrong profession. Why don't you become a doctor of the spirit?"

"That's just what I meant. You give smart advice, without interfering. You simply offer another direction. No thank you, Mama. I dreamed of my path in life back when I was reading the Talmud, bored, impatiently awaiting Papa's orders. Right now I'm doing exactly what I want to do."

"I've been thinking, since you're going to England, why don't you see about King George the Third? I've heard he's suffering from dementia." I couldn't help but recall the mercenaries, and tried to stay calm.

Nathan looked at me reproachfully. "Don't worry about the royal palace, Mama. I have no intention of taking part in their sickness. I think I'll focus on what I'm good at, commerce."

"You're right, son. Commerce fits you perfectly. We knew it would even when you were a little boy. Even Buderus prophesied it."

"Well, Mama, I haven't proved myself yet, but I certainly intend to try my luck." He fell silent, looking at me. I looked back at him. "You should know," he said, "that Papa is always on my mind. In everything I do, I always ask myself two questions: One, what would Papa do? And two, what would he say about what I'm doing now?" He smiled awkwardly.

"And do you provide answers to these questions too?"

"Sometimes. It's a bit confusing. See, Papa is a great, self-made man. He didn't have a successful father or grandfather to follow. Papa, an orphan, did it all by himself, with his own mind and hands, against all odds. Just think what measly chances this sorry ghetto provides, burying us under decrees from the days of Antioch, without a single enlightened man to stand up and say, 'While we're on the subject of progress, it's time to change this injustice to the Jews and toss out all those inhuman prohibitions and embargoes.' We can barely stick our heads out to breathe in some stale air. And where is this injustice taking place? In Frankfurt, the big, modern city, a destination for people from all over Europe. How dare the city treat us this way?" He paused, huffing. "I was going to discuss Papa and ended up talking about the Jews in general. Maybe it's because to me Papa represents the Jews. He proved that you can find the way to the top even if you begin in the gutter."

He started to laugh, and I held back tears. My son, who's had conflict with his father for so long, was standing before me, telling me about his hero father and what he represents to him.

Where was he all this time? Did he have to pack his bags in order to wake up and see his father's greatness?

Just as suddenly as he began to laugh, he fell silent. "Look, Mama, Frankfurt is the mother of all evil. I'm crowded here. I don't want to see the Judensau every day. As hard as I try not to look up, my eyes get pulled to the top of that bridge, and my heart tells me I must shatter this evil." He sighs.

I looked at my son. I thought of the Judensau, the "Jews' Sow," that hideous painted relief at the top of the bridge tower at the entrance to the city, and saw it through my son's eyes. A fat sow ridden by a rabbi lifting its tail to allow another rabbi to eat its excrement, while other Jews, wearing pointy hats as decreed by law, suckled from her teats. In the background the devil watches with glee.

So much suffering in his young heart. I wished I could take the suffering for myself and set him free.

"Papa did great things," he continued. "I don't know where he got the strength. We all have that same fervor. It's a pure Rothschild inheritance, without which we can't keep climbing."

He brushed a red lock from his forehead, which was ever widening with encroaching baldness. So young and already losing his hair. I'm sure this is a result of the mental effort he makes on a daily basis.

"Sometimes I tell myself, 'Papa would have treated this customer gently,' and maybe for him that is the right way. But I can't do that. I agree that sometimes Papa's patience and his ability to smooth things over are necessary for the success of a transaction. But I often pose an ultimatum to a customer, which causes them to hurry up and make the deal. Then I pat myself on the back, but simultaneously I wonder, *What would Papa say? Would he pat my back too, or would he tell me off?*"

The light beaming from his face while he spoke of his father told me that he accepted his criticism forgivingly.

I hope his father accepts Nathan's decision to leave with the same forgivingness. I hope he understands his son is not abandoning him, only getting some distance and expanding his horizons.

Thursday, September 6th, 1798

Nathan decided it was time to reveal his big secret. It was at the end of a family dinner. The little ones were already in bed, and the older ones lingered as usual with their father, quibbling about Torah portions. As Rabbi Shimon said, *Three men who have shared a table and spoken words of Torah over it have eaten in a palace.*

I returned from the kitchen after making sure the dishes were clean, the ceramic plates in one closet, the cups in another, and the cauldron and pan hanging from their regular spot on the wall. I took my usual seat in the chair near the window. A routine glance outside presented me with a dark, empty street. Everyone was indoors. I turned to face the others, my ears alert and my hands knitting a blanket for my granddaughter Rebecca in preparation for winter.

Nathan turned to his father. "Papa, I need to talk to you."

"I need to talk to you too, son."

"Since my matter is of great importance, you'd better start, and then we can move on to me," Nathan offered.

"My matter is also of great importance. As great as the size of England, actually. Who should go first, then?"

We have seen some surprises around this table, but the mouths that gaped around it now had never looked so big.

Everyone's eyes were on Meir. Nathan's face showed the shock of this surprise. He screeched, "Huh?"

"You meant to surprise me and are now surprised yourself, aren't you, dear son? You worked so hard on your plan, thinking over every detail, but you overlooked one."

Nathan's face filled with questions. He looked at his father, his mouth paralyzed, his eyes clinging to the man's lips. He couldn't move.

I had no questions. In fact, the goings-on in our home in the past week, which I admit I should have noticed, were suddenly clarified. I felt awful, knowing I hadn't seen, realized, and warned my son in advance. I stifled an urge to get up and hug him, stroke his hair, shake and break the tension in his body.

I could see Meir's face, but what I saw in his face must have eluded Nathan, for he was focused solely on this unexpected turn and could not concentrate on anything else in these critical moments.

Meir looked at me and nodded lightly at my pleading face. *Be gentle with him,* I whispered voicelessly. Shards of hope fluttered within me.

"Look, Nathan," Meir began, and I clenched my fists. "These past few days, I've been pleased by a new image, one that has surprised me and motivated me to do some detective work. I didn't have to work too hard—you made it easy for me. You were so preoccupied you didn't even notice that you had created this new picture with your own behavior."

He was speaking in riddles, but I was most concerned with the reproachful tone that accompanied his words. I pitied Nathan. Why torture him this way?

"This new picture is of a tranquil home full of smiles and kind words, free of conflict and teasing. A heartwarming image, no doubt, and quite pleasing. But that isn't my home. It's an illusion, I told myself, unless something is going on right under my nose. I do not like surprises. I turned to myself and to you and said, 'I do not understand what's going on. Something is not right. What is different?' But I received no answer. When I repeated myself, using different wording to phrase my question, the answer still didn't come. I began to snoop around in my own home, inside the study. From the very beginning, all signs led to you, Nathan. It became clear that you were the one who had changed. Where did all the anger, teasing, bickering, criticism, and roaring disappear to? How could everything be running so smoothly at home and in the study? Could you truly be approving of all of our decisions? How could it be that whenever you look at me, your father, or at your siblings, all those usual wrinkles of discontent are gone, your forehead as smooth as a baby's?"

My heart ached for Nathan. I knew his father's lengthy preface was not helping his growing nervousness. The air in the room thickened. Nathan reached for the saltshaker and turned it distractedly in his hand. I realized Meir did not intend to make things easy for his son, and was in no rush to finish. He would not miss out on this perfect opportunity to teach him a life lesson, especially if his son intended to embark on a new, long road.

"Like I said," Meir continued, as smug as one who was about to conclude his speech before a large crowd at the synagogue. "You over-looked one important detail: routine. If you wanted to surprise me, you should have made sure to act normally, like any other day. You left too many clues, all suspicious. It was as if you'd lit all the candles, stood in the center of the room, and yelled, 'Come look for me!' You see? I didn't need to search for you. You were right there. All I had to do was look. Where you went, I followed, but unlike you, I made sure not to leave any tracks. I pretended to behave as if it were any other day. I did not give you the slightest clue that I knew. That is how you keep a secret—you behave normally, attracting no fire."

Now Meir turned his face away from Nathan and addressed Amschel and Shlomo. "Remember that, you two. If you do not want to be exposed, you must project 'business as usual.' We must never show our weakness or let our emotions get the better of us. Self-control is the key to success. Self-control is necessary for many occasions in life, including negotiation. Do not lose your temper, even if you feel like ripping the head off the extortionist standing before you. Speak to him with respect, with friendliness, all while continuing to check internally whether the transaction is worthy or not. Remember, do not dampen their excitement, but restrain your own impulses. Beware of walls, against which enemy ears might be listening. Behave so that even the greatest manipulator cannot divulge a single fact from you. The desire to know is man's natural inclination. That's true of all of us. Unlike others, we have to make sure to keep information to ourselves on the one hand, and on the other hand use it as leverage toward wealth. The more we find out before anyone else, the more our knowledge becomes a weapon."

I fixed Meir with a look of rebuke. He'd pulled out all his heavy guns at once, even those that had nothing to do with what was happening with Nathan. These were all things our children had known from their first day of work, but it wasn't like Meir to miss an opportunity to remind anyone of the rules, certainly not his son, fruit of his loins, who seemed to be headed for battle.

Meir's eyes met Nathan's. Nathan appeared to be searching for the perfect angle for the saltshaker, turning it slowly.

The boys fidgeted uncomfortably, exchanging confused looks and moving their compassionate eyes from Nathan to his father, and back. My eyes darted between them all.

"Before I give you my opinion of your idea, do you have anything to say in your defense?" Meir asked Nathan, resuming his cold tone.

Nathan looked up at him, searching his face for his meaning. He put down the saltshaker and interlaced his fingers. "I was going to say several things," he said hoarsely, "but they all seem redundant after your preface." He carried on in the voice of a man finding his bearings. "I will say only this—I must correct you on one point. More than I meant to surprise you, I thought it best to prepare the ground and present you with as clear a picture as possible, in order to persuade you to welcome my decision."

"That argument is valid, although I think the idea of preparing the ground sounds more like your mother's than yours."

"Guilty as charged; it was Mama's idea."

"Let me point out that it isn't a bad idea at all. Only its execution was faulty, as you must already understand."

"Perhaps."

Nathan's impatience was beginning to show. Short statements are his signature. The final threads of restraint were being torn away. I began to worry that if Meir postponed the moment of truth any longer, this opportunity might slip away. Meir must have sensed that too, and he acted accordingly.

"As for your idea . . . moving to England, conducting commerce there and sending fabric over here . . ."

We were all holding our breaths, awaiting the big moment. Meir let his words linger on Nathan's face, which again looked as still as a statue.

"It's a good idea, son. You have my blessing."

The air trapped in our lungs was released with one unified sigh. Meir, embraced in Nathan's muscular arms, gave me a cheerful look, as if to say, *I had you worried too. You deserve it for trying to keep secrets— trying and failing.* I can't say for sure if he wanted to say all that in that moment, but that is how I felt during the loud and happy celebration that followed in the living room at that late hour, with all the sleeping children jumping out of bed, rubbing their eyes at the peculiar sight.

NOTEBOOK 2

Tuesday, September 18th, 1798

My new notebook is a mark of a significant milestone in my family. The first accounting ledger, which I'd received from my father at age fifteen, thirty (!) years ago—is full. Many things have happened in my life and my family's, and they have all been documented and saved in my notebook in legible handwriting. I began writing again in my first notebook when I fell in love with Meir, a love that has stood the test of time, the years bringing with them new and beautiful tones that improve the good, old ones. The first notebook marked the beginning of a new life, life in the company of Meir Rothschild.

Today, I begin a second notebook. I made sure to find a matching one, identical to the old one I loved, a notebook that is a true friend, to which I open all the secrets of my heart: my worries and joys, my thoughts and deeds, as well as the deeds of my family. My handwriting has changed, my letters growing plump and taking up more space. It is no wonder, as my eyesight isn't as sharp as it once was, though I must thank the God above for granting me satisfactory vision. At the same time, I must admit that the larger letters do not translate into better handwriting. On the contrary, it is not as handsome as it once was, and at times I must work hard to decipher my own words. Since I cannot ask anyone for help, I may have to put more effort into writing legibly.

I will start with the morning after Nathan's big announcement. He made his preparations, and was two days away from his departure to England. For the first time, a son of ours, flesh of our flesh, was about to leave the house, the city, the country, the Holy Roman Empire. For the first time, our business was literally crossing borders, all the way to England. If this is not a milestone, what is?

Nathan prepared thoroughly and carefully. He calculated many details, large and small, and Meir added his own. In fact, the two of them did nothing but prepare for the trip to England, heads touching, Meir's arm around his son's shoulders while his other hand ran over the map or sketched one of the ideas their minds were constantly producing.

I committed these images to memory, since the house would soon empty of them.

The other boys looked displeased. They wished to participate in the preparations, but had to make do with peeking in and receiving partial updates in between dealing with the suddenly increased workload.

Meir thought long and hard about an appropriate companion for his son's voyage and early stay in the foreign country. Everyone believed de Worms was the man for the job, but Meir's choice was Seligman Geisenheimer, our bookkeeper, who is skilled in accounting and fluent in five languages, including English. In addition to vital assistance with numbers, Geisenheimer will serve as Nathan's voice until he learns the new language.

Our home is very busy. From young to old, no one escapes the turmoil. Take Yaakov, for instance: whenever he takes study breaks, which are now growing longer and longer under the smiling approval of Dr. Michael Hess, he runs over to the two planners, sniffs their papers, runs his little finger over the sketches, asks and investigates and receives answers, and when he is satisfied, climbs up Nathan's back and asks for a ride. "You'll be leaving soon, and I won't have another horse like you," he cries from his brother's back, waving an imaginary whip in the air and calling out, "Giddyup! Take me to England!"

Meir tries to keep a straight face. Only when we lie in bed at night, far from the eyes of the family, and especially of Nathan, does he set his thoughts free.

"You know, Gutaleh," he said one night, turning toward me, pulling one hand from under his head to take mine. I clung to his hand. I needed his touch in order to make sense of my own thoughts. I too have a chest of thoughts with an open lid, and it fills up every day, every moment, until it is about to burst.

"Our Nathan makes me proud. This bold, ambitious boy gives me hope. He is only twenty-one years old, and already has extraordinary aspirations. He is unlike Amschel and Shlomo, or any other boy I know, for that matter. I've never felt surer of any decision as I am of giving him my blessing and a respectable starter fund. He will succeed. I don't have any illusions about things getting easier between us. I know Nathan is Nathan. Even a geographic distance can't put an end to our disputes. They may even get worse as he learns and experiences the big world out there. But he's got a good mind, our boy, and that's what matters to me."

I noted the tremor in his voice. His emotional state made my stomach rumble. I loved his words. I loved the trust he put in our son. The father admires his son as the son admires his father. I only wish they would tell each other.

"Do you understand, Gutaleh?" Meir continued to verbalize his thoughts. "Do you understand what it means to reside in England, navigating our business from there? Do you understand the kind of starting point he's picked? A fine one. This is the best possible choice a man from Judengasse can make. I know he isn't the first to immigrate to England, or the last. More and more people jump on this wagon these days. But he is going to do what no one else can even imagine. And as long as he does it before others get a chance to, he can expect success, because one accomplishment leads to many others."

Meir keeps referring to success in business. He admires his son, but his measure for admiration is embodied in a single key word: business. It reminded me of our wedding night, but this time I was not vulnerable. I knew him inside and out. He and business were one and the same, living with each other in peace, inseparable.

Suddenly he sighed, kissed me, and whispered, "Good night." His hand fluttered over my body until it stopped. He was asleep before I had a chance to say a word. I brought my mouth to his ear and whispered, "Nathan loves you. He admires you and needs you." He said nothing, his quiet snoring attesting to the peace of mind of a proud father.

Wednesday, September 26th, 1798

Yesterday we said goodbye to Nathan. Suitcases and bags were loaded onto the carriage. The coachman sat up front, holding the reins. Nathan boarded the wooden bench in back, restraining his excitement, trying to hide his flushed face that had been kissed and pinched endlessly. Geisenheimer took a seat beside him, also excited by this new beginning. His effort to project the confidence of a man who realized the size of his responsibility was apparent.

The velvet chest containing the unfathomable sum of 20,000 pounds was hidden beneath the floor of the carriage. A sum entrusted by Meir to his son. The majority of the fortune was Meir's, and a small part was accumulated by Nathan through his work. This was Meir's way of expressing his hope for this adventure, and expressing the high expectations he had for the match between Nathan and England.

Nathan had been informed of the amount two days earlier. Almost half of the capital registered in the books. Who knew numbers better than him? He looked at his father and clumsily wrapped his arms around the man's shoulders.

"Papa," he whispered into his ear. "It's too much."

"That's right, son. I expect the profits this money will yield to match your appreciation of the amount."

He pulled away a bit to allow his eyes to run along Nathan's face and body. Our son looked at his father and nodded, restraining his emotions.

In the parting moments, the Rothschilds—including my parents, my siblings, their spouses, and children, Moshe (Meir's brother) and his grown children—all gathered around the carriage.

My father kissed Nathan.

"Grandpa, the tefillin you gave me for my bar mitzvah is safe in my bag," Nathan said.

"Good—never forget it. It will always keep you safe, dear grandson." He placed a bony hand on his grandson's head, mumbling a blessing. My mother walked over, hugged Nathan with all her might, her stifled tears muffling her words. "Take care of yourself, dear Nathan," she finally managed.

"Dear Grandma, thank you for everything you've done for me," he whispered, then turned to his father.

Meir placed both hands on his son's shoulders, looking into his eyes. "Now listen to my request and my demand. You must write to me, keep me abreast of every single detail. Remember, I am the head of this business, and I must be up to date on everything."

"All right, Papa," Nathan answered through a choked throat, walking over to me and taking my hands in his, a slight smile on his lips.

"Take care of yourself," I said, my voice strangled. "Beware of those who wish you ill. Be vigilant. Lock the doors of your home. Do not let in strangers. And always remember we're your family, that we love you and will always love you, unconditionally. Promise me that you won't hesitate to come home whenever you want to. Our arms are open to accept you at any time."

"All right. Please don't worry. Take care of yourself, *mama-lieb*, and keep sending me strength from afar. You are the best mama in the world."

We hugged for a long time. My tears stained his shoulder.

"Now, have my blessing for your journey," Meir said, placing a hand on the hot head, whispering some final wishes. When he was finished, he kissed his son and placed a piece of parchment in his hand. "This is the Traveler's Prayer," he said. "Read it when you're aboard the ship."

Nathan looked at the parchment, nodded, and buried it in his pocket. From the pocket of my dress, I pulled a talisman I'd prepared. It bore these words: *Peace, peace, to those far and near. May the Lord bless you and guard you. May the Lord make His face shed light upon you and be gracious unto you. May the Lord lift up His face unto you and give you peace. So they will put my name on the Israelites, and I will bless them.* "Here, son. Keep this safe, and it will keep you safe. Go in life and peace and may the Lord illuminate your path." I put my arms around him, preparing for another lengthy hug, but he pushed me away tenderly. I took a few steps back, longing already making its way into my heart.

Suddenly, as if on cue, the entire family pounced, showering him with hugs, kisses, well wishes, and declarations of love. Vendeleh wouldn't let go until the last person to say goodbye, Nathan's good friend, Benedict Moshe de Worms, came over, and she stepped aside for him. The paths of the brothers-in-law, which had converged and budded in our home, would continue even when they were miles and miles apart.

Nathan and de Worms had made a plan for a business collaboration. Late at night they sat together at the table, and between sips of apple wine devised a plan for the establishment of a textile importing business. Moshe would take care of the local business in Germany, while Nathan would run the business from England. They would not lose touch.

My son has gone on his way with the help of God, and I carry a prayer in my heart. I must have the girls read Psalms.

The journey is long, and a first letter from Nathan can only be expected many days from now. How hard it is to bear the days.

I imagine my son crouching in the belly of the ship, pondering the secret future awaiting him far beyond the horizon.

On Yom Kippur, which took place a week ago, before I started my day, I turned to heaven and asked the kind Lord to protect my son.

Thursday, November 15th, 1798

Waiting for news can feel like an infinite state. We've had nerve-racking weeks waiting for a letter from Nathan. But I mustn't feel bitter for what is in the past, now that a letter has finally arrived. Here is the letter, verbatim:

> *My dear father, my teacher and rabbi, and* mama-lieb,
> *Here I sit, fulfilling my first duty on foreign land by composing a first letter to you.*
>
>   *Eight days ago, after a long journey by sea that took longer than expected due to different malfunctions that do not pertain to me, we arrived safely in London, the English capital. I shall only mention the dizziness on the ship, caused by the wind, which had all of us throwing up. How good to know it is behind me.*
>
>   *In spite of the cold of early winter and the fog covering the city, to my surprise, London has accepted me quite warmly. I must be accurate: I am not referring, of course, to Englishmen, but to our people, the English Jews. To be accurate, as you have taught me to be, Papa, I should mention the leaders of the Ashkenazi Jewish community.*

This is the time to explain a matter that has been secretly shared with me. The Jews of London are divided into two groups: those who came from Spain and the Mediterranean, and those who came from France and Germany.

I cannot understand why the two sides have not united. We are all brothers. But the reality here, which I am still learning, has developed a rivalry and a harsh divide between the two groups. This is demonstrated by separate synagogues: the Sephardic Jews pray at Bevis Marks Synagogue, located on the outskirts of the City (as Londoners refer to the center of town) while the Ashkenazi Jews pray at Duke's Place. I have no interest in the roots of this divide, which I cannot fathom. At any rate, as an émigré from Frankfurt, I was taken under the wing of the Ashkenazi community, and led to the synagogue at Duke's Place.

My friend Seligman is a great help when it comes to the English language, and serves as my voice wherever I go. And yet, I am determined not to become too attached to this lifesaver, though the temptation for comfort is great in light of the fact that the language spoken here might as well be Chinese as far as I'm concerned. I must do everything possible to become independent. I have already consulted with the welcoming community leaders, located the financial leaders, and ended up at L. B. Cohen and Levy Solomons. It turns out, Papa, that your perception is as astute as ever. The Londoner banker you chose to work with in recent years is no less than the number-one banker.

Well, *I'm getting to know him quite well. Levy Barent Cohen is a kind, smart, guileless Jew. I was lucky, being the son of Meir Rothschild of Frankfurt, and having the help of the heads of community, and Levy Barent Cohen agreed to teach me the secrets of English commerce. He treats me fairly. I must become proficient in the field, and hope at the same time to learn the language as quickly as possible. Who knows, I might surprise you with a letter in English one of these days . . .*

Though I am in a hurry, all my instincts pushing me to act, I think I'll spend a bit longer with Mr. Cohen before diving into the deep end.

Dear Papa, my first steps in this faraway land remind me of your life and your first steps in the business world, which had also begun by moving away from home. Hanover, far away from Frankfurt, was where you decided to take action, equipping yourself with the first tools that led you to greatness. Your success strengthens me and my faith in your way.

My sense is that I've come to the right place. Unlike my place of birth, as I walk in this strange and foreign land, the bells of liberty echo within me. I needn't worry about prohibitions and embargoes. I am just like anybody else.

I will end this letter with a hug, dear Mama and Papa, a hug for you and my beloved brothers, and kisses for my sisters and nephews and nieces, whom I miss dearly. Mama-lieb, *stop worrying. As you can see, I am safe.*

I will try to write as I have been told. I would also love to receive a letter at the address appearing on the envelope and learn more about the events at home and at M. A. Rothschild.

Yours,

Your loving son, Nathan Rothschild

I read the letter a dozen times. Isn't it wonderful to receive written words from my son who is far away, and learn that he is doing so well? I believe the combination of his special personality with the appropriate place and our prayers to God above is a blessing and a benefit.

Bless the venerable Levy Barent Cohen for the generosity he is showing a young man, with whom he has nothing in common other than his faith. Nevertheless, he offers him a seat at his table and shows him the finest hospitality.

This does not mean I am no longer worried. I reread the letter, waiting breathlessly for the next.

My heart contracts and groans. The letter is destroyed. "We mustn't leave a trace," Meir said before tearing the paper into small bits, burying them among the peels of the potatoes I had prepared for lunch, and throwing it all out in the large garbage can.

The words of my faraway son, which emerged from an excited heart and became etched into mine, are now mixed with dung and filth.

Thursday, May 30th, 1799

Meir, Amschel, and Shlomo work as one. They stride along at full speed in the banking and textile business, importing medals and coins from the Near and Far East, as well as a new product that has only recently been permitted for Jews to trade—wine.

Their speed has the appearance of a maddening dance to the beat of rumbling drums. They jump from one task to the next, gliding, hovering, then landing and taking off again. Perhaps I should sew three pairs of wings to attach to their wonderful arms. How much blood flows through their veins! It is as if a river of blood runs through their bodies. Nathan's absence forces them to utilize their full powers in the limited hours of daylight, and only sunset stops their work. At night they plop into their beds, drained, submitting to sleep like helpless babies. And I let myself walk over quietly and kiss their foreheads. They won't feel a thing, anyway.

The office team, now fully female until Geisenheimer returns from England, has been working nonstop as well. My daughters Schönche and Isabella and my daughter-in-law, Eva, have all demonstrated great responsibility in their work, and seem to be competing to see whose contribution is the greatest, all while maintaining a pleasant atmosphere. There's no doubt they add a graceful aspect to the office, through which severe-looking men stride frantically on their way to the next destination.

Nathan's letters are the epitome of our expectations. It seems that all of our frantic daily activity is nothing but preparation for the arrival of a letter from England, and life on earth, full of busyness, is conducted for the redemption of the letter that comes every three weeks.

His most recent letter, which came yesterday, announced his departure for Manchester. His new address appears in it. Who ever heard of this place? He speaks of it as if his presence there is obvious.

Upon first read, I spotted all sorts of odd words and indecipherable sentences. I wrinkled my forehead, and Meir watched me with the amused smile of one in the know.

"Were you able to read this, Meir?"

"Of course, Gutaleh. I don't see the problem. Don't you recognize your son's handwriting?" He took the letter from me and pretended to read it again, his head moving from right to left to match the direction of Judendeutsch, unlike German, which is written from left to right. "Everything's fine, I see nothing wrong."

He was clearly teasing. Suddenly, I remembered. "How could I forget? Confusing the enemy, that's what he's doing. Well, he's managed to confuse his mother too." I picked up the letter again and tried to read through the bizarre script.

The rules of letter writing were agreed upon in the early instruction Nathan received from his father. As long as he wrote about mundane affairs, there was no reason not to write simply and directly. But when he described business affairs that had to be kept secret from information-thirsty censors, specific rules of coding had to be followed. The Judendeutsch—our unique language that is unfamiliar to strangers—already poses some considerable difficulties for a foreign reader. But we could not underestimate the risks—the letter might be handed over to someone who speaks our language, and we would be doomed. The

Rothschild recipe, composed of Judendeutsch, Hebrew, Aramaic, and a touch of German, forms a stew that suits the family's stomach, but can cause an ulcer to anyone not used to consuming it.

Nathan's letter from Manchester is filled with words designed to confuse the enemy—a signal that there have been some developments that must be hidden from the eyes of strangers. Here is the letter, after careful decoding:

Dear Papa, my teacher and rabbi,

I hope this letter finds you well.

I was grateful to receive your latest letter and glad to hear your hands are full of fruitful work.

Let me begin by asking you to send all future letters to my new address. I must inform you, dear Papa, that my adjustment period is over. I could, of course, prolong it as much as I wanted. Mr. Levy Barent Cohen is a dear, gracious man who has touched my heart, and it's safe to assume he likes me too. He tried to keep me for a few more months under his wing, but as you know, an idle life does not sit well with me. I cannot spend all my days learning and receiving guidance. Those things are not sufficient to quench my thirst and fill my large stomach. Though the guidance did include experiencing the work itself, it is no longer sufficient if it does not yield fruit. Moreover, I feel that what I've learned thus far of English business theory is enough to start me off on my new path. And experiencing the work firsthand would be the finest teacher (even if the experiences of independent life can sometimes cost a pretty penny, and who knows that better than you, my father, my teacher).

*What can I tell you, beloved Papa? I walk in this free
land, in which all people are equal. We are all God's creatures, and even the changing image of God between one
faith and the next cannot distinguish between humans.
There are no ghettos here, no chains, no humiliations. I
am no longer anxious about being Jewish. I am not afraid
of hearing cries of "Hep! Hep!" or "Jude, mach Mores!"
And there is no* Schutzjude *tax, either. The space is open,
and I am free to live where I choose. I can hold my head
high. I am a free man. I may not be as light as a bird in
flight, but I am allowed to walk where I please, and the
feeling is worth a fortune.*

*As I have learned, Manchester is the industrial city of
England and of Europe, in general. Therefore, my rightful
place is here, in the heart of the matter. From the moment
I arrived here in the beginning of this month, I have not
ceased to be impressed with the possibilities in trading at
the center of the textile industry. The prices here are far
lower than in Frankfurt, and I intend to make calculated
use of the money you gave me (it is someplace safe, in a
velvet box hidden in the back of my room and concealed
in the same manner as your treasure. The apple doesn't
fall far from the tree, even if it is currently higher, eh?).*

*I have developed a method for trading in fabrics, the
purpose of which is to lower our costs and increase our
income. I hope you catch my drift, as I must take every
measure of safety, as you have guided me in your wisdom.*

Well, *the theory is simple: the production of goods
is a three-phase process. At first there is raw material.
Then color is added, and finally the production process
is underway. So I thought, if these are the three phases
that turn raw material into a finished product, then I*

can profit from each and every phase. I approached the manufacturer and offered to provide the raw material and the color, and in return he would provide me with a finished product. There is no doubt in my mind that you have already comprehended the efficiency of this method. But since Amschel and Shlomo are also reading this letter, and their perception is not as fast as yours, I will explain my manner of thinking more slowly. Please focus. In a single transaction I have made three separate sales: first, I sold raw materials. Second, I sold paint. And third, I sold a finished product. A three-sale profit!

Because whatever another man can do, so can I. This is what you were thinking back in Hanover, isn't it?

To sum up: since I have the upper hand when it comes to calculating expenses and income, we are able to lower fabric prices in Frankfurt, take over the market, and increase our profits immeasurably.

How lucky it is that people's thinking is so often slow. If it hadn't been, others may have acted as I have, spoiling my advantage.

You will receive the first shipment of linens next week. Please let me know when it arrives.

Farewell and kisses, Mama (I love you and miss you). To my beloved sisters Schönche and Isabella and my dear sister-in-law, Eva, please enjoy a pat on the back for your loyal work at the central Rothschild headquarters. Babette, my gentle sister, I salute you for offering so much help around the house and for the warmth you exude over your little siblings. Sweet Julie and Henrietta, I have included English dolls for you in the fabric shipment. Kalman, you will soon finish your studies and join the expanding family business. We need you. Little

Yaakov, the latest letter from home informed me that you are doing exceptionally well at school, and for that I am proud of you. School will help you in the world of business when you get older. To Amschel and Shlomo, keeping the flame alive—Amschel, I understand you and Eva are still stuck at Mama and Papa's home. The good life is hard to leave behind, eh? To my brother-in-law, my friend, and my business partner—Moshe, congratulations to you and Schönche and the children for moving to your own little home. I am certain that traffic is lighter there. And to my lovely nephew and niece, Binyamin and Rebecca, I hope to have more just like you soon.

 Love,
 Nathan Meir Rothschild
 Manchester, England

My son is satisfied with the advantages of open space, and is functioning in the way he had expected and hoped for before he embarked on this new path. But I couldn't help but notice that his vanity had remained intact. He is aware of his merits and flaunts them without modesty or consideration. I worry about the moment when Amschel and Shlomo, who are meant to return from Kassel tomorrow, read the letter and rebel against the sharp arrows shot at them. I regret the fact that Nathan's bluntness has not dulled, and that his first order of business in his new career path in England is to lash out at his siblings. It turns out that even the great distance between us is not enough to change him. A man who has always mocked his siblings will not cease to do so just because he has changed his address.

And there is something else that saddens me deeply: the short life span of Nathan's letters in our home. I never thought my potato peels would have any kind of function, certainly not as camouflage. I must put off cooking any potatoes on days when we receive a letter.

Sunday, December 28th, 1800

It has been about a year and a half since I last wrote in my notebook.
The previous entry was made in the late 1700s, and for the past year we
have been in a new century, the 1800s. Such a leap.

I have news that I must report. Our family has expanded, but the
head count in our home has gone down. How is this possible? Our
Shlomo married the sweet, eighteen-year-old Caroline, the only daughter of our neighbor, Shmuel Hayyim Stern, a successful wine wholesaler.
The happy father of the bride has granted the couple a handsome dowry
in the sum of 5,000 gulden, and has also promised, as is the custom on
our street, housing for the first two years. As a result, although Caroline
has joined our family, Shlomo has left our home, and now lives in obvious joy with his wife at her parents' house.

I must point out that before Shlomo was married, when Meir went
knocking on Mr. Stern's door, and in the days after Mr. Stern gave his
consent to the match and accepted the terms posed by the Rothschild
matchmaker and head of the household, I was plagued with doubts,
fears, hesitations, and worry.

In the days meant to fill a mother's heart with joy, rather than strut
like a peacock, I moped like a sad puppy. I was afraid that Shlomo

would repeat Amschel's mistake. Amschel chose not to wait until he found his heart's desire, and rushed to satisfy his father's wishes, which translated the family honor into money. As a result, he is now miserable in his marriage.

Amschel gets his lust for life from three compensating sources: One is his work and partnership at M. A. Rothschild and Sons. The second is his growing religious fervor, which leads him to treat even the tiniest decree with the utmost gravity. He likes to say, "Every day that goes by without performing a mitzvah is a wasted opportunity." The third is the charitable work he does as part of the Freemasons, whose ranks he has recently joined. *They have freely scattered their gifts to the poor, their righteousness endures forever.*

Shlomo's excitement about Caroline made me worry that it might originate from the honor she would bring to the family, as the daughter of a wealthy man. Shlomo needs love and is entitled to love by virtue of being human and of being sensitive, caring, and of striving for peace and camaraderie.

For days after they announced their engagement, I sniffed after the two of them. I could not find a fault in their relationship, but my fear did not let up, gnawing at me day and night. I stared at her, averting my eyes only when she met them with a questioning look. When the wedding date was chosen, I decided not to hold back anymore, and to share my concerns with Meir.

Our deepest conversations have always taken place in our bedroom, preferably in bed. When I initiate them, I must hurry to inform him of my intentions before he falls asleep.

I slipped into my nightgown and lay down beside him, taking in some of his body heat. "Meir, do you remember how hot our love burned even before we married?" I worked my hand under the pointy sleep cap on his head, and thought for the umpteenth time how lucky I was to have eventually received my father's permission.

Meir awoke to me. He kissed me tenderly, and his hands moved over my body. "I will never forget that burning, my love. I think we are still on fire. Come to me, let us satisfy the flame." He pulled me closer, reaching for the hem of my nightgown.

I stopped his hand, kissed it, and sat on the edge of the bed. "Just imagine that the 'court banker' title you received from the landgrave Wilhelm had been delayed for a year or two. By that time, I might have been married to another."

"Who, for instance?" Meir asked teasingly, pulling back his hands. The flame diminished on its own, making way for another awakening. "Let me think. Who were my poor, heartbroken competitors? I do not recall seeing them around."

"Don't brag, Meir Rothschild. You came to me when I was just a young thing, making my head turn. You decided, as was your custom, to beat the others to the punch. Before they could even plan their visit to my parents' home, I was already out of there."

He laughed. "Say, Gutaleh, have you ever been wrong? How is it that everything you do and say and explain is right? I, for instance, cannot attest to having never been wrong. Just look at all the mistakes I've made. Take Hirsch Liebman, for instance," he sighed.

"Don't start sighing on me now. Laughter becomes you more."

He smiled and beckoned for me to continue, clearing a small stage for me, a stage I do not often take advantage of.

"I learn many things from you, Meir. Now please accept a lesson from me. A person who does nothing makes no mistakes. You are a man of action, and action entails some errors here and there. Their function is to make you open your eyes and buff your diamond a little more. But they are so few that if we weigh them against your success, the scales would tip so hard in favor of success that they would collapse and shatter."

Laughter returned to his face. "Oh, that's better," he said. Then he stopped laughing. "What's on your mind, Gutaleh? Why are you so worried about Shlomo? He loves Caroline and she loves him. I want you to smile and look at the picture from the correct angle."

Even now, after thirty years of marriage, this mind reader sharing my bed is still capable of surprising me. "I don't know, Meir. Everything looks good, and yet my concerns won't leave me. I have studied Caroline. Other than the obvious fact that she is beautiful and that she comes from fine breeding, I have noted her intelligence and sensitivity, two vital qualities that make an excellent starting point. She has the potential to become a splendid homemaker, and I have no doubt that she would also fit in at the office and do her share. But I need to know how much they truly love each other. I am afraid he might be marrying her only to please you."

"Look, Gutaleh. I can see that work is taking up too much of our time, leaving us too little time for conversation. I forgot to share my agreement with Shlomo with you. He was the one who insinuated that the two of them had made a connection and that the time had come to take things to the next step. Everything I did was for him and by his initiative."

"And how do you know he did not tell you these things just to please you? Might I remind you that Amschel was also the one who initiated approaching Eva's parents?"

"Oh, the two cases are very different. Amschel was lackluster throughout their engagement. You were anxious from the very beginning, and with good reason. I believed time would do what nature failed to, and that was another one of my mistakes to be placed on the scales. But just look at the light in Shlomo's eyes. You cannot mistake it for a ploy for my sake. Only love can spark a light like that. Trust me, I have some experience in this."

Now it was my turn to sigh. "Perhaps, perhaps." I rose from our bed, walked over to the Star of David on the wall, and ran my hand over it.

Well, the two are married. The wedding was joyous. It is a mitzvah to rejoice with the bride and groom, and a double mitzvah to rejoice with the impoverished.

The familiar glow adorned their faces, illuminating their surroundings. How lucky that sweet Caroline is not aware of my early misgivings. *There is no need to examine the body of a bride with pretty eyes.* And how lucky that Shlomo does not know either, and that Meir has promoted their marriage, uniting the two lovebirds under the chuppah.

I could not have hoped for a better daughter-in-law. She has another virtue in addition to the ones I have already listed. This virtue is the greatest of all: love. I get to see her each day as she reports for duty at the study. She is working alongside Schönche, Isabella, and Eva, and Babette has also recently started to lend a hand and handle some of the multiplying tasks piling up on the bookkeeping desk. My daughters and daughters-in-law are a more efficient and reliable workforce than any made up of strangers, which pleases the company's founder to no end.

Well then, I have experienced in the flesh the importance of one of Meir's staunchest rules: keeping a secret. Keeping my mouth shut when it came to Shlomo and Caroline has proved to be a crucial choice in forming trust between mother-in-law and daughter-in-law.

I have further learned that she who loves my son instantly wins my love.

May the good and kind Lord grant them luck and blessings, wealth and honor, and may He allow them to bring children into this world and raise them under the light of the Torah and good deeds, and lead them into a holy chuppah, amen.

Sunday, February 6th, 1803

My family is accumulating titles at the same rate that I wash our laundry. Before we have a chance to get used to one title, adjusting to its appearance, its color, the impression it makes on others, another is accepted, and the one after that is already knocking at our door.

Before I list the myriad of titles puffing Meir and his partner-sons' chests with pride, I shall report two pieces of news that make my own chest puff.

The first piece of news: my Isabella is married. After Schönche, Amschel, and Shlomo, it is our second daughter's turn to stand, sparkling and breathless, under the chuppah. Bernhard Sichel, her husband, might not be the son of a court banker, but his father is a wealthy timber merchant, which Meir likes. Most important: he and Isabella are in love. The heart does not succumb to the rules of matchmaking. It does not ask whether one is a court banker. Once it has found its twin, the two break out in a lovers' dance.

In the very delicate changes in our environment, where hushed voices whisper bitterly about mixed couples—a Jewish man marrying a gentile woman, or a Jewish woman marrying a gentile man—Meir chooses to ignore one demerit for the benefit of another, such as making sure the groom is a kosher Jew. His father's pocket better also contain some money, even if he does not carry a dignified title. "My children will never marry gentiles—and I do mean every generation of my children," he announced to the family in one of our festive and well-attended get-togethers. The little grandchildren fixed baffled eyes on their sweet Grandpa Meir who was suddenly speaking with severe decisiveness. His sons and daughters nodded in agreement.

My second piece of news: I am grandmother to four grandchildren. I must point out that I do not feel old in the least. I will be fifty this summer, and I feel forty at most, and thus the road ahead is still rather long. I have no plans to leave this world anytime soon. I still have things to accomplish in this life.

Well, last month dear Caroline, Shlomo's wife, gave birth to a darling baby. Anselm is his name. In his very first days on this earth he has captured a chamber of my heart, just like my three older grandchildren. My grandmotherly emotion provides a warm reminder of my maternal love.

I must also report an additional change, minuscule and yet meaningful. Meir's name has undergone a small adjustment this year, in favor of his relationship with German businesspeople.

He has changed the spelling of his name from Meir to Mayer. His name is now pronounced with a German inflection, another seal of approval from the German business world. From now on, Mayer Rothschild is a great tycoon who must be treated with the utmost respect.

One of his latest benefactors is no other than the Holy Roman emperor, Francis II.

I must clarify that this honor on behalf of the empire was not simply handed to Meir on a silver platter. It was preceded by initiative and hard work. Meir, may God take care of him for many years to come, sat down to write a letter to Francis II. In poetic, ingratiating (and terribly broken) German, he listed the many services he has provided to the great emperor's military, servants, and allies. The number of items on the list is large, and the number of mistakes, I imagine, is no smaller. In conclusion, Meir requested to be granted, in return, the title of crown banker from the empire. His request was accepted, along with a permit for carrying a weapon, a waiver of quite a few taxes, and freedom of movement all over the empire.

And if that is not enough, my family has enjoyed another special attention from the court of the landgrave. The skillful services Amschel and Shlomo provide to the court in Kassel have readied the ground for their appointment as honorable bankers of the landgrave's wartime accountant's office. Of course this appointment was facilitated by Buderus.

My sons received this appointment with flushed excitement, like children donning floral crowns on their birthdays. I watch them and get carried away with their emotion. They deserve it. They are such good children. Shlomo has recently joined the Freemasons, following in Amschel's footsteps. Meir is proud of his sons' activity in an organization promoting brotherly love, aid, and truth, or the values adopted by the French Revolution: *Liberté, égalité, fraternité*. Though their hands are filled with work, they allot a fair deal of time to public aid and charity work. Pure Rothschilds.

And what's more, last winter, Meir received the title of Oberhofagent, head court banker, the highest rank ever to be given to a court Jew in Kassel. Truth be told, Buderus's recommendations were not enough to secure this title. It had to be bought with a sum equivalent to 5,000 gulden.

It seems that Buderus's work and Meir's money further strengthened the appreciation the landgrave felt for Meir's fast and efficient handling of loans. The landgrave, who is said to be the biggest moneylender in Europe at the moment, required Meir, Amschel, and Shlomo's fast camouflaging services in order to hide the money transfers from suspicious French eyes and continue to present a neutral appearance.

Meir took careful care of the bonds, whose value was close to 5 million gulden, most of them intended for the kingdom of Denmark, which has been impoverished by the French, as well as for Darmstadt-Hesse. He managed to conceal the source of the money, which had all come from the landgrave's court.

I hope, for Buderus's sake, that he procures his own coveted title, a title of nobility to set his mind at ease with regard to the future of his children. Buderus has made sure to leave a respectable, tidy inheritance to his six children. He bought a handsome estate on the outskirts of Hanau, and at Meir's advice, wrote an official letter to the Austrian emperor, applying for knighthood. The request has yet to be approved. I must have the girls pray for him.

As for us, it seems as if the whole world is watching the titles falling upon us like stars from the sky, thinking up new ones to grant us. And now Amschel and Shlomo have received two new stars: Kassel court banker, and Thurn and Taxis court banker.

As they held their title permits with clumsy hands, Amschel and Shlomo were showered with a flood of tiny stars: court banker permits from the skies of small, bankrupt princedoms, tied with string to an ingratiating letter asking for a small loan of Rothschild proportions.

As part of this ongoing shower of stars, Amschel also received a court banker title for the Order of Saint John, whose assets were confiscated by the French. Amschel parted with 200,000 gulden, the amount stated in the attached letter, with hope mixed with doubt that the sum would be returned to him in time.

The count of the Isenburg-Birstein princedom was also given a similar amount, while the duke of Aschaffenburg was informed that his request for a loan had been approved, and would be granted in the form of a supply of grains and hay.

And there are even smaller princedoms that wish to drink in a few golden droplets from the Rothschild home, with which to revive their emptying treasuries.

Well then, the tables have turned. If Meir had to ingratiate himself to the rest of the world before, now the world is ingratiating itself to him. Can a leopard change its spots? And if so, for how long?

The last piece of news I have for the time being is one I had reported to Nathan in my letter:

> *My dearest son Nathan,*
>
> *I am fortunate to announce some great news. The changes and vicissitudes in Europe are finally approaching Frankfurt too. A great change has occurred at the gate to the city. The gate and the Judensau relief that have made your blood boil for so long have been removed! The shame is gone.*
>
> *You are welcome to visit us in Frankfurt and witness the wonder with your own eyes. I am sure that this time, as you enter the city, you will break into a smile.*
>
> *I wish so much I could see your face light up when you read this.*
>
> *Love,*
>
> *Your Mama, Gutle,*
>
> *Wife of the venerable Meir Amschel Rothschild*

I did not get to enjoy the sight of his face lighting up as he entered the city.

Nathan received my letter and hurried to visit Frankfurt on business. His first visit since abandoning his hometown for the sake of England. At our doorstep, the emotion was still apparent on his face, though some of it could be attributed to seeing his family after over four years apart.

I tried to separate both elements and rejoice in both. I patted myself on the back for my twofold success. With maternal cunning, I had pulled the strings of my son's tender heart, lifted his spirits with the happy news, and simultaneously enticed him to come see us, so that I could enjoy the sight of his face and relieve my heart of its yearning.

I took him in my arms and breathed him into his special chamber, which fluttered in a dance.

Truth be told, beauty is not one of Nathan's qualities, and it is my fault. The years have played a part in this as well—they do not agree with him. His forehead grows bigger and a bald spot is revealed when he takes off his hat. His face is flushed and round with fat, his paunch hangs off his belt like the belly of a woman in her fifth month of pregnancy. All this, along with his modest height, emphasizes his stocky appearance.

But my heart melts at the sight of him. And I know for certain that all the faults I have just listed take nothing away from his confident, powerful presence.

My son, who is smart like his father, who runs worldwide businesses, comes up with ingenious solutions for the problems that constantly pop up, problems of a scope previously unknown; this son falls like ripe fruit into the net of his little, longing mother.

And I, in fine spirits, have no qualms about the small scheme I had concocted around him.

Sunday, April 22nd, 1804

Moshe de Worms, my kind son-in-law, has been brilliant in his use of Nathan's English business dealings in Frankfurt. He receives goods on an ongoing basis, passing them on to his customers with a swiftness that expedites shipments. From questioning my daughter Schönche, her husband's confidant, I have learned that the two men, de Worms and Nathan, who have only grown closer with distance, are in the midst of an ongoing correspondence, and seem to be working in perfect harmony.

There is, of course, also a line of goods shipped from Manchester to M. A. Rothschild in Frankfurt, but it has been facing obstacles. The scope of business has been growing exponentially, and friction has been occurring just as frequently. Although the supply of goods from Manchester produces satiated smiles on the faces of the Frankfurt Rothschilds, that is not sufficient to prevent conflict.

Meir is worried about Nathan's conduct, and Nathan in return writes brief letters expressing impatience, sketching the sensitive state of affairs in England in general terms. The main difficulty stems from the fact that countries that have commercial relationships with Britain have been conquered by Napoleon. In this situation, Nathan needs cash and is forced to borrow money quite frequently.

To Meir, this seems wasteful, while Nathan is convinced that he is behaving appropriately, beating the competition and providing his customers with the fastest, most efficient service. "I must let the customers feel that they are the most important thing," he asserts in his letters to his father.

Nathan's wastefulness drives Meir mad. In his letter, he rumbles, "What do you mean? Does this argument alone justify treating every lowly customer as if he were nothing less than a prince? If every customer receives a gift for his wife as well as special conditions for transfer of goods, what will you be left with? In a short while, all the money I gave you would be gone, and nothing would be left for future goods."

Amschel also added a few more lines of oil to the burning fire of Meir's preaching.

But in spite of the dispute between father and son, M. A. Rothschild is flooded with textile products, fine cotton, and wool sent from Nathan in England, as well as other products he buys in its colonies, such as fabric dye made of the indigo plant, tea, dried fruits, sugar, coffee, tobacco, and wine.

I read the correspondence between the adversaries, and Nathan's reply conjures up the image of an energetic, confident man who knows clearly what he must do, takes risks with eyes wide open, and is in such a rush he grows impatient with the complaints from home. He is in the midst of high-risk transactions with magnates, while his father and brother protest from afar about everything he sees up close.

I have in my hand his most recent letter, which arrived yesterday. Over and over again, I read the bottom line written in his strong handwriting before it is destroyed.

> *Your letters are filled with pettiness and ignorance. I can't be bothered to deal with you. I am in the great city of Manchester, and am forced to read frivolous thoughts sent from the small ghetto in Frankfurt.*

As time passes and letters are written, Nathan becomes even more Nathan. He has returned to his old ways, making not the slightest effort to soften his style. Unfortunately, his blunt attitude has not been tempered in refined England, but I can forgive his behavior due to his results.

And yet, I cannot lie. My son is vain. He treats his brothers as a master treats his subjects. The boastful comparison he makes between Manchester and our ghetto burns me. At this rate, he might forget his origins. He speaks of Manchester as if he'd created the place, but it was there for years before he received approval to tread its land. We must stop him before it's too late. He must always remember where he came from. I must protect my son.

I debate with myself about how to treat him. There's no point in arguing. Criticism and reproach would only make it worse. We must find a way that will not undermine his authority.

I walk on tiptoe, presenting Meir with the situation from Nathan's point of view. "True, children must obey their parents," I say to his surprised face. "But Nathan is the one wearing the shoe, and he's the only one who can say where it pinches. He's acting alone and quickly against all obstacles in his path. He does not have the advantages you've got here. Not only is he not fluent in English and impaired by his heavy German accent, but he must also face exterior difficulties that have nothing to do with him and everything to do with international relations, wars, and conflicts, maneuvering among them all. We'd best not burden him further with our anger."

My words seemed to have touched my man. Judging by my experience as a silent partner observing the company and its manager, I cannot confidently determine the longevity of their effect. But a short-term effect is good enough for me. After that, I will come up with another small and imperceptible intervention.

In the meantime, I have returned to my old habit of sewing Nathan's shirts. I picked up a collection of fabrics and headed to the tailor's. I must renew my habit and mail him ghetto-made shirts. From now on, every package I send to my faraway son will carry the aroma of home. The next shipment will include the shirts and my letter to my son.

> *My dear son Nathan,*
> *I am including six shirts and two scarves for cold days. Take care of yourself and never go out into the cold wind without a scarf on. Also, please write me the dimensions of your dining table and I will make you two tablecloths, as well as some white sheets for your bed.*
> *I found a sermon from Rabbi Shimon: "Man must always be soft as a reed rather than hard as cedar."*
> *I wish you good health.*
> *Your loving mother, Gutle,*
> *Wife of the venerable Meir Amschel Rothschild*

Sunday, September 23rd, 1804

I have Nathan's letter, which arrived today, on my lap. I have yet to let go of it. Could this really be my son, moving through a foreign country with the grace of a dancer, going from one city to the next as if it were nothing more than calling upon a neighbor? I read it, trying to settle my lifting spirits and adjust to the fact that this is, in fact, my son pulling the reins and striding forth, fearlessly.

> *My time in Manchester is coming to an end. This will mark the completion of the first chapter of my life in England. I am about to begin the second, more meaningful chapter. Though the textile center in Manchester is like a fertile vine, its opportunities endless, I mustn't rest on my laurels. It is time to attack from the front lines. I am returning to London. Commerce is not enough. I must combine commerce with banking, which must be run from the large city of London. The center of the world. I will move there next month, with the hope that it will be a high enough springboard from which I will be able to observe the financial market and calculate my steps wisely.*

I would love to have your blessing, dear father. At every step of the way I see you before me. You will always serve as my model of hard work, a developed business sense, and long-term thinking. My eyes are always cast ahead, my body leaning forward, ready for battle.

I read the letter over and over again before it is doomed to go the way of the potato peels. The letter fills my heart. Nathan, his father's bright student, has absorbed all tools and rules, and even the lingo of war has been etched deep into his being. But this springboard he's climbing is incredibly powerful. How high does he wish to go?

Sunday, July 21st, 1805

I am concerned about Meir's travels. The large and growing business and his insistence on beating the competition are making his travels more frequent, causing him to devote most of his days to sitting in the uncomfortable carriage. He wears a jacket in spite of the heavy heat, dons a wig, carefully places a top hat over it, and goes to Kassel, where the landgrave and Buderus reside, or to Munich to close a real estate deal, or to Hamburg to convince Lowitz that his 500,000 gulden loan for the kingdom of Denmark is superior to the one offered by the Bethmann brothers.

These transactions and many others push him to travel for a week in each direction. The carriages are mostly built as long, covered cars, and the hard benches on each side are not kind to miserable buttocks that must bounce against them with every bump in the road. There is not even a rope to hold on to. In the summer the carriage raises pillars of dust. In winter the road is muddy and the trip slow. The carriage often becomes upended, forcing the passengers to spend the night at a roadside inn under poor conditions. When the delays become problematic, Meir stuffs some money into the coachman's hand—a proven remedy against delays.

I include in his travel bag a pillow stuffed with wool to soften the ride for his behind, thinking sadly about his suffering and about our diminishing number of shared mornings, and the matching reduction in the number of good-morning coins. I was hopeful that the wool would soften his hardship somewhat, but when he returns home two weeks later, it turns out it did not, either because the bench was too hard and the bumps in the road too many, or because Meir was too embarrassed to use it. It is also possible that his condition is so bad that only bed rest can correct it, but this kind of cure is unattainable with a man like Meir.

In the last few weeks he's been plagued with pain, a fever, and debilitating fatigue, and his piles have been driving him mad. Upon his return from each trip he waddles in like a duck, holding on to his behind, sighing. The hemorrhoid epidemic in the ghetto has given birth to many consultants and a long line of remedies whose efficacy, regretfully, is doubtful. The medicinal salves given by order of a doctor or a doctor's synagogue friends are attempted hopefully, accompanied by a strict diet, only to fail miserably. The warm baths, followed by the anointment of the area between the buttocks with an oil-soaked bandage relieve the pain to a certain extent, but not for long.

The partner-sons offer to take over the long trips. "Papa," they say, "we'll do the traveling and you'll work in the study."

But whenever one son takes over a trip, his father finds another necessary trip on which to embark. I swallow a sigh and look at darling Kalman, my seventeen-year-old, who has recently joined the family firm, and whose contribution is becoming more and more apparent, though he is not yet trained to work independently in the business battlefields away from Frankfurt.

It is hard for me to watch Meir suffer. "You have brought us honor," I tell him, my face straining under the force of my husband's pain. "Your reputation precedes you. Rest. Enough now. There's no replacement for good health."

"Have you ever seen a coachman pause in the middle of riding up a hill?" he answers, not attempting to conceal the spasm of pain that interrupts his speech, twisting and turning his body like a Hanukah dreidel that has lost its cheer.

"And where is the summit of this hill? Have you asked the coachman? Where will you stop to set your flag?" I insist, my eyes running over the tortured dreidel.

"Oh, I have asked indeed," he plays along with a groan. "The summit continues on throughout life. As long as there is breath in my lungs I will continue to climb. When I leave this world, hopefully headed toward heaven, you will know I have reached the top."

"In that case I do not want you reaching it so quickly. Fine, do not stop, since blessing is nowhere but in the actions of man. Just slow down, please. Climb slower. One step at a time."

"Know this, Gutaleh—those who slow down on an upswing risk tumbling. It is dangerous. And at the bottom are the sharks, who would love nothing more than to watch me fall. They would devour my flesh and drink my blood without a second thought. I have no desire to descend. I am going at full force, and will do my best to maintain this speed."

I accepted his opinion with submission. This is the man with whom I share my life. Nothing can stop his stride. He will continue, even if it costs him his life. According to his worldview, without new ambition, life loses its meaning. He therefore continues on his journey, accompanied by his aching bottom.

All that is left for me to do is search for new cures, or at least for ways to alleviate the pain. I have yet to find the perfect solution.

Meir behaves as one who has made peace with his condition. The pain does not weaken him or dampen his spirits. His entire purpose is to climb, and like a young man after his lover, he is pulled up, one more step, then another, then another.

Nevertheless, he steers clear of other temptations. For instance, an incredibly enticing offer that arrived from the Frankfurt Senate, to be appointed Baumeister—head of the Jewish ghetto, an honorable appointment by any measure. I accept his rejection of this offer, though I regret the missed opportunity. On the one hand, this appointment carries power and responsibility in measures he has not yet known, when it comes to public office. It is a twofold honor. First, an honor given to the rich, and offering it to Meir signals that we are part of that group, headed for the same summits where the lords of the ghetto reside. Second, it is an honor given to scholars, and even if Meir is not a scholar in the pure sense of the word, he does have appreciation for learners, and does everything in his power to enable more children to live up to their academic potential. That in itself is a great honor.

But on the other hand, this position requires long periods of sitting, which does not bode well for his poor bottom. It is therefore clear that he had no choice but to turn the offer down.

In his letter to the senate, which begins with words of gratitude for the generous and flattering offer, Meir attached medical notes to strengthen his argument for rejection.

In his worrisome state of health, his position as head of the Jewish Welfare Board is more than enough. This is a public honor that matches his financial honor nicely.

Monday, July 22nd, 1805

It has been nine years since the great fire, and our street is still not sufficiently restored. Other than a few partial repairs, it stands neglected and ashamed, its eyes still webbed with sleep, overlooking the remains of lonely homes, scorched and sooty, inspiring a longing for the days before the fire. The view from our window offers no solace. The street is scratching its scabs, wallowing in the insult of its abandonment, enveloped in heartrending sadness. The houses are deserted and tired, yawning with boredom. The gray sky also seems to be lamenting the days of the past that will never return. Many former residents still live outside of the ghetto. The number of people convening on the street has gone down significantly, and there are whole hours when not a living soul can be seen. My eyes are filled with the memory of incinerators, bringing ruin and leaving their marks of eternal disgrace.

I think about our Jews. Many of them rise above their filthy floors, raising their heads, flexing their bodies, shaking off the dust, and mixing in with the gentiles in the Frankfurt business community. Why would they return to this dark place? There, outside ghetto walls, they are free to pursue their financial initiatives and bring honor to themselves and their families.

Meir tells me that among his Christian friends who own large businesses, some have told him in secret, "Know this: you, the Jews, have played an important role in the financial development of Frankfurt. If it weren't for you, Frankfurt would not have flourished." And to this notion Buderus adds, "God help you and help us. Bless the God of the Jews."

There are, indeed, upward-climbing Jews, and yet the ground of the ghetto remains filthy and unchanged, as has the humiliating treatment of Jews. The laws and restrictions of the senate, which has no intention of changing, are still in effect.

The senate contacts Jews who have lost their homes and left the ghetto, and demands that they return. "The period permitted for living outside the ghetto has expired. The homes have been repaired and the ruins have been partially repaired," it informs them. But its voice goes unheard. The Jews have no desire to return home. Why would they? To be reminded again and again of the degrading laws imposed on them?

The issue of the mail is also degrading. Letters addressed to Jews are delayed for long periods of time due to censorship. The Frankfurters read and censor the letters, and until they finish reading, the Jews must wait. The only thing they can do during this prolonged period of waiting is look at the envelopes to recognize the senders. The letters are like Hanukah candles, meant only to be looked at.

Meir paced the room, his face toward the distance. "We must leverage this permission," he said. "I'm sure there's a way out," he continued to encourage himself.

"What good is there in knowing that a letter has arrived from Nathan if we can't read it?" I answered his musings, trying to help move him toward a budding idea.

He fixed his eyes on me. Their silent message was, *Go on*.

I did. "We have no idea what the state of the market is in England. Without any hint or update our hands are tied."

"That's it, Gutaleh, you've hit the mark." He pounced on me, grabbing me by the waist and twirling me in a dance to the sound of the children's clapping.

"Look, Gutaleh, we must know what the state of the market is, that's all. We do not need to read an entire letter for that. A hint or a mark would be enough."

I realized he had an idea, but couldn't guess what it was. He rushed to send a letter to Nathan and did not answer my question. A smile stretched across his face.

The days went by, until one day Meir asked me to gather the boys. A new idea is best presented in a family forum.

We all gathered together in the study: Meir, Amschel, Shlomo, Kalman, Isabella, Babette, and Eva.

"Our hardship is a blessing in disguise," he announced inside the closed study and looked over his children's faces.

Everyone's eyes turned to me.

"Don't look to Mama for answers. I expect you to think about this yourselves. How can we make fast and efficient use of the postal system, a use that is quicker than opening a letter?"

"Papa," said Shlomo, "we've got no time for riddles. One way to become more efficient is for you to tell us the idea so we can begin acting."

"Well then, let's begin acting. Come with me."

"But what is the idea?" Shlomo insisted.

"The idea will become clear from the action," Meir replied. "Come on, let's go."

Father and sons stepped outside, and I was left behind with pointless guesswork.

From that point on, the Rothschilds went to the post office every day, and every day took decisive action: buy or sell. Their decision whether to buy or sell was proved right again and again.

The flushed faces of my husband and his partner-sons beamed enthusiastic complicity that involved no one but them. The secret gang confided in no one, not even in me, an expert in deciphering Rothschild expressions who this time admitted defeat.

The Frankfurt merchants gaped at the success of the Rothschild firm where they themselves failed again and again. The other merchants' attempts to track the actions of the Rothschilds were all for naught. They always missed the first step. When they saw that the Rothschilds had bought and decided to do the same, they found the exchange rate for the British pound already changed, and they had to sell.

I staked out my team of men, peeking and testing them. I eavesdropped on their whispered conversations. But I could detect not a single revealing detail. I heaped layers of guesses on top of each other, and all of them collapsed in overwhelming failure.

"Are you bribing the postal workers?" I asked Meir.

"Gutaleh, what are you talking about? Bribing? That's immoral."

I tried with Amschel. "How are you opening the letters?"

"Mama, who said we are opening the letters?" my son said, pretending to be naive.

"Well, Shlomo, pay respect to your mother by telling me the secret."

But Shlomo's mouth remained sealed, then opened just a bit for a kiss before running out on his next mission.

Two weeks later, when the group returned with special cheer after an immense success, I asked Meir, "How did you know the exchange rate was up?"

"Because the envelope was red," Meir answered with a smile.

"A red envelope," I said, thinking out loud. "And what color is the envelope when the rate goes down?"

"Now you've got it, my dear. Blue means down."

"That's brilliant, Meir. No need to open the envelope. It's enough to look at the color."

"Indeed. It even saves the time we would have spent reading the letter. We go out to take action immediately, always first on the scene."

"He who knows first, acts first," Kalman, who just walked in, concluded.

The boys' post office runs are conducted with special care. We must never miss a piece of news. The color solution has proved to be fast and efficient, and is being used by our family on a regular basis. Nathan showers us with colorful envelopes, and Meir behaves according to the color of the day and continues to leave his competitors reeling. It has happened more than once that when an envelope was finally permitted to be opened, there was no letter inside. Meir forgives this, even laughing about it. "Oh, Nathan, Nathan. And I wondered how he could have found the time to write so many letters. An easy task indeed," he grumbled amiably, his face beaming.

But let me return to the main point. I was describing the prohibitions and limitations imposed on us, the Jews of Frankfurt, specifically, the Jews of the ghetto. I must be precise. In addition to the special permit for a brief glance at the sealed envelopes of the letters we receive, we have recently been informed of another new permit: we are now allowed to leave our street on Sundays. This appeared to be thrilling news. In fact, I almost added it to my list of exciting events in the history of Judengasse. But I mustn't get ahead of myself, seeing as this blessing comes with an unavoidable curse.

What is this all about? Well, this newest permit has been deemed "temporary," and in order to enjoy it, we are forced to pay a new tax, the Sunday Tax. I suppose the regular list of taxes imposed upon us due to our religious beliefs no longer satisfies the Frankfurt Senate, and they demonstrate intense creativity in inventing new taxes.

And nevertheless, I must take heart. Another change for the better has happened. A change that does not entail any kind of creative punishment. And it must be attributed to the French, as well as to the unlucky Mr. Cohen.

So it goes: about a year ago, a French Jew naively walked into the forbidden paradise—the Frankfurt Public Garden. The militia recognized him as Jewish, and in order to verify they asked his name. The man answered simply, "Cohen."

"There," they said, looking at each other proudly. "We've got him, and our instincts were right."

But the militia missed one important clue. In their joy of revelations, they didn't bother to dig a little deeper and find that this Jew was not a Frankfurter at all, but French.

Therefore, poor Cohen was forced to feel the full force of the law on his flesh and bones. The militia men, thirsty for battle and eager for this opportunity to veer from their dull routine, charged upon him furiously, mercilessly beating the unkempt man as if he were the enemy of all mankind. Unfortunately for them, the event reached the ears of the French. Enraged, they condemned the attackers.

The militia men were harshly disciplined, put in custody, and required to apologize to Mr. Cohen. The French commander, Fouquet, even sued them for damages. People on our street have been saying that this shocking development was reported in the French *Journal de Francfort*. This goes to show that what is considered routine in one place is perceived as shocking in another. These French truly do seem to adhere to their motto of *liberté, égalité, fraternité*. I like them, especially in light of the fact that this devotion is a benefit to us.

And this brings me to the happy results of this unhappy event. Because of the difficulty of making a distinction between one kind of Jew and the next, there was no longer any point in enforcing a law forbidding Frankfurt Jews from visiting public gardens. While this decision does not nullify the law itself, it is the most significant change we've seen in centuries, as far as I'm concerned.

I jumped into action. I wasn't going to miss this opportunity before it was taken away. Who was to say how long this French influence on Frankfurt habits would last? I've already seen the tables turn and know that political revolutions can happen at any moment.

So I went out to make a childhood dream come true.

In the afternoon I headed eagerly to my parents' home. I went straight to my mother's chair and took her hand gently. This hand, shrunken with age and covered with tired wrinkles, painful to the eye and to the touch, made me shiver, and I let go for a moment.

The fangs of time have been leaving their mark on her, now more than ever. My heart ached at the sight of her face, suddenly so worn out, and the slowness with which she moved her limp limbs. My father is also a far cry from the strong, impressive man he used to be. He has grown thinner and shorter, dragging his tired legs through the rooms of the house, using a cane to walk slowly to the synagogue, the only place for which he goes to the effort of leaving the house.

I took a deep breath and reached out hesitantly to take the old hand in mine. "Come, Mama, let's go for a walk," I said quietly, as if a walk was something we did together every day, as if it had not been several years since we last left her home together. This realization dawned on me suddenly, with full force and very bad timing. I looked at her apologetically.

I forced myself to stop this downward turn of spirits, determined to raise them back up. I led my mother slowly to the end of the street and toward the carriage parked on the side of the path. I wrapped her hand around the railing and turned to speak to the coachman, who was in the midst of tightening the shaft. I whispered to him to take us to the public garden.

"Let's get up there, Mama, one, two, three," I said cheerfully, supporting her as she boarded the carriage. I sat beside her and wrapped my arm around her narrow shoulders.

She obeyed without asking any questions about what we were doing, where we were headed, or why.

On the way there, I noticed that the streets of Frankfurt all had lamps, though the lights weren't on right now, in the middle of the day. I wondered if and when Judengasse would be lit up, since we too experienced darkness. This thought was cut short when the carriage paused at the gate of the park. The sun burned bright. We would have to submit our bodies to the heat for twenty or thirty steps before we could cool off in the shade of trees.

I turned to take a look at my mother's pleasantly surprised face, but she was frozen in her seat, her legs like pegs pierced into the floor. She narrowed her eyes and looked around, terrified. "What are you doing, Gutaleh?"

"I want to walk in the garden with you."

"What's wrong with you? Are you mad?" The tremble of her body matched the one in her voice. "Take me home, right now." Her voice took me back to childhood. "Get that crazy thought out of your head and never repeat it again," Mama had told me years ago. A lump of pity fluttered through my stomach. Pity for my mother, for myself, for Judengasse.

I glanced at the horse. It stood peacefully between the carriage's shafts, as if awaiting a decision.

"Mama, we're allowed," I whispered in her ear, trying to smile to cover my pain. "We can walk here, and no one will hurt us." I fought off other emotions that suddenly rose in me, threatening to erupt. I mustn't spoil this fine day. This is a day to make things right. Making one of the many atrocities we have suffered right. Today we must celebrate.

"What do you mean, 'allowed'? Have you forgotten where you are, Gutaleh? This is Frankfurt, not Paris."

I felt proud of my mother for being aware of the French values of equality and fraternity. "Yes, Mama, you are right, we are in Frankfurt. But thanks to the people of Paris, we are now allowed as well."

"Are you . . . sure?" Her eyes left mine and wandered. Her fear had not yet evaporated, but the terror had lessened.

"Yes, Mama, I'm sure. Perhaps the word 'allowed' is not exactly right, because the law you speak of still exists. But believe me, *mama-lieb*, no one in the world can stop us."

The coachman, who had listened in on our conversation from his seat, now turned to me quizzically, and I nodded toward him. He stepped off, walked over, and placed the wooden step on the ground. I stepped off lightly, then gave Mama my hand and did not let go as she slowly descended from the carriage. She stood firmly on her feet, linked her arm with mine, and looked down to make sure she truly was standing where she thought she was. Arm in arm we walked along the paved path. I was strolling with Mama where the noble ladies of Frankfurt strolled. I could not help but think of this great privilege, to make an old dream come true, together with my mother.

We paused to look around. "It's bigger than I had imagined," Mama whispered, echoing my thoughts. *The horizon was far here too,* I thought, thinking of Meir. In spite of the cluttered horizon of Judengasse, his gaze always saw for miles. It occurred to me that often, outside of our street, he must pause to glance at the wide horizon, where the sky kissed the earth, inspiring his imagination.

"Look, Gutaleh, how pretty this garden is." Mama tightened her grip. Her eyes sparkled. I looked at the glory of the garden. A carpet of beauty spread before me, as if to say, "Here I am! And where have you been this whole time?" My eyes took in the sights. All the wonders of the world could not compare to the splendor of this place. I felt I had to hurry up and drink in this luscious view. I feasted my eyes on the green trees towering over the old mounds of earth, the branches rubbing shoulders with the rays of the sun, the thickets of tiny bushes, like children holding on to the low branches that peeked out of their mighty parents' trunks, the colorful variety of flowers, the wide meadows that called for me to run and frolic in the grass. I did not know the names of the trees, the bushes, and the flowers, other than the tall cypresses, and beside them, the pine trees, the cheerful siblings of my own poor pine that had died in the fire. But I was so close to them now, and had to fill the empty space in me created by their absence during all those years.

I took in deep whiffs of the blossoms' scent that was carried through the open air. I sensed the presence of another smell, which I could not identify. I took in all the aromas, for myself and for those who were not lucky enough to smell them in their lifetime. I regretted the fact that there was no way to deliver smell from one place to another. One day, when there is a way, I would transfer hefty amounts of this fresh air into our street.

Suddenly, I felt sad. The thought of all we had been deprived of until now filled me, pushing away the brilliance before me, threatening to take hold of my mind. Our people's cruel fate was knocking on the door to my heart. I watched my mother, her burning eyes. She was living the moment, leaving the past behind. I must be like her, enjoy these moments to capacity. I mustn't wallow in darkness. I must regain my senses.

At that moment, I recognized that other smell. It was the aroma of freedom. Freedom smells intoxicating, superior to all other scents. I would always remember my first whiff of freedom.

Was this heaven on earth? Was this what the biblical Garden of Eden looked like? Where did the snake tempt Eve? In this place, one could easily be tempted. It is no wonder Eve couldn't resist, and Adam followed suit. I knew these were foolish thoughts. Why was I thinking about the Garden of Eden? And yet, I allowed myself to linger in the sense of miracle. Here I was, strolling through the forbidden garden, which was temporarily permitted.

I sat Mama down on a bench and took a seat beside her. She needed rest, and so did I. I felt like one who had just performed an enormous task. A few brave rays of sun filtered through the foliage to cast light on the paving below. A thick branch sheltered us, drawing a long shadow on a patch of dirt. I picked a handful of green weeds that had made their way out of their territory and toward the bench. I held the buds to my nose and inhaled deeply, and then passed them under Mama's nose. She took hold of the fragrant bouquet, trembling, and breathed in their scent, as if trying to take all of it in. Illuminated tearful beads flickered in her eyes.

"Gutaleh," she spoke to me, her eyes continuing to drink in the space around us. "I've spent years trying not to think about this place. But the thought never left me. When you told me, so many years ago, that you wanted to stroll here, I was horrified. You expressed my wishes exactly, but I couldn't let you keep thinking about something that was unattainable. I had to stop you from nurturing false hope. And then you came to me today to show me that night can indeed turn into day. It is a wonder I never thought I would experience."

Mama hadn't spoken this much in a long time. I rubbed her hand. I was so happy for her. I was so happy for myself.

We sat quietly, giving our faces over to the expanses opening up to us. Our ears were attuned to the rustle of leaves and the flapping of birds' wings. From time to time I glanced at her to make sure her eyes were still lit up. Squirrels chased each other around the tree. Colorful butterflies fluttered among the flowers. Green cypresses stretched their necks, as if trying to blend in with the blue sky. Vines twisted over their trunks, looping and gripping each other, as if making love. Birds hopped on treetops with cheerful chirps, moving their heads to and fro. In the distance, a fountain threw its twinkling arms all around. Shiny showers glimmered in the sunlight, looking like a fluttering bridal gown.

I looked over at the women strolling along in their fine garb, their dresses cinched at the waist and then ballooning from the hips down. Their heads were adorned with fashionable hats, and they walked with straight backs and exposed necks. Their movements were feminine and masterful at once, as if to announce, "The whole wide world belongs to me."

I looked forlornly at my own clothes, examining my dress, my body shrinking on the bench, wishing to become invisible. I couldn't help but compare. My clothes were outdated, though the fabric was good. My hair was covered by a coif, its ends tied under my chin. My dress, which widened at the waist, blurred the shape of my body. I was a model of the Judengasse landscape. I looked at their faces and recalled what Meir told me when we had first met. Indeed, there was color in their faces, but I did not know whether to construe it as the color of life or the color of makeup. Either way, I paid mind to the fact that some of them were beautiful, in contrast with Meir's report. I don't know if he told me they were not pretty in order to make me feel better, or if he didn't know how to tell beauty from ugliness, his understanding of women being tenuous at best.

I looked at my mother. Her dress also belonged in a museum. It screamed antiquity. I moved my eyes to her face. She was still gripped by the entrancing vision, drinking in the sights, paying no mind to the thoughts running through my head. I must do as she does, not waste my thoughts on fashion.

Mothers pushed prams along the paths. Beside them, small children scampered about, governesses at their sides. Such was life in paradise. The mothers strutted on high heels, while the servants did the lion's share of the work. Now they too chose a bench to rest on. The delicate Frankfurt women were tired from idleness. They gathered the ends of their dresses and sat down, making sure to keep their long legs together and slightly tilted to the side, turned their heads carefully toward each other, and carried on in their restrained conversation, probably spoken in perfect German and with a varied and impressive vocabulary. The babies, the prams, and the children running happily, without restrictions, all these were under the care of the governesses.

I would go mad with boredom if other people did my work for me, especially the work of raising my children. Well, the truth is, my older children helped me care for their younger siblings, but governesses? Who needs them?

Some women walked with their dogs. Now another moment threatened to break the spell. I couldn't stop making comparisons. How is it that dogs have always been allowed in this park, while Jews have been forbidden for generations? Does this mean we are inferior even to dogs? A wave of fury climbed inside of me, trying to break through to the open, prohibited space. Or prohibited until recently, anyway. A few dozen years ago, Moshe Mendelssohn walked into Berlin through a gate meant for Jews and beasts. As God is my witness, I had no desire to break the tranquility, but I felt I no longer had a choice. I fidgeted restlessly on the bench.

I had to get hold of my emotions. I scolded myself. *Why is it that when the world offers you a hand, you resent it for not having done so earlier? Be glad for today, do not cry for yesterday.* I looked at my mother, trying to catch her calm. She was planted on the bench, her eyes devoted to the garden, the smile never leaving her face. I kissed her hand that held on to mine, rested my head in her scrawny lap, and took her in.

It was almost time to leave. The last rays of sun caressed the flowers. A light breeze made the treetops dance. At the sound of their rustling, layered with the songs of the birds, we crossed the park back to the entrance, arm in arm. When we reached the gate, Mama paused, looked back, and gave the view a final look. "Thank you, Gutaleh, you've granted me one final moment of grace."

I rejoiced in her happiness, though I didn't know why she said "final moment of grace." Mama is very careful in choosing her words. I wanted to tell her that my conscience plagued me for not finding the time to grant her more graces. I promised myself I would try harder, for her sake.

We boarded the carriage again, leaving the magic behind.

Thursday, October 17th, 1805

We must show gratitude for the degree to which the French have taken an interest in our well-being. They do their best to implement their advanced ideas any place they have influence and investments. They call Judengasse "a medieval ghetto." Finally, someone cares enough to try and salvage the forgotten object from the scrap heap.

Meir goes into town to sniff around. As expected, the Frankfurt banks and guilds are not happy about the French intervention. Meir's competitor, the famous Frankfurt banker Simon Moritz von Bethmann, warned that granting equal rights to Jews might hurt the livelihood of the lower class and lead them to leave the city.

The Jews inside and outside of Judengasse are quoting the words of Abel, the representative of the senate in Paris, and end up confused. On the one hand, Abel said, "The French have no right to intervene in the affairs of Frankfurt Jews, which are purely internal affairs." On the other hand, he suggests permitting Jews to leave the ghetto and live in houses that are more befitting of human habitation. What might we glean from these conflicting statements?

Our natural tendency is to hope the senate adopts his suggestion, so Jews can live happily and content. Time will tell.

Meir, of course, has no influence over the decisions of the senate. Nevertheless, he continues to write letters.

But when it comes to the Jews' own education, Meir has done something great: he founded a school that teaches in the spirit of enlightenment. This was a controversial choice, which, for the first time in his life, made the community's old-fashioned members turn against him, as well as Rabbi Zvi Hirsch Halevi Horowitz, the son of our great rabbi and teacher Pinchas Horowitz, may his memory be a blessing, the community rabbi and head of the advanced yeshiva who died three months ago and was buried with great lamentation in our cemetery. His son now fills his place as the head of the community, and follows in his father's footsteps in objecting vehemently to the Enlightenment Movement.

In spite of the loud objections to the opening of this school, I feel at ease. I have already learned that many great developments are received with doubt or aggression at first, but with time, their value seeps into the public awareness. I believe this is the case here.

But I'm getting ahead of myself, as usual. I must take a step back and put some order in the events.

For generations, our teachers have used the same methods, passing textbooks from generation to generation. But ever since the publication of Moshe Mendelssohn's translation of the Bible, an unending dispute has plagued Judengasse: Should we preserve the traditional ways, or should we move with the times?

Wealthy families send their children to school outside of the ghetto, to the Frankfurt Humanistic High School, while our old *heder*, adjacent to the synagogue, is still attended by the children of the poor, along with the children of the families that adhere to traditional scholarly methods.

Meir avoided taking a stand on this issue for a long time. Though he was aware of the limitations of the old methods, he didn't want to anger the rabbis. Having refused outright to send our children to a secular Christian school, he solved the problem temporarily by getting

Yaakov his tutor, Dr. Michael Hess, in accordance with the recommendation of our accountant, Seligman Geisenheimer.

About two years ago, in October 1803, an event occurred that brought a change in Meir's attitude and led him to take a decisive, influential stance.

On one of his visits to Marburg in Hesse, a skinny boy standing on a street corner and singing Jewish songs in a clear voice caught his attention. Meir paused to listen to the moving song. Passersby dropped coins into the boy's hat, which was lying on the ground. Meir's eyes examined the boy's torn and unpatched clothes. He placed a handful of coins in the child's hat and asked his name.

"Moshe," the boy said.

"You sing wonderfully. Where are you from?"

"From Galicia."

"Where are your parents?"

"In a better place."

The statement startled Meir, awakening a forgotten memory in him. This child standing before him was younger than Meir had been when he was orphaned. He smiled at the child. "Who taught you how to sing these wonderful songs?"

"My mother, may her memory be a blessing."

"I see. And where do you live? Who takes care of you?"

The boy lowered his eyes and pursed his lips.

"I can tell you're a bright child. Would you like to come with me to Frankfurt?"

The boy looked up into Meir's face, surprise in his eyes. Meir ran his hand over the boy's head. "I can take you in and put you through school."

The child continued to look at him, perhaps to test the seriousness of his words, or perhaps because of the dilemma the unexpected offer raised in him.

Meir came to his aid. "I suggest we go see your adoptive parents right now and ask permission to leave." As he spoke, he took the child's hand like an old acquaintance and led him to the carriage.

The adoptive mother, who turned out to be Moshe's aunt, was sitting on the floor of her small kitchen, her legs on either side of the laundry pail, her body leaning forward and her hands working furiously up and down the washboard, while her children gathered around her like a flock of chirping chicks. As she worked, she told off one, threatened the other, and demanded with a huff that the eldest one take her little brothers outside. With a light complaint she got up on her feet to greet the uninvited guest who had been brought in by Moshe. After a brief introduction, she returned to the pail, carried on with her work, and refrained from asking too many questions before answering Meir with a fervent yes as if fearing that any delay would cause him to regret his offer. It seemed she would have been friendlier if he had agreed to take one or two of her own offspring, as well.

Meir smiled at Moshe, and once the squeaky door was closed behind them, he whispered in his ear, "We won." It was as if they had just left a wrestling ring with the upper hand. The boy put his little hand in the large hand offered to him, and again the memory of orphanhood was aroused in Meir.

Meir brought the boy he had pulled out of the murky water into our home and tasked Geisenheimer (who had already returned from England) with making sure he found Moshe a place in an appropriate educational establishment.

Meir never imagined the effect this action would have. He never thought that bringing in the orphaned, penniless Moshe would serve to change things for so many other children. How right the Sanhedrin had been when it determined that he who saves a single life has saved the world.

For a while, Geisenheimer had been talking about the idea of starting an innovative Jewish school. Moshe's arrival pushed him and

Meir to bring thought into action. Geisenheimer was joined by three energetic men who were passionate about education. Leaning on the financial foundation offered by Meir, they started a committee for the establishment of a new school for impoverished Jewish children. They suggested that for the time being a temporary school be built inside the ghetto, until the construction of a larger, permanent school was completed outside the ghetto walls. The name suggested for the school was the Philanthropin.

The entrepreneurs spent hours in our home office with Meir, poring over their list of school goals. The main goal was the spreading of human love. Teaching would be performed according to the theories of the great Swiss educator Johann Heinrich Pestalozzi, "Learning by head, hand, and heart" (Meir had devoted many nights to reading Pestalozzi's four-volume book, *Leonard and Gertrude*), and according to the spirit of enlightenment. Along with holy studies, the children would learn the ideas of enlightened French philosophers and writers Voltaire and Jean-Jacques Rousseau, German poet and philosopher Johann Gottfried Herder, and Moshe Mendelssohn, one of our own.

Dr. Michael Hess, Yaakov's tutor, was appointed school principal and head teacher, and Seligman Geisenheimer became a member of the board of directors. Moshe could take pride in being one of the three first students in the new school. The number of children enrolled is growing daily. The school teaches German, French, geography, natural studies, and modern philosophy.

The Philanthropin has stirred up controversy, as has any new idea that comes to our old-fashioned street. It's obvious the debate will continue for a long time yet, but Meir is determined. "I will continue to be a conservative Jew my entire life," he declares patiently yet persistently to anyone who addresses him on the matter. "But the need for modern education is unavoidable. We mustn't continue to ignore the new needs of the world, of which we are an inseparable part."

The father's words echo his son's, who has moved a long distance away in order to adapt himself without interruption to the needs of the new world.

The school outside the walls of the ghetto is in advanced stages of construction. Its building and furnishings are funded by Meir Rothschild, my venerable man, and this is his dignified contribution to the future education of our children.

Tuesday, June 3rd, 1806

Mama died, may she rest in peace.

Mama-lieb, you are no longer with us. The gates of heaven have opened to receive you. Though her condition was deteriorating, and although the doctors had prepared me for an imminent separation, when the time came I was totally unprepared. How can anyone prepare for the death of a loved one?

I haven't written much about my mother, due to the events that have been shaking the lives of my family. I now wish to repent. I should have mentioned her from time to time—her concern, her devotion to her grandchildren, her knitting, the sweet cookies and buns she made for them with such love and care. It was my duty to describe her love for my husband and how much she admired him.

Therefore, to the black list of my sins I add my sorrow for the awful lack of attention to my loving parents. I spend all my time caring for my children, but I haven't done enough for my parents. While one of them sat down to tell stories to their grandchildren, I took advantage of the children being under their loving care and turned to complete one of the many tasks that pile up at my feet every morning, noon, and night. Every day, I am in the midst of a frantic struggle to complete more and more missions, big and small, and I never thought to join that family tableau, which included my aging parents, and lend an ear to the details of their personal stories, which are part of their feelings, dreams, and aspirations. I am too late. The craters that have opened up between us can no longer be filled.

They never remarked on this behavior. On the contrary, they kept expressing their discomfort for not being able to help me enough with the running of my life. But I cannot forgive myself, as I should have put them before my own needs. Love must be expressed before it is too late, through words and actions, while one's loved ones are alive.

My beloved mother. I suddenly realize that all the signs were there. The dragging of the feet, the tired eyes, the betrayal of the body. They all seemed to say, "Take note, Gutaleh, evening is descending." But the signs blurred in my eyes. Or did I blur them purposefully, wanting to delay the end? Why would I? Because I wanted God to let her stay alive a little longer? I did, and yet I did nothing in order to see her more often. There were always more urgent matters that demanded my attention.

I was foolish. And worse yet, I was selfish. If I could turn back time, I would have behaved differently. I would have rearranged my days according to different priorities, ones that would put my mother and father first. I did not do my job as the eldest daughter. My devoted sister Vendeleh took my place at my mother's side and made sure to visit, along with her children, until the very end. Now Vendeleh will turn her love on my father. She won't allow the tiniest bud of guilt to take hold of her. Her heart is pure. Looking at my father's face, body, and conduct, I can see he will soon join his wife. He keeps silent, as if to announce that his interest in this world is a thing of the past, and all his attention is devoted to the other world, the one to which Mama has departed.

My beloved father, the man responsible for my writing in these notebooks, would have probably loved to receive a few spicy nuggets of the many hidden between these pages. But the truth is, he never asked me to share them with him. Now I can add this guilt to my list of sins: that I never let him know the side of me I put in these pages. Nevertheless, my heart tells me that he knows.

How great is the torment of regret. Will it stay with me my entire life? Oh, Lord, if only You had given me the wisdom to see and understand when the time was right, when I could still fix things. What good is regret when it can only serve to prick my heart?

Will I ever find solace?

During the seven days of mourning, as I was forced to pause in the speedy journey of my life, I summarized matters for myself and found that many of my habits were learned from my mother: my affinity for cleanliness and order, my love of language, my sensitivity to the children's needs. I am so attached to her, and now that she is gone, she continues to remain embedded in my soul.

The memory of our stroll through the public garden is etched into my heart. Until the time of our visit to the garden, Mama was independent in simple routine actions, which she carried out slowly and heavily. But the significant change in her health occurred after this visit. Mama seemed to have made up her mind that visiting the garden was the fulfillment of all her wishes, and she was prepared to part from this world and move on to the next one. She refused to eat. Her body grew limp, moving from standing to sitting and then to lying down, without strength.

Through different ruses, Vendeleh was able to persuade her to eat one crumb after another, crumbs of life that fed for several months, until the end.

Mama, thank you for everything you gave me and my children. Please forgive me for the many hours we missed spending together. If my heart were more understanding, I would have walked hand in hand with you down Judengasse, listening to your opinions, your advice, your ponderings, and singing the praises of your wonderful grandchildren, lighting your extinguished eyes and putting a smile on your wrinkled face.

But you aren't here. And I did not walk down our street with you, the street where you were born, where your mother was born, where your children were born. Mama, my heart weeps.

Is this the way of the world, filling us with guilt upon the departure of our loved ones? I seek out a way to console my conscience, and allow myself to sneak one single satisfaction into the pain, a kind of reward to raise my spirits. I give myself a small merit point for making her dream come true, for making *our* dream come true. Though I didn't carry you into the garden on a litter, Mama, the light that shone in your life is tantamount to all the golden chariots in the world.

I will fix things. I am accustomed to mending. I will fix things with Papa. What I didn't do in your lifetime, Mama, I will do in your death. I will visit Papa and try to shake off his boredom with the grandchildren I will bring along with me, with your recipes that I will cook especially for him. I will take his hand in mine and warm it with my body heat, and rub his head the way you used to before your hands shook and your body betrayed you.

And I will come to you too, Mama, for a visit. I will visit your eternal resting place, kneel down, converse with your soul, and receive your blessing for the future. Your virtue will protect us.

Farewell, *mama-lieb*, and rest in peace. Your offspring will continue to succeed, each in their own way.

Sunday, November 2nd, 1806

I am cold. I stay close to the hot water bottle, moving it from my legs to my back, then between my thighs, and so on and so forth. The hot water bottle is an extraordinary invention, and I owe a fortune to the anonymous inventor for granting me this comfort. I need the bottle in spite of the pleasant heated room. As the years go by, I stay closer and closer to heat sources in winter, and to the fan in summer. I wonder if this is caused by a change in the climate of our area, or if it is an unavoidable outcome of my age. I am fifty-three years old and orphaned. Papa passed away a month ago and was buried next to Mama. I will now speak to two adjacent graves, unfolding my life to them the way I do in my notebook. My parents are the most trustworthy confidants on earth, or should I say, under it.

I kept my promise to my mother, but didn't have to keep it for very long. The Lord took care to fulfill my father's wishes, and quickly delivered him to a better place. For three consecutive months I visited my father daily, sometimes alone, other times with my grandchildren, and often with my sister Vendeleh. We sat at his side, sharing hold of his hands, each holding on to one of them, or rubbing his head and talking to him as if he were completely up to date on life in our world. Only the painful looks passed between the two of us attested to the fact that the contents of our words did not enter his failing mind. Nevertheless, we felt his ears pricking to take in the sounds of our voices, which granted peace to his closed eyes. His caretaker never left his side, making sure to give him food and drink in small increments, not deterred by his grumbling that she should leave him alone.

Rest in peace, dear Papa.

A glance at the window during these cold days reveals the still view of snow piled up in the street. Nobody bothers to shovel. In the days before the fire, when the street still teemed with life and the snow piled high, I loved watching flocks of people with sharp picks and shovels, clearing a path along the street. But now no one makes the effort, and the white blanket continues to cover us, uninterrupted, blocking the doorways.

I warm my hands on the water bottle and turn my thoughts to Nathan.

My Nathan, my beloved son who is so far away, is deepening his new roots. He has married a Jewish woman named Hannah, English born, a flower that had budded and blossomed in a pretty garden, becoming an honorable lady of manners who projects amiability all around her. Her regal look places a barrier of respect everywhere she turns. My new daughter-in-law has two other virtues: her love for Nathan, and her position as the daughter of Mr. Levy Barent Cohen, the greatest banker in London, who had greeted Nathan when he arrived and served as his consultant and guide on his first days in the new place. Her father, in his great generosity, also gave the couple a handsome dowry.

It appears that while Nathan was working with her father, his eyes were drawn toward little Hannah, six years younger than him. She was fifteen when he first met her, and she captured his heart. When he lived in Manchester, whenever he was in London on business, he found an excuse to visit the Cohens. Hannah grew older, prettier, and smarter, and developed feelings for him too. I do not know if she stood expectantly at the window the way I used to, hoping to see my Meir, though I assume that in her own way, she waited for him to come and cure her longing.

When Nathan made a home for himself in London two years ago, the lovers' rendezvous became easier to arrange, though my son still spent most of his time preoccupied with the battles of life.

This year is a year of growth for Nathan. This year he has received the status of an English citizen, his business has doubled and tripled due to the decision of the French to close British ports to merchandise. Luckily, he was able to come up with some creative ideas on how to get around these prohibitions.

And this year he also married Hannah.

We did not attend our son's wedding celebrations in London. I do not leave Judengasse, and the fast-evolving events in our area required Meir and his partner-sons to remain on guard in difficult spots. But the single explanation that pushes away all excuses, the plain truth, is this: Meir and I were born and raised on Judengasse, and even if our son has wandered far away, our roots are here, and he must come see us here and introduce us to his chosen one. We obviously agreed to the match.

And indeed, after their wedding, the two came for a four-day visit, and I could indulge in my son's happy face and warm my heart in the features of his pretty bride.

Nathan, and sometimes Kalman and Yaakov, all served as translators in order to solve the challenge of verbal communication between me and Hannah. But I needed no translation for what counts the most. The language of the body and the eyes requires no words. I listened to this boundary-breaking discourse, to the tenderness with which the two of them treated each other, and my curiosity was fully satisfied.

There is great strength in Hannah's softness, a rare instrument for softening Nathan's hard exterior and gloomy expression. Like a hot iron smoothing down fabric, she smooths the wrinkles of rage, bitterness, and impatience that fill the space between his brows, ruffling his hair with hints of youthful cheer that have been woken from their slumber.

And as for his razor-sharp tongue, she seemed to have picked up a handkerchief and wiped the corners of his lips from the leftover bluntness that had stained them, leaving them clean. Where was the hottempered, unstoppable Nathan? Where were the pulsing veins in his temples? What happened to the grouchy grooves in his face? Where were the eyes glazing over with restrained fury? Oh, how I love to see his face so calm, the light blooming in his eyes! Even the concentration with which he devours the food placed before him.

I gave Hannah ten Gutaleh points for the appearance of my son, relaxed and glowing, an unusual combination all owed to his miracleworker wife.

And Hannah has also granted us another significant, unprecedented honor. For the first time in the history of our family, we have the pleasure of hosting an outside noble. True, there is another honorable customer who visits our home—Buderus, of course. But though his appearance speaks of dignity, I never forget that Buderus comes from the countryside, unlike Hannah, who has been anchored in a stable, respectable home from birth. I cannot say this takes anything away from the way I feel about him. On the contrary. Of all of Meir's foreign connections, he is my favorite. He is a true friend, a partner who offers the longest helping arm in the climb to the top, never letting go.

Well, the way Hannah carries herself inside our home, her amiable demeanor, her elegant table manners, her tailored outfits (my skilled eyes immediately noticed that her refined silk dress, as well as the rest of her clothing, was artfully handmade by an expert tailor), her chiseled body that attracts all eyes to it and from it to the bracelet adorning her delicate wrist, even the way she tilts her head back—these all send the message of nobility.

It seems that the narrow, unassuming lair in which we live did not deter this daughter of silver spoons, nor lead her to exhibit any sort of condescension. Moreover, this lair appeals to her, turning her attention to valuable items that catch her eye. If she has been struck with even a hint of doubt with regard to our small, crowded home, she has not shown any sign of it. She gracefully leaned forward to examine, ask, and show her reverence for such items as my wedding bouquet, which is kept on a small wooden dresser at the back of the parlor. "It's so sweet, Nathan, isn't it?" she asked, gently squeezing his hand. The look she gave him made me feel immodestly proud for having kept this bouquet for the past thirty-six years.

This is Hannah. The English language rolls naturally on her tongue, adapted to her general, unique style. I noticed that when she pronounces certain sounds, her tongue pushes against her teeth. I do not know whether this is a speech impediment or part of the pronunciation of English. I must ask Nathan. Either way, the sound is graceful and pleasant to the ear. I'd best begin to learn the language too, or at least the finest of its words.

Parting from the young couple has left me missing my son and new daughter. Hannah had captivated me, and another chamber of my heart opened up to contain her alongside my children and grandchildren.

This chamber opened when we were saying goodbye. The newlyweds took a seat in their elegant carriage. Hannah, so refined, with her curled black hair parted, framing a handsome, round face, a fashionable English hat atop her head, and a bow around her tiny waist, smiled at us, deepening the dimple in her cheek. She waved her right, gloved hand, her short sleeve puffed and its ends accentuating her smooth arm. Her left arm was wrapped around Nathan's wide waist. Nathan was adjusting his narrow top hat upon his head, his left hand holding on to the strap dangling from the ceiling of the carriage, and wrapping his right arm around Hannah's narrow shoulders. This seemingly innocent, routine image captivated my heart. My eyes fixed on it, not wanting to let go, committing it to memory. The two drove off, and I kept my eyes on the dust rising behind them. For the first time, it occurred to me that Hannah has two roles: the role of wife and the role of mother. I have passed on the baton to conduct Nathan's life. Thanks to her virtues, I feel that she can put my mind at ease and set her shoulders to carry the burden of his supervision.

The carriage was on its way, and I was pleased to know that among the banknotes and gold bars in one of the suitcases, I had managed to squeeze a few Judengasse-made shirts for my son.

◆ ◆ ◆

These are days of political turmoil. Napoleon is in a crazed march of conquest. It seems that the obstacle the English have set is driving him mad.

Our family is working in the eye of the storm, quietly and surreptitiously, with multiarmed maneuvering, its sole goal to benefit financially from the international chaos.

Nathan has been supervising the events in and around London, and Kalman has joined him to provide some help. Amschel and Shlomo are getting set up on the coasts to receive smuggled goods from England and its colonies. Meir, in spite of his shaky health, continues to supervise the work and make sure all the long lines are tightly fastened.

Our little Yaakov, who had his bar mitzvah only last year, has also made his way into the bustling business, pushing his father to treat him like a man who is ready to perform the decrees of Judaism, including the decree of work. Meir tasks him with more serious and dignified missions every day. Yaakov is becoming necessary and important to the business, and I am surprised to see in our little boy the same signs that had appeared in his brother, Nathan.

Sharp thought, overarching sight, boldness, determination, and the ability to squeeze the most out of time. It seems that Yaakov will follow in Nathan's footsteps, and that it will happen sooner than we think.

Occasionally I am plagued by the question of the decency of using international affairs as a springboard for our success. Meir pauses in his striving to soothe my conscience and his: "We are not the ones who created these problems. We only move through them, taking what the adversaries toss into the sea." Then he continues, full steam ahead.

"Yes, Gutaleh, smuggled goods," he said in answer to the persistent question that took hold of my furrowed brow. "When a man declares himself emperor and sets loose his ambition for unbridled conquering, even going so far as to prohibit the shipment of goods from England, when a man like that allows himself free rein, then another man is permitted to make a fortune off his whims. Only the one and only who resides up in heaven has an exclusive right to the world. Man is nothing, and if Napoleon boasts qualities that do not belong to him, he shouldn't be surprised to find their validity temporary."

"And does God up in heaven watch these events unfold with equanimity?"

"The Almighty has given man wisdom to look around with open eyes and be ready for action. Where those who see themselves as superior to man and God stumble, man has the right to use the springboard these fools have put at his feet in their moments of weakness."

Monday, May 9th, 1808

My family, the Rothschild family from the modest Frankfurt Judengasse, is fully dedicated to extensive, cross-country business activity. The founder and his five sons move quickly in their carriages, while the daughters and daughters-in-law, and I too, all take part in the merry activity.

I don't know where to start. There has been much political turmoil, and we have played an active role in its financial repercussions. It is a baffling whirlwind. The names of Napoleon and of the kings of England and Prussia have become familiar to our tongues, as if they were our neighbors, some friendly and others malicious. And I?

Dear God, I am getting old. Everything is moving too quickly.

My son Nathan, my pride and joy, who knows no fear, is feeling fully at home in England. From his London office he navigates, guides, transports, sends, receives, overtakes, rakes, praises, scolds, celebrates, goes wild, whoops, then navigates again. And in Frankfurt and elsewhere different people receive, report, send, transport, worry, and rejoice.

Yes, I am speaking in riddles, I realize that. Oh, how difficult it is to write. My thoughts scamper all over the place and I must gather them.

But what right do I have to complain when Meir and my sons are the ones charged with the truly difficult tasks?

I cannot say that Nathan has become fully assimilated in London in all aspects. His English, still broken and clumsy with a heavy German accent, is miles away from sounding like the graceful English in Hannah's mouth. And society life in London does not suit him. Kalman and Yaakov, who visit him often, speak upon their return of his appearance, which is so different than that of cosmopolitan men, and about his rejection of the unspoken rules of hosting and chitchat. I understand my son, who was raised on different habits. It isn't his fault that England has adopted strange customs that are not common on Judengasse. Luckily, the social responsibilities fall mostly upon Hannah, and according to Kalman and Yaakov, she runs her share of the business in an awe-inspiring manner, enjoying many compliments and words of ingratiation from high-ranking guests.

"Hannah looks like a prestigious product in fine packaging," Yaakov says.

And Kalman adds, laughing, "And next to her, Nathan looks like spoiled goods, not worth the price of the box it came in."

And I rush to summarize: "You've got to admit it's a priceless package deal, and the two items should not be sold separately."

"When you're right you're right," Kalman admits, and Yaakov adds, "The truth is, both sides cut a profit."

Only when they finish teasing do they reach the heart of the matter, and offer a single conclusion: "Nathan is a wizard, and anyone who spends time with him falls under his spell."

Indeed, I knew Nathan would never become an English gentleman, but he has proved to all the English gentlemen, all buttoned up, speaking as if they were superior to everyone else, that he can achieve the goals for which he'd come. Moreover, he succeeds in a foreign country in what they have failed to do on their own turf, and that is more valuable than all the decorum in the world.

From now on, he told us, he would pronounce his name "Nay-than," as the British do, and not "Nah-than," as we do. This way, he said, the sound would not be offensive to sensitive gentlemanly ears. I see this as a testimony to his casting roots in the new place.

Here in Frankfurt, things have changed. In the fall of 1806, we learned that the Holy Roman Empire of the German people has breathed its last. After centuries' long rule, things have finally changed. These tables, too, have turned.

As far as we on Judengasse are concerned, we had expected this change to lead us to redemption. Our status as the king's sharecroppers has been annulled, and now we have to decide on our new status, its name and form. Frankfurt, which is no longer the capital of the Holy Roman Empire of the German people, is now one of sixteen German states united as part of the Confederation of the Rhine, established under the patronage of France.

So now we, the Jews of Judengasse, gaping at these revolutions and curious to the bone about the future, look up expectantly at the man who will determine our condition: Karl von Dalberg, elector of Mainz.

Dalberg, a senior administrator in the Holy Roman Empire, collaborated with Napoleon to found the Confederation of the Rhine, a third German power to face the two others—Austria and Prussia. Due to his involvement, Dalberg was appointed by Napoleon as prince primate of Frankfurt and its surrounding area. We had good reason to believe that Karl von Dalberg would support us and deliver us from sorrow into joy.

First, he is open about his tolerant views, and most prominently his belief in religious freedom. Evidence of this can be found in his being a declared friend of the enlightened Goethe, Schiller, and Herder. Second, as soon as he arrived in Frankfurt, Karl von Dalberg petitioned to allow Jews entrance to the public gardens.

Third, he fights for the rights of all faiths—Lutherans, Catholics, and Calvinists—to serve in public office. We Jews will likely be next.

Fourth, Dalberg's business relationship with Meir Rothschild, one of the most influential Jews in our area, is going very well for both parties. Not only that, but Meir has helped Dalberg out of the financial duress into which he had fallen. Because his expenses as prince primate of Frankfurt and the area add up to hundreds of thousands of gulden per year, he had turned to different bankers to request loans, but had been turned away. His savior was Meir, who stood by his side, meeting his many needs. In return, Meir asked one thing of Dalberg: to grant Jews the status of equal citizens.

Unfortunately, this support turned out to be unreliable, and our tower of hopes collapsed before our eyes. While the Lutherans, Catholics, and Calvinists were declared fit to serve in public office, we Jews were sentenced to make do with protection from humiliation. Meaning, the critical changes taking place all around us have no effect on us. Our history goes on uninterrupted.

This news hit us with the full force of its ugliness. The street, shocked with pain, crouched down, gritting its teeth. Meir was seething at Karl von Dalberg. The latter, who needed continued service, tried to appease the former by promising that Meir himself would instantly be granted personal status as an equal citizen. This offer made Meir even more furious. "I demand nothing for myself," he muttered. "I demand what my people all equally deserve."

With his request from Dalberg rejected for the time being, Meir sought alternative routes. He sniffed around and discovered that a formal event was slated to take place in our area. "Excellent," he said, and sat down to outline an impressive plan.

This was just before Napoleon was scheduled to visit Frankfurt in July 1807. Meir gathered the key players of our street in his study. "This high and mighty man," he told them, "who is coming from enlightened Paris, which supports equality and fraternity, is the man who can help us." Meir described his plan and made their eyes twinkle with a new light.

Sleeves were rolled, and shoulder to shoulder, our people built a triumphal arch for the great man. Preparations for the arrival of the emperor filled the streets with small shards of new hope, which managed to conceal its dimness for a while.

The coveted day had arrived. In the morning, a delegation of Jewish dignitaries reported to the gate of the city to greet the emperor and his entourage. Among them, of course, was Meir Rothschild, our son Amschel, and the chief rabbi.

The description of the following events was told and retold afterward, and every grain of information was ground to dust. For days and weeks the story took wing through our street, and with each retelling another shade was added to glorify the details. Not a soul seemed to have missed it. Many gathered around the gate where they were allowed to stand. Some watched from the street itself, and a few looked through their windows. Though they couldn't see the goings-on, they heard the sounds and let their imaginations fly when envisioning the events in their minds.

Yaakov took my hand and led me to the crowd. For hours on end, the delegation stood in the blazing sun, their foreheads dripping with sweat, and their fine clothing stained with moisture.

Just before six o'clock in the evening, we heard the horses' hooves approaching. The delegation straightened their backs with renewed formality. The crowd that had gathered, blocked by police officers, followed the action curiously. The crowd's density was hard to bear; everyone faced a single direction. Yaakov supported me lest I stumble, and I felt his hand trembling on my shoulder. We had never experienced anything like this.

The guards marched in first, tall, straight-faced, left-right, left-right, straight legs, equal steps, sparkling shoes, and pressed uniforms. They were so different from the French soldiers who had marched through our street sixteen years ago. Behind them was the magnificent carriage of his highness the emperor Napoleon, harnessed to four noble horses, fitted with steel cranks, strutting in slow motion. Finally, there came the carriage of the guard, harnessed to two horses.

The emperor's procession surprised us. Mute looks of wonder passed from one to the other. The venerable emperor, whose name was formidable, was surrounded by guards that were so much taller than him that we could barely see him.

But this wasn't enough to take anything away from the regal majesty of his appearance. He wore a shiny white uniform adorned with a row of sparkling buttons sewn on in an unfamiliar fashion. The white pants, tight against his body and folded under the knee, revealed tight, white silk socks. His feet were clad in narrow, shiny boots. The sleeves of his white shirt were fitted and his cuff links were crimson. His shoulders were decorated with symbols and marks, and he had a black hat on his head, striped with gold down the middle and ending with long, narrow edges. In his hand was a golden scepter sparkling with silver.

I felt as if I had stepped into one of those fairy tales I used to tell my children.

A blast of horns broke the silence, adding even more dignity to the affair. I took my eyes off Napoleon and turned to look at the Jewish delegation. They looked as if they were all holding their breath as they saluted the emperor, their heels clicking dramatically. Silence fell all around. The whole world seemed to be part of this momentous occasion, lowering its head respectfully.

The delegation speaker cleared his throat and began. In spite of the endless rehearsals he'd performed to his friends in the past few days, the tremble in his voice echoed through the standing air.

The emperor, wearing a severe expression, nodded lightly. I watched his face. Not a muscle twitched, no sign of him taking any interest in the events unfolding around him. Did his highness realize that all this was for him?

One by one, each of the three delegation members recited a song of praise for Napoleon, one in German, one in French, and then Meir, who read it in Hebrew. His reading was fine, though touched with nervousness, which I'm certain no one but me could sense. I was proud of him. His posture was a bit hunched, but his stance was steady and confident. He stood perfectly still.

The emperor held his scepter in his right hand, and I imagined him trying to drive it deep into the hard pavement. Slowly, he raised his left hand and waved it in the direction of the speakers, nodding his head to the same rhythm. He seemed to be lost in his reveries, and this entire ceremony was like a bothersome fly to him. One could imagine that during these pestering moments he was busy planning his next conquest.

I shifted my eyes from Napoleon to Meir. The two were so similar. Both of them, my Meir and the emperor Napoleon, were cut from the same cloth, an ambitious cloth that made their blood race, sent them out to battle, and never gave them rest. Each new goal only sped them on to the one after that, and their desire knew no end. But their goals were inherently different: the Jewish one was racing to conquer the peak of dignity that twinkled with silver coins and banknotes, while the elevated gentile aspired to territorial conquests at the price of human lives.

This noble man cleared his important schedule to come see the Jews of Frankfurt. But could a man who eats, sleeps, and breathes like any other concern himself with only one thing—conquest? What did he wish to do with all the territory he occupied? What would he do with all the dead? Where would he find a large enough cemetery? On Judengasse, for instance, space in the cemetery was minuscule. Graves were heaped atop each other, separated by layers of dust, so as not to defile the bodies by allowing them to touch. Our pleas to expand the cemetery have all been ignored.

And what about those declarations of liberty, equality, and fraternity? Did they not contradict the man's great appetite for land at any price? In the meantime, soldiers on all sides continue to die.

I looked once more at the glamorous man's face. A hint of fatigue had made its way in. I thought about how this single man—who, at the moment, was tired, swallowing a yawn—determined people's fates, and that no one in the entire world could say a thing. What about his mother? Did she not have any influence over him? Poor thing, I suppose she didn't. I felt sorry for the Corsican mother who had to see what had become of her son. Her dear son, whom she had nursed, helped through his first steps, taught his first words, whose clothes she washed with bony hands, and whose food she cooked, all while dreaming of him growing older and choosing a noble profession. And now what? Was she proud of her son who had become a great general? Or did she follow his actions with bitter disappointment, her aching heart saying, "This is not what I had yearned for, my son. Not the harlot widow you married, six years older and with two children that are not your own, nor your obsessive conquests that bring pain and grief to whole families."

And what about his wife, Josephine? Is she pleased with her husband's choices?

I looked at the horses. They too were their master's lackeys, just like the people that surrounded him as if he were a spoiled baby, following his every move, rushing to fulfill his every whim. Those dumb horses stood there, awaiting orders with submissive boredom. I would have at least expected them to neigh, disturbing the respectful silence that fell over the place, or even drop a few fragrant bits of manure to the ground, breaking the emperor's infuriating façade of smugness, if only for a moment.

The satisfaction of our Jewish delegates did not match the disappointment I felt. Their great intentions, the excitement coursing through them, and their naivety did not allow them to take a real look at the emperor and see what was hiding beneath the exterior. Their hope was false. I felt for them. I felt for Meir.

Now the emperor whispered something to his bodyguard, who rushed to fulfill orders. The short ceremony was over.

The entourage was on its way. As an echo to the neighing of the awakening horses, the crowd called out rhythmically, "Long live the emperor! Long live the emperor!"

I recalled the banishment of the French in 1792. "Down with the French! Long live the king of Prussia!" our friends on Judengasse had cried back then. And now, sixteen years later, the tables have turned.

◆ ◆ ◆

Now we must accept another disappointment. Our hope for redemption at the hands of the emperor has vanished.

The few changes made for our benefit after the French invaded Frankfurt were trampled under the weight of prohibitions that have remained in place. We, the Jews of Frankfurt, who have grown accustomed to paying a special tax for the simple fact of being Jewish, were carried away with the changes that swirled all around us, indulging in the hope that their agents would glance in our direction too, and remove the atrocities from our midst.

But the exterior changes seemed to keep their distance from us.

We must continue to pay the tax. We must accept the allotment of prohibitions enforced upon us for generations, such as the prohibition against sitting at cafes, or crossing central squares in town, or, at the public bathhouse, touching towels that were imprinted with the words "Christians Only," as if we were lepers. I wonder what those Christians have that we don't. Or should I ask, what is it about us that seems so wrong to them? I suppose we ought to remind them what their esteemed origins are. They worship Jesus, their savior. Was he not one of us? If they take offense with circumcision, they might consider that

Jesus was circumcised too. And if that does not change their minds, then I understand nothing.

I'll let it go. I now feel sorrow for Amschel's heartbreak. His request for a permit to live outside the ghetto is rejected again and again. The self-righteous people of Frankfurt know there are no available apartments in Judengasse, and yet they continue to harden their hearts to us, refusing to permit him to live in other parts of the city. How long will my son be forced to live in our home with his wife, as if he were a child? They have been married for twelve years. If Eva had been able to have children, they might have had almost ten by now. But as fate would have it, I will have no grandchildren from Amschel. My heart aches at the thought. If only he had enjoyed a bit of compassion from the authorities and been able to buy his own home outside the ghetto. My poor son. Even his innocent request to publish a weekly journal in Hebrew or Judendeutsch has been rejected for fear that the journal may serve as a vehicle for anti-Christian propaganda.

Monday, April 2nd, 1810

Meir waited breathlessly for Dalberg's new Jewish Law to be posted. He hoped that the French wind that blew on Dalberg's face would make its mark in Frankfurt too. He paced through the house restlessly, moving his hands from his bottom to his hips and then back to his painful bottom, hypothesizing about the reliefs we would soon enjoy.

On January 4th, Dalberg's new Jewish Law was posted, replacing that damned one from 1616.

A week earlier, all homes were decorated, prepared for the festive news. But the decorations came down, collapsing under the constant snow, their hanging remnants swinging from side to side like a miserable memory.

On the big day, the neighbors all put on their holiday finest and went out into the street. With white, ironed shirts peeking out from under heavy winter coats, we mingled in the street, the falling snow piling up. People did not go to work, and stores were empty. It was a joyous holiday, appropriate for a change that had been dreamed of for two hundred years. Everybody's hearts seemed to beat together as one, faster than ever. The moment was finally here, and the Jews would have happiness and light. Some spoke of the earlier generations. "It's a shame they aren't here to experience this historic moment with us," they said.

Rabbi Zvi Hirsch Halevi Horowitz arrived with a rolled missive in his hand. All around him, men, women, and children gathered, trying to get a look. He stepped onto the podium at the synagogue and faced the crowd. I stood at a distance, following his every move along with everyone else. People shushed each other all around. Silence fell. Our street had never been so full, or so quiet.

The rabbi removed the seal and unrolled the paper. His eyes fluttered over the words before reading them to the public that awaited with bated breath.

Suddenly, he grew weak. His face, which was always pale, now whitened like the snowflakes that fell from the heavens. The missive seemed to burn his hand and he almost dropped it. His feet lost their steadiness. Two men came to his aid. They took the letter from his hand and spread it open. Rather than fighting over the paper, they each seemed eager to be rid of the damned thing.

I didn't need to hear the words that passed between the two and the people that crowded around them. The rabbi wrung his hands, and the people who were holding the letter followed suit. One of the old men let out an awful cry and collapsed into the arms of the people around him. They carried him out, the crowd parting to make way for them, and led him home. Other people cried too, a sharp, unified wail emerging. I covered my mouth with both hands, and moved my frightened eyes to Meir.

I worried for his heart. Rather than the list of easements he had hoped for, he found words that shattered those hopes. As Amschel wrapped his arms around his father's shoulders, tears were running down their faces. The two set out for home, our other children following suit.

I made a path for myself through the sea of pain.

Leaning on Amschel, Meir climbed up the stairs to our house heavily, his limp hand dragging along the railing. I followed them up, never taking my eyes off the beaten body that was pulled upward distractedly. We arrived at the living room. His tired eyes turned to me, then moved to his own faltering legs. He fell into the chair. "It's impossible, Gutaleh," he sighed, closing his eyes.

I came closer and kneeled before him. I stroked his hair and took his cheeks tenderly in my hands. Hatred burned inside me. How dare Dalberg be so cruel to us? How could he have betrayed Meir's trust? Was this how he repaid him for his loyal service?

One by one, enraged people entered our home. The parlor swarmed with people, and the puddles of melting snow pooled over the floor. Their anger searched for a way out. Words were muttered into the thick air, questions with no question marks at the end, cries without exclamation points. Sighs and groans of a common destiny. The unity of torment. The unity of rage. The unity of acceptance of our miserable fate. Hands sought out hands, clinging to each other, squeezing with painful force.

Someone wished to give voice to the injustice. Others hushed him. What for? Were the events of the day not enough? Why hurt our ears with further reminder?

More people demanded that the new law be repeated, so that the horror could trickle down, so we could remember who we were and what our destiny was. The voices grew louder. Arguments gave way to anger. Here was a suitable channel for its expression. Shouts mixed with each other, hands let go of their clutching and were raised to the sky, toward the one who remained unnamed, who remained silent in light of this horror. The gates of heaven were closed. The cries mixed together to form one single scream, and heads were turned upward. The ceiling was struck with a mélange of words, a lamentation that did not form coherent sentences.

Someone began expressing a sentiment, and others repeated his words, their voices rising louder: "My God, my God, why have you forsaken me? Why are you so far from saving me, so far from my cries of anguish . . . Break the arm of the wicked man, call the evildoer to account for his wickedness . . . Have mercy on us, Lord, have mercy on us, for we have endured no end of contempt . . . Deliver me, rescue me from the hands of foreigners whose mouths are full of lies, whose right hands are deceitful."

When the storm ended, there was quiet. One man at a time approached Meir, placed a gentle hand on his shoulder, and left. The condolence of mourners was over for the time being.

This entire time, Meir was curled up in the chair, his back hunched, his head lowered, his lips pursed. His hands lay limply in his lap. Four of his sons stood guard around him, remaining restrained. And only I, on the floor, my elbow against Meir's thigh, recognized beneath their polite appearance my sons' anxiety about their father. I felt anxious too.

Slowly, soft flakes of contentment filtered their way into my tormented heart. They appeared, fell away, then appeared again. My dear sons knew how to be in the right place at the right time. They did not leave their father's side, standing around him like a protective wall to cushion the blow of his shattered hopes. Their tightly closed lips and their eyes that shifted from a cold and direct look at the visitors to a worried glance at their father, were a familial picture of loyal sons who care for nothing more in this world than their father's well-being. They were ready to pounce whenever the situation required them to, in order to ensure his continued health. I gave silent thanks that Nathan, so far away, was spared this scene. The news itself would be enough to rekindle his old resentment of the city of Frankfurt.

Meir broke his silence only after the last of the mourners left. "Betrayal," he whispered, gritting his teeth. "I gave that man everything, and he gave me nothing. Napoleon was no help, and neither were all the services I provided that traitor, Dalberg. All our efforts are for naught."

The words themselves were unnecessary. Meir knew this too. Who better than him to recognize the mood of a place. And nevertheless he felt the need to speak them. I looked up at him, following the movement of his lips, these lips that spoke wisdom every day. Confident lips, hoping for the best. His weak voice and pounding temples hurt me. Suddenly I realized that Meir Amschel was flesh and blood, imbued with human weakness. His greatest weakness being his inability to handle defeat. Of course no one wants to be defeated, but Meir's body lacked that unique mechanism that allows people to admit and accept defeat.

And I loved him for his humanity. And I ached for him, so much. Exile is harder than all other evils put together.

Wednesday, August 22nd, 1810

I've decided to devote my entry today to Wilhelm, the landgrave of Hesse-Kassel. Recent events remind me of Marie Antoinette, whose demise proved how fickle fate is, mocking and warning us that no one is immune. Even kings and princes cannot rest on their laurels. Just as they have risen to greatness, they can fall from grace, as worthless as chaff.

Well, we have learned about the matter of the landgrave with time, by following moods and rumors, especially the ones shared by Buderus, Amschel—who is posted in Kassel—and through Meir's direct involvement. The landgrave's recent matter began four summers ago, when the war between Prussia and France broke out. Many months earlier, Wilhelm had vacillated between sides. On the one hand, he did his best to please the Prussians, transferring twenty thousand soldiers to fight for their cause in exchange for 25,000 pounds, which he happily added to his loot. On the other hand, he made the French believe he was neutral, and in exchange asked for control of Frankfurt and its surrounding area.

"When you chase two rabbits, you end up catching none," Buderus warned him, but it was no use.

In response, the French informed him that he would be appointed king of Hesse—the title that the landgrave had aspired to—as long as Hesse joined the sixteen German states in the Confederation of the Rhine, which was under their protection.

Wilhelm's refusal to join the confederation was the last straw, and Napoleon reacted quickly. Thus, at the height of the war against Prussia, Napoleon ordered his military commanders to turn west, toward Kassel, capital of Hesse, take over the elegant Wilhelmshöhe Palace, take Wilhelm captive, and seize his possessions.

The landgrave spent the months preceding the French invasion preparing for this very scenario. Buderus helped him look over his accounting ledgers, packing away any documents or bonds that might disclose his income and investments. A long line of servants and other employees in the palace toiled tirelessly, filling chests with silver and gold jewelry, valuable household goods, crystal chandeliers, and ancient coins and rare medals, many of which he had bought from my Meir's collection.

Buderus offered to deliver the possessions and documents by ship to the city of Bremen, not far from the North Sea, and from there to England. The plan did not come to pass because of the landgrave's refusal to pay the ship's captain fifty thalers, and so the 120 chests were in danger of destruction.

As a makeshift solution, the chests were hidden within specially built plaster walls in the palace and in two other castles: Oldenburg and Sababurg.

When he learned that the French soldiers were advancing toward Kassel, the landgrave, wearing civilian clothing and accompanied by his eldest son, his mistress—the Countess Karoline von Schlotheim—and six servants, fled in two carriages harnessed to six horses each. Deep in their luggage were hidden British account information documents and some cash. The two carriages made their way north under cover of night, crossing the Danish border and stopping near Schleswig, outside the mansion of Karl, Wilhelm's brother.

Buderus spent one more day and night in the palace, hastily arranging the final details, and then departed, disguised as a traveling cobbler. At the bottom of his pack he placed a bag containing Danish and English bond stubs, covered by work tools—an anvil, hammer, and nails. Luckily, he did not encounter any enemy.

But when he arrived at Sababurg, near the castle where some of the chests had been stashed, Buderus was met with an extremely unpleasant surprise. When he asked the peasants if any of them would be willing to rent him a wagon to continue his journey, he was shocked to find that rumors of the landgrave's treasure, concealed in the castle, had been swarming in the area. The secret had been revealed, and the French military leader, Lagrange, was on his way to capture the treasure.

There was no time to change the plan, and it was impossible to collect the treasure hidden in the castle. The peasant who had harnessed his wagon pleaded with Buderus to hurry up and leave Sababurg, explaining that Lagrange was close, and if he found out Buderus had rented his wagon, the peasant would be forced to pay dearly.

Indeed, as soon as he left, the formidable Lagrange arrived. Without too much effort, the governor uncovered the stash of money, gold, and coins.

Lagrange stood breathless before the sparkling sight, and in his eagerness, gave orders to have the gold and silver melted, and the coins sent to Paris to be auctioned off.

In the next few weeks, he spared no effort to track down additional hiding places, eventually discovering most of the chests hidden in Wilhelmshöhe Palace and in Oldenburg. Signs bearing the words "Neutral Territory," posted by the landgrave during his escape, made no impression on the military leader. He and his people broke into the palace, shattered the walls, and recovered the chests, all while causing no harm to the landgrave's wife and children, who stood watching, petrified.

Meir followed the events with great concern from our home. Other than he and Buderus, no one had a clear idea of just how much the richest landgrave in Germany owned. Meir's main worry was the financial status of the poor man, who was being stripped of significant portions of his possessions on a daily basis, so much so that he was facing the risk of being left penniless. Meir took pity on the man who had granted him his important titles, and with whom he had been collaborating for the past thirty-five years, growing even closer in the last few.

Moreover, Meir was concerned with his own future. He was afraid that the great accomplishments he'd achieved in his dealings with the landgrave would all fall apart. He had to be patient, waiting for a sliver of light to break through some hidden crack. Meir's head swung like a pendulum, his eyes on the horizon.

Nevertheless, this entire time, he never looked like a man on the edge of an abyss. He just continued repeating that they "had to find a way" and that they had to "find the enemy's Achilles' heel."

The Achilles' heel was found—in Lagrange himself. The leader had developed an insatiable appetite for the landgrave's treasure, and pocketed a considerable portion of it. With bold cunning he reported to Napoleon only 16 million gulden and proposed to the landgrave that he allow him to smuggle the rest of the sum—22 million gulden in bonds, bills, and contracts—out of the country, in exchange for a bribe of 1 million French francs.

Encouraged by Buderus, the landgrave eagerly accepted, transferred the bribe to Lagrange, and in exchange received the chests. Some of them arrived at his brother Karl's mansion in Denmark, where the landgrave was staying for the time being, and four others arrived at our home, care of Meir.

Meir was relieved to find that not all the money was lost, and that a considerable part of it was still usable.

I was so proud of Meir. I reached out in invitation, and he walked over and put his arms around my plump waist. I wrapped my arms around his neck and whispered in his ear, "Of all the many Christian bankers in Germany, the landgrave chose the perfect Jew from Judengasse to keep his treasure safe."

Meir spun me around. In my dizziness, I heard Amschel, who had abandoned Kassel to come home on the occasion of this transaction, laughing. Then he grabbed Eva's slim waist and spun her around as well.

I stopped, breathless, and sat down on the chair. Meir sat down beside me. We watched Amschel and Eva, who continued to dance slowly and smoothly, her head resting on his shoulder, her hands holding his waist. Other than a few rare exceptions, they have been spending their days together with acceptance and appeasement. It may not be happiness, but it isn't constant grief, either.

I have accepted Eva too. My eyes and my heart have grown accustomed to the good in her. I am grateful to her for correcting her ways in the early days of their marriage. All our lives we are destined to falter. When we take action to stop the faltering as it occurs rather than letting it recur, we must be satisfied.

In the past, I had trouble bearing her sorrowful demeanor with the eternal wrinkle between her brows. Melancholy had gripped her. And Amschel, with his gloomy expression, trapped in a failed marriage, also troubled me. His skinny body appeared shriveled. They looked like two people walking on opposite sides of the street, each of them looking down at the gutter, as if wondering if their lost joy was wallowing there.

Often, as we all sat together in the living room, Eva would shut herself in her room or wander the house on tiptoe, as if she had submitted to her fate. The cloudy sky of her life seemed to have no intention of changing seasons, and the weather that was forced upon her was dreary and dark. Gradually, she dared come closer to Amschel's spot and sit down behind him, hidden behind his back, her eyes wandering, tortured, over the room, searching for a place where they could rest without disturbing anyone.

I decided something had to be done. The sadness had to be lifted, patiently, slowly. This delicate situation required tenderness and care. One step at a time, I came closer.

One night, when her eyes met mine, I gestured for her to come over and pointed to the available chair I had placed beside mine. She obeyed with respect, trying to decide where to rest her hand. I took hold of her lost hand, rubbed it, and whispered, "Everything is all right, Eva. Everything is all right." She looked at me quizzically, doubting the earnestness of my words. I looked back at her affectionately. I would not divulge her secret. Her tormented regret and Amschel's suffering were punishment enough. Tears gathered in her eyes. She squeezed my hand softly and looked at me with gratitude.

One day, I even invited her into the kitchen, and promised her that Amschel knew nothing of what had taken place in her soul when she fell under the spell of Moshe de Worms, and that I trusted her and knew things were back as they should be, and that from that point on we would put the affair behind us. "You are my first daughter-in-law and you are dear to me," I concluded.

She fell into my arms, releasing the thicket of emotions that had tangled deep inside of her. Her sobs were accompanied by my tears of compassion.

As the days wore on, the barrier that had formed between the couple was lowered, and they shared an expression of melancholic acceptance. Eva had adjusted to her life like a baby that grows accustomed to the taste of new foods. A taste, a frown, another taste, a swallow. Even her treatment of dishes around the dining table had changed. At first she would slam them onto the table, but now her touch has softened, and she places them down soundlessly.

And I had long ago removed my cloak of anger and scratched the remnants of ire from the walls of my heart. I had rid myself of my inclination to judge her harshly, and my attitude toward her is now anchored in a message of peace and forgiveness. My piercing eyes were replaced with pardoning ones, and my severe tone with a warm voice. From the moment I shared the cooking process with her, the ice broke, and she had become part of the family. I do not regret the way I looked at her at the time when my assertiveness was necessary, but I no longer hold a grudge, and I am doing my best to help her remove whatever is left of that gloomy atmosphere, put the past behind her, and gradually widen her weak smile.

I have noticed something odd. Eva's appearance has grown more appealing to my eyes. A person's character must determine to a great extent our judgment of their looks, for better or worse. But I still regret the fact that she lives out her days without enjoying the fragrance of a baby. I am sorry that my son will never have a son of his own to say the kaddish prayer over his grave. I find small comfort in their continued life as an amiable couple under the same roof.

Tuesday, October 16th, 1810

I've been smiling often lately. The race of our lives leads us up a steep incline, and in spite of the effort required, the view from each step of the way is breathtaking, and calls for us to keep climbing upward, revealing what is yet to come.

Fortunately, Meir received a permit from the landgrave to use the contents of the chests he had received for safekeeping. The transactions made using the landgrave's treasure have increased our income exponentially. From this point on, Meir is the single trustee of the landgrave's fortune. The tables have turned, and the fear regarding Wilhelm's deteriorating financial state has made way for a significant leap for the Rothschild Bank.

But I must go back and tell things in order.

Wilhelm's first days in exile, in Gottorf Castle in the Schleswig-Holstein district, with his brother Karl, made him depressed. The proximity of Napoleon's troops and the fear of being taken prisoner made him morose.

The man who stood by his side and helped him during those hard days was Buderus. He lifted his spirits and kept him abreast of the news received from Meir about the business, informing him that his capital was continuing to bear fruit, a fact that was enough to bring a bit of light back into his dark eyes. This time, Buderus was able to appease the landgrave and make him understand that in these complicated times, it was best to entrust his possessions to the hands of one man and one man alone—Meir Rothschild, who had proved his reliability, his devotion, his loyalty, his professionalism, his openness to taking risks, and his discretion.

Meir himself did not sit idly by. He prepared a safety net in the form of a letter written in broken German. Buderus glanced at the letter and roared with laughter. With the remains of laughter still on his face, he slipped the letter back into its envelope and promised to deliver it, assuring my husband, "Don't worry, Meir, the landgrave himself writes with terrible spelling mistakes. He'll be glad to learn there's somebody out there who writes even worse than him."

Confirmation of this was provided in a lengthy, intimate letter. Buderus's examination proved that after losing 21 million gulden, Wilhelm was still at the top of the list of richest men in Europe, with 30 million gulden to his name.

Equipped with power of attorney, which was passed through Buderus, as well as with the document attached to the letter, Meir hurried to collect interest from the landgrave's debtors in England and Austria. Each day he worked on two sides: the English side, from which he deducted the landgrave's bills and charged interest, and the Austrian side, which had to transfer the interest payments in exchange for a large loan given to the Austrian emperor. The collaboration between Meir and Buderus in tending to the landgrave's affairs became even closer, and the wheels turned faster than ever.

Buderus had trouble working from within Denmark. He returned to Kassel, risking being caught by the French. The purpose of this trip was to help his family prepare to move to the new mansion he had built in Hanau. The geographic distance between Meir and Buderus had shrunk once more, and the short trip from Frankfurt to Hanau gave rise to extensive secret activity between the two: Meir was in charge of collection, and Buderus of managing the books. The two worked together to bring back the landgrave.

Due to their fear of the French police, which had been trying to track the exiled landgrave's moving funds, Buderus and Meir decided to maintain duplicate accounts, a task at which Meir excels. Meir's double accounting is meant to present the French, if need be, with the appearance of minor financial activity on behalf of the landgrave, nothing that would be of interest to them.

Buderus has taken a lesson from Meir, and built hidden compartments in his home for the confidential material. As an additional protective measure, he only stashes the accounting ledgers in the compartments. Interest receipts, cash, debt bonds, and other sensitive materials related to the landgrave are sent directly to us, and Meir, with the swiftness of a bird in flight, directs them to their destination: some money is invested, by orders of Buderus, in the Rothschild Bank, and the rest is buried deep in the chest in the cellar leading to our neighbor's home.

Indeed, the French soon appeared at Buderus's home. They arrived at his mansion for a surprise audit, eager to uncover evidence that could be used to convict the landgrave. When they found nothing, they grew furious, and when they grew tired of Buderus, they began to harass his friend, Meir Rothschild of Judengasse.

I must say that the patriotic winds blowing through Frankfurt were working in our favor. Thanks to them, the French officers were forced to search our home in a way that wouldn't anger the clerks of the local government, who sent their own representatives to supervise the search. Ultimately, this search, backed by a fine tip from the household to the visitors, uncovered nothing.

The French officers opted for seduction. They used a few moments when the local government representatives were lingering in one of the rooms of the house, and made Meir a tempting offer: a commission of

25 percent in exchange for any English landgrave funds he transferred to them.

The head of the search crossed his arms and must have been pondering the moment, not too far in the future, when he would finally rub his hands with satisfaction. But Meir stuck to his story that he was not in possession of the landgrave's English money, and his accounting ledgers confirmed his claims.

The matter grew to such proportions that a need arose for a reliable contact who could connect Meir and Buderus and handle the landgrave's affairs. The man chosen for the job was our Kalman. Due to his position, Kalman had a daily travel routine for handling ongoing and overall management: taking care of debt bonds, charging interest, making deposits, and passing messages. For his errands, Kalman used a carriage with a false bottom, built by a professional carriage maker in Hanau, a reliable man who would not reveal his customers' secrets. The valuables were buried in the hidden compartment of the carriage, including not only financial documents, but also political information and messages passed between the three men: Meir, Buderus, and Wilhelm.

Soon, Kalman found himself taking care of more and more personal requests of all kinds on behalf of the landgrave and his companions. He became the main transporter from Hanau to the point of exile in the Danish castle, delivering groceries according to a list given to him upon each visit: bottled water, honey, clothes, shoes, books, scissors, corkscrew, and other items that made me seethe, because the rude landgrave thinks that though he is now a mouse hiding in his dark hole, he can behave like a master of servants, and my son Kalman is no servant, but a top-tier banker, the son of the leading banker in Germany.

But the brunt of my anger is directed at his incorrigible mistress, Karoline von Schlotheim, who shares the landgrave's dark lair, pops her head out, and demands that my son add her own items to his list, some of which would have been best kept inside of her twisted mind and never put in writing.

"Do not get those things for her," I scolded my son, as if it were his fault.

He said, "But she'll complain to the landgrave, and I'll have to do it anyway. What good would this do? I would have made him angry and given her what she wants. She would come out on top."

My blood boiled. "Then at the very least put it off, tell her you couldn't find what she asked for, that you didn't have time, that you couldn't do it, that you would try again next time."

And so Kalman does not share his lists with me anymore. I do not know whatever became of the mistress's requests. My smart son finds efficient ways to hide them from me. I don't like to tell my children how to do their jobs. Their father is their professional mentor. But the matter of the mistress deviated from my son's realm of responsibility, and I couldn't just stand on the sidelines and allow that clucking hen to behave as if she were the queen of the birds, treating my darling son so degradingly.

I do feel sorry for the landgrave's wife. I have a lot of sympathy for that miserable woman, left behind in the empty palace, who must be spending her days and nights in tortured guesswork about what her husband and his mistress must be doing together.

Enormous sums are transferred to her by Meir, according to Wilhelm's orders. If I ever left the ghetto, I would go see her and comfort her. But, on second thought, I wonder if she would have accepted me. Perhaps she would think a Jew from Judengasse had no business comforting a weeping Christian in the palace in Kassel.

Once again, I learn that life in a palace is not all fun and games, and that happiness does not depend on the number of rooms in one's home or on the materials coating the walls. Something mysterious causes life in palaces to go awry.

The landgrave's business had led Meir to start a branch of the Rothschild Bank in Hamburg, in order to allow Kalman to perform his job more comfortably and efficiently. The landgrave was pleased with this decision, and in those very same days, the spring of 1807, bought a home in the small Danish village of Itzehoe, near Hamburg. Meir would spend several weeks at a time in Hamburg, and was able to visit the landgrave in his new mansion. Walking side by side like old friends on the expansive lawns of his garden, the two had an opportunity to consult on his investments.

The close connection between Meir and Wilhelm was meant to reinforce their relationship, giving us a sense of stability. I believed Meir should be able to rest on his laurels. But the following developments shocked me and proved just how fickle and fluid human relations can be, shedding further light on Wilhelm's instability.

At first, the kind Buderus tried to hide the embarrassing chain of events from Meir, saving his friend the heartache. But since the matter was not resolved, he was finally forced to include him in it.

Wilhelm was extremely satisfied with the service he had received at the Rothschild Bank, and had decided to no longer engage the services of Rüppell and Harnier, the largest and oldest bank in Kassel. This decision was reinforced by the founded suspicion that the owners of the large bank did not handle his money with integrity. But, in accordance with his fickle nature, he was suddenly having second thoughts about the decision Buderus had led him to—to use none but the Rothschild Bank. Wilhelm was uncomfortable with the thought of sealing the fate of his relationship with the Bethmann brothers, the venerable bankers of Frankfurt, and one of the biggest in all of Germany.

One day, the landgrave ordered his servant to summon Buderus. Standing above Buderus, hunched over due to his arthritis, with his plump belly and unsteady legs, Wilhelm scolded him harshly. He made it unequivocally clear that he would not be parting ways with the

Bethmann brothers. "You and Rothschild are conspiring against me," he accused.

Buderus did not take this lying down. "I suggest you go to sleep now," he said, "then wake up tomorrow morning, check how your money has been handled again, and compare the conditions other bankers are offering to the ones you're receiving from Rothschild, then apologize to me for the way you just spoke."

He said this with express calm, which only exacerbated Wilhelm's rage. "You will do as I say, and you will leave Hanau and come live here, in Hamburg. I forbid you from distancing yourself from me."

"No," Buderus said plainly and left.

A month later, Buderus was summoned. He stood before his master again, and like a teacher instructing his imbecilic student, listed, one by one, Rothschild's virtues: his integrity, his punctuality, his energy, his resourcefulness, his imagination, his convenient terms, his efficient service, his availability at any time for any matter, and his discretion. As evidence of this, he reminded Wilhelm that even when the French made Rothschild a very compelling offer, he did not fall into their trap and disclose the landgrave's assets.

Wilhelm said nothing, and Buderus added, "The loyal Rothschild family, which stands undeterred before any challenge of weather, time, cash flow, or low commission, is doing everything in its power to please you. Most important, Rothschild is offering you the most money, delivered in the safest manner."

The meeting ended without resolution. When Buderus arrived home in Hanau he wrote and mailed a brief letter of resignation, which he closed with the line, "Lack of faith in an honest man is a lethal ingredient."

This letter put an end to the affair. The landgrave's rage dwindled, Buderus took back his resignation, and from that point on, the Rothschild Bank was the only bank that handled the affairs of the richest landgrave in Europe, and the financial balance of the M. A. Rothschild firm has been in constant ascent. Kalman's older brothers, Shlomo and Amschel, came to his aid, and have been assisting him in collecting enormous sums from the landgrave's debtors, while for the time being only a small share of the sum has been delivered directly to the landgrave. Meir assured the man that he would receive the money in time, but that it was best if he held on to it while Wilhelm was in exile.

Meanwhile, we have received news of unprecedented success on the part of our English operations. Nathan does not write often, but the reports he trickles to us attest to extensive activity, the yield of which is in direct contrast to the dwindling number of letters he writes. Perhaps it is because he is working so hard that he cannot find the time for such frivolities as correspondence.

Sunday, December 2nd, 1810

My Dear Son Nathan,
I hope and pray that you and darling Hannah are well.

Praise the Lord, we continue to excel through hard work. Amschel, Shlomo, and Kalman have been demonstrating strength, vigor, and wisdom.

Demand for English goods in Frankfurt is unprecedented. All the white fabric that had been kept in storage for three years has run out. I think I have a solution for the shipment of goods. Try a route through Holland. We are swamped with orders. Do your best.

Mama sends warm kisses to you and Hannah. And I add mine.

Write more. We are eager for any information about you and our financial situation.

Love you,

Papa,

Meir Amschel Rothschild

These are decoded excerpts from one of the many letters sent from our home in Frankfurt to Nathan's home in London. In the exchange of letters between the two, many more are sent to London than are received here. But, unlike Meir, I feel no qualms about Nathan not writing enough.

Meir is supported by the wide net of his children, who work to promote the firm, and so he can make time to retire to the secret cellar whenever he wishes to put pen to paper, in a careful mélange of languages. Nathan, on the other hand, is working alone, taking many risks, and can spare no time for writing.

Amschel, Shlomo, and Kalman also write to Nathan, letters containing information about the price of gold, of securities, and of goods in European markets.

Nevertheless, our temporarily British son makes the effort to write and ask his father to take more care with his letters. In the future, his personal letters can still be written in Judendeutsch spiced with Hebrew, and it is a good idea to use a pseudonym for the landgrave and use an Italian nickname for himself. The code word for investments ("fishing rod") is appropriate and makes him burst into laughter that causes the clerks to look at him imploringly. But letters revolving around accounting must be written in English, and better yet, by Seligman Geisenheimer, if Meir wanted the accounting team in Nathan's office to understand the information he wished to convey.

The intense chill forced me to rise and add some wood to the fire. I rubbed my hands over the flames and filled the hot water bottle. While the heat spread through my body, I pondered the act of writing. I never imagined that the words in my private accounting ledger would ever make their way outside of my home and outside of Judengasse. But now the words break through to the street, crossing the country and touching the great big world, which is wondrously connected to my family.

Well, I take hold of the pen, dip its tip in ink again, and return to describe the situation that reaches across this great distance from our home.

Meir's personal letters to Nathan keep him up to date on politics, as well. Commerce has developed a great dependence on politics, and is handled according to the political climate. For example, back in the spring three years ago, Meir told Nathan that Alexander, emperor of Russia, had conferred with Napoleon in Tilsit and signed a treaty, and that this might be a hopeful sign of peace.

Two and a half years ago, he wrote that it looked like Sweden was about to form an alliance with France and Russia, and if this indeed happened, it would mean the end of our business transactions with Sweden.

And so, Meir and his sons—Amschel, Shlomo, Kalman, Nathan, and Yaakov—are aware of international affairs, and peace or war between different countries in Europe have a great effect on the financial developments in our firm, for better or worse.

Of course peaceful days are days of financial flourishing—that much is clear to all. But, wonder of wonders, Meir's worries about Napoleon's lingering war have been found to be baseless. The war, which has been going on for years with no end in sight, has done nothing but good for the cash flow at M. A. Rothschild and Sons—our family firm's new name.

Well, Napoleon had made a decision that was supposed to close doors to us, but Nathan reassured us from London, reminding us that if a door closes, we should open a window.

How did this happen? Let me lay out the events of the past four years.

Napoleon, artist of war, who miraculously defeats any rival, has not accepted the British persistence to remain fortified against him. In a great fury, he ordered an embargo. Four years ago, we became familiar with the Berlin Decree, which ordered the closure of all ports in Europe to British goods. Any merchandise smuggled against this decree was confiscated.

Austria, Prussia, Sweden, Denmark, and Russia all accepted Napoleon's request for collaboration on this matter.

Meir came home, behaving like a man who had lost his pants. He put his hand on the mezuzah and seemed to have forgotten to remove it. The sight of him made me anxious—Meir's work in Frankfurt is largely based on goods imported from England.

He gathered the boys for a conference. For hours on end the five of them stayed in the study behind closed doors. They then spent days gathering intelligence in the field, and when this operation was over, they reconvened in the study.

Finally, we heard the wing flapping of news. While our men at home appeared helpless, considering possible solutions, redemption came from Nathan. In an initiative that Meir defined as "financial genius," Nathan had turned the harsh conditions of war into a once-in-a-lifetime opportunity. Nathan had utilized Meir's famous sniffing skills thoroughly and meticulously, without missing a single detail of the many he used to spin his thick, tight web.

Our financial genius based his masterpiece on two pieces of information.

One: The growing demand in Europe for goods from Britain and its colonies had encouraged ship crews, freighters, and merchants, to take risks.

Two: The French embargo was not impermeable. A man with cunning eyes and ears could locate breaches.

Nathan was graced with such cunning, as well as a few other strengths, which together have created the necessary conditions for success in this dangerous adventure: verifying information, keeping secrets, forging documents, and bribing hungry clerks.

This is all written in retrospect. After the fact, anything I say and explain will sound convincing, perhaps even commendable. But at the time, we in Frankfurt had yet to understand the atmosphere in England and had not yet learned of Nathan's plan. Tension in our office and home was higher than ever before, and the sight of Meir and the boys pacing purposelessly through the rooms repeated itself often. I sensed that if I lit a candle too close to them I could start another fire.

Fortunately, the boys did not have the option of staying at home. They were busy with work: Amschel in Kassel; Shlomo in Amsterdam, Hamburg, and northern German ports; Kalman in Prague (where the landgrave had moved); and Yaakov in France, the ruling country at that point.

Nathan realized he had to take all possible measures in order to keep his secret. He knew the family was under close watch due to suspicions of collaboration with the landgrave, and that the French were awaiting higher orders to summon us all into interrogation. Therefore, in the early days, he chose not to share any information with us.

During that time, the French issued a warrant to have our home searched. Their officers, like guard dogs that had received orders to attack, strode right in.

This warrant was given due to the landgrave's sad involvement in Kassel. From his seat in Prague, Wilhelm funded a rebellion against the French. The rebellion was planned to start in Kassel, the capital from which he had been exiled. Unfortunately for him, the plan failed and his involvement was discovered. Since he was abroad, they couldn't arrest the landgrave himself, and the easiest man to arrest was Buderus. Under custody, Buderus was cross-examined, and though the examiners found nothing, he was not released. Their next destination was our home.

Karl von Dalberg found this to be a proper time to partially redeem himself of the disappointment he had caused Meir and the people of Judengasse. He informed Meir of the French delegation's impending visit and leaked a few details. This is how we learned that the French police commissioner, Savannier, had intended to arrest Meir for the suspicion that he was running the landgrave's business, and for his assistance in transferring the landgrave's money for the purpose of funding the failed rebellion in Kassel. But Dalberg's involvement prevented Meir's arrest, and as a compromise, Dalberg gave his permission to search our home, under limited conditions. In return, Dalberg earned back a few Rothschild points.

This took place on May 10th, 1808, two days after Buderus's second stint at Mainz Prison. Amschel was in Prague at the time, where the landgrave had recently moved, while Kalman was on duty on the Danish coast.

Meir ordered Shlomo and Yaakov, who had arrived for a brief visit, to go down to the hidden cellar and transfer the landgrave's chests through the secret tunnel into our neighbor's home. But it turned out the chests were too wide and the tunnel too narrow. In a flash, we all gathered to empty the chests and scatter their contents in different hiding spots throughout the house and the cellars.

From the cellar, we heard the new voices moving through the house. The officers, led by the tough commissioner Savannier, had invaded our home, while another group of officers waited outside. This certainly was an unusual sight on our street. The officers, filled with the fervor of their mission, found the man of the house, elderly and sick, lying in bed. Meir did not need to pretend. Unfortunately, he truly was sick, and had just undergone surgery. Shlomo and Yaakov went up to the study and were told to stay there. The commissioner accompanied the search on behalf of Dalberg to make sure the investigation was going according to the predetermined procedure.

Shlomo presented them with the accounting ledgers, which have always been carefully edited in expectation of an unwanted visit. In his interrogation, Meir claimed to remember nothing. He wasn't even sure of his age. "About sixty-seven," he answered meekly. When asked where his other sons were, he stuttered, "The boys? Where are the boys . . . let me think. Nathan, oh, yes, Nathan lives in England with his wife. What is her name? I can't remember. When did he move there?

I can't remember. Eight years ago. Maybe ten? Kalman . . . Kalman is in Copenhagen. Amschel is in Vienna. Or maybe Prague. He intends to come back."

"Are your sons partners in your business?"

"No, certainly not. I am the owner of the business. The boys help me."

"You are good friends with Buderus," Savannier determined.

"Buderus? No, I am not friends with Buderus."

"Yes, you are. The two of you meet often."

"We aren't friends. I'm his banker."

"And what were you doing in Hamburg? Did you and Buderus open a money-changing business there?"

"Oh, Hamburg. Let me think. Yes, of course. I went there to settle a problem with some merchandise I had ordered. It was accidentally registered as smuggled goods. I had it released and came home." He sighed and cleared his throat, then turned away and closed his eyes.

Savannier shook his head and looked up as if to say, "I know he is lying, but have no way of proving it." He looked around him, and his eyes fell on me. They lit up for a moment. He seemed to think he had found easy prey from which to milk the truth.

"Frau Gutle Rothschild, who are the businesspeople whose money your firm handles?"

"Forgive me, sir, but I am a homemaker. All I can offer is to show you my recipes, and if you've got some time, I'd also be willing to demonstrate my cooking skills."

"Thank you kindly, maybe some other time. Now, tell me about your husband's business."

"I have no hand in my husband's business. I take care of his meals, his clothes, and his health. I'd be happy to offer you the *kugelhopf* I just pulled out of the oven, or some gefilte fish with a bit of sweet, steamed carrot on top."

"You are very generous, madam. We'll put that off too." His voice was desperate. "What do you have to say about your sons who are not home?"

"My sons cannot come home due to a shortage of carriages. Who knows better than you that war does not agree with everyday life. I worry for my sons who linger outside of the home."

Savannier folded his papers and ordered the officers to leave. The withering stare I offered them at the doorway made them apologize for the bother. I watched them, thinking about how powerfully they had entered and how meekly they were now leaving.

In the copy of the report we received were nothing but useless details, among which one sentence flashed: "The Rothschilds are clever and cunning." Meir forgot all about his sickness, and broke into a liberating laugh that swept us all. The sounds of laughter crossed our threshold and invited our kind neighbor to come in and take part in our victorious joy.

Now we could go back to focusing on Nathan's action plan. By his order, we transferred a major part of the landgrave's funds to him. Nathan used this money to buy linen, food, and other assorted goods. Through his web of contacts, he reached the breaches he had located in advance, made deals with sailors, freighters, and traders, and used them to transfer the goods.

Napoleon must not have foreseen this. If store shelves in Germany, Scandinavia, the Low Countries, and France itself could rejoice, it would have been the greatest celebration in the world. If they could speak the name of the one who had made them so happy, they certainly would have offered our own Nathan Rothschild. News reached the doorsteps of millions, who rushed to the stores in spite of the exaggerated prices. The shelves overflowed with cotton and other fabrics, tobacco, coffee, sugar, and other groceries.

Nathan had an entire fleet of freight ships at his disposal to ship the goods from Kent on the banks of the channel to the ports of Germany and Holland. One or two of my sons waited at each port: Kalman in Hamburg, Shlomo in Dunkirk, Yaakov and Amschel in Amsterdam. At the ports they rubbed shoulders with sailors and loud porters, befriending even the most brutish of the lot, with only one goal in mind: assuring the continued shipment of goods to Frankfurt and other distribution centers in Europe.

While customers swarmed over the valuable products, clearing the shelves, I imagined Nathan rubbing his hands contentedly, looking toward the horizon, and thinking, *Thank you, Napoleon, for creating such optimal conditions for profit. I never thought I'd be able to sell for these prices.*

Here in Frankfurt, our warehouses empty out and fill up with dizzying speed. Orders passed from Meir and the boys to Nathan impatiently await mail days. Frankfurt had never known such blossoming sales of English goods as it had since the embargo had been announced. The Rothschild cashbox—in Germany and England both—had never known finer days.

But every rose has its thorn.

The smuggling served as a model for other merchants, and the festival of goods spread through Frankfurt and all over Europe. Napoleon was unable to do anything to stop it. He wanted to punish the British, but found that they carried on, unmoved. On the other hand, the residents of areas under the control of the undefeated French emperor now suffered from rising inflation and severe economic recession.

He had no choice but to put his pride aside and announce two new ordinances: one, a lowering of limitations on imported goods, and the other, the granting of licenses for imported goods.

These two ordinances not only did not resolve the crisis that had weighed so heavily on Napoleon Bonaparte, but rather caused a sharp rise in importing from Britain and its colonies, in spite of the high prices.

The new ordinances have allowed the bold Nathan and other adventurous merchants to locate additional loopholes through which to enter the markets without undergoing the inspection of the clerks. The success boosted the smugglers, and now smuggling rates are even higher. *The more they were oppressed, the more they multiplied and grew.*

I wish I could see the worried expression on Napoleon's concerned face. It must look entirely different from the one he wore during the Jewish delegation's welcome. A suitable punishment for the way he insulted us in those moments when he lost himself in reverie, the entire ceremony no more than a bothersome fly.

I must admit, I'm worried too. I am proud of Nathan and the whole Rothschild clan, united around a new goal. But at the same time I worry that he might be caught and punished for his transgressions.

When it comes to those, I would like to make it clear that I have not the slightest regret. Nathan and the other merchants reacted in an appropriate fashion, combining determined patriotism with the unique opportunity to act on behalf of the large number of people that required groceries. At the same time, he was able to grow his capital. Even the British government, Nathan reported, had been encouraging the smugglers, offering special incentives to anyone who took part in thwarting Napoleon's plans.

Napoleon had no choice but to come to a new decision. It came late enough to allow our forces to continue sailing the waves of smuggling.

The results of this decision were felt in the largest commercial city, Frankfurt, the center for trade of English and colonial goods. Meir, Shlomo, and Yaakov made sure to stash the goods in the cellars of warehouses in advance. But even as they did, they knew for certain that not everything could be concealed. Amschel and Kalman remained away from home, directing the goods that arrived at the ports.

Shlomo was the first to storm in. "The city is full of military battalions, police, cannons. The gates are manned by a sea of custom clerks. Everyone is being thoroughly checked."

A message was sent to Nathan, Amschel, and Kalman: "Stop shipping goods." Yaakov went out and then returned. "All warehouses are being searched. Goods are being confiscated, fines are high," he breathed.

Shlomo went out to sniff around the warehouses, and returned with the latest rumors. "Everyone is suspected of collaborating with the enemy. Spies and informers are everywhere, camouflaged in plain clothing."

The French even reached some of our warehouses. The fine for the goods they found was set at 20,000 francs. We breathed a sigh of relief. The great Napoleon had failed once again, in spite of using his army of officers and clerks, and the forces of spies and informers padded with money and promises. But the overall fine charged in Frankfurt reached the respectable sum of 9 million francs (360,000 francs of which were taken from renowned banker von Bethmann), but it was meaningless in light of the astronomical sums that would have been charged if all the goods had been discovered.

The landgrave, whose money is an inseparable part of our transactions, offered his intense appreciation of Meir's actions from his exile home in Prague.

Nevertheless, the French emperor was able to hit us where it hurt the most. Last November, the French soldiers produced an extravagant show in the center of Frankfurt, publicly burning some of the British goods that were found in the warehouses. The soldiers, riding on horseback, circled the site of the fire and made sure no one tried to put it out. Merchants and locals stood around, watching the goods turning into ashes in gloomy silence. The fire raised painful memories of our burning Judengasse. Just like then, the fire was the fault of the French.

Rumor has it that the value of the goods was no less than 1.2 million francs. The thought of all those goods lost in the fire makes my heart ache. Would it not have been better to donate them to the poor?

Monday, December 10th, 1810

Meir's health is deteriorating. The signs have been there for years, but he ignored them, putting up a strong front.

I was tempted to put the matter out of my mind, but it would pop up occasionally, without invitation, and take hold of my heart, refusing to evaporate, making terrifying scenarios run through my head. His long journeys were detrimental to him, but all I could do was try to extend the periods between one trip and the next.

When he began to stay longer in Hamburg, I was thankful and never complained about the intense longing that was more than my loving, tender heart could bear. I had made a rule for myself, to put health first. Fewer journeys meant more comfort, more comfort meant less illness. Sometimes we must do things for the benefit of our body, and as a result strengthen our souls as well.

Meir stayed in Hamburg the last few months of winter and into the spring of 1808, and would meet with the landgrave frequently, staying in his home in Itzehoe. Their conversation was meant to revolve around money issues, but took a sharp turn and ended up focusing on the landgrave's dire mood. As the days wore on, Wilhelm received more and more hints from his brother's palace about just how unwelcome he was. The insinuations were light at first, then clearer and accompanied by a visible shortage of smiles. Eventually, there came a direct statement, ordering him to leave at once. The poor landgrave was heartbroken.

Meir found himself fulfilling a new duty as the guard of the landgrave's wounded feelings. At least thirty of the people who stayed with him in the Danish castle searched for a way into his heart, with no success. And now, the Jew from Judengasse was turning out to be not only a master of money but also a friend who offered a comforting hand to the aching heart, while still maintaining the great respect he had for the man who, to him, was still the great landgrave of Hesse-Kassel.

On mail days, we received letters from Meir, in which he hinted about what was going on between him and the landgrave in Itzehoe. The last letter from there was hard to decipher, camouflaged with thick layers of secrecy. After some complicated decoding, we learned that the landgrave had left Denmark that spring and had gone to Prague after receiving a promise for asylum from Franz I, emperor of Austria.

Before he embarked on this dangerous journey through French-occupied territory, the landgrave entrusted Meir with four chests full of debt bonds, contracts, and valuables, and asked him to keep them for him in his home. Amschel made plans to join the landgrave's entourage in Prague.

Meir's journey home lasted ten days. Ten whole days before I got to see his exhausted face. That face was emanating pain, which matched the appearance of his body. Shlomo and Amschel supported him as he climbed the stairs. Kalman was out of town, and Yaakov had been sent by Meir to see Nathan in London, as a way to test his youngest son's skills.

Two helpless arms waved from Meir's shrunken body.

"Stop!" I cried.

Amschel and Shlomo paused, surprised.

"Listen to what he has to say."

I noticed a slight signal in his eyes and came closer.

Meir whispered, "The chests."

"But Papa, let's get you inside first," said Amschel.

"Now," he mumbled. The word was meant as an order, but all the authority had gone out of it, and all we could hear was a hoarseness that led to some coughing.

"Do as your father told you," I said. "I'll stay here with him."

The boys moved their eyes from me to Meir as if we were both mad, then, with displeasure, went to take care of the landgrave's chests. Julie and Henrietta came down the stairs and helped me carry their father to bed.

"Julie, go get the doctor, and tell him to hurry." Julie was on her way before I could even finish the sentence.

I kneeled beside him, my hand never leaving his. With my other hand I checked his forehead. He had a fever. I placed the cold compresses Henrietta handed me on his forehead, wiping away his sweat, then replacing them with new, clean ones.

"The road is long, and . . . ," Meir mumbled.

I completed his sentence for him: "And rough."

He nodded and turned his attention to a spasm of pain.

I could tell he wanted to describe and blame the harrowing journey, but he was unable to. I prayed for the doctor to come. I had to keep my composure. My hand was still in his, refusing to let go.

Julie walked in, followed by the large case carried by the doctor.

"I'd like you all to step outside," he said, and I looked around, astounded. *When did everyone get here?* Our small room was crowded. Everyone was there—Schönche, Moshe, Amschel, Shlomo, Eva, Isabella, Bernhard, Babette.

Stifling. Get out. Give Meir some air. Everyone left. Eva and Isabella put me on my feet, leading me out. The door closed.

Lips were pressed against the closed door. Psalms were mumbled. The mumbling mixed with sobbing, as if that too was quoted from the Bible. Whispers were the only signs of life from within the room. We could not decipher any of the words exchanged between the doctor and his patient. Perhaps we had only imagined them.

I wanted to go inside, to take Meir's hand during the long examination, but Isabella put her hand on my shoulder. "Be calm, Mama, let the doctor do his job." Why did she think I would interfere? I did not mean to be a burden, only to hold his hand, to feel it, warm and alive, inside mine. I closed my hand around the doorknob. Schönche and Isabella pulled it away, and Shlomo dragged over a chair. "Sit down, Mama," he whispered authoritatively. Since when do my children order me around? What do they know? What do they even understand? Meir needed my hand now, and I needed his.

I gave Shlomo a reproachful look, but he forced me into the chair nonetheless. I plopped down with my immense weight of worry, and realized I could not stand a moment longer. Shlomo accepted the grateful look I gave him through my wrinkles of pain, and turned his attention to his father, behind the door.

Now the door opened. The doctor was standing there. I jumped up to get a look at Meir's face.

"Prepare the carriage, he must have emergency surgery."

"The carriage is ready," Amschel and Moshe said as one.

"One moment," Meir said almost inaudibly. I walked over to him and he whispered, "Will."

"Papa wishes to prepare a will," I told the boys.

"We cannot wait," the doctor said, nervously. "We have to get him into surgery."

The boys looked at me imploringly, and I nodded at them. They were out in a flash, and returned shortly with the lawyer to have the will signed lawfully.

"Now come here, both of you, and pick him up carefully. You, hold him under his arm, and you, grab his legs. Let's go." The doctor seemed to have lost his patience.

They were out quickly and the path to the carriage was clear, pedestrians having moved aside to make room.

"What's wrong with him, Doctor?" I dared ask, trying to keep up.

"His high blood sugar has damaged a few vital organs," he said ambiguously and rushed to Meir's side to run a hand over his forehead.

I hurried after him. "The operation, Doctor. Will he survive it? Will he live?"

The doctor's face clouded over with discomfort. He quickened his walk and so did I.

"Doctor?" I urged him.

"Well," he said, fidgeting, "Madam Gutle Rothschild, that is a question for the one in charge of life and death."

"I will speak to Him, but I must also know what your intuition is, Doctor. Please, give me your answer."

"Madam Gutle, I feel that Meir has been made from strong material. He may survive the operation. The question is how he plans to continue his life."

That was all I needed. I boarded the additional carriage that had been ordered. It sped after Meir's carriage, which also contained Amschel, Shlomo, and the doctor. Julie and Henrietta came with me. We arrived at the hospital, said goodbye to our doctor, and Amschel stuffed a pile of cash into his hands. *"Asia demagan magan shavey,"* he whispered in Aramaic. A free doctor is worth nothing.

Professor Ledig, the great surgeon from Mainz, received the patient. Meir was led inside, and we said goodbye to him, hoping we would see him again in a few hours.

The prolonged wait and not knowing what was happening in the operation room almost drove me mad. The only thing that kept me sane was reading Psalms. I focused on the words and felt myself becoming charged with hope.

Professor Ledig's face, which suddenly appeared before us, confirmed my intuition. I sighed with relief before he said a single word.

"The way things are looking right now," he said carefully, "the operation went well. He will need time to recover and a long convalescence." The surgeon looked like a kind father. He looked at us with affectionate eyes. All that was missing was for him to approach each of us, rub our heads, shush, and say, "Go to sleep, my little one." I thought how lucky his children were to have such a caring father to shower them with love.

Two hours later, we all stood around Meir's bed. His eyelids slowly separated, opening to see us, then immediately closing. From the depths of the fatigue on his face peeked small signs of vitality. I searched for his hand, enveloping it with tenderness. His hand was powerless in mine. I smiled at him, though his eyes were closed. He nodded, though he wasn't able to smile back.

"He'll smile at you yet, do not worry." It was the kind doctor, standing at my side and following what was happening.

"He'll have many reasons to smile, Doctor," I assured him and let my eyes wander to the horizon. In my mind's eye, I imagined Meir sitting in his study, giving orders with his familiar determination. A return to life meant a return to work.

Meir's initial convalescence period was moderate. I spent most hours of the day at his side, taking care of him. In spite of the physical difficulty, his spirits never fell and his sense of humor was not diminished. This was the first time in our lives that we had the opportunity to spend so much time together without the disruption of travel.

In the first days after the operation he had no appetite. He pushed away the soup that he always loved so much. "I see you're concocting ways of getting rid of me, but this is not your lucky day. I won't put that poison in my mouth," he said jokingly, pulling away from the bowl. When I shrugged and brought the spoon to my own mouth, he stopped my hand. "What did you think, that I would give *you* up? Neither of us will touch that poison." Then he said we ought to feed the soup to the neighbor's dog, who barked constantly, interrupting our sleep.

In the next few days, as he tested the strength of his legs, he moaned, "Oy vey, Gutaleh," making me race over from the kitchen as fast as I could, anxious that he might have fallen from the bed. "You're always complaining about never having seen ducks in real life. Well, here is your opportunity to spend some time with a human-sized duck." Meir was waddling around, rejecting every offer of help, falling and getting up and waddling some more. "An intelligent duck, falling and getting up again," he boasted, eliminating the embarrassment I felt at the sight of his weak body.

When the pain medicine did its job, his brain began to churn once more and he demanded that his sons be brought to speak with him.

"They aren't home," I said, surprising him.

"What do you mean, they aren't home? Where are they?" He raised a brow.

I searched his face for signs of frivolity, but found none. "They're at the ports, Meir, shipping Nathan's goods."

The memory resurfaced. "How stupid of me, where else would they be?" Then a new thought occurred to him. He asked me for the accounting ledgers, and in contradiction to the doctor's orders, decided to continue to rule his kingdom from his sickbed.

"Meir, rest," I pleaded.

"I assure you, Gutaleh, I will rest in my own way," he said, looking at me, amused, like a child preparing for mischief. He leaned on the cushions I had plumped behind his back and placed one of the accounting ledgers on his lap.

"You are confusing recuperation with idleness. When a man rests in order to recuperate and recover that does not mean he is being idle," I tried.

Meir looked at me with surprise. He considered this for a moment, then muttered, "Gutaleh, we haven't fought all these years, it would be a shame for us to begin now. Let's leave that kind of thing for people who are more skilled at it than us."

"Does this mean you intend to sabotage your health now?" I asked. I realized he was right, that we hadn't before, except for two budding fights that had never ripened, one after the first night of our marriage, the other when he became involved in the landgrave's mercenary deal.

He put the book on top of the pile that took up a considerable part of the bed, and gave me a long look, as if in expectation of judgment. Then he opened his arms. "Come to me, my beloved wife, and don't worry so much."

I leaned into him lightly, careful not to hurt him. I kissed his forehead. "I love you, Meir, with all my heart and all my soul."

"I guess it took a dangerous operation and almost reaching the gates of heaven in order to get a confession of love out of you. Did everyone hear that?" He turned to an imaginary audience. "Gutaleh loves me! She has taught me to speak words of love to her, but has exempted herself of her own rule all these years."

"Wasn't it obvious?"

"Of course it's obvious. I know you love me. But now I hear the words coming from your mouth, and that's so much better, my love. Even a man needs words of love," he said with a laugh and gathered me into his lap again.

Sunday, December 16th, 1810

After Meir's surgery, I had guests. My beloved grandchildren stormed into the kitchen, and I rushed to close the notebook and slip it into the bottom drawer. I opened my arms and they huddled around me, overtaking me with hugging arms and kisses, sprinkling me with joy. I gave them a generous amount of candy and slices of *kugelhopf.*

Then I took them to see Grandpa Meir. *Visiting the ill helps them live.* The smile on his face is the surest sign of life.

After four months of convalescence, Meir rose from his sickbed. He had slowed down once he accepted the fact that his sons were fulfilling their many duties in a satisfactory manner, but he seemed worried.

"I must take care of the future of my children," he told me one morning. "I don't want to leave any loopholes that might cause disputes within the family. I have to put into writing what each of them is in charge of and what each of them gets in return. We must make sure the business continues to thrive. Thanks to the boys' involvement, it is flourishing. But the process must continue, even after I die, even with the next generations. We need a contract. We must convene the boys."

A few days later they all convened, all except Nathan, to receive their new partnership contracts. These replaced the old ones, drafted fourteen years ago, according to which Meir ran the firm while Amschel, Shlomo, and Nathan were defined as junior partners. This time, the boys' roles were extended, and from now on it was agreed that they were authorized as firm representatives and signatories. The money was divided so that each son—Amschel, Shlomo, and Kalman—received the appropriate share for his age and seniority. Yaakov was promised his share when he reaches twenty-one.

The new contract preserved Meir's status as the head of the firm, while Nathan's name was not included. Nathan, the most important branch, "our wise teacher," as his brothers had nicknamed him, was now a British citizen, and was therefore considered to be living in enemy territory. Wanting to maintain a clean image from a political standpoint, Meir avoided involving Nathan in the division of wealth. But Meir did prepare a secret addendum, according to which he was obligated to keep Nathan's share of the capital. The official document bore four signatures—Meir's and the three sons': Amschel, Shlomo, and Kalman. But all five boys signed the addendum.

Meir even took care to form terms of inheritance. "Gutaleh, who knows better than you that I love my daughters no less than my sons. But those who carry the business and pull it upward are the boys. Therefore, and please do not be upset about this, only they have a right to inheritance."

"And the girls?"

"Gutaleh, you can see for yourself that I am not abandoning them. Every daughter who reaches marriageable age receives her inheritance in advance in the form of a wedding gift, and will receive an appropriate allowance in due time."

Everything was phrased very clearly in the contract, leaving no room for doubt.

Meir has therefore harnessed his sons to his glorious chariot, which flies down straight and twisting roads, its driver slowly letting go of the reins.

The less time Meir spends working for the firm, the more involved he becomes in public service. As a representative of the Judengasse Council, made up of five dignitaries, he misses no opportunity to try and influence the fickle Dalberg to change the Jewish Law. He was filled with renewed hope when Dalberg received the title of grand duke of Frankfurt. He met with him and presented him with the bitter situation. "Of all the people of this city, only the Jews have remained deprived of full civil rights."

Dalberg sighed. "What can I do?"

"Well, for one, you can allow us to live in a better part of town."

"I would allow *you* that right now, Meir, but you're so stubborn."

"Let me remind you I'm speaking to you as a representative of the Jews of our street. I am asking for nothing for myself, only for my people."

"Who sent you? God? Are you Moses now?" Dalberg bellowed in fake laughter.

"Don't be smart, Dalberg. It's time to keep your promise."

"You never give up, do you?"

"Only those who fight for their freedom deserve it."

"And how long do you wish to fight for?"

Meir chose to ignore the scathing tone and respond in a placating one. "I'm glad you have risen to greatness, and I give you my congratulations. It is an honor to stand here before the grand duke of Frankfurt. I had hoped that from this elevated position, you would begin to implement Napoleon's laws and the French declaration of civil rights in our city. But instead, you have chosen to come out with a public statement that 'giving the Jews full civil rights would be dangerous.' And to make matters worse, you gave the most bizarre reasoning for your statement: 'Because Jewish political and moral culture does not compare to that of the Christian faith.'"

"What's wrong with my explanation? Do you deny there are differences between us?"

"First you bind us, then you complain that we cannot walk."

"It isn't that simple, Meir. As a skilled trader, you know everything comes at a price."

Meir felt himself grow angry. "I never heard of anyone trading in human rights in France."

"France is France and Frankfurt is Frankfurt. If you want to move forward, you must see my position and move forward with me."

Meir chose to move forward. He named a sum, but was turned down on the spot.

"I do not speak for myself, either. I don't need money for myself, but for my government, and my government needs more."

Meir knew about the large debt that Dalberg's government owed the French government. He himself had assisted by offering very comfortable loans. Now he realized that in Jewish suffering, Dalberg had found an additional source of income.

Dalberg explained himself simply. "If I give up my protection fee, I'd be losing my regular income from you, the Jews, which comes to twenty-five thousand gulden a year. In twenty years, it would mean a loss of a million gulden. I can't afford to give that up without replacing it with another fee."

Meir's eyes burned. "What are you talking about?" he hurled. "The money you've charged us all these years, calling it 'protection fee,' was pure evil. Now that it is time to repent, you dare ask for something in return? Doesn't it make more sense that we would be the ones deserving of a refund?"

"Meir, slow down. I'm not talking about simple logic here. I'm talking about a complicated situation, and the situation is, there is no money in the coffer, and the French government, the one pushing us to grant equal rights, is also demanding its due taxes. It is very convenient to say pretty words like 'equal rights' without proposing a way to turn this declaration from words into action without my losing my job."

"And you want me to feel sorry for you and say, 'Oh, poor you, you owe money, and we must understand your distress and help you out.'"

Dalberg fidgeted in his seat. "You think this situation is comfortable for me? I did not create this, I was merely chosen to come here and establish some order. Without money, I've got nothing to do here. I'm willing to compromise as much as I can. I won't ask for the entire million gulden, and I won't charge interest. I'll only charge half—five hundred thousand gulden."

Meir knew he had to grab the line before he lost it. The trader in him rushed to negotiate, and the sum was lowered to 440,000 gulden.

He came home and stood at the door to the living room, gloating and beaming. "Gutaleh, we've come to an agreement. Equal rights. Can you believe it?" He walked over, dragging his leg a bit, and reached out to me.

I put the knitting needles down on the chair and rose to meet him. "That's wonderful, Meir," I said, carefully curling up between those beloved arms. The image of our previous defeat with the new Jewish Law rose in my mind. *Who knows if Dalberg will stay true to his word this time?*

"The amount is high, four hundred forty thousand gulden," Meir explained after leading me to the sofa and sitting beside me. "But I'm sure it will be accepted by the community. This afternoon, I will gather the council and tell them the news. I'll be paying one hundred thousand of the total amount."

Meir depicted his meeting with Dalberg, their verbal battle and the forced reconciliation. That entire time, as my ears were attuned to his words, my fingers closed painfully around the knitting needles. Meir's cheerfulness made me worried about another disappointment.

As Meir had predicted, the community gladly accepted the agreement.

And as expected, Dalberg's part of the deal was postponed.

Sunday, May 12th, 1811

Meir cut his trip short, came home early, and parked his carriage in the stables outside the ghetto gate. I watched him through the window as he made his way home with excruciating slowness. With him was the messenger, carrying his cargo.

"I have come full circle," he announced as he walked in, his blue eyes shining, camouflaging his lack of strength.

Before I could say a thing, he began coughing and massaging his chest. He smiled at me to conceal his pain, and I wondered at his heart-rending efforts to keep me from worrying.

I kissed him and suggested, "I'll make you a cup of tea, and then I'll want to hear all about this circle."

He nodded with a crooked smile, and I hurried to the kitchen, swallowing the lump in my throat.

"My dear man, what say you?" I asked after he sipped his tea and I looked him over to make sure he was feeling better.

"Well, today, still strong, and with the landgrave reliant on my services, I was able to go see him and come full circle."

"What do you mean?" I asked, wondering why he was mentioning being strong when he was physically so weak.

"I went into the landgrave's office, and he accepted me as one would a dear friend. Finally, I didn't have to remind him of who I was and what I did for him. He hugged me and said to his ingratiating friends, 'Do you know who this man is, standing before you? This is Mayer Amschel Rothschild, the leading banker in Germany, and the man about to take over Europe. Do you have any idea how much he and his children do for me and how much I owe them? It is immeasurable.' Then he hugged me again and said, 'Thank you, Mayer Amschel Rothschild.' I said, 'I'm merely keeping my promise.' He looked at me and asked, 'Promise? What are you talking about, my dear friend?' and I said, 'When I was ten years old and standing by your carriage in Judengasse, I told you, "I would be glad to provide you with my services when the time is right."' Of course, the landgrave had no recollection of this childhood memory, but I told him every detail until he recalled the scene. He fell into my arms with an unrestrained show of affection. I feared I would buckle under his weight and signaled to his servants, who came to rescue me from the terror of his body."

"That's a nice ending to the fairy tale," I said quietly.

"That isn't the end of it, Gutaleh. Before I left, he said, 'Dear Mayer, we have both kept our promises to each other. I have made things hard for you and you stayed loyal to me the entire time. Now it is my turn to make a promise: from this day on, all of my business in this generation and the following generations will be handled by your family, the Rothschild family, for all its generations.'"

"You have come full circle, Meir," I said, thinking about the end of the fairy tale and the end of his travels.

"I have disarmed, and I feel light as a feather," he said, laughing. "Of all my weapons of war, I saved this one for last, a reminder of what the landgrave promised me when we were both children. And you know what? Not only do I not require this weapon any longer, but I don't think we would need Wilhelm to fulfill his final promise to use the services of the Rothschild family for generations, because I think the Rothschild dynasty will continue to flourish, while Wilhelm's offspring, as many as he may have, are not destined for greatness."

NOTEBOOK 3

Tuesday, June 25th, 1811

My dear father, if you only knew. I am starting a new notebook—a third one. And I've decided to begin it by describing your youngest grandson.

Our youngest child, Yaakov, who has just turned nineteen, has matured so much. So much so, that three months and three weeks ago, he moved to Paris, to continue the story of his life from afar. He has visited Paris several times in recent years, but this time he has moved there for good. Dear God, my youngest child has embarked on a new journey. Please keep him safe. I place him in Your kind hands.

The family council has decided that the precedent set by Nathan in London must be repeated in another important location—the most influential capital in Europe, Paris, whose emperor is conquering more and more territories all around the continent.

"From now on, I will call myself James, a name that has better odds than my Hebrew name," he informed us in his letter. I try to spell his new name. J-A-M-E-S. I roll the name on my tongue and feel its foreignness on the roof of my mouth. To me, he will always remain "Yaakov." He treats his new name with reverence, as if that in itself is enough to assimilate him into the new world. I'm hoping James will be able to accomplish in France what his brother Nathan has accomplished in England. The similarity between them is the boldness to embark on a new path at such a young age. Nathan did this when he was twenty-one years old, certainly a young age, and now Yaakov is doing it at nineteen! From this point on there are conditions that worked in favor of Nathan, and there are conditions that work in favor of Yaakov.

England welcomed Nathan warmly, openly, equally. A great Jew, Levy Barent Cohen, who later became his father-in-law, helped him take his first steps there. Our accountant, Seligman Geisenheimer, who joined him for a while, was also a great help. These factors made his life much easier.

On the other hand, Nathan arrived in England without knowing the language, and this disadvantage continues to plague him. He isn't a native Englishman, which is very apparent in his conduct.

Nevertheless, and against all odds, Nathan has climbed to the top. He has been appointed the financial manager of the landgrave in England. For a discounted commission of 0.33 percent, as opposed to the English bank's commission of 0.5 percent, he invests the landgrave's hundreds of thousands of pounds in low-rate English stocks, then sells them for a high rate. The profit gained is incredible both in numbers and in its simple brilliance. No more trading, but instead playing the stock market. Rather than the complicated research needed to buy and sell goods, one can take a few simple, thought-out actions with stocks. Thinking replaces labor. How easy! What quick profit! How suitable for a quick-minded man like Nathan, and how foreign and incomprehensible to me.

And as for Yaakov, France has been placing many obstacles in his path. The suspicions he raises in Napoleon's people are bringing him no end of misery. But our Yaakov is fluent in French, and that is no small thing. I believe speaking the language will help him fit in.

I recall the image of the French marching down Judengasse. Yaakov, just a baby at the time, clung to me, his tiny body awakened at the sight of the soldiers. And now my son resides in the country from which these soldiers came, boldly forging his path. Is this not a miracle?

Before moving to Paris, Yaakov underwent an eighteen-month training period with Nathan in London, where he went in order to remove some of the burden from his brother. I missed my son dearly, and always added my longing and strong desire to see him again to the letters Meir sent. Nevertheless, in longing-free moments I adopted his father's line of thinking and envisioned the great benefit he would receive from time spent in the company of his wise brother, a model for international business.

During Yaakov's long stay with Nathan, Kalman returned from one of his London visits, his face troubled. I assumed this had to do with one of his many business affairs and put it out of my mind. Only when he followed me into the kitchen did I realize his concerns were more than just business related.

Henrietta and Julie were clearing the table and about to get started on the dishes.

"Girls," I said, "let Kalman help me with the dishes." I took the towel from Henrietta's hands and passed it to Kalman. The two girls, who were used to kitchen heart-to-hearts, evacuated the premises with skillful swiftness, leaving the two of us alone.

I picked up a plate and scrubbed it slowly.

"What's going on over at Nathan's? Tell me."

Kalman passed the towel slowly from hand to hand.

"I'm worried about Yaakov."

"Yaakov?" I jumped, dropping the plate into the sink. It did not break (I always get angry when dishes break. I find no relief in the notion that a broken plate signifies a blessing. To me, it means nothing but waste).

"What happened to Yaakov? We just received a letter from him today and he didn't mention any problems. How odd, he always reports every little detail, even taking pleasure in the wordplay he shares with us."

"True, Mama. But there is one matter he has been keeping to himself."

I looked into his eyes. "And how did you find out about it?"

"Some things can be understood even without words."

"Is he in love?"

"You win!" he joked without smiling.

"She's a gentile. Is that it? She isn't Jewish?"

"Unfortunately, it's worse."

"Worse? What could be worse than falling in love with a shiksa?"

"It is worse to fall in love with a Jew we love and admire."

"Oh no, is it Hannah?"

"Exactly. He's distressed. He can't take his eyes off her, moping along after her wherever she goes."

"And how does she react?"

"She treats him like a sweet, younger brother. I think she realizes he loves her, but she attributes no meaning to it. She must think of it as a passing thing, and is behaving as if everything is normal."

"That is wise. Well, it's no wonder he fell for her. He's young and confused. He'll get over it when he comes home. I'll ask Papa to summon him back."

I wasn't too worried about this infatuation, but just like the Eva debacle, I had no doubt it must be nipped in the bud. He had to be kept away from her. Out of sight, out of mind.

Yaakov came home the very same week.

The thought of sending his youngest to Paris occurred to Meir many months before it was put into action. Our business was booming, so much so that now Meir's financial maneuvering was inseparably intertwined with national and international affairs. As always, my

Rothschilds are masters of sniffing and tracking down every bit of information, and the collection of details puts together a picture that requires quick and thorough analysis and the drawing of conclusions about the most effective means of action.

But no sniffing was necessary to track down the information about Napoleon. It is in the papers for all to see; it is the talk of the town. Napoleon seems determined to have France take over all of Europe. His decision to banish his wife, Josephine, due to her barren womb and marry the young Marie Louise in the hope that she would give him an heir, shows us just how determined he is.

"Nothing can stand against his will," Meir muttered, pacing the living room, bleary-eyed and facing the horizon. "Import from England is drawing its final breaths," he continued. "It will soon hit rock bottom. Nathan is acting correctly. He is parting ways with his previous success and moving directly into this new opportunity that is opening its doors to him."

From his seat in England, Nathan is channeling his resources into the war effort. Years ago, Meir offered General von Weimar, who was in charge of supplies for the Austrian military, his services caring for the needs of the soldiers fighting against the French. Now his son was putting himself at the service of the British military deployed in Portugal and fighting the French under the command of Arthur Wellesley of Wellington.

I am astonished at the great generals' modes of operation. They go out to battle so easily, equipped with flesh-and-blood soldiers, and only halfway through the battle do they open their eyes and realize something is missing: von Weimar needed supplies for his soldiers, and now Wellington needs money to pay his soldiers. He has had to borrow money from bankers in Malta, Livorno, and other places whose names I cannot remember, taking out loans with elevated interest. In exchange, Wellington has been handing over British government bills.

This information motivated Nathan to urge his brothers to go out on a focused sniffing mission. Shlomo, Kalman, and Yaakov pounced on this opportunity for a new adventure, and in a short while lunged at those British government bills, bought them for a low price, and transferred them to Nathan through Yaakov. Nathan walked powerfully into the Bank of England, dropped the bills on the counter, and received in exchange sums that carried enormous profit by London scale. This might sound like child's play, but I can only imagine how much gumption, forethought, and attention to detail were required to pull it off.

Now Nathan had a lot of money on his hands, and he began the dance of rolling it into the next transaction. "Money shouldn't be held on to, but put into efficient use to yield even more money"—this is one of Meir's oldest sayings, and now Nathan was acting on it. The most profitable coin is gold. Therefore, Nathan approached the East India Company, handed over 800,000 pounds, and received gold in exchange. With the sparkling cargo in his chests, he addressed the British government and offered his services. His application came at just the right time, when Wellington was so desperate he was considering a retreat from Portugal. Now here was a solution for him: quantities of gold, ready to go. The deal was completed on the spot, and Nathan even had a solution for the transfer of the gold: "The Rothschild family has extensive connections everywhere. We can arrange shipping."

This extensive network included a team of smugglers who had just completed their duty of transferring Nathan's goods to different European ports and were now eager to fulfill the shiny new mission. They shipped the gold across the channel, where our three boys— Shlomo, Kalman, and Yaakov—were waiting to deliver it from Paris to Portugal.

"It is time to act," Meir resolved. "We have to gather the boys. Those who are too far away to come will receive word."

Amschel, Kalman, and Yaakov sat around the large desk in our new office. I settled near the outside wall. The air was filled with secrecy.

"Look," Meir began, breathing hard like a boy after a sprint. "I'm glad you're here. We're about to make another leap in conquering Europe."

"We have a new Napoleon in our midst," Kalman joked, trying to break the tension.

Meir protested. "Napoleon chose a path of occupation and bloodshed, while we have decided to conquer trade targets and collect money."

"That's what we've been doing," Kalman insisted.

"Shut up and let Papa talk," Amschel scolded.

"Oh, look at that, we've got a new Nathan in the study," Kalman teased.

"Settle down," their father hushed. "Let's get going. There is a lot of money to collect and time is of the essence."

Amschel looked at Kalman beseechingly, and the latter raised his hands in submission. All eyes were on Meir.

"Look, I've discussed the matter with Nathan. Meaning, I sent him a garbled letter. I was inspired and must have included every possible language but ancient Egyptian. The landgrave would have been appalled had he known we'd given him a Jewish pseudonym. Napoleon would have me beheaded if he discovered his Hebrew name. Nathan supported my views. His letter was short but to the point." He felt for the envelope bearing Nathan's handwriting. "Needless to say, everything said here must remain between us. Also, we must inform Nathan and Shlomo of our decision as quickly as possible."

The boys leaned closer to their father as if listening to an adventure story.

"Look, we are here in Frankfurt, and Nathan is in London. Those are two stable anchors and they have done well so far. It is time to drop another anchor. We need a family representative in Paris. All signs point to the fact that in the near future important decisions will continue to be made in Paris, and we ought to have our own footprint there."

Everyone around the table nodded.

"Who were you thinking of, Papa?" Amschel asked. "I was thinking the best man for the job is Yaakov."

All eyes turned to Yaakov, who choked, tried to take a sip of water, but missed the mark and spilled it down his neck. He coughed with embarrassment.

Meir looked at him with kind eyes. My own eyes were wet.

"But Yaakov is young, he's still a child," Kalman said, then added, "France is not a welcoming country, certainly not for a Rothschild."

I didn't have to say a thing; Kalman took the words right out of my mouth.

Meir spoke calmly now. "True. Yaakov is young, and we cannot expect Paris to welcome him with open arms, especially in light of our connections to England and the landgrave. Nevertheless, we must take into account the fact that Yaakov has already been tested by our firm, and has had several opportunities to prove that he is just as brave as Nathan." He moved his eyes between his boys and finally rested them on Yaakov. "Besides, we all know Yaakov is talented, sociable, scholarly. These are all crucial factors. They could assist him in blending in. And what's more, he has studied French, and there is no finer time than the present to prove that this was a worthy investment. It's time it brought some benefit to our firm."

From my seat, I followed the conversation around the desk with mixed emotions. I looked at Yaakov, who had just returned from London. To the description of my son, I should add that Yaakov Rothschild is as handsome as his namesake, the biblical Jacob.

"Papa," Amschel said, shifting in his seat. "I agree with everything you said, but I think that, at least at first, we should send Kalman and Shlomo with him, so he doesn't have to be there alone."

"I agree," said Kalman, "and I'm willing to go with him. Don't forget that Nathan didn't go on his own, either. He had an excellent accountant with him and a successful Jewish banker to rely on."

"No," Meir said. "I need each and every one of you. I do not have ten sons. I only have five and it is too late to change that now."

I interrupted the burst of laughter from my seat. "As a reminder, the daughters and daughters-in-law also have their hands full at the firm. Each of them makes a considerable contribution. Or perhaps you would prefer to hire outside secretaries and bookkeepers."

"Mama is right," said Meir. "Know this: Mama is always right. That's been tested. The women in our family deserve a medal for their hard work, their persistence, and their patience. There isn't a doubt in my mind that our business would not work without them. Each part of the carriage has a function. When a wheel is missing, the vehicle can go nowhere."

"All the parts are important, but the coachman is the most important one of all," said Kalman.

"You have spoken wisely. Look, two are better than one, and five are better than four. I need five coachmen to steer five different carriages, the fleet of M. A. Rothschild and Sons. I need a family representative in every important hub in Europe. Each one will be run by one of my five sons, and with constant, ongoing collaboration between all hubs, we will become the largest firm in Europe."

"Papa, if I may, I think this new vision is more fantasy than reality," Kalman dared say after a long silence.

Meir looked at me for a long time, and then said, "I know it sounds crazy, but it will happen. I may not be alive to see it, but you will, and if not in your generation, then in the next."

I stood up and walked over behind Meir. I leaned down to put my arms around his neck. I kissed his forehead and turned to the boys. "Papa is right. By the way, Papa is always right. That's been tested."

Meir smiled at me and then turned to Yaakov. "And what say you, my son? Will you accept this mission?"

"All I can say is thank you, Papa," the young son said hoarsely.

Wisdom reposes in the heart of the discerning.

Wednesday, August 28th, 1811

Yaakov's departure was postponed by a few months while we waited for just the right moment. The right moment was provided by no other than Napoleon Bonaparte himself.

Surprisingly, any step the emperor makes for his own sake ends up promoting our agenda. The noble French emperor, who married the young Marie Louise in the hope that she would give him a son, finally celebrated the birth of his coveted heir. Many dignitaries were invited to the royal baptism of Napoleon Francois Charles Joseph Bonaparte, including Karl Theodor von Dalberg, the grand duke of Frankfurt.

And now we were ready to enter the fray.

The royal visit, which the grand duke refused to miss, involved financial expenses that were far beyond what his emptying pockets could afford. The Frankfurt traders Dalberg contacted for a loan turned him away, and as usual, his search ended at the Rothschild Bank.

Meir, who put on a show of equanimity in light of Dalberg's torment, followed closely every leg of the latter's journey, fearing that one of the other traders would suddenly grow soft and consent to his pleas. His impatient, yet restrained wait ended with Dalberg approaching Meir, out of sorts.

Meir lent an indulgent ear to Dalberg's groveling, spoken in poetic terms in order to express his full appreciation for his friend's kindness and integrity. At the end of the ingratiating speech, Meir granted the request, adding with the same breath two conditions for its realization, both to do with our Yaakov.

The terms were soon settled. Dalberg received 80,000 lifesaving gulden with a very flexible return date, while Meir left with a legal passport for Yaakov, as well as lovely letters of recommendation addressed to treasury clerks in France.

Yaakov looked over the passport and other documents for a long time, his face grave. He then placed them carefully in his briefcase, as if they were fragile, and looked out to the horizon. I watched my young son and waited for a smile to appear on his face.

When his countenance lit up, the long-awaited smile finally appearing, I had trouble containing the lump in my throat. The words emerged from his throat, clear and confident: "I am going. Papa, I will always remember I mustn't let you down. I know this place is a stepping stone for me and for our whole family. As you have said, we will work together and show the world the power and honor of the Rothschild family."

I had trouble bearing the emotion that gripped me. Before me was a confusing figure. The voice was Yaakov's, but from within it emerged a second voice, Meir's. I wrapped my arms around my son, rested my head on his shoulder, and wept. He didn't push me away. He lent me his shoulder for as long as I needed it.

The crying resumed in our moments of parting. All was quiet around the carriage, leaving room for my sobs. Yaakov stroked my face and kissed my head over the coif. I wiped my face on my apron and looked up at him. "Do not forget, son, meet your brother Nathan in England before continuing on your way, and remember to give him my letter," I whispered. It would be better for him not to meet Nathan in his home. He must avoid seeing Hannah. He would surely find a young woman to distract him in Paris.

"I'll do that, Mama," he answered.

I added, "I already miss you, my dear son."

"Mama, I promise to write a lot, and I will do my best to visit too, though that might prove more difficult."

I knew he would write. Being with us here, he knows the importance of letters in soothing our longing souls. I have no doubt he would always make sure to deliver updates in his fine handwriting. I will memorize the contents of each letter by heart, using his words like a pillow on which to rest my head.

He hugged his father, and suddenly I noticed how tall he'd become. Meir patted the boy's back and sniffed to fight off the lump in his own throat. He slipped a copy of the Traveler's Prayer into Yaakov's pocket, and his hands slid gently over his son's jacket, holding on for a long time.

I took a break from writing to have lunch with Meir, rinse the dishes, and walk him to bed. I nodded at the final words he mumbled before closing his eyes—the only action strong enough to inspire the shutting of his mouth. Lately, the need to talk has been getting the best of him, and since the pairs of ears around him have dwindled, I offer mine happily. Now that he was in the fog of his afternoon nap, I listened for the sound of his snoring and got up from the bed carefully. I turned my back on the seductive charms of sleep in favor of different tasks, such as writing. I follow the words of the rabbi who said man should not get more sleep in the daytime than a horse. And how long does a horse sleep? Only a few moments. I reserve my sleep for nighttime.

Well, my Yaakov, my mad longing, my youngest son, so handsome, so educated, so smart and sociable, has gone on his way, equipped with the necessary documents. My last image of him is etched into my mind, my eyes, my heart. In his white shirt, black jacket and tie, his red hair glowing in the sunlight above his beaming face. A sweet boy in the costume of a cosmopolitan man. He pressed the Traveler's Prayer against his chest and boarded the carriage that had been loaded with trunks and suitcases by the firm's employees, and was on his way with God's help. Well then, we have sent along another son, bless his soul. I prayed, "Please, dear God, watch over my dear son in his distant travels. Protect his heart, his body, his soul. I entrust him in Your hands, kind and merciful God, for You know the weakness of a Jewish mother's heart."

Two weeks later we received a letter from Nathan, and two weeks after that we received a letter from our new navigator. As expected, Yaakov stopped on the shore of the English Channel to receive Nathan's blessing, along with some direction and final words of advice before he dove in.

In his very first letter, Yaakov reported in a mélange of languages that would put the Tower of Babel to shame: "I must take all safety measures and keep away from the French police, which has caught wind of me."

He lives on Rue Napoleon 5, and rumor has already spread among the bankers that young Rothschild is in possession of bonds from London.

Unlike Nathan, our Yaakov was not as quick to make his way into the Jewish community and be invited to prayer at the synagogue. Nor did he make any connections with a successful Jew who might be able to support him lest he stumble in his early steps.

Yaakov had to hold his head up high and become acquainted with experienced gentile bankers, who may serve as anchors to help him expand his banking activity in the new city.

He quickly took advantage of his connections with the first bankers he met, Guillaume Mallet and Jean-Conrad Hottinguer, both Protestant and Swiss-born, with excellent credit, entitling them to some advantages over many other bankers.

Yaakov's first transaction with the two of them was meant to prove to us and to himself that he was a natural Rothschild who knew how to utilize his environment. The next gold bars he received were transferred to his two new friends, and in exchange he received bills bearing the seals of banks in Spain and Portugal. The bills were given to General Wellington, who rejoiced as a drowning man who has been saved.

The transferring of money to Wellington has now become routine, with Yaakov-James managing the entire operation with brilliant ruses and control. My baby, who sat on my lap and gurgled at the sight of Napoleon's soldiers marching down Judengasse, is now coming up with ruses in favor of the British Wellington, who is fighting against Napoleon. The wonders of life are beyond what I am able to grasp.

One of Yaakov's frequent letters has told us that it is no longer possible to hide the enormous number of gold bars crossing the channel and arriving at the hands of the new Parisian resident known as James Rothschild. The eagle eyes of the French treasury have already spotted these shipments.

My days and nights were devoted to the frightening thought that we might have been caught. *What will become of my son? Will he be punished? If so, what kind of punishment?* I shared my concerns with Meir, and he tried to put my mind at ease. "Do not concern yourself. *The wise prevail through great war.* Don't you trust Yaakov's wisdom?"

"I trust his wisdom, but who can assure me he'll make it safely out of this tangle? All I want is to see my son alive, well, and free."

Luckily, my concern was short-lived. Before long, we were informed that the tables have been turned in perfect coordination with the plan outlined by Yaakov-James. His ruse took shape and was successful. I sighed with relief.

It was an illusion, an act of trickery, though I must admit that in addition to my son's astute business sense, he was assisted by the fact that the Rothschilds have become famous as financial navigators, inspiring admiration wherever they set foot.

Once again I am struck by the surprising notion that life still has new lessons to teach me. Even in my old age, nearing sixty. The fact that I am constantly learning makes me feel lively and young.

The guineas, the British gold coins, have been regularly moving from Nathan's hands to Yaakov's, from one side of the channel to the other, through a regular team of middlemen.

Additional Parisian bankers have been added to the roster. They receive the British guineas, and in return hand over bills of exchange withdrawn from the Bank of England.

My five sons' eyes are wide open, their noses in constant sniffing mode, their ears pricked. They are engaged in a hunt for information and in its transmittance. In spite of the fact that their letters are opened and read by censors everywhere, they reveal not a single disclosing detail, while still reporting all necessary information to their brothers, who rush to make intelligent use of the details.

Meir and Amschel stand guard in Frankfurt. In addition to the British gold coins, they are also handling French silver coins, transferred by Shlomo and Kalman.

Kalman makes his way through the Pyrenees mountain range, which serves as a border between Spain and France, carrying British banknotes intended for General Wellington. He then returns along the curving paths to hand over the papers signed by Wellington, and so on and so forth.

The steps taken by Kalman are supervised by Shlomo, who is present whenever his brothers' actions must be kept secret, maintaining an illusion regarding the purpose of the transactions in the eyes of the French.

Thus money is transferred to General Wellington, and the interest makes its way into our coffers.

And now, a question: How did the great French generals fall into the trap?

Well, it's all about how one views the picture. Two people can look at the same image, and while one would see the pastel color of flowers as a sign of a severe water shortage, the other would see it as signifying a springtime bloom.

The French minister of finance has read the situation in complete contradiction to the way Hiever, the commander of the French police in Mainz, near us, had. The first swallowed the bait and told Napoleon that he believed we Rothschilds were famous for procuring information first and taking advantage of the sensitive situation of the British government. Meaning, the revaluation of the guinea would collapse the British economy.

Everything, then, was done out in the open, right under their noses. The police crossed their arms and watched the transfer of funds by the Rothschilds from England to France with glee, eagerly awaiting the fall of the British enemy. They are not familiar with the passage *Do not gloat when your enemy falls; when they stumble, do not let your heart rejoice.* And what's more, this enemy had no intention of falling. That was only the illusion Yaakov was selling the French.

I must make one thing clear: not everything goes right under their noses. For instance, the flow of cash on a scale of millions of pounds transferred over to the English general Wellington in order to fund the war against France.

As a result, five men are the top funders of the British in their war against France, and these five men are my sons. If they wish, they can tip the scales either way. As it appears now, the scales are tipped in favor of the British. I envision Napoleon's face and imagine how its expression must have changed since that sleepy day when he came to see us. His face must now assume a combination of rage and confusion.

My family is involved in money transfer to every part of the continent. England has transferred 15 million pounds to its allies—Austria,

Prussia, and Russia—all with the complete and quick involvement and careful supervision of Nathan and my other sons. Thank the Lord, while these transactions fund my family's business hubs, the exchange rate of the British pound remains stable.

I had never been closer to seeing, really seeing, how true one of Meir's many sayings is: "Unity is power." Our people's history has already proved as much. We were few against many, and we won. But I never thought the few could be so few as to be one single family.

Monday, December 30th, 1811

And the Jews had light and joy.

The Jewish street has never experienced such unbridled joy as it has during this God-sent period, which began the day before yesterday with the greatest news of all: we are equal-rights citizens.

For a long time, Dalberg did not live up to his word and failed to grant us the equality we had yearned for, and for just as long, Meir did not give up, sending many reminder letters to the grand duke of Frankfurt. The situation seemed hopeless, and a deep fear settled over our street: the fear that the Jewish Law would continue to prevail for all eternity.

At the beginning of the new Jewish year, Meir sat down to compose a new kind of letter.

"You could have one of your clerks do the writing," I offered. Ever since he has accepted my suggestion to narrow the scope of his business activity, I have found myself offering a piece of advice or two from time to time.

"No, Gutaleh. The letter must be personal, written with blood. It must bring attention not only to the words and form, but also, and mostly, to the spirit of things. Every spelling error or grammatical mistake, every illegible letter, can awaken the reader from his slumber."

I love my old Meir. He has not changed since the days when he first wrote poetic letters riddled with mistakes to the landgrave. I thought, if it worked with the landgrave, it might work with Dalberg too.

> *To:*
>
> *His Highness Karl Theodor von Dalberg, Grand Duke of Frankfurt am Main,*
>
> *I allow myself to address our merciful ruler and remind him that in our most recent conversation, he has posed some difficult conditions in exchange for granting the Jews under his rule equal civil rights. At the end of lengthy negotiations, we have reached an agreement that satisfied both parties.*
>
> *In spite of the great difficulty of withstanding payment terms, I had accepted the Jewish Community's obedient consent to the agreement made between us, since the thirst for equal rights is more powerful than any obstacle.*
>
> *From that day on, I have received countless applications from the people of Judengasse, who wish to find out what has become of our agreement.*
>
> *I must give them an answer.*
>
> *It would give me great pleasure to inform them that the declaration of equal rights has been approved and signed by his highness the grand duke.*
>
> *I am certain that a signed declaration from the grand duke would win him a blessing from heaven for his immense generosity. I also hereby assure him that the payments we had agreed to will be paid in full.*
>
> *I await a signed declaration with bated breath and pounding heart.*

Respectfully,
Meir Amschel Rothschild,
On behalf of the Jewish Council
Judengasse

A response was received within two weeks, on February 7th of this year. Meir hurried home, waving the newspaper. The smile on his face had us all convening in the living room, listening as he read the printed words out loud.

We stood around him, drinking every word. The grand duke of Frankfurt, Karl Theodor von Dalberg, had announced equal rights.

The declaration first refers to all city residents, and later addresses Jews, including some limiting conditions, the fulfillment of which would lead the declaration to include them as well.

The last thing I wanted was to spoil Meir's jubilation. But why was the first obligated party the Jewish party? Wasn't it enough that we, unlike people of other religions, would only receive our rights under limiting conditions, being forced to pay for them? Now Dalberg was adding kindling to the fire within us, as if to say, *You Jews cannot be trusted. You must first fulfill the conditions, while I, Dalberg, am known for keeping my word.* How eager I am to remind him of what became of the Jewish Law!

But Meir was in a fine mood. He quickly sat down to write Dalberg how grateful he was for this public declaration, and how hopeful he was to be able to see the Jews enjoying their big day.

A direct answer from Dalberg was received on December 11th. Meir's letter had touched his heart. He admired his persistence and his care for his people, and has therefore decided to ease the terms, offering a more generous payment plan.

Meir moved his eyes from me to the letter, and read the brief response again. He jumped up on his feet and sat back down with a grunt of pain. Bursts of laughter and tears emerged between one grunt and the next. He looked like a madman. I realized that a happy person is somewhat insane. Otherwise, he would not have made it this far.

It happened two days ago. The seal of his highness the grand duke has led us into a new era. God, in his great mercy, has turned Dalberg's heart in our favor.

We are spreading our wings, ascending into the sky, filling our lungs with fresh air, observing each other's smiles, making sure this is reality and not a dream. Cheers of glee emerge from dry throats. Parades are underway. A song of praise is carried down the street, up the stairs to our home, embracing Meir, who is described as "almighty" and "our savior."

"The Lord of Lords alone does great wonders," Meir called out to the crowd, searching for a seat.

"The Lord has done it this very day; let us rejoice today and be glad," a cheerful chorus of men answered.

Suddenly, the sounds of a violin were heard, and a cheerful tune burst out, urging the men to form tight circles, stomp their feet to the beat, and cry out with joy.

The rabbi raised his hands into the air and called, "The Lord foils the plans of the nations."

Meir sat back on the sofa, his hand gripping the armrest. He nodded at the celebrants, his eyes sailing over to the horizon, as if the two of them were old friends sharing a secret.

I thought about his unique brand of determination, the one that had led him on his path toward honor and empowered him in his public service. I looked at him and saw young Meir, an ambitious, energetic man who had managed to convince my stubborn father to give him his daughter's hand in marriage; who, on the first night we had strolled together, said clearly, "Dignity is a powerful thing. We shall use it to break through the walls of the ghetto and set ourselves free." I laugh now, a hoarser laugh than the one of the young girl who had replied with wonder, "Break through the walls? Leave the ghetto? You're out of your mind." To which he had replied, "I know it sounds crazy, but I'll make sure it becomes a reality. We *will* leave the ghetto. *Everyone* will leave the ghetto. If not in our lifetime, then in our children's."

I look at Meir. He is weak and ill—old age has taken over all at once—but he has had the fortune of seeing his dream come true in his lifetime. We have equal rights and may come and go as we please.

The celebrants leave and I suggest that Meir lie down for a bit. These last few hours had required effort—a pleasurable effort, but an effort nonetheless.

Sunday, April 19th, 1812

Our small home has not expanded by an inch, but it is now less popu-
lated, and the fewer people that occupy it, the less furniture and possessions fill it, as well, for they have lost their purpose.

Our children, other than Kalman and Yaakov, have each married
and left their lively nest in order to build their own, unthinkingly leaving behind a pair of elderly people staring at the great, quiet space
before them.

Amschel and Eva now live in luxurious Frankfurt, and so do
Shlomo and Caroline. Yaakov-James is excelling in Paris, pricking my
heart with both pride and longing, each emotion fighting the other for
dominance.

I pace the rooms, imagining I can hear my children's breathing, the
sounds of a full house, envisioning lively comings and goings through
the tight spaces of the house from sunrise to slumber.

In our bedroom are soft, lace-fringed sheets and plump pillows. In
the living room are curtains of darkness and light.

The traffic of visitors in our home has also decreased since our
home study has been abandoned in favor of a much finer office at the
end of the street.

Though the memory of days of noise and vitality in our home fills me with yearning, I find peace and pleasantness in the silence between our walls. I had never known quiet in my life, and now it smiles at me, rubbing my head, soothing me. The change of offices has done me good.

Two years ago, three of our partner-sons—Amschel, Shlomo, and Kalman—decided to purchase a lot at the northern edge of Judengasse, the area that had been damaged in the fire and never rebuilt.

The empty lot, sprawled in its abandoned, dreary indignity, had lit up at the sight of the Rothschild trio that had come to revive it from its deathly slumber. In exchange for about 9,300 gulden passed from a cheerful hand to a happy hand, my industrious men adopted the lot near the Hinterpfann, Meir's place of birth, and began to enliven it with all the necessary tasks: clearing the rubble, turning over the soil, digging, pouring foundations, and constructing the skeleton. Meir was appointed supervisor, and his duties entailed a daily tour of the construction site. But rather than give advice or praise, he would fish a handkerchief from his pocket to wipe away the tears in his eyes. He looked back upon his life at Hinterpfann, the home where he'd grown up, which was now nothing but painful ruins. If only his parents could come back to life to see that their son, who had freed himself from the ruins, had started an international business empire.

His longing for his deceased parents and siblings was awakened with a new intensity during construction. I walked him to the cemetery and prostrated myself with him on the graves of his family. Then I left him alone with his memories and walked toward my own parents' graves. I rested my head on their tombstones and carried on a conversation with my beloved, silent parents.

A stone house was built on the lot—stone and not wood—rising into the sky, with windows on both sides. One morning, Meir invited me to join him there. He took off his hat, adjusted his wig, and bowed at me, a smug smile adorning the corners of his mouth with charming wrinkles. I saw before me young Meir, the way he had looked when I had first met him, with a short, black beard, bowing at a girl waiting at her window with yearning persistence. A young man with light in his eyes, who has produced a full life of success. I slipped my hand onto the inviting arm of the man who had aged and hunched, whose face was now adorned with an impressive gray beard, and headed out with him onto the road leading to the new building.

We paused in front of it, looking around. Four levels, bright white, standing out in the depressing landscape that surrounded them with scorched remnants. The heart that had just opened up to joy now crumples with gloom. The eyes that opened with a twinkle for a new gift collapse with exhaustion.

Meir could feel the change in me, and he tightened my hand's grip on his arm and hurried to lead me inside. I pretended to drag behind him, all the while trying to detach myself temporarily from the bothersome surroundings, while never taking my eyes away from his heavy legs, in case they tripped on the stairs.

I had a tour of the house. The rooms were fine, as were the windows that let in plenty of light. My sons' intention was to designate the first three floors to the firm and have us move into the fourth floor, with its spacious rooms.

"What do you think, Gutaleh?" Meir asked.

"The house is well lit and elegant, darling. It would be a wonderful place from which to run your business. But if it is up to me, I have no desire to replace our modest home with any other."

"Well put. Your wishes are my wishes. We have always been in perfect harmony." We therefore turned down the boys' offer.

Amschel was unhappy with our decision. "I don't understand you. We all work outside of the office, some of us outside of Germany. But you, Papa, are in charge of its daily management. Why, in your state, should you have to drag your feet from the house to the office every day, when you can avoid this unnecessary bother? Leave that old house and enjoy your new home."

"Amschel, darling, my kind son," Meir answered, unwavering, "your father must work at an office every day so he doesn't forget how to work, and walk home every day so his legs don't forget how to work."

Each morning, Meir leaves for the office, returning home for lunch and a midday rest. In the afternoon he goes out again and returns in the evening. At the office, Meir also takes care of the public service duties that take up most of his time.

In February, Meir was invited, along with eighteen famous Judengasse heads of families, to the office of Guiollett, the mayor of Frankfurt, to be sworn in as a citizen. They were the first families to receive this honor. Two weeks later, Meir enjoyed another honor, being appointed by Dalberg as a member in the Council of Frankfurt, along with his enemy, Simon Moritz von Bethmann. I would have thought it a sign of the end times.

In spite of his poor health, Meir continues, as financier of the community, to be called to duty and solve new problems: Should Jews, who are now official citizens, be obligated to do mandatory military service? What about those who live on Judengasse—should they enlist into the French military, invading deep into the Russian Empire, and join the battling forces near Bialystok? Meir traveled to Dalberg's castle in Aschaffenburg, demanded his immediate involvement in this matter, and returned with a promise for a temporary postponement of military service.

"All that is left is to watch Napoleon's downfall, after which we will be exempt from service anyway," Meir concluded, keeping a close watch on the progress on the French-Russian front.

Now that Meir's travels have come to an end, the number of good-morning coins beside my pillow is growing. Meir always remembers his first love, the love of coins, and makes sure to share it with his beloved. I kiss each love coin before dropping it into its special chest.

And I, who have time and health on my side for the time being, praise the Lord, continue to manage my household—cooking, cleaning, washing clothes, sewing, patching, and practicing efficiency and thriftiness.

Any of my grandchildren's clothes that are slated to be tossed out must receive my approval first, after a careful examination of their deterioration. My family members adhere to this rule, and I believe they do so because of the upbringing they have received and internalized through the years, and not because they defer to my authority as the elder of the tribe.

I continue to place nostalgic gifts in Nathan's packages: new shirts, carefully folded, made by Judengasse tailors. I do this in spite of the fact that London's tailors are in no way inferior in their sewing and stitching to our skilled tailors. Hannah has written to me that every delivery awakens Nathan's longing. "He speaks about you until the small hours of the night, until his eyes close and a smile envelops his lips." Unlike Nathan, and as if to compensate for his shortcoming, Hannah writes warm, heartfelt letters, in which she provides many details about my faraway, numerous grandchildren. They are miles away, but close to my heart.

At the same time, I continue to improve the appearance of my home and its tools. A fine home and fine instruments expand the mind of a person.

Well, I have improved the furniture in the living room, replacing the chairs that have performed their duty for decades. The only thing I have not replaced is the sofa. It remains in place, upholstered with the same green velvet I have taken such good care of, preserving it in near new condition. From the ceiling dangles a long, copper chandelier, and in its concave bottom I place a large candle that sheds a ring of light over the table and sends dull arms all around.

Whenever one of our sons visits London, I slip a list of items I want him to bring me upon his return: a serving set, silverware with ivory handles, coffee cups with matching saucers, pot, and tray. These are special items, and their price is incomparably lower there than it is in Frankfurt. I lay them out on our table, and they inspire us.

I have asked for nothing from Paris for the time being. Perhaps I will when it turns its face toward peace.

Wednesday, September 30th, 1812

My Meir, champion of my youth, crown of my head, my man and my love, admirable father of my ten children, is gone.

There are times when all the words we know cannot come together to properly express the turmoil in our hearts. The heart has its own language, and no verbal communication can give it full expression. Spoken language is superficial by its very attempt to make itself suitable for all people. But the language of the heart is personal, and contains a singular inner gurgling belonging to its owner and understood by him or her alone. It cannot be shared. Only two souls that have come together can conduct a dialogue of the hearts, understood by the two of them alone.

Ever since he left us, I have found that silence is the best choice for mourners. There is grief only in one's heart. Silence has conversed with me intimately, gripping the root of the bleeding wound.

My Meir is gone. How could it be?

Upon my return from the cemetery I stared at the plate of the *seudat havra'ah*, the meal of consolation, a round plate with Hebrew words inscribed along its edges, moving my eyes around the plate in circles: "A contribution to mourners—eggs and lentils."

When the heaps of lentils and eggs are consumed, the bottom of the plate reveals an image of figures serving the plate to a pair of mourners. The halacha has defined a ritual of consolation. At times of heavy grief, neighbors are obligated to feed the mourners. My neighbors are performing their duty with admirable dedication, preparing food, entering quietly, and carrying it into our home, the mourners' home, with a few crumbs of words.

But whose job is it to open the mouths of mourners? My mouth is shut to words and food. During the days of the shiva my home swarmed with people. Consolers came and went, never allowing me a moment alone. Everyone spoke to me, but I was attuned only to my loneliness. My grieving children, sitting around me like a herd without a shepherd, take nothing away from the wave of loneliness. All the words of comfort cannot console a grieving soul.

I sit at home, wearing my black mourning dress, a black coif on my head, its ribbon choking my throat. I sit like this, waiting for him to come home from the office. My ears are alert for the sound of his footsteps climbing up the stairs. My eyes are open to see the smile that precedes the kiss he plants on my lips whenever he comes and goes. My heart is ready to receive his report of the day, bring life into our home. To share in his pondering. To rejoice in his joy. To take pleasure in his happiness. To ache with his pain.

I am filled with anger. Why did he leave? Why did he give up? Why did he leave me alone? A man is only dead to his wife. We walked under the chuppah together, but when he rose to the heavens our paths diverged.

Then I grow angry again, a different anger, at myself. For my selfishness. *Why do I complain about him? How he suffered before he departed. How he loved this life. How he wished for the road to the top to never end.*

Forgive me for my anger. Forgive me for your suffering. Thank you for everything you've done. Thank you for everything you were.

For strengthening me. For keeping your promises. For the honor you brought the family in your life and after your death. For your love.

For forty-two years you were my loving husband. Now it is time to rest. You've done enough. In the sixty-eight years of your life you have managed to come a long way. If anyone can measure how much work you did and how many accomplishments you've achieved, they might think you were an entire battalion. Who could believe that all these achievements were made by one person, and that person is you? Not everyone enjoys two advantages, and you have had both: wisdom and wealth.

A man has three loves: his sons, his funds, and his good deeds. And you left this world with all three at your side.

Rabbi Yaakov said, *This world is a corridor to the next. Make yourself comfortable in the corridor so that you may enter the parlor.* Now the doors of the parlor are open to you. Make some room for me there, and when I arrive, introduce me, as you used to do in the corridor of our world.

I yearn to see you. I long hopelessly for your being.

But I would not be truthful if I complained that you had been plucked before your time. You died at a ripe old age. When you were a young man you already behaved as an adult—mindful, smart, experienced. As the years ticked by, you challenged the clock, with each year doubling, tripling, and quadrupling your allotted time.

Now your climb up the mountain is over. You have reached your destination, leaving the keys in the hands of your children. You took only your life with you as you emerged into your new world. Rest in peace, my love, you have done enough. The next generation will do the rest—you have prepared it in advance.

I dragged myself to the dresser by our bed, opened a drawer, and dug through it. There was the envelope. I took hold of the letter you wrote me the first morning after our wedding.

If my busy schedule will not allow me to declare daily just how much I love you, I hereby declare in advance my great love for you on this day and on every day that follows. Please remember this whenever your soul desires words of love and affection when I am not at your side.

Now you are not by my side. You've asked me to remember, and I do. I remember every single word of love. They are etched in all the chambers of my heart. They will give me power. I shall treasure the words of your life and the pain of your leaving, and carry on where you left off.

◆　◆　◆

I must describe everything from start to finish.

On September 16th, Yom Kippur, Meir rose early and prepared to head out to the restored synagogue. His face was pale, his hands supporting his lower back. I wanted to ask him not to fast this year. His health was more important than faith.

He looked at me assertively. "Do not ask me to do that, Gutaleh. No one has ever died after not eating for one day."

I knew nothing would change his mind. There was no point in making him angry on our holiest of days.

From my seat in the women's section, my eyes followed his every move. He was praying standing up. I wanted to ask him to sit down. Praying while sitting down is still praying. My eyes ran over the central bimah and from there to the chiseled wooden seats surrounding its four sides. Some of the worshippers were standing up and others were seated. My eyes returned to Meir and his stubborn standing. There was no chance of catching his attention. He was entirely lost in prayer, his eyes on the book and his lips moving.

Amschel stood by him. I sent my granddaughter Sulka, Schönche's little girl, who was running around with her friends, to speak to Amschel. Amschel leaned down and looked at me. I signaled for him to step outside.

"Have you noticed your father insists on standing all through the prayer?"

"I asked him to sit down or go home and rest, but he refuses. He thinks the deeper he prays, the better it would be for his health."

"Try again. Tell him I asked you to."

"All right, I'll speak with him, but Papa is especially stubborn today."

Meir responded to his son's pleas. He alternated between sitting down and standing up, but stood up for too long, and sat down for such short spells that my temper grew short too.

In the evening, I began to set the table for breaking the fast. My hands did not obey, and the glasses slid out of them, almost breaking. Henrietta and Julie, my beloved daughters, carrying my future grandchildren in their wombs, sat me down on a chair and worked around the table, distracted and silent. The smell of stew began to rise in the room, and along with it rose the level of anxiety.

The door opened. Meir, supported by Amschel on one side and Moshe de Worms on the other, climbed up the stairs to the house. The rest of the family followed suit, returning from the synagogue.

I rushed to Meir's side, putting a glass of water to his lips, but he shook his head. "Wine," he whispered, then collapsed.

The men laid him on the bed. I placed two pillows under his feet. "Meir, open your eyes," I begged.

Meir's eyelids fluttered, and I quickly dampened his lips with the wet cloth Schönche handed me. He opened his eyes, searching for something.

"Bring the wine for havdalah and the candle," I said.

Moshe borrowed a flame from the chandelier in the living room and returned with a lit candle. He placed it on the golden saucer on our tiny bedside table, and the flame trembled and cast flickering shadows on the walls.

In the golden goblet in Amschel's hand, the wine sloshed and threatened to spill over. Amschel said the blessing in a voice that was not his, and everyone answered, "Amen." He sipped the wine, dipped the tip of his finger in it, and spread it over his father's lips. Meir ran his tongue over his lips. The goblet was passed from one hand to the next.

The holy act that sealed Yom Kippur seemed to fill Meir with renewed strength. He willingly accepted a piece of bread and a cup of tea. His face grew livelier and his pain seemed to have dulled. Shortly thereafter he fell asleep, the sounds of his snoring more pleasing to my ear than any music.

In the morning, I awoke to a rustling. Meir had left the room and his heavy footsteps could already be heard descending the stairs. I hurried toward him. "Good morning, Meir."

He turned to face me, and like a mischievous child, he wore a weak smile, his hands gripping the wooden railing. He began to lean forward in order to climb toward me, but I raised my hand. "Stop! Here I come." I came down to meet him and kissed his cheek.

"I'm going to see Amschel at the office. It's been a while since I've visited him."

"Wait. Let me wash up and get dressed and I'll join you."

"No need, my dear. It's going to be a quick visit. By the time you get ready I'll already be back. I'll give him and Eva your best."

"I suggest you stay close today. You need to rest up."

"Please don't worry, my Gutaleh. I'll take it slow."

And already he was walking carefully down the stairs, and I turned back toward the bedroom. I was uneasy with the thought of Meir going out into the street unaccompanied, but I knew his uncompromising insistence, and I knew any further attempt on my part would only bring unwanted results.

I turned to my morning routine. Two coins winked at me from the pillow. I picked them up and closed them in my hand. I sat on the edge of the bed and lost myself in thought. One coin was a gift owed from yesterday, the holy Yom Kippur, when money must not be handled, and the second was for today. No reason is good enough for Meir to break his ritual. How much longer did I have to enjoy this morning routine? His body was in constant deterioration, but his mind was clear and leveled. He was still full of curiosity and passion for life in general and for his sons' work in military and financial fields more specifically. Now he was heading over to see Amschel and hear the latest from the Rothschild arena and the international arena, such as news of the war between France and Russia. Just a few days ago, the street discussed the bloody Battle of Borodino, near Moscow, unsure who to name its victor.

The latest. How much longer would Meir be able to hear the latest? And what would be the very latest, the news to end all news and accompany him to his grave?

I stood up at once. What were these thoughts filling my mind? Dear me. My Meir, the undisputed hero, would beat this illness. He had many more missions to accomplish. It was much too early for eulogies.

I shook and fluffed the comforters with determination. I stretched the sheet as taut as I could and tucked its ends beneath the mattress. I went to the bathing corner in the kitchen and washed my face with plenty of water.

When I slipped a piece of bread with a wedge of cheese into my mouth, I grew weak and lost my appetite. I put the bread back on the plate, rested my arms on the table, and took my head in my hands. I had no more energy to deny the unease inside of me. No morning activity was powerful enough to lift it. I sensed that something was wrong. Meir had sensed it too, and his tortured smile was an attempt to alleviate my worry.

I jumped up at the sounds of voices approaching the house. I rushed to the stairs, taking them two at a time, ignoring my old age and the frailty of my body. I saw our neighbor approaching, carrying Meir in his arms. Behind them was the doctor, ordering, "Be careful, don't shake him."

I heard a scream. I looked around. *Who was that?*

The doctor said, "Gutaleh, be strong, he's alive, please don't."

I blocked my mouth with my hand and came closer to Meir, now beside me, observing his pale face and his closed eyes and looking at the doctor imploringly: *Are you sure . . .* He answered impatiently, "Yes, he's alive." Then he told the pallbearers, I mean, the people carrying the patient, "Lay him down on the bed, carefully."

The door closed and I stood behind it. Schönche and Babette dragged me to the chair. I sat down, my eyes fixed on the door. Julie brought water to my mouth. When did everybody get here? Now Amschel arrived. He opened the door to the bedroom and disappeared inside.

What about Meir? Why was the doctor taking so long? Why was nobody saying anything? What were they hiding from me? I should be the first to know.

I demanded to know that he was all right, that he would make it, that he was alive.

I closed my eyes in prayer. *Heal us, Lord, and we shall be healed. Save us and we shall be saved, for You are our glory, and therefore bring complete recovery to all of our afflictions.*

"He's all right. He needs some rest."

I opened my eyes. The doctor was standing over me. He gave me the news first. Good news. I looked into his eyes and cried my gratitude. But beyond my tears I could tell his eyes did not share in the good news he had just delivered.

"What was wrong with him?" I asked.

"The site of his operation opened up."

I stood. Schönche and Julie rushed to take hold of me, leading me to the room. The doctor followed us inside.

Meir lay on the bed, his eyes cracking open and closing alternately, but his mouth was mumbling into Amschel's ear.

Amschel signaled us to come closer. "Papa wants to change the will. I'm going to see the attorney."

Meir reached out his trembling hand and brought mine slowly to his face. His lips clung softly to the back of my hand and did not let go for a long time. If I had only known I was receiving his last kiss.

He asked for my ear. I brought it to his mouth, then jumped as if bitten by a snake.

"The notebook."

Dear God. My breath caught in my throat. With my hand on my bosom, I realized I mustn't lose his attention. I had to keep up a calm appearance for as long as possible. I brought my ear to his mouth again.

"Destroy it. The first two, as well."

"You knew?" I tried to whisper the words, but my voice broke out as harsh as a crow's.

He smiled at me mercifully. What a fool I must have seemed to him. How did I never realize that Meir, mind reader and secret keeper, knew all about the notebooks? How obtuse could I have been?

I scanned his face. It showed no anger. In it, I recognized the last bit of sharing that narrowed the only gap remaining between us. A new light glowed in his eyes.

I found no words, but I didn't need them this time. Meir made them unnecessary. "You write well," he whispered. "Accurate." A fit of coughing cut him off. He recovered and continued, as if he knew time was limited. "You must remember not to leave it out in the open. Too many secrets. Write and then destroy."

I looked at him. I wanted to know more.

"I loved what you wrote. It made me feel peaceful, especially in the days after a particularly long business trip. I never missed a beat, all thanks to the words you never spoke, but wrote down with endless devotion."

How contented those words made me. How much tenderness and refinement was in the way he excited my heart with this surprising revelation.

I had to fulfill his request. I would destroy the notebooks before I died.

"Don't be too upset about me. You've always said I'd done enough. You were right. Now it's my time."

What could I say to that? I was silenced. My man never ceased to surprise me, on his last day on earth as on our first day together and in all the days in between. His body was in the midst of the distress of parting from this world and moving on to the next, but his mind was attuned to my sorrows in this world.

The attorney arrived with Amschel, sat down on the chair, and pulled out his papers and stamps.

With a clear mind and a hushed, slow, and calculated voice, as a man who knew his last lines by heart, Meir dictated his corrected will. From time to time he moved his eyes from the lawyer to Amschel and repeated his warning: "I am entrusting my precious treasure to your capable hands, knowing you will be able to grow it. Never fight each other over inheritance or anything else. Make sure to pass my will to future generations. The work I have done will grow generations of wealthy men who will continue to bring honor to the Rothschild family. This will all happen if you make sure to preserve the basic rules I taught you all these years.

"Continue on your way, love people, give to charity.

"Obey the faith of Moses and Israel.

"Build your life on three foundations: unity, integrity, and hard work."

Even in his final will, Meir kept the secret of our wealth. With classic Rothschild sophistication, he sold his part of M. A. Rothschild and Sons and the whole of his assets to his five sons for a total sum of 190,000 gulden, to be passed on to me and our five daughters. By force of the will, the entire business will belong to our five sons.

The attorney listened and took down the clauses, and the will was lawfully signed. Turning to leave, the attorney noticed that Meir was lost in reverie. He sat back down and waited, like us, for him to speak. For a long moment, Meir stared up at the ceiling of the room as we all stood around him silently, waiting.

When he turned his face back toward us, his eyes twinkled with a new light. "I'd like to make one final request: give me a modest funeral."

This statement landed another blow of silence upon the room. I watched him while listening to the voices inside me, all speaking at once. Voices of compassion and pride. Sorrow and admiration. Pain and wonder.

This was my great man, with the two sides of the coin of his life. One side pounced on the sources of life, drank their water thirstily, and was never satiated. The other side was modest. A man who did great things but kept his life small. He garnered honor but lived simply, and as was his way throughout his life, he sealed his wondrous journey with a humble funeral.

Two days later, on his deathbed, before he spoke the final Jewish sentence, I whispered my final statement to him: "Meir Amschel Rothschild, you have brought us great honor."

He nodded and shut his eyes tightly. Then he whispered, "Shema Israel, Adonai Eloheinu, Adonai Echad." Hear, Israel, the Lord is our God, the Lord is One.

The doctor came near, put his ear to Meir's chest, and shut his eyelids.

My Meir returned his soul to his maker on Saturday night. I put his date of death on the last page: September 19th, 1812. His face was peaceful.

The funeral took place the following day, on Sunday afternoon, eve of Sukkot. The procession walked down the entire street, the street where he was born, where his ancestors were born, where he worked and left lots of work for his offspring.

The procession began modestly. Four men—Amschel, Kalman, Moshe, and Bernhard—carried the coffin. They were followed by men in black, and then by the women. I was supported by Isabella and Babette, and with us walked Schönche, Julie, and Henrietta, my sister Vendeleh, and her daughters.

Women and children stood silently and respectfully on the sides of the road. More and more men joined the procession, filling the street. When we arrived, I looked around, imagining the entire People of Israel standing around the open grave. It was dug near the grave of Isaak Elchanan, his great-great-grandfather, which Meir liked to visit from time to time.

I cannot remember the funeral. Passages from the Talmud were read, as well as a song from Psalms. We begged the deceased's forgiveness. Spoke the kaddish prayer. Tore a bit of our clothing.

As Meir had instructed, there were no eulogies. The eulogies were spoken silently in the eyes of his many friends who had come to say goodbye. When people cry over a righteous man, the Lord counts the tears and keeps them in His treasure trove.

When the grave in the crowded cemetery of our street was covered, I thought, *Meir must know this is not the end of his heritage.*

Sunday, December 6th, 1812

After the shiva, Amschel convened ten rabbis, the best on Judengasse, who prayed and said the kaddish day and night. Amschel did not work, grew a beard, ate almost nothing, and spent his time sitting with the rabbis, praying with them, and performing charitable work for the ascent of his father's soul.

We had promised Meir not to say eulogies over his grave, and so the eulogies appeared after the burial, at the end of the seven days of mourning. With time, they appeared in newspapers and journals, at intimate meetings and mass gatherings. They all said what I had already known, that Meir was not mine alone—he belonged to everybody, to the entire community, and beyond. Meir, who cared for the education of the children of our community (the Philanthropin School he started eight years ago for children of the poor had become an invaluable institution for many enlightened families that believed in education and reform). Meir, who performed charity for the less fortunate—Jews and non-Jews alike. Meir, who brought freedom to the people of Judengasse. Meir, who put the Jews on equal footing with the gentiles.

A journal placed in my hand bore the following headline:

The Life of Deceased Jewish Banker Meir Amschel Rothschild, a Symbol for a Life of Justice and Morality

Righteous men are greater in death than they were in life. May we all enjoy this same privilege.

Every night I lie in bed, close my eyes, and move over to my side of the bed to leave room for Meir. He drops in for a brief visit, curling beside me, and listens to the events of the day. I tell him everything that happened and shower him with pride for the Jewish memory he left behind. "Your soul continues to shade our children and imbue them with power," I whisper to him.

In the routine of our life, when everything still moved in familiar paths and things seemed so obvious that there was no need for words, I didn't often praise him for his actions. From the beginning of our life together, my ears and my heart had been trained to fill a more active role than my mouth. I had gotten into the habit of listening. Now that he is gone, I am left with a box of words, tied with a bow, sealed with the label of the manufacturer: Gutle Rothschild. I open it and out burst the words, eager to breathe fresh air. They squeeze their way into my daily reports, dancing before Meir with twirls of flattery, praise, and song. And I, with my eyes closed, imagine him surprised at the generous burst of words charged with love, admiration, and exaltation; whole, confident words, without filters or blockades.

All I had never said to him in his lifetime, trusting that he already knew all that was in my heart, I say now, every night. I whisper words of love to my Meir. I remember how his heart rejoiced at my declaration of love, a declaration that had arrived so late, inspiring him to confess, "Even a man needs words of love."

If only I had known how important it is to tell a person kind words in their lifetime, how important it is for even the obvious to be occasionally spoken, not kept in a box until they are gone.

I am repenting, my Meir. Though I know you knew the words that were filling my heart, I should have spoken them to you sooner.

Thursday, August 4th, 1814

Dear Meir,

From now on, this notebook is dedicated to you. I will keep you abreast of all that goes on in our lives, and thus writing will continue to connect us, and I can keep feeling you by my side.

Well, darling Meir, as you know, I am tired of arguments and of the well-meaning delegations of our sons, daughters, sons-in-law, and daughters-in-law urging me to leave Judengasse. I do not intend to leave Judengasse, period.

I have no desire for a large home, no wish to spend the rest of my life at a prestigious place, and absolutely no interest in getting to know new neighbors. My kind neighbors are enough. I have been friends with them for years and can see them whenever I wish. Though some of them have left the ghetto and others have left this world, the few that remain fill all of my social needs. No, I have no interest in the blooming gardens in the yards. The planters smiling at me from the windowsill are quite enough.

The children's pleas were no good, not even Amschel's, who had done more than anyone to try and get me out of the ghetto. "It is time to bid farewell to your old house locked within poverty and meet another environment of life, breathe some new, fresher air," he said.

My answer was unequivocal, if repetitive. "I will never abandon the stagnant air of our street."

When his pleas and reasoning didn't work, Amschel grew impatient and adopted a new tactic, riding on his rising waves of anger. "All these years, we have fought for our right to leave the ghetto and choose where to live according to our own wishes and not according to some medieval dictates. And now, after Papa managed to procure this historic right, and the entire community celebrated him for it, you wave it off as if it was all pointless. Worthless. I don't understand your stubbornness. You are mocking Papa's efforts and achievements."

My fury burned. My heart wanted to explode. I brought my frown close to his face. "Where do you get the nerve to speak to me this way? Never repeat these malicious things you so foolishly said. Who appreciated your father's work and his achievements better than I? I stood by his side and supported all he did for years before you came along to learn the alphabet of life from him. You . . . you are not authorized to explain to me what contribution your father has made to our community."

"I—" Amschel tried to respond.

I cut him off. "I have no interest in what you have to say." I fled from the living room, slammed the door to our bedroom, and leaned against it from inside, catching my breath.

Minutes ticked by. On the other side of the door, Amschel whispered like a frightened child, "Mama, forgive me, I'm sorry. I want to talk to you."

The door stayed closed. He apologized again, but I wouldn't open it.

Slowly, the thoughts began to find order in my mind. The family's persuasion efforts have sickened me, and now I've taken it all out on Amschel, that chamber of my heart that bore the title "Devotion."

"Mama, please, let me in. See me. I am so sorry, Mama. It was so insensitive of me to say such harsh, wrong things."

I opened the door and let Amschel in. I buried my face in his neck. "I'm sorry," I managed to say, a brief, angerless sentence between wails. I lingered against his warm, loving, devoted, calming shoulder.

I settled down, more or less. At least I was able to let go of him and find that I had drenched his shirt and he now had to change it. "Come sit," I said, taking his hand the way I did when he was a toddler taking his first steps. We sat on the edge of the bed. "Amschel, do not torment yourself. We were both out of line," I said softly.

"No, Mama, I was out of line. All I wanted was what's best for you. I wanted to give you a better, more comfortable life. But I, such a fool, what did I do instead? I hurt you. I hurt the person I care about most, my mother."

I rubbed the back of his hand, stopping new tears from coming, tears for the two loves that had been taken away from him, the love of the woman at his side, and the love of his children that would never be born. I tried to appease him, but he did not want to stop his confession, and so I let him release what was in his heart.

"Who knows better than I what a strong bond you and Papa had? If only I could take a lesson from the two of you and create it with me and Eva. I will never forgive myself for the pain I've caused you. I deserve all the punishment in the world for each tear I made you shed."

"Amschel, listen to me." He looked at me, tortured. I tried to control my tears, so as not to deepen his guilt. I spoke quietly. "I thank you and your brothers for your goodwill. I know there is another life out there, a more comfortable, glamorous, indulgent life, and much, much more. But if you truly want what's best for me, and I know you do, there is only one thing I want."

"Anything. Name it, *mama-lieb*."

"Try to put an end to this campaign of persuasion to get me out of here. Have the topic removed from the family agenda. I am here for the rest of my life."

Amschel looked at me carefully to confirm my seriousness, and his face fell. He looked like a man who had expected a bowl of hot soup and received instead a plate of lukewarm mush. I felt sorry for him again, but I was not about to offer him any other dish. "Mama, I'll do anything you say, but let me ask you one last thing, and I promise not to bother you about this again. I must know why you refuse to leave. Understand, it is hard to accept your explanation, 'This is where I was born, this is where I met your father, and this is where I will die.'"

"Well, my son," I said calmly, "some things belong to the heart, and their sentimental value is high. As long as they remain in a person's heart, they are kept safe and can affect them and their surroundings. But when they leave the realm of the personal, they lose their power. And I wish to preserve the power of the things that belong in my heart, for their positive effect on my beloved family."

Amschel said nothing, awaiting further explanation, something to lift the fog. When the silence wore on, he fixed me with baffled eyes.

When Amschel left I remained alone with my reveries. I will never reveal to anyone the real reason behind what they see as my stubbornness.

Well, the real reason has to do with something my mother told me as a child, when I wondered why the Frankfurters had sealed the windows of our homes. Mama told me they were afraid of the evil eye and left it at that.

That statement was etched inside me, and I was often reminded of it during the course of my life. If the great Frankfurters were afraid of us hurting them, then we must fear their hatred and conceal our success. We mustn't be too ostentatious, or it might come back to hurt us.

My feet are on the ground and my eyes are open to the changing reality. Our children have grown up in our home, on my humble lap.

But their encounter with the outside world, the one yielding fine business results, is also the one that pulls them into different norms, which fit their new financial and social status. They live in two worlds at once. On the one hand, they swear allegiance to the heritage you have taught them: honoring both our holy Torah and the rules of the financial-political game. But on the other hand, they live in ostentatious castles. Among them all, Nathan is the most moderate. He still maintains a certain sense of modesty, but I know it won't be long before he too will give in to the new dictates of life and make his home and his children more comfortable. In spite of his relative moderation, even he, with the help of Hannah and the company of servants, hosts dinners for world leaders, showing off the contents of his home, the fine dishes, and the concoctions that only those with means can afford.

I have never intervened in my children's lives, and I have no intention of starting now. It would be imprudent and unfair of me to advise them to live in a small home and a simple environment. And I have no doubt that they wouldn't listen, either.

All I have to do is protect them from the evil eye. As long as I live in my simple home on Judengasse, I can shelter them and balance the extravagance.

I must keep this to myself and never reveal it. By keeping this thought to myself, I'll be able to protect my children, who are great doers, but naive when it comes to understanding the depth of secret beliefs.

Tuesday, June 27th, 1815

Oh, Meir, Meir, a tragedy has befallen us. Our Julie is gone.

Julie, our little girl, who had just tasted the flavor of motherhood, is gone, leaving us lost and powerless.

An entire chamber of my heart is wrapped in shrouds. A chamber twenty-five years of age.

It's as if she was born only yesterday. Only yesterday she stood under the chuppah with Meir Levin Beyfuss, you and I at her side, wishing her the best. It's as if her eldest son, Gustav Beyfuss, a three-year-old who has recently joined the *heder*, has just been born. Her second son, Adolf Beyfuss, is not yet one year of age.

Their young mother grew ill and was torn from her small children, and already she is lying in the dirt.

Where is the force of the Rothschilds? Here comes death to slam us with the helplessness of man. No amount of money in this world can save us from the Angel of Death.

My Julie is on her way to see you, Meir. Or perhaps she has already arrived.

I will take our motherless grandchildren under my wing and dull the pain of her absence. At night I will soak my pillow with tears, and in the daytime I will envelop myself in the love and tenderness of my little Gustav and Adolf. I will look at their faces, bearing the smiles and laughter of our Julie, and find some small comfort in the fact that they are here to continue her legacy.

Woe is me for the fate that has dragged my faltering legs to stand before the open grave of my daughter.

Sunday, October 22nd, 1815

In the shadow of the ongoing grief over the death of our Julie, I wish to inform you of the downfall of Napoleon. You predicted this would happen before you died. You are a prophet, Meir Amschel Rothschild. So many of the peculiar things you have said over the years have come true.

I am well informed in the events that have led to his defeat.

It was the Battle of Waterloo that tipped the scales. The French military, led by Napoleon, was larger and more experienced than the British military, led by General Wellington, but this only pushed Wellington to come up with a trick to challenge the French enemy. The trick he found seemed so simple to me. On the right, Wellington's forces waited at Hougoumont farm on the mountain ridge, all around it a fortified wall with embrasures concealed by bushes. On the left were the Prussian forces. And so it was Napoleon's fate to lose the battle. A month after his defeat, Napoleon was exiled to Saint Helena, and so ended his conquests. I do not think there is any chance of him escaping from there to renew the fighting.

Though you know what is in my heart, I feel the need to share my opinion of the ousted French emperor.

There are two sides to my opinion. One side pays homage to and has appreciation for the man identified with civil rights. Napoleon Bonaparte, unlike small, wavering cowards like Dalberg, has always remained steady in his ideas. All along, he adhered to his motto, that all people were created equal and have the right to their own possessions. What matters to me is that we Jews are included in this declaration. All the people of the Judengasse, who now have equal rights, must admire him for that. I myself will continue to respect him for it, and I therefore feel compassion for the humiliating way in which he ended his career.

But then there is the other side, which has to do with my nationalist sentiments. Being a resident of Frankfurt, born and raised, I see the French emperor as a conqueror in the full sense of the word. And Nathan, as a resident of England, sees him the same way. Must we, as a Jewish minority, remain faithful to our homeland? I think the answer is yes. Though the place where we live is bad, we must protect it against foreign invaders trying to seize it and attach it to their own land.

I wonder at what point our Yaakov-James will begin feeling like a French patriot. What kind of conflict would this create between the brothers? I must make sure their relationship perseveres.

I have mentioned that General Wellington has used some wartime trickery. Now listen. Our Nathan, I found out later from Amschel, had also devised a trick, a Rothschild-style trick, in order to turn the results of the war between England and France into another stepping stone in his financial battle. You must be curious to know how.

As everyone knows, the Rothschilds acquire new information before everyone else. Nathan has relied on this fact and made rather sophisticated use of it.

The first to learn of the crushing French defeat, Nathan went to the London Stock Exchange and began selling. Rumor of Nathan Rothschild standing at the counter and selling English stocks over and over found its way to other shareholders, and the clear conclusion was that England must have lost the war.

A response wasn't long in coming: one by one, big and small shareholders sold their stocks. The market was swamped, and the value of English stocks decreased exponentially. A few moments before the English public learned the truth, Nathan bought an immense number of stocks at dirt-cheap prices. Our Nathan made a fortune in a single day—the largest profit he'd ever made.

The upset stockbrokers could only be appeased by the sweet flavor of the news itself—that their military had beaten Napoleon's. England had won. How I would have loved to see Nathan rubbing his hands with pleasure over both outcomes.

Thursday, June 6th, 1816

Darling Meir,

Praise the Lord, my eyes have lost some of their clarity, but I mustn't complain. I can see anything I want to see, and my legs can carry me around without a hitch. From the height of my sixty-three years, I must admit that the function of my vital parts is satisfactory, showing no signs of special weakness, for the time being.

I may not be as pretty as the moon or as pure as the sun, and age spots have made their marks upon my face, but I mustn't grumble, having come this far, but rather thank the kind Lord and accept my looks as they are. My black hair that has turned gray and thin. The two symmetrical wrinkles running from the corners of my nose down to my chin, which I assume will deepen the more years God allots me on this earth. The thin lines that occasionally appear on my forehead, as if still seeking their permanent placement.

But it is underneath my clothes, on my modest parts, that the years have dared leave more of a mark. My full, upright breasts, which had been through a long line of pregnancies, births, and breastfeeding, seem to have realized their job is done and are sagging toward the earth, and finding a rather comfortable resting place on my stomach. And speaking of my stomach—the muscles have loosened, they too understanding that this is the finish line in their ongoing service in the name of the next Rothschild generation.

Well then, I have described the way I look, but no one can see it beyond my dress, especially with the corset, which I never had to use before, and which is now serving me well on Shabbat and on holidays. As God is my witness, I feel completely stifled inside it, but I cannot resist the shapely form it grants me. On weekdays I leave the corset in the closet and tuck my body into the wide dress that leaves plenty of room for my worn-out limbs.

In spite of the functions of my body, which I boasted about earlier, I cannot deny the daily reminder that old age provides, naturally dragging me to keep new habits. Submitting to a quick nap after a few tasks are completed is the most prominent one. The midday nap is my newest ritual, and now that I have learned the pleasure of slipping into sleep in the afternoon, I will never give it up again.

Old age carries some advantages that youth does not. Every passing day grants us another point of wisdom. Those who reach grand old age have so many points to their name.

I therefore do not wish to turn back time. If I have made it this far, accumulating so many points, why should I want to start all over again? Praise the Lord, I am still able to run my household by myself.

As the matriarch of the glorious Rothschild dynasty, and in light of my position as the tribe elder—in addition to the sorrow that fills me to this day due to our absence from Nathan's wedding in London and the fact that you are not by my side anymore and I am deprived of my long-term right to carry out your orders—I have come to a new conclusion.

Our sons are growing roots in cities all over Europe: Nathan is in London, Yaakov is in Paris, Shlomo and Kalman are looking around for new destinations, and Amschel is keeping watch over the bank here in Frankfurt.

On holy Shabbat, after dinner and after Amschel said the after-dinner prayer, I asked everyone for their attention. "I have something to say."

Schönche, Isabella, and Caroline began gathering the small children lest they interrupt and were about to lead them toward the bedroom.

"No, I want all of you around for this. Even the little ones."

They quickly obeyed. The children sat down, flummoxed at this new development. The Rothschild clan all curled up, bleary-eyed and silent around the table.

"What I'm about to say applies to the entire family, and as long as I live, you must obey this order. One single order." I felt my body filling with strength. I looked over everyone, my beloved family. Blood of my blood. Chambers of my heart. Their eyes seemed to say, *Go on*.

"Look, darlings. You know that this is my home and that I will not be leaving. You also know that I do not intervene in your choice of where to live. You may live wherever you please and come visit me whenever you wish, at your convenience, and never need to feel guilty about it."

I paused before the blow.

"But in return for all the freedom you receive from me, there is a single thing I will never give up: the right to meet my children and grandchildren's chosen ones and witness their marriages. From this point on, I must see each and every one of you wed, and if you must have your wedding far away, the bride and groom must stop by my house, here in Judengasse."

Silence fell. My darlings looked at me.

"Take this as an indisputable order, more powerful than any written agreement," I concluded and said no more. Sometimes the silence that follows a declaration is more powerful than words.

The following day, I put this same order down in writing to be delivered to Nathan and Yaakov.

Wednesday, January 14th, 1818

Darling Meir,

You know how impatient I am when it comes to ceremonies. It is so lovely to continue life in my home, without changing my habits or wasting my hours on the insignificant rules dictated by high society. Why do people who consider themselves progressive and enlightened put so much weight on frivolities such as clothing and social rituals?

Well, this is about our sons, bless their souls, who all share in this affliction. But this time the focus is on Shlomo and Kalman, our Judengasse duo, who have risen to fame and have proven capabilities when it comes to the stock exchange and problem-solving. They have only one shortcoming: their ability to mimic these social rituals is deficient, not to say nonexistent, and their attempts at adapting are dire.

This is how things came to pass: the new French government is suffering a severe budget deficit, and two years ago it announced the issuing of an enormous state loan in the amount of 350 million francs. The loan was handled by Gabriel-Julien Ouvrard and Baring Brothers, and both enjoyed impressive success.

Last year, a new issuance of debt bonds was decided, for an amount of 270 million francs, and the leading candidates were once again Ouvrard and Baring Brothers.

Of course, our boys did not sit idly by. They filled their brains with data, parsed out the information they had, and concocted a suitable recipe for change. Their conclusions were as follows: their battlefield would be the Congress of Aix-la-Chapelle. The representatives would be Shlomo and Kalman.

The two of them arrived by separate, elegant carriages, their horses clean and sparkling. Packed into fine suits, they entered the magnificent parlor, where world leaders rubbed shoulders, overflowing with ceremonial etiquette. The quality suits our sons wore so well were not sufficient to hide their embarrassment in light of the noble manners demonstrated all around them. The others watched our boys with ridicule, expressing their impressions of our two clowns' unseemly behavior. Then they ignored them, resuming their festivities.

Shlomo and Kalman were insulted and humiliated, but did not let their emotions get the better of them, and decided to follow their initial plan. They thought being ignored might actually make things easier.

They walked aimlessly through the hall, pretending to be harmless, while making sure their assistants did not attract attention.

While taking dainty bites of the hors d'oeuvres, the mannered celebrants were distracted and failed to see what the assistants were doing on behalf of the innocent-looking Rothschilds. What they were doing was acquiring the debt bonds printed by Ouvrard and Baring Brothers.

Thus, the congress passed, the stronger party enjoying the pleasures of life, while the weaker, outcast party was busy with hard, dedicated work. Days and weeks went by, and finally the boys were in possession of enough debt bonds to prepare for an explosion. One stormy winter day, Shlomo and Kalman burst into the stock market and flooded it with an enormous accumulation of debt bonds. The walls shook. The stronger side was terrified. It had weakened in the span of a day.

And our boys? They were received like kings. Their lack of manners was cloaked by a golden robe, and their hands took hold of magic wands, which overturned everything. The ridiculing looks were now replaced by expressions of appreciation and appeal.

Oh, how the tables have turned.

Wednesday, November 4th, 1818

Darling Meir,

You must have noticed that I haven't been writing much lately. On the one hand, I feel the urge to continue to describe the wonders taking place in our family. On the other hand, my skin crawls at the thought that I would have to eventually carry out your order and destroy these pages, so as not to divulge our secrets.

Therefore, I do not write much, though I could fill whole pages every day, describing the lives of our loved ones. Still, I cannot stop writing altogether. Through the years, it has provided such comfort and release, and continues to do so today.

I curl up in my woolen robe, sit near the fireplace, having fed it with woodchips, the hot water bottle on my lap. I have just rubbed my hands together to warm them up, and now I can hold the pen steadily, though my handwriting is changing, growing more similar to that of my late father. As the years pass, I grow closer to my parents.

My ascent up the mountain is not over yet. As you wished, your death did not put an end to the Rothschild climb. Our children continue up that mountain, and have no intention of stopping.

Amschel, our eldest son, who was more attached to you than the others, trying to be like you, runs the Frankfurt branch of the Rothschild Bank with wisdom and care. Nathan continues to succeed in London, and has even received the title of "baron." I must point out that, unlike Amschel and Shlomo who proudly carry the title given to them by the Austrian emperor, and are now known as "von Rothschild," Nathan does not use the title he has received from the British Kingdom, preferring to be called Mister Rothschild. Yaakov is managing the Parisian bank, Shlomo the Viennese bank, and Kalman is in Naples.

Our children have drawn away, though they make sure to visit me. They have grown paunches and parted ways with their birth names. Amschel is the only one who stayed in Frankfurt, the only one who preserved his birth name, and the only one who has remained skinny. Nathan has been Nay-than for a long time. Yaakov is James. Shlomo is now Solomon, and Kalman answers to the name Karl. New name, new status.

I do not resent them for it. You changed your signature too. And yet, I must ask: Is a name powerful enough to let them become assimilated in their new countries? How do they feel there, so far from home? Money does not solve everything. Our children, who have been used to life on Judengasse, cannot change their skins completely, and even if they could, deep in their veins flows Judengasse blood, never mixing with another.

I pray that our children be happy. Their contentment is so much more important to me than the contents of their pockets.

But then there is Yaakov. In spite of his humble upbringing, he makes every effort to fit into Parisian life. He throws horridly elegant balls, arousing the wrath of Nathan, who criticizes him: "Stop romping around, you must restrain yourself. You went to Paris to work and make money, and yet you are wasting your time at parties all night long."

Our youngest son is quick to refute the charges. "I am working. I am making money. Making money in Paris is different than it is in

London. The moment I clink a glass of wine with a mogul at a ball is the moment I hook another fat fish, adding him to the list of people who may help me get ahead."

They are so alike, those two, with their hot tempers and original thinking. Your sons, Meir, their father. I smile. Let them bicker. It is an excellent release, and best done within the family, among relatives, always followed by a warm reconciliation.

Yaakov came to visit me a few months ago, granting me the grace of some private time together. In spite of how busy he is with work, he sat with me in my small kitchen, undid his top buttons, and opened his heart. My ears pricked to catch every one of his words, and his presence was a sight for sore eyes. I gave silent thanks to the kind Lord for giving me the chance to tour the mind of our little-big son, and get to know his stormy soul.

I learned that, being alone in the heart of the most fashionable capital in Europe, wanting to fit in, he has been doing all that is in his power to adopt their grandiose mannerisms, which are his entry ticket to the condescending society. These include things we had never encountered in the ghetto. His clothes are sewn by the greatest tailors in Paris, and he has learned to dance (I can just imagine him taking a woman's hand and twirling her around). Since it turned out that horseback riding could earn him a few more social points, he has started riding lessons, already paying dearly by falling off the horse and breaking his ankle. I hurt for him, but also loved to hear how Nathan worried about him, writing, "Be careful, dear brother. I cannot bear the thought of you confined to your bed, your ankle agonizing you. I hope the pain passes soon and that you can get back on track. I love you as I love myself, your brother, Nathan."

"You know, Mama," he told me, "I have no anger toward Nathan, Amschel, or Shlomo. Even if we disagree, I know they will be at my side whenever I need them, fighting with me through thick and thin."

"And I have no doubt you would do the same for them. Yet you *are* full of anger. Who is it directed at?"

His face flushed over. "The high society in Paris, all those snobs and anti-Semites hindering my progress merely because I am Jewish."

I thought about the disturbing, growing number of converted Jews. They convert not because they find Christianity to be superior, but in order to remove the obstacles standing in their way. Now my Yaakov was facing some of the same obstacles, but he never imagined taking the easy way out by leaving his mother's side in favor of a gentile faith. I am so proud of him. Even four of Mendelssohn's children have converted, while all of our children have married Jewish women.

"Tell me, son, about your life in the big city."

"Mama, try to imagine an elegant hall full of lights, gowns, suits, and wine. In short, glamour. The latest fashion is balls thrown in elegant parlors."

I noticed his eyes shimmering. My son loved this life, even if his official reason for partaking in it was business.

Then a shadow passed over those eyes. "I participate in some of them," he continued, lowering his voice, "but sometimes I am kept out. Laffitte, a socialite, threw a ball and invited everyone who is anyone. I was the only one he left out."

"Why?" I asked, a wave of anger rising in me over that evil Laffitte who had dared humiliate my son so.

"He is envious. The more our family grows and our financial influence increases, the more envious people like him become. They don't want the Rothschilds to continue to gain wealth and influence."

"And what does my Rothschild do in this type of situation?" I knew he wouldn't let this blow over without an appropriate response.

"Well, *mama-lieb*, I did not take it lying down. I knew I had to get ahead of Laffitte and shock him. *The wise prevail through great war.*" I smiled. I thought about your sayings, Meir, which the children were now putting into action.

"I arranged a dinner party and made sure to hold it a few days before Laffitte's ball. In the list of honorable guests I included Duke Wellington. The duke was glad to come, seeing as how we singlehandedly saved his army from disbanding and defeat in Spain and Portugal. His appearance in my house amazed everyone, especially Laffitte. This was my first, immediate feat."

Meir, are you proud of your son?

"But there is another, more important accomplishment here. Thanks to Duke Wellington, I enjoyed the protection of Elie Decazes, the minister of police. So this is one relationship that's important to maintain."

"Two accomplishments from a single ruse," I said, impressed.

"Three, Mama," he corrected. "The third is adding a new face to my growing collection of business contacts. I have my eyes on a new bank customer, Louis Philippe, duke of Orléans. I predict he's going to become important for all of France. I won't let him get away."

"Papa must be looking down proudly at you," I praised, rubbing his shoulder softly. "Tell me, Yaakov, are you comforted by these accomplishments?"

He cleared his throat and ran his hand over mine. "Papa is always with me. I feel him every step of the way. I ask his advice and feel him giving me strength."

How alike two brothers can be, I thought, kissing his wide forehead.

"To answer your question, Mama—every victory pushes me onward. That doesn't mean I don't worry, but I choose to focus on progress and do not let these bothersome thoughts take up too much of my time."

"Speaking of progress, I was glad to hear about your move to Rue de Provence."

"Thank you, Mama. Your letter of congratulations is on my desk. It's been a year since I moved there, and it was the right choice, situating myself in the financial hub of Paris. But I already have more news. I am about to move to a bigger place, suitable for hosting more guests."

"You aren't leaving Paris, are you?"

"No, Mama, people don't leave Paris. I am moving to a house on Rue d'Artois. Guess who used to live there?"

"Napoleon," I joked.

"Close. Hortense, Josephine's daughter."

"Josephine, the empress who left one husband after he was sentenced to the guillotine and was abandoned by her second husband, Napoleon, in favor of a younger, more fertile woman. Why would you put your healthy head in a sickbed? You must have forgotten how she ended up."

"Mama," he laughed. "It isn't a sickbed, and my memory is not betraying me, either. It isn't Josephine's house, it's Hortense's. What did she ever do?"

"I'm not telling you what to do. You know better than I. Just remember that the Parisian royalty's life of debauchery was anything but pure."

"I tend to believe that royal families all over the world have some degree of corruption, but that's got nothing to do with me."

I felt as if I were being transported back in time, an entire generation. Do you remember, Meir, the similar claim you had made? *I am not responsible or involved in the way nobles and rulers live."*

"You're right, I must congratulate you for this imminent move too," I agreed.

"Thank you, Mama. I need your blessing. You cannot imagine how many reputable people will be my guests—politicians, artists, court people, musicians. I am planning to take over France, attend all the respectable parlors, and host dinner parties the likes of which they've never seen before."

"And what about keeping kosher, son? Do you keep kosher during these fancy meals?"

"Mama, do not worry. I don't go to these events to eat. I always arrive after a hearty meal, and in order to show my respect I have some wine and eat some fruit and vegetables."

I stifled a sigh.

I have reservations about my son's attraction to glitter and extravagance, but I accept it. I am preoccupied with something else. I don't understand why Yaakov lingers on and on instead of finding a wife. All of his brothers have families. Two years ago, Kalman married the beautiful Adelheid Hertz. He is a handsome thirty-year-old and she is eighteen, the daughter of a wealthy merchant from Frankfurt, beloved by all who know her, and in charge of hosting balls and dinners, a vital role in these new times.

Only our Yaakov remains single. "An eligible bachelor," as the others call him. Just recently, he came close to putting a ring on a woman's finger. Under Nathan and Amschel's coercion and Shlomo's direct influence, there had been talks about uniting our family with the von Eskeles family, a Jewish-Austrian family that also has a noble title. Meir, you ought to be proud of our efforts. This potential bride answered three entry conditions: she is of our religion, the daughter of nobles, and of a wealthy father. But the negotiations, which had given us all hope, reached a dead end after Yaakov announced unequivocally that he was not ready to link his life to another's just yet.

Meir, you are up there, closer to God. Please, do something. It would be best if our son's efforts to blend into fashionable Parisian society would be performed with a woman at his side. It is a man's duty to court a woman and not a woman's duty to court a man, and women want to marry more than men do.

Our children visit me regularly with our sweet grandchildren, and I love them all equally. In secret, I will admit that one of our granddaughters has taken up an especially large chamber of my heart. That is my Betty,

Shlomo's daughter. She lives with her parents in a castle in Frankfurt and often comes to Judengasse to spend time with me. My Betty has been traveling with her parents and her brother, Anselm, to Vienna, for Shlomo's work. Though she is visiting me less frequently, she clings to me as if we have always lived together. The mannerisms she brings with her from Austria charm me, and her curious questions please me. Her brother attended the Philanthropin, the fine Jewish school you established in Frankfurt, while Betty was educated by the best tutors in the city. She takes after her father, but is more polished and refined, as befits a girl, and her pretty face is completed by a charming personality, intelligence, resourcefulness, sweetness, and sharpness of mind.

Wednesday, May 12th, 1819

Darling Meir,

A few months ago, Amschel told me something that exemplified Yaakov's statement about Rothschild unity. It was a story that began with a check Amschel gave Nathan.

Nathan went to the Bank of England and gave the check to the teller to be cashed.

"This cannot be cashed," the teller said, returning the check to my son. "Why not?" Nathan asked, surprised and peeved.

"We don't cash checks from private entities," the poor teller explained, unaware of the mess he was creating for the bank.

"The Rothschilds are not private entities," Nathan shouted, then took the check, returned home, and began to plan the lesson he would teach the bank.

The next morning, he appeared again before the same poor teller. This time he handed over a ten-pound note.

"Gold in the value of the note," he ordered the teller.

Gold in the value of ten pounds? the teller must have wondered, moving his eyes between the note and Nathan.

Nathan stood there, staring at the ceiling, waiting for his demand to be fulfilled. Finally, the man had nothing left to do but follow instructions and hand over a tiny amount of gold.

Nathan accepted the gold with one hand, and with the other handed the teller another ten-pound note. "Gold in the value of the note," he said.

The teller, who realized this was anger talking, hurried up and did as he was told.

Thus Nathan spent all day long at the bank, handing over ten-pound notes and receiving gold in return. All those long hours, the other nine windows were occupied by nine of my son's loyal clerks, who had been equipped with the same notes and instructed to make the same request: handing over one note and receiving gold in return, handing and receiving.

Of course, the tellers were then unable to service the long lines that dragged on behind Nathan and his clerks.

The next day, the same group appeared at the bank again, their wallets filled with ten- pound notes.

The manager of the bank came over and whispered in Nathan's ear, "How long do you plan to carry this on?"

Nathan answered without batting an eye. "Rothschild will continue to question Bank of England notes as long as Bank of England continues to question Rothschild checks."

From that point on, all of Amschel's checks were received and cashed.

Our Nathan had taught the bank an important lesson: the Rothschild family shall not be disrespected.

Sunday, August 8th, 1819

The older I get, the more partings exceed meetings. My child Julie is already resting in peace, and my heart knows no solace. I said goodbye to my mother and father years ago, and to you, Meir, in body but not in spirit. And my elderly neighbors are also departing, one by one, to a better place.

Tonight, Shlomo came to see me, grieving and distraught, his eyes downcast. He fell into a chair and could not raise his head. I walked over quietly, took a seat beside him, and took his hand in mine.

"What's wrong, Shlomo? Who is it this time?"

He looked at me through dark eye sockets. His lips twisted, as if refusing to release the name.

I rubbed his hand. "Who is it, son? Who must we mourn today?"

"Buderus." The name fled from its prison.

"Buderus, dear God." I squeezed his hand. "But he was fine. What happened to him?"

Once the name left his mouth, a long string of words followed. "He turned sixty this year. True, his body was healthy, but his heart must not have been able to carry the burden any longer. The daily stress was too much. One day, in the middle of work, as he sat behind his desk and handed a bill to a customer, he was felled by a heart attack. He didn't suffer."

"Poor Buderus, he was a loyal man. Loyal to his family, to the landgrave, to Papa, to us. He didn't deserve this. When did it happen?"

"Three days ago. I'm just coming back from a visit to his family. They can't believe he is gone."

"He was a good father. He loved children."

"I remember him playing cat and tiger and lion with us. We always loved him."

"So did I."

"I know. I think he was the only gentile you liked."

"He was the only gentile who came to my home and showed me there were worthy non- Jews out there."

"You know, Buderus built his family a grand home, a proper mansion. He took care of each of his children, leaving them enough money to live with dignity. He made sure they had everything they needed. He knew he wouldn't live forever."

"Who wants to live forever? But he deserved a few more years of happiness."

"Mama, he is like Papa, may his memory be a blessing. He couldn't sit still either. He was always thinking about how to get ahead."

"Well then," I concluded, "Buderus grew up with a fine reputation and died with a fine reputation."

Shlomo went home, and I stayed and reminisced about the times Buderus had spent at our house of life. Then I got up and lit a yahrzeit candle in his memory. May his soul be bound in the bond.

Sunday, October 3rd, 1819

I know there will always be trouble. I am familiar with our suffering, with those who wish us ill, who insult us, beat us, and degrade us. And yet I hoped those dark days were behind us, that the times of our abuse at the hands of gentiles were gone. We Jews are flesh and blood, we have a soul and a heart, and we feel. And now ugly days have come to prove to us that the wheel of evil keeps on turning. Judengasse is troubled again. Once again the Jews have no safe haven and no way of knowing what the future might hold.

As pogroms break out, I make a single plea to God: Please, open Your gates of mercy. More Hep-Hep riots are upon us. Damage to property, physical harm, and emotional damage. Our walled homes are exposed to evil winds caused not by nature but by the talons of humans who have forgotten their human form. The lively noise of our street has been muted by a sudden ruckus. An angry gang of savages broke into homes and stores, crying "Hep! Hep!" and destroying everything in its path. Old people and babies, men and women, were trampled in an instant. Others crawled into their lairs until things died down.

I watched from my window, horrified. I wanted to open the window and shower them with the wrath of the ghetto. They were holding bats, pitchforks, and axes, their eyes terrifying. They were in the mad throes of ruin and corruption, so much so that they did not notice an old woman watching them, testifying to the God of man.

Ever since the Congress of Vienna, we have experienced a deterioration in our status. The restoration policy has reversed the progress in the treatment of Jews.

Once again, we hide in our homes, keeping our heads down, waiting for the storm to pass. How lucky that at least some of our children, those who have left Germany, are spared this danger and humiliation.

Monday, October 9th, 1820

The visits to Vienna have paid off. Our son Shlomo, the third Rothschild offspring, took his wife, Caroline, and his two children, Anselm and Betty, settled in Vienna, and opened the fourth Rothschild branch in Europe. This branch joins the ones in Frankfurt, London, and Paris. My Shlomo has been living in the elegant Romischer Kaiser on Renngasse in Vienna. My Betty is enthralled with her Viennese teachers, and I can just imagine how eager she is to learn more and more. They must be surprised by this thirst for knowledge in a fifteen-year-old, and eager to plant in her the cultural seeds of the new world.

This time, the parting was natural, as if I had seen it coming. A few pricks in the chest, wet eyes, a hug and a kiss, and watching the carriage pull away.

But when I returned home I felt another chamber of my heart preparing for longing. I have found that every problem has its solution, but I have yet to detect the solution for longing. Oh, I am rich with longing indeed, and the harshest is my longing for Betty. I have so many memories of her. Mundane memories: her hand distractedly running over mine; her smooth forehead wrinkling suddenly in an effort to understand something; her laughter, which pulled me along after her; her eyes looking at me reproachfully; her head shaking at the sight of all the food I had made without asking for help; her request that I close my eyes as she slipped a spoonful of a new dish in my mouth and demanded that I guess what it was.

Oh, my Betty. Grandma misses you so.

Tuesday, October 10th, 1820

My Meir, how often did you warn your children to keep our secrets? "Secrets are the most important weapon," you said. "Beware of walls concealing enemies' ears."

Well, Nathan slipped.

One night, he left his home in Stoke Newington and parked his carriage near his office in New Court, where he met his associates to discuss an important matter.

A few moments later, a drunk man stormed into the conference room and fell to the floor, helpless. Nathan and his people rushed to him, carried him to the sofa, poured cold water on his face, spread scented oil on his forehead, and massaged his legs to get the blood flowing. Nothing worked. The man lay splayed, unmoving. He seemed to be in a deep sleep, and so Nathan and his people continued their meeting. They were discussing new information that had come in from Spain, and had decided that the very next morning they would buy stocks that were liable to bring in enormous profit.

At the end of the meeting, Nathan instructed his employees to mind the drunk and help him on his way home when he awoke. He boarded his carriage and returned home.

As soon as the carriage drew away, the drunk got up, wobbling, and rejected the offer of help. He thanked the men for their generosity and was on his way.

It turned out the name of this man was Lucas—a stockbroker and Nathan's Stoke Newington neighbor—and he had followed Nathan there. He made haste and acted according to the information he had learned while he feigned a drunken stupor during the meeting. When Nathan went to purchase the stocks, it turned out that Lucas had already bought them all. Lucas made a great profit, and taught Nathan a lesson in caution.

Wednesday, August 4th, 1824

We mourn the premature death of Abraham Montefiore. Henrietta's kind husband was plucked in the prime of his life, only thirty-five years old. How many broken hearts he left behind: the hearts of his mother and father, his wife and their four children—Nathaniel, Yossef, Louise, and Charlotte. And the hearts of his acquaintances and friends, and of his uncle, Moshe Montefiore, the Jew who was famous for his grace and mercy, and who had married Judith Cohen, the sister of my daughter-in-law Hannah, daughter of Levy Barent Cohen. And my own heart, the heart of Gutaleh, crying onto her notebook.

I feel such sorrow for my Henrietta, who has had the ground pulled out from under her feet. And I feel sorrow for their children, who no longer have a father. I regret how far away they are, in Paris. I take comfort in the love of her dear ones in the sparkling city whose face has darkened. Yaakov will not abandon her, and the dignified Montefiore family will fill her with its strength.

I feel for you, my dear daughter.

Sunday, October 3rd, 1824

My darling Meir, please rejoice and offer your blessing.

What brings me to the notebook today is a piece of great news: our youngest son, bless his soul, Yaakov-James, the French member of the Rothschild family, is married.

And who is his wife? It is my beloved Betty, our dear granddaughter. Shlomo gave his consent right away to his nineteen-year-old daughter marrying his thirty-two-year-old brother, and gave her a dowry in the unthinkable amount of 1.5 million francs.

There was good reason for the delay in Yaakov's announcement of a bride. His partner was young and they had to wait until she came of age. I know this is a perfect match, set by God Himself.

I sat expectantly at the window. The royal couple arrived with their entourage and parked their fancy carriage outside the northern gate of Judengasse. The bride walked slowly down the narrow path to our home, wearing a glamorous gown, cinched at the waist and ballooning toward the bottom. One gloved hand held the ends of her dress, while the other gripped a bouquet. Her lace train was held by the tiny hands of her two little bridesmaids, Louise and Charlotte, Henrietta's daughters, who had recently lost their father. Their hair was tied with pink ribbons. The groom, wearing a top hat, an elegant suit, and white silk socks, fluttered his hand around his bride's small waist, taking signature Rothschild bows toward the well-wishers. A long row of friends and admirers followed them down the street, transforming its impoverished appearance with their festivity.

I pulled myself away from the window and hurried to the doorstep to welcome them, a hand on my heart, as if keeping it from jumping out of my chest.

Indeed, our son, the sworn bachelor, who stood steadfast against the norms of society for years, has finally given in to its dictates, and has accepted the sentence of the marriage establishment at age thirty-two.

And what a wonderful choice he's made. It is God's doing. You, Meir, appeared in Yaakov's dream to direct his heart. Now you must be watching your young son, who has taken France by storm, who for the past two years has held the title of "baron," granted to him by the emperor of Austria. Your new daughter-in-law meets all the requirements, and has one more virtue: she is flesh of our flesh, blood of our blood, and so the family capital remains pure of foreign interference. How sublime is the power of God!

The first to fall against my fluttering chest was my darling Betty. I took my beloved granddaughter/daughter-in-law into my arms, touching her necklace and breathing in the smell of her hair. She bawled against my shoulder, calling me "Grandma" and then correcting, "Mother-in-law," then "Grandma" again. She was getting confused, and I shushed her and rocked her like a baby in my arms, whispering, "Congratulations, my girl. Take care of your makeup. Don't spoil it."

I recalled my own tears after our engagement, and my mother, may her memory be a blessing, who let me sob freely. But I hadn't been wearing any makeup.

My delightful grandchild was born in Frankfurt, grew up in Vienna, and was now moving for the third time in her life—to Paris. She wiped her pretty eyes and button nose obediently, and I curled up in the arms of Yaakov. I rested my ear against his heart, cherishing its beating, giving myself over to the captivating touch of his hand on my coif.

"You've done well, son. Papa is proud of you," I said, wiping away a tear.

"I know," he said, shedding a tear of his own.

I let him and his tears be, and turned to Shlomo to wipe my eyes well so I could look at my son, now also my in-law, and see him in a new light, perhaps because of the gleam in his eyes. He swayed as if drunk, and I opened my arms to support him.

The next to be hugged and kissed was sweet Caroline, my daughter-in-law and now Yaakov's mother-in-law. What an odd position to be in, familial warmth bursting from every corner to protect us. The moments of embarrassment were resolved by the laughter that took hold of our home.

But at night I cried my restrained emotions into the pillow, saying a blessing for the order I had given our children and grandchildren. This was the definition of happiness. Was I happy before today? Of course, but there are many kinds of happiness. This is a happiness mixed with great sorrow for my daughter Henrietta, who arrived wearing black and fell into my arms, choking on her tears, mixing her pain with my own, pushing its way into the thicket of joy to demand its rightful place.

Such are our lives—happiness and sorrow are intertwined.

Sunday, November 28th, 1824

Darling Meir,

Throughout my life, sadness and joy have gone hand in hand. Now it is once again time for bad news.

I am in mourning. Our eldest, Schönche, has been taken from us. She has breathed her final breath, plucked from this world at the age of fifty-three.

Our daughter, our pride and joy, the kind beloved of my heart, has departed to the world of truth. My Schönche, who gave birth to her own eldest on that hellish night of the great fire, demonstrating incredible strength, has joined you, Meir, and her sister Julie.

A few years ago, she changed her name to Janette, but my heart will always bear her original name, Schönche.

I have no power to write. The pen is leaking tears, and yet the words continue to moan from the pit of my stomach into my trembling hand.

My Schönche, ever since you were a little girl you served as a little mother to your siblings. You told them stories, sang them lullabies, got them dressed, fed them, bathed them, and ran a fine comb through their hair to keep away parasites. As they grew, you worried and cared for them as a mother would, wished them well, and stood beside them when they needed help. You were the first one to assist Papa in his study, were an exemplary wife to your husband, and a mother in body and soul to your sweet children.

You, who cared and watched and devoted yourself your entire life, how could you have hidden your illness from us, denying us the opportunity to care for you with the same level of dedication with which you cared for all of us? My soul wails. Where was I when you cried your pain in the dark? I would have wanted so badly to stand by your side, hold your hand, place a damp cloth on your forehead, collect your sighs and your coughs!

You succeeded in everything you did. Everything you touched turned into a pearl in your magical hands. And so even at the end of your days you managed to bottle the pain inside, never letting anyone know or touch.

Why, my child? You deserved loving care too. If only in the end of your life you would have given up your habits, allowed yourself to receive, and enjoyed the devotion of your loved ones.

We did everything together. You shared your secrets with me, my child. You have the right of the first child. Your coming into this world filled your father and me with joy. You were the first to make me feel that miraculous maternal emotion. I recollect days, waiting for Papa to return from the fair, laughing giddily as he showered us with love, tickling you until you got away from him, only to return and wait for him to tease you again. I remember you caressing the baby in my belly, your brother who never lived. And when your other siblings came into this world, one by one, they were lucky enough to receive anything they wanted from you, learning from you to admire the beauty of the world.

Oh, Lord, is it my fate to bury my children? Would it not be more fair for children to bury their parents, rather than the other way around?

Tuesday, November 20th, 1827

Darling Meir,

Yaakov and Betty came to visit me in our home, straight from Boulogne-sur-Seine, their new home in the heart of Paris, for a few hours of family comfort.

I'd like you to know, Meir, that there is no shortage of visitors in our home. Though our family has spread its wings to faraway points around the continent, we have remained united, mostly thanks to you.

Well, I enjoy frequent visits from our children and grandchildren, but when visitors arrive from afar, the taste is twice as sweet. This visit from my son and my granddaughter-turned- daughter-in-law was a precious gift. Better yet, I could breathe in the scent of my two new grandchildren, whom they have brought with them: Charlotte, who is two years old, clutching her doll and fixing me with big eyes seeking to be close to me; and baby Alphonse, crawling all over the house in search of its treasures, every item thoroughly tested by his nose and his mouth—clear signs of his belonging to the sniffing Rothschild family. The two little ones are cared for by the governess who has joined the family on their trip.

During their three days in Frankfurt they stayed in Amschel's castle. He allocated an entire wing to them. Our home, which used to house a pair of parents and ten children, and sometimes even a son- or daughter-in-law and a couple of grandchildren, now seems too small to contain a family of four, along with their governess and their porter. How the needs have changed!

The picture of Yaakov and Betty's life came into relief through our conversations.

My Betty is a woman of valor and a lady in mind, body, and soul. In spite of her young age, she has adapted well to the burden of running the large, respectable home Yaakov had purchased in Boulogne-sur-Seine as if she had been groomed for it. The biggest part of the job is hosting, which she does in an exemplary manner, enchanting her guests both with the Viennese manners she had acquired in her childhood home, and in the way she treats luxuries as obvious possessions.

Unlike Yaakov, who handles his guests clumsily, my Betty treats them with ease. Her father Shlomo and her mother Caroline gave her a well-rounded education. Her French is fluent and devoid of a foreign accent. Her fingers are experts at embroidery and painting, and slip smoothly over the keys of a piano. Through accompanying her parents on their many trips, and through her habit of reading, Betty has acquired varied knowledge, and is able to converse with her guests about philosophy, art, nature, even politics. There is no dull moment when one is in her presence.

Well then, Yaakov's Betty, just like Nathan's Hannah, fulfills the dictates of nobility, enjoying compliments on her hosting habits. But even she, like Hannah, is unable to camouflage her husband's Judengasse ways. Though Nathan is rougher than Yaakov, our youngest son follows in his brother's footsteps in his lack of refinement. This causes him some difficulty in fitting into a society founded—according to my family's stories—on indulgence and criticism.

Yaakov is not to blame. A shoot from a tree that is planted along other trees will clearly grow a tree identical to the original stump, not a tree that matches the ones around it. Yaakov's Judengasse trunk contains none of the etiquette expected in aristocratic Parisian society. Now, as a wealthy man of influence, he is expected to act as they do. But why should he know their art and literature? How is he supposed to appreciate artifacts or oil paintings? Does this make him deserving of the mocking looks of high society? I would like to know how a society is measured, if not through decent treatment of one another, including those who are different than they. Is there a rule that says everyone ought to be the same? If there is, why would God make us so different from one another? And I, I wish for my son to be as he is, not to try and be what he is not. Attempting to resemble others is destined to end with a chuckle.

Why does the crow dance? One day, the crow saw a pigeon walking more beautifully than any other bird. He liked the way the pigeon walked, and thought, "I will walk like her." He broke his bones walking, and the other birds mocked him. The crow grew ashamed and said, "I shall return to my original walk." He tried to, but couldn't. He had forgotten his original walk—he could not walk as he did at first, or as he did later—and so he began to dance.

I tried to gauge Yaakov's views on this infuriating matter. Yaakov, my healthy, wise son, shook off my anger.

"As a Rothschild, I am skilled in acts of survival," he said. Then he clarified: "It is true that I know nothing of artifacts or oil paintings. But I know one thing infinitely more important: I know people. I sift through them to pick the ones worthy in my eyes, and I bring those closer to me. That way, I live in peace and comfort with myself and my surroundings. I let people with know-how and experience handle matters of vanity, each according to his own expertise. The architect designs my home and my office, taking care to buy gilded furniture and fine decorations. I make sure he orders works from the greatest painters to hang on the walls of my home. Carême, the famous chef, who worked for the English crown prince and the Russian czar, supervises my kitchen and the foods and drinks served to guests with tender palates. The stable workers tend to the elegant carriage on which my name is printed in golden letters, and to the four spotless horses. And let us not forget the most important thing of all: my wife, bless her soul, is in charge of making an impression when it comes to art—literature, music, painting, and the rest."

"Very impressive, son. Please, tell me, who are the guests visiting your castle?"

"About thirty people attend lunch, and twice as many come to dinner. The guests around the table are usually politicians, diplomats, royalty, nobility, and top-tier artists."

"And my Betty is in charge of them all?" I cried.

"*My* Betty is in charge of them all," he corrected, and we both burst out laughing.

"I see she plays a pivotal role in your business."

"Certainly, Mama. I don't know what I'd do without her."

"So what do you think about married life now?"

"You were right, Mama. It's real life: a woman like Betty at my side and wonderful children scampering around. But I don't regret waiting longer than you had hoped. There is a time for every season. I had to go through the whole process in order to want a change. Besides, if I'd married another woman, who knows if I would have been as happy as I am now, with Betty. I suppose I would have had to wait anyway, for Betty to reach marriageable age."

"I respectfully concede. Especially in light of the fact that you love her."

"I did not know what love was before I had the privilege of experiencing Betty's love."

"Well said, son."

Indeed, this marriage of my granddaughter and her uncle appears perfect. This precedent should be adopted in the family: familial and business cohesiveness.

You, Meir, would surely have agreed with me.

Sunday, October 5th, 1828

I do not need any help.

I do not need servants. Why can't my family understand that?

Why do I not have the freedom to wander through my own house without some *piltzil*, some housekeeper, blocking my path, bowing constantly, offering me all sorts of frivolities, like placing my shoes at my feet. For heaven's sake, can I not put on my own shoes?

Or making tea, for instance. I can make tea for myself and a hundred guests, if they should visit. I do not need her cup.

Nor do I need a servant to announce the arrival of a neighbor. Do I not have eyes to see that my neighbor, old Schiff, has come to visit? Do I really need her standing there like a porcelain doll, announcing him?

I can still prepare my own meals, bake my own *kugelhopf*, serve myself, sweep the floor, dust the furniture. I have excelled in these tasks my entire life. Why should someone come by to take them away from me? I am able to perform any task in spite of my advanced age of seventy-five.

"Leave me alone. Let me live out my life as I wish. Who invented this nonsense of 'servants'? I do not want them. I have no room for them." I repeated this to my children and grandchildren, who seem to mean well. I spoke clearly, and was undeterred by their baffled looks. "You've all gone mad, throwing away money as if it has come from the sky." Then I added, "My old age might wrinkle my skin, but boredom would wrinkle my soul." And also: "If I sit idly by while others work around me, I would die sooner rather than later, and I have no such intention."

In general, this new lifestyle adopted by our sons doesn't please me one bit. I am often invited to big dinner parties and have turned down the invitations. I have only slipped once, accepting the invite because the phrasing of it was so sweet. That same time, I regretted my choice. These dinner parties are so dull. The conversation is boring and exhausting. The women seem to be coming for one single purpose: to show off their party dresses. The only diversion I allowed myself during those dead hours was a careful observation of the silent competition between the women, and the mutual shots taken by one woman against another. I remember you, dear Meir. You would not have noticed. You were never an expert when it came to women.

But this kind of amusement is short-lived. I therefore have never accepted another invitation for this kind of questionable experience, and that is the end of it.

And as for servants, I had sent them away, one by one, until everybody finally got the message.

And what has this earned me? More frequent visits from my family. I am surrounded with love. That is what I need—love, not help.

Perhaps what they wanted was to be rid of me on the one hand, and on the other hand to assuage their consciences by ensuring I would be surrounded by people who would care for my needs.

But I need no strangers around me. At my age, all I need is the warmth of the Rothschild family.

Tuesday, December 1st, 1835

Amschel and Eva, who remain childless, live in their lifeless castle, working for the sake of the family and the community. Amschel has transferred our Frankfurt bank to Bergheimer Strasse, and is running the offices in the best possible manner. His noble title adorns him like a cloak of pride, and he wears it all around, forgetting to remove it when he is with family. I am not oblivious to his nephews' attitude toward him. On the one hand, they appreciate his honest concern for them and the gifts he showers them with, and on the other hand, they do not enjoy his uncompromising involvement in their affairs. They are put off by his stern attitude regarding religion and his frowning upon anyone diverging from his opinions and instructions, and they improvise ways of cutting short their time with him.

I am proud of our granddaughter Betty. She is worthy of our shared pride. On the one hand, according to the rules and dictates of Parisian high society, she is filling her role as a salon matron flawlessly. On the other hand, she devotes many hours to humanitarian work, as becomes a Rothschild offspring.

On the third hand, which I should have started with, in spite of all this, she never ceases to surprise me with her attitude toward the most important role God has given us women: the role of devoted mother. Now that their son Solomon is born, I see once again how maternal our granddaughter is. She is still young, thirty years old, and will most likely carry more Rothschild offspring.

Betty and Yaakov were the first in our dynasty to marry within the family. Following suit, other Rothschild brides and grooms are now marrying each other. And you, Meir, must be watching from above, rubbing your hands with satisfaction.

The second interfamily marriage has also occurred within Shlomo's family. Betty was first, and the second is her brother, Anselm. Our talented grandchild, marvelously reminiscent of his father, and like him a man of peace and kindness, is a working man dividing his time between Frankfurt and Vienna.

Well, he has married his cousin Charlotte, Nathan's eldest. This was nine years ago. They came to see me in their wedding best, letting me take pleasure in the beauty of our granddaughter, her curly hair and what is hidden beneath it—a wise mind, charged with knowledge and enveloped in an extraordinary musical sensitivity.

And soon to arrive is the latest interfamily match: groom Lionel—Nathan's son—and (seventeen-year-old) bride Charlotte—Kalman's daughter. I look at these cousins, these dear grandchildren, and my heart sings.

Sunday, July 31st, 1836

I am grieving.

Our Nathan is gone. He was fifty-nine when he died. Is this punishment from God—grieving for my children?

I should have gone in your place, my brilliant, brave, powerful, groundbreaking son, his father's clear successor.

The cemetery inside of me cannot contain this new death. He should have stayed alive. My tears stain the page. I shall let them flow. Oh my.

Darling Meir, I must tell you how Nathan died. I wonder if it was my fault. I am so tortured about it. You can be the judge.

As you know, I demand that all marrying couples in our family stop by to receive my blessing. Amschel has adopted the same rule, and—as is his manner—he was more stringent, demanding that all Rothschild weddings be held in Frankfurt.

And so we were in for a more opulent wedding than we have ever seen. Our Londoner Lionel, Nathan's eldest son, has married his cousin,

Charlotte of Naples, Kalman's seventeen-year-old daughter. Another pure Rothschild match. Distance makes the heart grow fonder.

Meir, I am so sorry you could not have been here. Our five sons, scattered in five European capitals, all came together for this celebration. Elegant Rothschild carriages, resembling mobile palaces, filled with family and friends, dowry and gifts, decorated with glittering gold, took over Frankfurt: Nathan and his London entourage, Kalman and his Naples entourage, Yaakov and his Paris entourage, Shlomo and his Vienna entourage, and of course the entire Frankfurt branch of the family, led by Amschel and myself. I left my house on Judengasse and traveled into our great city (and Frankfurt is impressive, without a doubt).

When the carriages arrived and parked along the street, a large, uninvited audience was there, staring, astounded, at the moving palaces that had popped up. You would think that all of Europe dropped everything it was doing to pay mind to one thing and one thing only: the wedding of Lionel and Charlotte Rothschild. The Frankfurt hotels were filled with our dynasty and with the distinguished guests that traveled in from all over the continent.

The bride and groom, the most beautiful on the planet, stood there in their wedding best, greeting the people gathering around the chuppah with lovely smiles. Amschel and I enjoyed the royal honor of standing on the podium, me at the end of the women's row, and Amschel at the end of the men's. The rabbi said the blessings and the audience answered, "Amen."

My eyes ran over the audience filling the hall. Many of them were our offspring, shoots of the Rothschild House, but many others were unfamiliar faces—friends from finance, politics, and art—who all treated our sons as if they were the kings of Europe.

To my left was the mother of the groom, dear Hannah, with whom the years had agreed, adding even more grace to her appearance. I recalled Yaakov's childish love for Hannah. I thought, *She must have broken several more hearts, Nathan's beauty*. Beside her was the mother of the bride, the refined Adelheid, Kalman's wife, and next to her my princess, Charlotte, a white wedding gown revealing her pearly white shoulders, her sleeves puffy and her waist cinched. I squeezed Hannah's hand, transferring some of the heat waves inside of me. Hannah squeezed back and whispered, "May God be at our side."

I leaned over to glance at the groom's face. It was beaming. Ever since his arrival, Lionel had enjoyed praise for the way in which he had blended into the business as his father's successor in the enormous Rothschild firm in London. Before the wedding, Lionel used his trip to Frankfurt to stop in Belgium and the Rhine cities with his good friend, gifted composer Gioachino Rossini. He told me the two of them had met when Rossini visited London, during which time he came to their home often to teach his sister Charlotte to play the pipe organ. "Papa bought her a pipe organ made entirely out of gold," my grandson told me, describing my son's odd life in London.

My eyes were drawn to Nathan. The heart rejoiced for Lionel and the eyes cried for Nathan. Our stubborn son insisted on traveling here for the wedding in spite of his weak health. On his way from England, Nathan already began suffering intense pain. When he arrived in Frankfurt one of the best doctors in Germany was summoned. He determined Nathan was suffering from an abscess and ordered him to rest. "You mustn't attend your son's wedding," the doctor emphasized.

Nathan chuckled. "Nothing can cause me to spoil my son's joy."

"You are putting your life at risk," the doctor tried again, surprised by his patient's determination, though he already knew Nathan was the stubborn one in our family.

Oh dear, I thought. *Why does my son have to be sick, and why did God choose such unfortunate timing?*

I tried to persuade him. "Nathan, you would be spoiling Lionel's joy by worsening your condition. Listen to the doctor."

"Mama, do not worry. Nothing can bring me down," he answered decisively, punctuating his words with a burst of laughter.

But he did not put my mind at ease, neither with his determination nor with his contrived cheerfulness.

Oh dear, my mind continued to torture me. *I am finally seeing him after so many years apart, and I cannot bear to watch his pain, it reminds me so much of yours, darling Meir.*

Nathan put on a show of robustness under the chuppah, but I could not ignore his efforts. *He does everything well,* I thought. *He can successfully take on the most influential people in the world, but is now failing to pretend.* He faked the appearance of painlessness, but behind his mask was the truth: he was utterly exhausted.

While the rabbi spoke the seven blessings, I turned to God to say a prayer for the health of the father marrying off his son.

The blessings were over, and so was my prayer.

But it did not help. Nathan's fever continued to rise. After the ceremony he swayed over to the nearest chair and plopped down, with the help of Hannah, who shifted her eyes between him and the event we had gathered to celebrate. Lionel pushed his way out of the surrounding crowd, approached Nathan, and touched his forehead. "Papa, we must call a doctor," the newlywed said, afraid.

"Forget it, Lionel, it's just the wine. I had too much to drink. Go dance, have fun. This is a happy day."

He pushed Lionel away, and the groom, who was once more becoming surrounded by embracing well-wishers, put his father out of his mind.

But I did not. "Amschel, take him to my house and call the doctor," I instructed. And to Hannah I said she should stay to fill the role of both host and hostess. Hannah's eyes glazed over, and I put my arms around her and whispered, "Get yourself together, dear, for Lionel's sake."

Amschel obeyed my order and whispered with his nephews, who surrounded Nathan and me, clearing a path to the door, and so we were able to leave the hall straight onto the carriage.

Along the way, Nathan seemed to be delirious. My hands were occupied changing the cold compresses I was given to cool down his burning forehead.

We arrived at home. Nathan was laid down on the bed, away from us, lost in his dreams. The doctor arrived shortly thereafter and decided on immediate surgery.

Nathan was operated on. The abscess was in his rectum, and the surgery did not improve his overall health.

Our grandson Anthony, who looked so much like his brother, Lionel, sent a messenger to summon Nathan's personal doctor, and we waited for him to arrive from England.

The fallen face of the British physician, Dr. Benjamin Travers, told us that the worst had happened. "The infection has invaded his bloodstream," the doctor explained, and I realized my world had ended.

I cannot fathom where Nathan got his strength from, though I have seen such precedence in our home before. I have no doubt it is too much work that felled him. If he had taken some time off, he would have taken care of himself before disease took over completely.

In the next few days, between delirium and awakening, Nathan gave Hannah and the children orders for the wording and delivery of letters.

Our home swarmed with people. Nathan was surrounded by his family's love. Hannah and the children never left his side. His mother also waited on him hand and foot, disrupting his work. The days wore on with the hopes that the infection in his blood would clear up. His heart was strong, and could withstand a war for his life.

Our powerful son fought for two weeks against the enemy within his own body. For two weeks he persisted and did not give up. Days of suffering and pain with no complaint. But when they ended, his sentence was cast. Our Nathan, strong as a rock, was gone. He parted from us with the words "Good night forever," and said no more.

I stood over him for a long time, opening and closing my eyes. "The place where you were born," I whispered, "is the same place where you have returned your soul to your maker, just like your father and your sisters. I am saying goodbye to you, but cherishing your being in my heart until my time comes to join you."

I wonder if I should accuse myself for my son's death. Had I not supported Amschel's insistence to hold the wedding in Frankfurt, Nathan could have received treatment from his London doctor in time.

Or perhaps this was our son's fate. If a man is destined to drown, he would drown even in a spoonful of water. Perhaps God has made His calculations, as He had with you, and concluded that this man alone did in a lifetime what normally takes many men to accomplish. And so He brought him closer to His side, leaving the rest of the work to his offspring.

I recall the memory of little Nathan, who, in the middle of a fight, told his older brother, Amschel, that just because Amschel was born first did not give him any special rights other than the right to die first. That grumpy, naive child did not know that not everything in life works according to logic and justice. Some are born later and die earlier.

Oh, my Nathan, how I'll miss you. How we'll all miss you. Behind your stubbornness and bluntness were tender human values. Your treatment of your siblings is forgiven when weighed against your love for them and your insistence on family unity. You never minced words or greeted people politely, but you donated generously to those less fortunate (who are as prevalent in London as they are in Frankfurt). Beneath your cold, hard exterior hid a modest Nathan. Though you have risen to greatness, become a mogul, and received many honors, you vehemently refused to be addressed as "baron" and never wore any decorations on your body. You abhorred these mannerisms of opulence.

Your exterior gruffness did not prevent policymakers from investing you with authority. You were not full of tact, and yet the Austrian Empire appointed you general consul of London.

Your simplicity always pleased me. You were never tempted to buy ornaments only because those of finer tastes approved of them. "I cannot waste my money on pictures," you said frankly, though your coffer was never empty.

You defended your privacy and never let strangers in. I loved the answer you gave anyone who asked why you had moved to London: "There was no room for all of us in Frankfurt." I liked your joking little lies.

Son, you had the power, courage, and determination to stick to your beliefs and maintain your family's honor. You were even able to stand against the Bank of England. I recall Amschel's story about the check he gave you. You taught that big bank a big lesson: the Rothschild family is not to be belittled.

Our son was buried in London. His city received the bitter news with shock. His coffin was carried over the Thames in a steamship. From there, it was transferred to his office palace in New Court, in order to allow his many admirers to pay their respects. A large crowd of people dressed in black participated in the funeral procession that dragged from the Ashkenazi synagogue at Duke's Place to the cemetery. Amschel said no English citizen had ever received such a large and dignified funeral as Nathan. Amschel, Shlomo, Kalman, Yaakov, and Nathan's sons—Lionel, Anthony, and Nathaniel—followed the coffin. Among the other participants were the mayor of London, city council members, nobles, ambassadors of Austria, Prussia, Naples, and Russia, and other dignitaries, along with a massive crowd.

There was one group among the participants that stole my heart: a group of Jewish orphans who had been supported by Nathan walked in the front of the procession, reading Psalms. Nathan had done so much in his life for poorer people, but never discussed it. Just like his father, he gave charitably in secret.

Darling Meir, our Nathan has followed in your footsteps. His will instructs his sons to become partners in the firm, obligating them to preserve unity. The boys are his only inheritors. And yet he has made sure, in his lifetime, to bequeath his daughters with large sums of money—100,000 pounds each. Like you, he did not mention the sum of the fortune he left behind.

Did you know that Nathan was also involved in education, donating to the foundation of a Jewish school? Amschel went to see it and returned with moist eyes, carrying me away with him. Our Nathan helped start the Jews' Free School, following which, similar seminaries were started all over London and its suburbs.

But unlike you, Nathan eventually adhered to the dictates of the higher class. Amschel had a chance to visit the mansion Nathan had purchased a year ago. Gunnersbury Park, according to Amschel, is a spacious mansion laden with lakes, swans, streams, lawns, flowers, bushes, gazebos, and benches, all surrounding a large, glorious house. Unfortunately, Nathan had little chance to enjoy it. He left this pleasure to our Londoner grandchildren.

Indeed, Lionel told Amschel as they strolled along the garden, "It is a fine location for a ball." Well then, Nathan is now with you and Julie and Schönche in heaven, while his children throw garden parties here on earth.

◆ ◆ ◆

I do not visit our son's grave. I must remain loyal to my decision not to leave Frankfurt, because that is the only way I can protect our heritage. It is hard to think of not seeing his grave, but I will not break my promise for any amount of pain in the world. God made sure I had a chance to say goodbye to my son when he was here, with me. And now, rather than physical distance, I feel an emotional intimacy that will accompany me for as long as I live.

I have the address, written in English in the handwriting of Lionel, my fatherless grandson, along with a Judendeutsch translation in Amschel's handwriting: *Ashkenazi cemetery, Whitechapel, London.*

Your roots, my son, have deepened in London, and that is where you are buried.

Monday, January 11th, 1841

Do not go about spreading slander among your people. All of Israel are responsible for one another.

Those are two important mitzvahs, one from the Bible, the other from our sages.

Our son Yaakov, in Paris, and our grandson Lionel, in England, in cooperation with kind and loyal Jews from all over Europe, have worked tirelessly to do all that was in their power to redeem their poor brothers in Damascus from torture they did not deserve. In doing so, they lived up to these two mitzvahs, determined by our holy Torah and our great sages.

In my heart, alongside the pain, sorrow, and fury over what occurred to our innocent Jewish brothers, is contentment with the deeds of our sons and grandsons in their efforts to alleviate the people's harsh fates.

It is a blood libel, one that rolled and grew and evolved, that has plucked so many of our people in Damascus.

The evil and false libel, entwined throughout a long and malicious history, according to which Jews use the blood of Christian children for the baking of matzo on Passover, has broken free from the boundaries of Europe and arrived at a Muslim country. In spite of the challenge of putting into words the lowly account that makes my blood boil, I will describe what happened.

It all began on Sunday, February 5th, 1840. A French monk and his Muslim servant vanished from the alleys of Damascus. A rumor spread that the two had last been seen in the Jewish quarter, and the Christians claimed that the two had been slaughtered by Jews, so that their blood could be used for matzo in the nearing celebration of Passover. Count Ratti-Menton, the French consul at Damascus, on behalf of the Christians, turned to governor Sherif Pasha, and demanded that he investigate the affair until the guilty parties were detained and punished. The count was also an active participant in the investigation in his own special way, which included bribing witnesses and cross-examining suspects with the use of violence.

A Jewish barber was the first in a series of wheels that descended down the slippery slope. The barber was arrested due to a rumor that the two missing people had been seen near his shop. In his interrogation at the French consulate and the governor's office, he insisted that he had not seen or heard either of them. After intense torture, the interrogators managed to glean a false confession from him, according to which seven Jews, community elders, had butchered the monk and his servant.

The wheel had rolled onto the doorsteps of the seven surprised Jewish dignitaries. When they were brought in for questioning, they denied the allegations, swearing they had nothing to do with the monk. Their denial made the interrogators angrier, and the seven were harshly tortured. Two of them could not withstand the torment, returning their souls to their maker, while the others were forced to admit to the false allegations. The malicious interrogators even managed to get one of them, Moshe Abulafia, to confess that he kept the bottle containing the monk's blood in his home.

The impassioned interrogators went to the home of Abulafia's wife and demanded that she hand over the bottle of blood. The poor woman was unable to provide them with something that didn't exist.

She received what Ratti-Menton saw as fitting punishment: he beat her to a pulp and dragged her to the prison, where she was forced to watch her husband lashed two hundred times. Moshe Abulafia fought to bear the pain, and fought even harder to bear the fact that his wife was watching. In his weakness, he rolled the libel onto the chief rabbi of Damascus. "I gave him the bottle," he blurted, exhausted, and asked to convert to Islam and put an end to his suffering.

The investigators went to see the chief rabbi and took him away along with two worshipping Jews who were with him. They exerted their rage onto the three, beating them until their skin separated from their bodies.

If that wasn't enough, Moshe Abulafia, who had already converted and wished to impress his new community, created a series of alleged proofs from the Talmud of the decree of using Christian blood in baking matzo.

Around the same time, some bones were found in the gutters and determined to be human bones. It was decided they must be the monk's. The bones were interred in an impressive funeral, and the tombstone stated it was the burial place of the bones of Father Thomas, who had been murdered by Jews.

But, dear God, the wheels did not stop turning there. After the burial, with tensions high, the spree of arrests was renewed. Among those detained were dozens of miserable children, bound in chains and starved in order to divulge from their poor little mouths the location of the bottle of blood.

The French consul danced on the blood of the victims, so to speak. He delivered his own angle to the European press—a twisted angle, it must be said. And though his story was anchored in lies, his words gave the misleading impression that he was dealing in actual facts. People do not tend to dig deeper and ascertain the truthfulness of rumors. Instead, they accept them as pure truth. Thus the evil rumor was heard by the

Jews of the world, including my Yaakov, the Parisian navigator. The shock was great, and at the same time the Jews were too helpless to help.

Who knows how much farther this would have gone if not for the case of the Austrian citizen?

Among those detained was a Jew named Isaac Picciotto. As he was an Austrian citizen, his family wrote to the Austrian consul in Damascus for help. The Austrian consul got Picciotto out of jail, and in return Picciotto extended his gratitude, along with a list of the atrocities taking place within the confines of the jailhouse. Upon reading these, the consul was touched by God, and realized he must perform a thorough investigation of the matter.

The Austrian consul—may God bless him and keep him safe—went through the acceptable channels and transferred Picciotto's list to the general consul of Austria, in Alexandria. The list worked its magic, and the general consul, bless his soul, demanded that Muhammad Ali of Egypt put an immediate end to the torture and hold a proper trial. Muhammad Ali agreed to the first demand, and upon his order the tormentors ceased their work, but not before they caused the death of four more Jews.

The kind Austrian consul did not stop there. He realized there was an urgent need to take care of Ratti-Menton, who had foolishly declared he condoned the actions taken to stop the Jews. This time the Austrian consul decided to take matters further, and rather than turning to the Viennese government, he turned directly to the Austrian consul in Paris, James Rothschild, who carried the title of "baron" given by the Austrian emperor on the one hand, and served as financial advisor to Louis Philippe, king of France, on the other. What's more, his wife, Betty, was close friends with Maria Amalia, the French queen.

From the moment our Yaakov-James entered the fray, he made this affair his top priority, and his Lafayette office became the center of activity for the redemption of our brothers in Damascus. Yaakov first turned to the French prime minister and the French minister of foreign affairs and requested that they become involved. Maddeningly, this request was denied. Yaakov did not give up, and, after consulting with Shlomo-Solomon in Vienna, decided to leak the story to the news, including the information in Picciotto's list.

The first result was an article about the blood libel in a Parisian newspaper, written by poet Heinrich Heine, the converted Jew who had moved from Germany to Paris. God bless him and forgive his weakness in converting.

Just as they would share their financial undertakings with each other, our family members collaborated in this humanistic matter of utmost importance. Our British grandchildren, led by Lionel, the late Nathan's son, reached out their long arm to place Moshe Montefiore— famous for his relationship with the heads of the British government— in the lead. Montefiore spoke to the British minister of foreign affairs, who sent an order to the British consul in Alexandria, according to which he must demand that Muhammad Ali hold a trial at once, punish the responsible parties, and compensate the families of those Jews who had been hurt.

Things also progressed hopefully on the French side. Heinrich Heine published another article, in which he revealed facts that blemished Count Ratti-Menton's reputation.

While our British Rothschilds were putting Montefiore into action, the French representative of our family turned to Adolphe Crémieux, the man who was working tirelessly for the sake of fugitives. At his request, Crémieux headed to the center of activity in England.

Thus formed a delegation of Jews from France and England, led by Moshe Montefiore. Financially backed by the Rothschilds, the delegation headed to Alexandria to meet and confer with Muhammad Ali and bring about the necessary solution.

After a battle of greats, our delegation came out on top. The accused parties were acquitted with the approval and signature of Pasha Muhammad Ali.

In late summer, the prisoners were released, physically and emotionally wounded, mourning their relatives and friends who were not lucky enough to survive, but—I assume—with a dull light flickering in their eyes, directing them toward the new reality of being recognized as innocent.

But Montefiore was not successful on all counts. He did his best to persuade the Turkish sultan to issue a royal letter clearing the Jews of all blame for ritual murders, and hoped the pope would agree to erase the words from the monk's tombstone that accuse the Jews of his murder, but the two turned him down.

Who knows, perhaps the future will succeed where these two great men failed.

And I am both grieving and encouraged. I lament the travails of my miserable people, living in exile, forced to prove their innocence of crimes they themselves abhor and that their holy Torah condemns. But I am encouraged by certain occasions, like the one at hand, in which justice was served. I think, darling Meir, about our family, who for the first time became involved in international affairs that had nothing to do with financial profit.

Thursday, August 18th, 1842

A surprise visit from our large family has brought new light into my already charmed life.

The gorgeous Charlotte, Yaakov and Betty's eldest, came to the house in her bridal gown, along with her handsome groom, Nathaniel, son of Nathan, may his memory be a blessing. Behind them followed a cheerful Rothschild entourage, and our small home trembled with contagious joy.

I looked over the faces of our grandchildren, the bride and groom, carrying on the tradition of united family unions, and thanked the good Lord for His blessings.

In the middle of this joy, my eyes were drawn to Abraham Binyamin Edmund James de Rothschild, Betty and Yaakov's youngest child. I fixed my eyes on his, unable to look away. What was it in his gaze that penetrated my heart? Something familiar that drew me in.

Suddenly, it became clear. This baby, only two years of age, was watching the horizon with mature eyes. It was the same gaze of his grandfather, my Meir. God! Meir-Edmund's eyes were staring into the horizon. What were they searching for?

Your grandchild will go on to do great things. That is my guess, judging by his eyes. But unlike you, Meir, I mustn't expect this baby to open his mouth and verbalize his thoughts just yet.

Where is this old soul in a baby's body headed?

Tuesday, September 10th, 1844

My family tells me I have grown grumpy. What they mean to say is, I do not treat my enemies amiably.

And why should I have to pretend? Would I be stoned for my frankness? I am an old woman, ninety-one years of age. I am allowed to behave as I please. My eyes, thank the Lord, continue to do their work on this earth properly.

What is this all about, you must be wondering, darling Meir. I shall explain why Amschel is cross with me this time. Well, I've had an unexpected and unwanted visit. It is a man whose name I do not wish to tarnish my notebook with, but I have no choice. Karl Marx. There, I've put his name in writing. I shall not do it again.

He appeared at my doorstep, removed his hat, and bowed deeply.

My anger burned. How dare he show his face at my door, after all the nonsense he writes in his articles, about the Jewish people in general, and the Rothschild family in particular? That scoundrel behaves so brashly, as if, being Lutheran, he believes he can enter any home he sees fit. But if his father, a Jewish rabbi, decided to convert to Christianity, his family no longer has any right to set foot in our Jewish home. Am I wrong?

He looked at me. He was young enough to be my grandson, but, unlike him, my grandsons will never be sinners. I turned my eyes toward the ceiling, taking the opportunity to ask God why He has sent me this heretic.

The servant, whom I had finally consented to accept under my roof, having sent away all the previous servants my sons had hired, stood beside him helplessly, awaiting my tirade.

"Does the venerable Madam Gutle Rothschild know who I am?" he began, choosing words that sounded arrogant to me, in spite of his use of the third person.

"And so what if I do?" I answered his question with a question, looking at him coolly.

"And so, please, allow me to come in."

"What is the purpose of your visit?" I asked, keeping him in the doorway, hoping he would turn to leave.

"I must speak to the venerable Madam Gutle Rothschild."

"What for? Do you have new ways of maligning us? Your pen drips with malice. Have you come here to complete your mission in person?"

He laughed as if I had just told a joke, and his laughter only exacerbated my fury. I quickly added, "If that is the case, I must tell you, you have done your job perfectly, to the satisfaction of all anti-Semites. Conserve your energy and refrain from all further efforts."

"Au contraire, madam. I come in peace. If she would only be so kind as to allow me to enter, I would be pleased to explain that I have come here wishing to acquire what I am unable to find anywhere else." As he said this, he entered uninvited.

I lost my temper. "Spare me your ingratiation. It does not impress me. I am used to visits from people of our faith, and yet you and your father have turned your backs on the decrees of the Lord, and so your footsteps sully my home."

He sat down on the sofa and lifted his feet off the rug. "There, I will not rest my feet on her flawless floor. Her home is pure because Madam

Rothschild is pure. She does not deal with money, money, money. Her children, I presume, have already offered her a place to live in one of their castles, but must have been turned down. Madam is not like them. She does not measure the world in silver and gold and the number of bedrooms. Madam is a woman of values."

"I am proud of my children and their accomplishments," I blurted. "How dare you criticize them so publicly? Why won't you let them be? They have acquired their financial standing with hard work! You cannot accuse them of being parasites!"

He responded quietly. "I have made it my goal to change the world, to make it better, a creative and productive world in which man can live up to the full potential of his humanity. And the endeavor madam's family has chosen is abusive in essence. This is the core of my criticism."

My blood boiled. "My children have morals and values founded in the holy Torah of Sinai," I cried. "It is a fact that none of them has abandoned Judaism in favor of financial advancement. They are not like your father, who turned his back on his heritage and pushed aside our Torah in favor of his profession. Your father chose the easy way out, and now his son is attacking us as if we were immoral and erroneous."

It seemed my anger did not deter him. On the contrary, he was enjoying it. The converted Jew did not fight me. Instead, he fixed his eyes on me.

I took pity on him. "You can put your feet down."

He nodded gratefully, placed his feet gently on the rug, and spoke calmly. "Reality forced him into that situation, so that he could work as an attorney. He had to feed his family."

"I know that. But he would have done better to fight against discrimination rather than give in to it."

He shook his head. "The problem, Madam Gutle, is that society is still prisoner to what I have defined in my writing as a kind of false consciousness. This society, plagued by estrangement, is not free enough to grant us full, equal rights, because it is not yet liberated itself. Until that day, some people make compromises. Such was my father's choice."

I must admit, I was touched by his defense of his father, which was almost as fervent as my defense of my sons. I think my face must have softened a bit. "But it is the basic right of any person, even a Jew, to be free. They must choose the professions they see fit, live where they wish, and walk freely," I insisted, my heart beating at the same time with my reservations regarding my children's ostentatious lifestyle.

"Until reality is transformed from its very core, I do my part by writing my articles in the newspapers." He spoke so quietly that I had to bring my head closer. "Madam is used to seeing only the beauty in her children, is she not?"

"I do not know what you mean. I am not blind. I know that physical beauty is not one of the virtues of my family. But this shortcoming is compensated for by a different kind of beauty, far superior to the exterior, and for that I thank the Lord. My sons love people, contribute to society, do charitable work, and giving in secret is an inseparable part of their lives."

"The manner in which madam defends her sons is admirable. Not in vain did I call her a pure woman. Her line of thinking is clean. The simplicity of her lifestyle attests to a purity of morals. She has all the money in the world to allow her a life of comfort and ease, but she has chosen instead to continue living as she always had. Show me another person who would choose to behave as she does."

"Just because I live in a small, old house, does not mean I do not live in comfort and ease. My home is fully equipped with amenities, and I require nothing more. What would one more room give me? More work, that's all."

"She could have given the work to a team of servants who would be happy to be at her service in exchange for such dreamy conditions."

"Servants? You too? What do I need servants for? If my daily chores are taken away, what would I fill my days with? Idleness?"

"She could avoid tiring housework, and still not live idly. There are suitable alternatives to work, such as cultural gatherings. Has it never occurred to her to attend a salon, listen to music and poetry, and rub shoulders with high society?"

"You are not speaking sincerely," I said with anger, though, I should point out, it was not nearly as intense as it had been just moments earlier.

"I do not mean today, of course, I mean when she was younger."

"Those kinds of gatherings are the ill of society. They do not truly exist for the alleged purpose for which men and women claim to gather in elegant parlors. Their outcomes ought to be examined."

"What does she mean?"

"You would be better able to tell me. A man like you, who attends the most exclusive salons in Paris, knows what I am getting at. Why don't you tell me about it?"

He cleared his throat and seemed unsure, but I stared at him pleadingly. "Madam must be referring to romantic encounters."

"That is a delicate way of putting it, but yes, you have understood my intention. What do you think of the exhibition of elegant dresses?"

"What's wrong with them? There's nothing like beauty to heal the soul."

"Then you, like all men, do not understand. Those self-righteous women, supporters of literature and art, all they care about beneath their cultural exterior is the desire to win the contest: who has the prettiest dress, the priciest jewelry, the best makeup. Their interest in the book or the piece of music or the work of art is a negligible afterthought."

"And so what about it?"

"God help us. I can't stand that artificial look. Hypocrisy makes my stomach turn. And I'm not a fan of modern fashion, either. Ladies' dresses these days are sleeveless, and on cold evenings they merely wrap transparent silk shawls around their shoulders. They sacrifice themselves on the altar of vanity."

"Then would the madam please tell me what she *does* like to do."

"I like to live real life, to let my hands play their role in this world. To pray daily for the well-being of my children, grandchildren, and great-grandchildren, may they live a long and healthy life. To feel satisfied with their achievements. To see the faces of the younger generation of my family, to drink up their joy of life and look through their eyes at the wondrous world God has made for us. To pick up the good book, dive deep into it, and discover each time—"

I paused. My eyes fell upon *Brent Spiegel* and *A Good Heart*. My two books, my close friends. They seemed to be warning me, and suddenly I felt tricked. How did I allow him to turn my head? We were conversing like old friends. Am I to forget his attacks on my family? Certainly not. I would not allow him to leave with the upper hand.

He was watching me, expecting my outpour to continue, but he seemed to also be noticing the change in me. "It seems I have taken up enough of her time for today. I must now say farewell." He stood up, grabbing the brim of his hat. I got up too and stood before him. "I would like to thank the madam kindly for these special moments. In this material world screaming all around me, I felt the need for a few moments of relative sanity. I shall return to Paris now. I am only in Frankfurt for a short visit, and I decided to stop by at her home and fulfill my need to experience a real, simple, true life. I am glad I decided to do so."

"And will you continue to tyrannize us with your pen?" I asked reproachfully.

"I wish Madam Rothschild wasn't so angry, and I wish she didn't attribute powers to me that I do not have. I am no tyrant and therefore cannot tyrannize anyone."

"The power of the written word, making waves, reaching many eyes, is greater than the power of any tyrant on earth. You are sprinkling salty words onto bloody wounds."

"It is my duty to present reality as I see it. Madam abhors hypocrisy. I cannot be a hypocrite, presenting an image I do not see as true."

"Since your eyes are clearly misleading you, you could simply avoid presenting the image without committing the crime of hypocrisy. Why must you write '*What is the secular basis of Judaism? Practical need, self-interest. What is the worldly religion of the Jew? Huckstering. What is his worldly God? Money.*' Are we so short of enemies that you felt the need to join in? Why can't you simply abstain?"

"I appreciate Madam Gutle Rothschild's perspective. I hope she does not think me rude, but I must disagree. Just as the madam lives according to her conscience, I too have a conscience pointing the way, and it demands that I warn my readers against certain situations, and mostly about the ills of society, all in order to benefit social justice. I am not among the haters of the Jews, but it is a plain fact that Jews worship money and petty trade. But it is not their fault. Reality is what led them to this state. They were forbidden from pursuing other professions, forced to focus on commerce and banking, and the result is that Christianity fulfills society's spiritual needs, while the Jews fulfill its practical side."

"And what is so wrong with that? Someone must take on the practical side."

"I suggest we leave that question open until I visit again during my next trip to Frankfurt."

"I have no desire to meet again. The scathing words you delivered in this first and last encounter were quite enough."

"I had no intention of hurting her. I regret that she sees things this way, but I respect her stance and appreciate her honesty in speaking her true mind." He bowed at me and turned to leave.

Only then did I notice Amschel in the doorway. The guest bowed at my son, who walked him outside.

When he returned, Amschel shot me a severe look. I felt him battling against himself not to shout the words that were waiting to burst from his mouth. The ones he chose in their stead were restrained, but I noticed the tone that accompanied them, which he could not control.

"Mama, he's a guest. You used to offer your guests a warm welcome."

"He is an uninvited guest," I corrected.

"You have many uninvited guests here, and none of them ever receive such an infuriated welcome."

"Do not start. You know he deserves every condemnation. I treated him with refinement and restraint, much more than he deserved."

"*Mama-lieb*, I love you," he announced, then added in a whisper, "especially in your natural state, projecting warmth and joy." After this declaration came a request: "I only ask one thing. Do not let anger and grumpiness spoil your hospitality. You have the reputation of an amiable woman, and this is not the time to change that."

I am proud of my son, though I don't agree with him. How gently he shot his critical arrow at me, so gently that I accepted it as an arrow of love.

Have I really become grumpy?

Monday, December 23rd, 1844

My Meir, I do not know what has become of me.

All of a sudden, new visitors are dropping by, in this old age in which one no longer desires new social engagements.

Only three months after that scoundrel's surprise visit, I enjoyed the visit of another convert, poet Heinrich Heine. I write "enjoyed" since this visit made me feel pleasant, and imbued me with affection for the man.

In contradiction to the feelings elicited in me by the previous visitor, my heart is not offended by Heine's conversion. I remember well how hard he fought for our brothers in Damascus. Rather than resentment, I felt compassion for his state. He seemed full of regret for having been baptized, a step he took, like many others, in order to enter Christian society. But his new society did not see his baptism as reason enough to treat him as equal.

He arrived wearing a black jacket over a white shirt with a perfectly pressed collar. This was one evening during Hanukah, as I was standing near the windowsill on which the menorah was positioned. It was the same menorah you knew, made of beaten silver and etched with upright lions on both sides. It stayed with me. The shamash stands tall while the other arms stand in a straight line at the bottom. Each arm holds a small cup filled with oil and a linen wick. The menorah and its decorations smile at me confidently, projecting stability, while I, with my legs sketched with blue veins and painted with varicosities, return a meek smile. My body has weakened, and it has become difficult to stand by the menorah.

From the moment he was invited in, he took liberties in examining our home, lingering by the white curtains I had hung over the window in celebration of the festival of light, and asked to stand beside me as I lit the candles.

I lit the shamash and said the blessing, and Heine answered, "Amen." Then I lit the other arms, said another blessing, and Heine said "Amen" again and finally joined me in song.

"The mitzvah of lighting Hanukah candles is a lovely mitzvah, and one must do it carefully, announcing the miracle, adding a praise for God, and a thanks for the miracles He has done for us," he quoted.

I looked at him with wonder. What business did a converted Jew have saying things like that?

"That was a quote from Maimonides," he clarified quickly, walking me over to the armchair. I sank into the beloved chair, already imprinted with the shape of my body. "Isn't it a lovely statement?" he asked.

"Everything Maimonides says is lovely and wise, and it is our duty to learn his sayings and abide by them," I replied.

"Mama Rothschild is right. *The Guide for the Perplexed* is worthy of profound reading, in spite of being controversial." He pointed at the menorah. "House of Hillel."

I wrinkled my forehead quizzically.

He laughed. I liked his laugh. Along with his flowing golden hair, perfectly combed and parted in the middle, covering his ears. "The House of Hillel and the House of Shamai had a dispute regarding the number of candles," he explained. "The House of Hillel argued that one must 'add in holiness rather than subtract,' meaning that one must add a candle for each day of the holiday, just as you are doing. The House of Shamai, on the other hand, determined that, as in Sukkot—when a smaller number of oxen is sacrificed each day of the holiday, starting with thirteen and ending with seven—so must we decrease the number of Hanukah candles."

"How do you know all that?" I couldn't help but ask.

He laughed his lovely laugh again. "I am a born Jew and a Jew in my soul. The exterior transformation of baptism takes nothing away from that."

"I believe you miss your origins." I noticed suddenly that he was still standing and gestured for him to come sit beside me. I looked at his long, pleasant face.

"That is the truth, Mama Rothschild," he answered and took a seat. "My origins are cast in stone. They are impossible to uproot. I even miss my original name, Haim."

"Your name is Haim, son?"

"Indeed."

"Haim. Your life, your *haim*, is still ahead of you. I wish you all the best."

"I thank her kindly for these words. I am not wholly comfortable with my choice. I have been baptized, but I live at the expense of wealthy Jews. I wake up at night and curse myself in the mirror. I tell myself that though I am baptized, I am not a Christian. Now I am hated by Jews and Christians alike, and am seen as belonging to neither community."

I felt for him. So sensitive and so talented. He read me some lines from his poetry, and two of them touched me deeply.

> *As my mind yearns for German*
> *I lose my sleep at night.*

Like my previous visitor, Heine now lives in Paris and has come for a homeland visit. He told me how preoccupied he was with Germany and its worrisome politics.

"Your writing is touching. Yaakov has read to me some of your letters. Where do you find inspiration?"

"I invent little poems out of great misery," he said.

I stopped my hand that wished to rub his, consoling his tortured soul. "You mustn't live in guilt. It is pointless."

"I thank her for her concern. God will forgive me, that is His duty." He smiled.

"Of course. You can be certain of that. God is merciful," I said, then recalled, "besides, He must have given you a few points for the way you came to the aid of those poor Jews in Damascus."

"I thank her for that as well. Wherever evil has spread, it must be uprooted."

"But are we able to uproot evil? Yaakov quoted what you said about burning books. Yours is not a happy prophecy."

"I fear the outburst of the barbarian spirit hidden within the German people. Burning books is a sign of things to come. Where they burn books, they will also burn people."

"Is that not an apocalyptic prophecy?"

"I hope the future proves me wrong. I hate to think my words might be validated, but my heart tells me the future is solemn." His face clouded over.

"Why did you come to see me?" I asked in order to help his tortured face clear up again.

"I am in Germany to see two precious women," he answered, seeming to accept the change of subject. "The first is my mother, a lonely widow whom I ache for having abandoned. Just as I had pulled away from the Judaism that still resides in my heart, thus my love for my mother is planted in my heart forever. The second is Mama Rothschild, whom I admire for her humility. I have much to learn from her about the true meaning of patriotism. She remains loyal to her place."

I waved him off, wanting to push away the praise I didn't think I deserved. I thought Yaakov must have been involved. It seems that Yaakov, who is the poet's patron, has exaggerated his descriptions of me, and Heine was falsely charmed.

He looked at me and my chair for a long time. "That green chair," he said, pointing at the ancient piece of furniture, "reminds me of her late son Nathan's chair. I now understand why he chose green velvet."

"That's a surprise. He never told me."

"It seems there are other influences she had over her children without them paying any mind to the matter. But I remember one occasion that has to do with Nathan's chair. I wonder if I should tell it or if she would see it as a bother."

"Tell it. I like to listen. It is a habit I have formed in my life. And my ears certainly prick up when the story has to do with one of my sons."

He took a breath and began. "I was in Italy, and as part of my trip I visited a podiatrist. As things happen, we found ourselves discussing the Rothschilds. The man told me he had treated Nathan's calluses at his home in Stoke Newington. According to him, Nathan sat back in his green chair, surrounded by his servants, his legs spread out, the rest of his body busy with one single action: sending messages to kings the world over. The expert glanced at him, returned his eyes to the razor in his hand, and thought with amusement, 'Here I am, holding the foot of a man who has the entire world in his hands, and I too have the power to influence the results. If I cut deeper, I shall anger him and thus affect the cruelty with which he treats those kings.'"

I looked into Heine's kind eyes. There he was, sitting beside me like an old friend, painting a vivid picture of my dead son. "He suffered from calluses? He never told me that either," I said, thinking about those baby feet I had taken in my hands, kissing over and over, growing callused.

"That isn't suffering, dear Madam Gutle. Nathan could afford to enjoy the delights of this world and have the dead cells removed from his feet to improve his blood flow. Just as James, her Parisian son, may he live long and prosper, regularly visits the hot baths of Europe with his wife, Betty, to allow the water to caress their bodies and ease their pain. These are just a few of the pleasures Mama Rothschild could have enjoyed if she had only considered the matter." He paused, then said, "I am moved by her superior character. Out of this whole story about her son holding the world in his hands, she has chosen to focus on his calluses. I did not mention my admiration in vain."

I waved him off again.

Heine ignored my protest and went on. "I wish Mama Rothschild would let me speak my mind. She lives in this house while her family is clad in gold and silver. If she wanted to, she could have moved into a glamorous home in a luxurious neighborhood."

"Why is everyone so concerned with my house," I protested. "Maimonides said a man ought only to eat when hungry and drink when thirsty. I have never felt hungry or thirsty for another home." I ran my eyes over the room and asked, with a wink, "Do you not like my home? Is it not warm and inviting?"

"That is precisely my point. Her home is the warmest home in the universe, and I hope she believes me when I say I have known many homes. It is a match for all the luxury castles I have seen when visiting literary salons and other cultural gatherings. I hope it doesn't anger her to hear me say outright that it is superior even to her son James's elegant palace, which I visit often. My admiration for her is founded in her normalcy, her projected humanity, her being a loving, peaceful woman. I too yearn for peace. My entire ambition is for a modest apartment with a roof over my head, a comfortable bed, good food, and flowers in my window. I saw the light in her eyes when she lit the Hanukah candles, and that was the first time I truly grasped the meaning of this act. Even in her advanced age, she continues to obey tradition the way she has her entire life."

"Is this a eulogy?" I joked.

"God forbid. I wish her many more active years."

Oh, that Haim Heine is a real mensch, I thought. "No, no, son. I do not need them. I thank God above for blessing my home and giving me many years of observation and satisfaction with my family's choices. My children are all independent and successful, taking part in international processes of which I understand not a thing. It is now time for me to say goodbye to this world. I feel prepared to go the way of all flesh. My Meir continues to take up a large part of my soul, and it is time I reunite with him in the afterlife."

I stood up. It suddenly occurred to me I didn't speak this way with any of our children or grandchildren, but now, talking with this stranger, the floodgates of my heart had opened. How did this happen? Silence is my home. I am not in the habit of revealing my secrets.

Heine stood up too, offering his arm as I walked him to the door.

"You know, I do not speak much," I said.

"In order to speak well, one must only say what is necessary, and nothing more," his words made me smile.

"You are correct. That I have done, only what is necessary, nothing more."

"Her husband, the late Meir Rothschild, is also dear to me. We both embarked on our paths as apprentices in the bank, and lo and behold, the apprentice who preserved his Jewish faith has risen to financial greatness, while the one who became a practitioner of law and was forced to convert in order to find work now depends on the graces of the former apprentice's son. I must say that James is a benevolent patron indeed."

"He loves you very much and appreciates your skills."

"I thank her for her kind words. Would Mama Rothschild do me the honor of joining me and my mother for dinner? She can trust that my mother, unlike her son, maintains a kosher kitchen."

"It is an honor to receive your invitation, and I would very much like to meet your mother, but I do not leave my house. I dine on my own cooking, which now carries the persistent aftertaste of indulgence, being served by a servant I was forced to accept into my home. Give my best to my children in Paris."

He nodded with understanding. "I am accustomed to spending time with James and owe him and his beautiful and demure wife, Madam Betty Rothschild, a debt of gratitude. It would give me great pleasure to return with greetings from his mother."

"Well done, son," I said with express pleasure, recalling his poem "The Angels," which he had written for my darling Betty. "And when it comes to Germany," I added, "do not worry, my children will not allow another war to start."

This time his laughter sounded best of all.

Amschel was standing at the doorway, a wide smile on his face.

Wednesday, May 2nd, 1849

I gathered the family.

Not everyone was able to take time off from their worldly affairs and travel from all over Europe, but many of my beloveds were there: children, grandchildren, and great-grandchildren. It is such a shame that Schönche, Julie, and Nathan are not here with me. And last year we sadly parted with my daughter-in-law Eva, as well.

I looked at them, my loved ones, and pondered for the millionth time what would have happened had my father not given you my hand in marriage. What would my family look like if I had married another man? What would the world look like had my children not taken part in the political affairs of this great green earth?

I have decided these will be the last pages I write before destroying this notebook and the previous ones, as I had promised you. I must leave no secrets behind. I shall burn the shards of my memories.

Babette and Henrietta made a festive dinner and set a gorgeous table. *The last supper,* I thought with a chuckle, stifling a tired cough.

My hand is not steady enough to hold the pen, so I will keep my description short. Surrounded with love, I spoke my mind: "Remember the decrees of the Lord and of your father and grandfather, Meir, the heritage he has left you. More than anything, save yourselves from assimilation. It is a mitzvah to maintain the survival of the Jewish people. Remember who your founder was and who is responsible for delivering you where you are today. Honor his wishes and his legacy, and pass them on to the future generations of the Rothschild dynasty.

"And I shall add this: your father brought honor to this family and you have increased this honor. Your father knew money carried power and could bring dignity to us and to the community, but he was never blinded by money. He continued to live his life with modesty and simplicity. You have rubbed shoulders with the outside world, and are influenced by a life of luxury, mimicking a bourgeois lifestyle. And nevertheless you are hardworking and tireless, and that makes me proud. I turn to the women among you: it is not the way of a woman to sit idly. *She watches over the affairs of her household and does not eat the bread of idleness.* Idleness is the mother of all evil.

"Let me be clear: you have wealth and honor. You have received mighty titles and influence over the leaders of Europe. You host feasts in your castles, dine on silver, and shade your windows with crimson curtains. Even Nathan, may his memory be a blessing, finally gave in and moved into a mansion, where he gave his children a small carriage harnessed to four goats. His eldest son, Lionel, bought fine purebred horses, as well as an Arabian steed from the sultan of Morocco. Though this life of leisure is not to my liking, I cannot make your choices for you. You alone can choose a life of luxury and social etiquette. I will ask you one thing: never forget where you came from. Love and respect each other. Do charitable work, for those who do charitable work will enjoy wise, wealthy, and brave children. Charity shall save from death.

"And one more thing: be wary of complacence. Just when you think the troubles of the Jews are over, new calamities surprise us. They happened in 1819, then in 1830, and once again last year. If there is quiet, it is likely temporary. It matters not how we live—impoverished on Judengasse or rich in castles—someone will always criticize and harass us. Heinrich Heine warned against what book burners might do: *Where they burn books, they will also burn people,* he said. Who knows, perhaps in fifty or a hundred years a new madman will rise to announce a new kind of pogrom, something we haven't yet heard of. If he chooses to return us to the ghetto, well then I will already be here, buried in its dirt. No madman will be exhuming my bones."

Amschel wrinkled his brow. "What are you saying, Mama? That there is no way out? Why don't we all just return to the ghetto now to wait for that madman you speak of?"

"You do not need to return to the ghetto. It is enough that your father and I are here. But there is one single solution for the future, and that is to settle on our land."

"I don't understand. You just told us not to return to the ghetto. Then what land do you mean?"

"The land of our forefathers. The Holy Land. That is where Jews belong. There, no one can destroy us."

"Us? In the Holy Land?"

"Yes, my son. If not in your generation, then in the generation of your children or grandchildren standing around me. Living in the Land of Israel is comparable to performing all the mitzvahs in the Torah put together."

A harsh cough shivered out of my throat. I asked to be led to the window and took deep breaths. "No doctors," I whispered. "Air." The window was opened and I took small sips of the light breeze that greeted me.

That's it. Now I'm alone. There comes that traitorous weakness again, besieging me. So stubborn, crawling over, taking hold, slowing my movements. *Rocks we had perched on in our youth have waged war against us in our old age.*

My handwriting is playing tricks on me. The letters dance on the page. I shall go to the window.

I have no strength to reach it. My hands tremble. My legs ache. Even the touch of my starched dress against my skin is painful.

I shall sit here and wait for my power to return.

I look about and see you in the distance, calling me over. Wait for me, I am coming to meet you.

◆　◆　◆

Gutle died at the ripe old age of ninety-six, on May 7th, 1849. Forty velvet chests were found in her house, one for each of her children, grandchildren, and great-grandchildren. The name of the inheritor was printed on each chest.

Once their locks were opened, each chest was found to be filled with a great treasure of coins. On top of the coins was a folded piece of paper bearing these words:

> *Dear descendant of the Rothschild family,*
> *This treasure is yours. It is full of love coins, some of which have passed through the hands of the dynasty's great founder, Meir Rothschild, the best of all men. Those coins are clean and pure, given with a loving heart, and to them I have added my own love coin each day.*
> *Since God has granted me many years of life, I have had the opportunity to fill these chests, one chest for each family member, each proud offspring of the Rothschild family.*
> *Save them for a fine opportunity, and remember always that the secret of this family's power lies in its unity.*
> *Yours with love,*
> *Gutle,*
> *Widow of the venerable Meir Amschel Rothschild.*

ABOUT THE AUTHOR

Sara Aharoni was born in Israel in 1953. She worked as a teacher, educator, and school principal for twenty years. She also spent four years in Lima, Peru, as an educational envoy of the Jewish Agency. Together with her husband, Meir Aharoni, Sara wrote, edited, and published a series of books about Israel, as well as six children's books. Sara is the author of the bestselling *Saltanat's Love*, based on her mother's life story and the winner of the Book Publishers Association of Israel's Platinum Prize, and the Steimatzky Prize–winning novel *The First Mrs. Rothschild*. Her novel *Persian Silence* won the Book Publishers Association of Israel's Gold Book Award.

ABOUT THE TRANSLATOR

Photo © Michelle Tong

Yardenne Greenspan has an MFA in fiction and translation from Columbia University. In 2011 she received the American Literary Translators Association Fellowship, and in 2014 she was a resident writer and translator at the Ledig House Writers Omi program. Her translation of *Some Day*, by Shemi Zarhin (New Vessel Press), was chosen for *World Literature Today*'s 2013 list of notable translations. Her full-length translations also include *Tel Aviv Noir*, edited by Etgar Keret and Assaf Gavron (Akashic Books); *Alexandrian Summer*, by Yitzhak Gormezano Goren (New Vessel Press); and *The Secret Book of Kings*, by Yochi Brandes (St. Martin's Press). Yardenne blogs for *Ploughshares* and served as *Asymptote*'s editor-at-large of Israeli literature. Her writing and translations have appeared in the *New Yorker*, *Haaretz*, *Guernica*, *Asymptote*, the *Massachusetts Review*, and *Words Without Borders*, among other publications.